A HELL DIVERS NOVEL

RHINO

THE RISE OF A WARRIOR

NICHOLAS SANSBURY SMITH

Printed in the United States of America
Originally published in hardcover by Blackstone Publishing in 2025

First paperback edition: 2025
ISBN 979-8-228-00063-6
Fiction / Science Fiction / Apocalyptic & Post-Apocalyptic

Version 1

Blackstone Publishing
31 Mistletoe Rd.
Ashland, OR 97520

www.BlackstonePublishing.com

To Colonel Russell Olson (Ret.)
Affectionately known as Spartacus, Colonel Olson
honorably served his country in Vietnam before
returning home to build a loving family and inspire
young minds as a high school history teacher.
A devoted family man, steadfast follower of Christ,
and patriot, he embodies the spirit of a great
American. Through relentless hard work, overcoming
trials, and acts of courage, Colonel Olson has selflessly
dedicated his life to service and family. It is in this spirit
that I dedicate my novel Rhino *to Colonel Olson. Much*
like the resilient protagonist in this story, Colonel
Olson's journey through hardship and triumph mirrors
the struggles and steadfast resolve that define the
heart of Nick Baker in Rhino.

"From the ashes of defeat, a warrior rises, stronger and more determined than before."

—Marcus Aurelius

PROLOGUE

Two hundred thirteen years after the bombs erased civilization, a violent geomagnetic storm rushed across the wastelands above a buried Industrial Tech Corp bunker. The 304 occupants living deep beneath the surface heard only the usual rattle of the ventilation systems that kept out the toxins and radioactive dust.

They went about their day, doing the tasks that kept the bunker going: routine maintenance on the water treatment plant, transporting salvage down the ninety floors for repurposing in the machine shop at the bottom, educating the thirty-two variously aged kids at the school, or tending the grain and vegetable crops growing on the farm.

Almost no one had any idea what lay two hundred feet above their bunker. But there were a few who not only knew but had seen it with their own eyes.

Ranger Mac McGee was one of those individuals. His role was protecting the bunker and the people inside—and not only from external threats. For humans weren't designed to live packed together like pomegranate seeds. They could always find reasons for conflict—some small, some not so small. His job was to dial down the heat and mitigate it all. Challenging, but it was the easier part of his job compared to keeping the bunker safe from the monsters above: ravening beasts, and men who were every bit as frightening, prowling the vast ruin once known as Houston, which stretched all the way to the Gulf of Mexico.

He would gladly take a conflict over rations between two screaming neighbors, or a brawl about a debt, before heading out into the wastes.

Today his job was none of those things. Today their sanctuary was about to experience something rare—a miracle, really.

The birth of a child.

As the storm rattled overhead, the howls of a woman in labor resounded up the stairwell from the thirty-fourth floor. Mac hurried down the corridor with a box of medical supplies under one arm, trying to appear calm.

"It's okay," he assured the concerned faces peeking out from rooms and doorways. "Everything's under control."

People were unaccustomed to hearing such anguished cries, for this was the first baby in three years.

Mac arrived at the medical bay, winded and sweating from the long haul down the stairs. He took a breath outside the open door, preparing himself. Inside, he was greeted by another scream from the woman contorting in a chair—Cat, just twenty-two years old. Her youthful, frightened eyes flitted to Mac, and she sucked in a breath, holding her round belly in both hands. Caring for her was Nixon—a doctor, if one could call him that. Now going blind with macular degeneration, he had the callused hands of a technician who had worked his entire life to keep the bunker's machines up and running. He also had some success in fixing broken or ailing bodies.

The two actual doctors had died during a great plague, and most of the community's medical knowledge went with them. Nixon was all they had now. He had retired from machines to teach in the afternoon, hoping to pass on what he knew to young-sters who might grow up to be doctors.

Mac walked up, clearing his throat for Nixon's benefit. The man wasn't losing just his sight. He was also going deaf.

"I have the instruments, Betadine, and sterile dressings," Mac said.

Nixon waved him over to a cart strewn with medical supplies.

"Put them down over there and bring the cart closer," he said.

Nixon put a hand on Cat's back. "The contractions are closer. That's good. Get back into bed for me, now."

She climbed back onto the bed with shaky legs, and Mac reached out to help her. She looked at him again. Along with the fear, he saw loneliness. So far, no father had come forward to claim the child, and Cat hadn't identified one.

"Breathe," Nixon said. "Now, push! Mac, bring the cart over here."

Nixon leaned down, turning on his head-mounted flashlight.

The door opened again, and Smitty walked inside. Though only in his early twenties, he was hunched over from scoliosis. He pulled on gloves as Cat wailed from another contraction.

"Breathe. That's it," Nixon said. "Hurry, bring those here."

Mac finished setting out the dilator, retractors, and forceps on a sterile mat atop the cart. He wheeled the cart over, and Smitty joined him by Nixon's side. She looked up at them all with fear in her eyes.

"Breathe," Nixon said.

He squirted gel on his gloves and reached under the sheet again. He was busy for several seconds while she grunted in agony. He pushed back and swiveled his chair, then got up and faced Mac and Smitty just outside the door.

"The baby is breech and must be delivered surgically," Nixon explained.

Mac understood what that meant, but Smitty shook his head. "What do you mean?" he asked as he raised his gloves to his hair.

"Don't touch your hair, man, and put on a damn mask," Nixon said.

Smitty pulled one from his pocket and strapped it over his face.

"What this means is," Nixon continued, "I have to cut her open, and I fear she won't survive the blood loss."

"Is this the only way?" Mac asked.

"It is if we want to save the baby."

In their confined world, hard decisions like this always factored in the overall good of the bunker. Cat was a fertile woman, but priority must go to her child—to help repopulate.

"It must be done," Nixon said. "Say nothing. I will sedate her, and I'll need both of your help holding her down. Do you understand?"

Mac and Smitty nodded.

They returned to the room, where Cat writhed in tears.

"Get Valkia," she whimpered.

"What?" Nixon asked.

"Valkia. She can save my child…"

Mac and Nixon exchanged glances. Valkia was not a scientific doctor, or a doctor at all. She was a witch, a sorceress.

"Valkia!" Cat wailed.

Nixon turned to Smitty. "Get the witch," he said.

Wide-eyed, Smitty turned and left as quickly as his hunched back would allow.

Nixon followed him to the door and then locked it. That was when Mac understood—the acting doctor had no plans to allow the witch in the delivery room. He was simply trying to give Cat hope.

Mac went over to the bed and peered down at Cat, who looked up desperately.

"It's gonna be okay," he offered.

Nixon went to her other side while Mac had her distracted. He stuck a syringe in the feed to her IV tube. Her head rolled to the side, eyes glossing over. As she drifted off, Nixon took a scalpel from the cart.

"She's out," Mac confirmed.

Nixon came over and pulled the sheet away from her swollen belly. He flinched as a voice called out from the hallway.

"I've got Valkia," Smitty said from outside the locked door.

Nixon ignored him and went to work.

Pounding came on the door.

"Open up!" Valkia shrieked.

Mac tried not to look as Nixon cut the patient open. Blood welled out from the incision. Within a minute, Nixon had her uterus open and was fishing inside for the child. He pulled it out—a boy.

A shrill scream filled the room.

"Oh God," Nixon said, holding the infant, who was still connected to the umbilical cord. Mac used the sheet to cover her body. She already saw the devastation, but her fearful eyes seemed to brighten at the sight of her child.

She raised a shaking hand.

"Let me…" she whispered. "Let me hold my baby."

Nixon leaned down with the boy, who gave a loud squall.

Cat used her last conscious breaths to soothe her son, pulling him to her chest.

"Give them hell, my son," she said.

PART I:
ITC STAR STATION

CHAPTER 1

The rattle of machinery woke thirteen-year-old Nick Baker at the same time every morning. It was the rickety old ventilation system coming to life.

Nick sprang from his pallet like a lizard off a hot rock. A faded lamp emitted a dim glow over his tiny living quarters, which were the size of a large closet. Just enough room to spread out the faded red sleeping bag that he was now rolling up. He stowed it neatly in the corner, then opened the doors to a storage locker. Inside were two shirts and pairs of sweatpants—blue with the silver ITC logo. Even the elbow holes seemed identical.

After shucking off the long underwear that kept him from shivering at night, he pulled on the pants first, then the sweatshirt.

Leaning down, he looked to the crack in the wall where his best friend visited him every morning. Sure enough, Timmy Tam poked out his whiskered face. Nick held out a morsel he had kept from dinner—corn bread, which he had most every night, and the same breakfast Timmy Tam came for each morning.

"You never get sick of it, huh, little guy?" Nick whispered.

Timmy Tam came farther out of the hole, sniffing, then

climbed onto his hand. It had taken months. For days, Nick would hold the morsels out and the mouse would venture a bit closer, then a bit more. If he should ever be caught, there was no doubt that Timmy Tam would end up on the menu. Mice, rats, even bugs were often part of the daily diet for the 321 people living in ITC Star Station.

Nick set his friend down and began his morning push-ups.

Ten…

Twenty…

By fifty, his bony arms were starting to burn.

By eighty, he was shaking.

His goal was a hundred. And not the weak, on-your-knees kind. He went all the way down, his chin hovering just above the cold concrete floor.

He glanced over at Timmy Tam, who watched as if to cheer him on.

At ninety-eight, Nick's body quivered and sweat stung his eyes.

Ninety-nine…

One hundred!

A knock came on the door, and Timmy Tam rushed back into his cave. Nick shot up—all five feet four inches and 102 pounds of him.

The door opened, letting in the banging and grinding from the workshops.

Eight-year-old Sofia stood outside, smiling. "Hey, you're late," she said. "Whatcha been doing in here? Jeez, you're all sweaty."

"Working out."

Sofia looked him up and down. "I can tell."

He scrutinized her to see if she was joking.

"Really," she said.

He dragged his arm over his forehead. "So, what am I late for?"

"You serious?" She raised a brow.

When he didn't answer, she reminded him. "Today a Ranger team is heading out for readings. Don't tell me you forgot."

Of course, Nick hadn't forgotten. He respected and admired the twelve Rangers who protected the bunker. He planned on someday becoming one himself. But he didn't want anyone to know that, not yet. They would laugh and call him a runt.

"I remember," he finally replied. "But it's all a joke."

"What do you mean 'a joke'?"

"They go out and take some readings for the council when they should be out exploring. Then they come back, and the council reports the same thing: not safe to go outside."

"Maybe today that will change."

"No, not until the Rangers are allowed to go farther—to actually poke around the outside world. That won't happen with Minister Creed in charge." Nick gestured to the door. "Can you move, please? I've got work to do this morning."

"But I came all the way down here to get you."

"Sorry." Nick nudged past her into the hallway. That didn't stop her from following. For the past four years, she had practically been his shadow. They had met in school, which he rarely attended now, so she made the long trip here almost every day to see him.

Their lives couldn't be more different. She lived up with most of the population, in the community space with her mother. Nick had been moved to the bottom of the bunker after the collective raised him through his younger years. An overseer decided he would be most useful in the workshop. His long, scrawny arms were perfect for reaching into the machines and lubricating and cleaning them.

If he were being honest, he did enjoy Sofia's visits. There weren't many kids in the bunker. He was the only thirteen-year-old, and while they had a five-year age gap, it didn't feel that way.

She was smart for her age. And kind. And he got lonely. Seeing her brightened his day.

He wasn't alone down here though. The other workers lived in the retrofitted storage rooms. He walked by a more spacious room, where Smitty and his wife, Ginger, lived. They had a bed, a desk, and even an ancient TV that worked.

"Morning, Nick," Smitty said.

Nick nodded at the humpbacked man who had been there the day he was born. He didn't blame Smitty for not saving his mother any more than he blamed the "doctor." He blamed himself for killing her during his birth.

Anger burned in his chest. Anger at being stuck in this prison that no one seemed to want to leave. Anger at also being trapped in this skinny body that didn't grow as fast as other kids'.

The sounds of machinery grew louder. He stepped into the sprawling, echoey workspace, where three men were already at work on various projects, ranging from rethreading a stripped screw or forging new nails to cutting glass. Everything in the bunker was used, reused, and often repurposed down here.

"I'll ask your boss if you can go up a few hours early," Sofia said.

Nick glanced over his shoulder to see her sly grin. She whipped her braid over her shoulder and then rushed through a door to the engineering room.

"Wait, Sofia, no!" Nick said.

She scampered across the cluttered space.

"Damn it," he grunted.

He followed her into the vaulted chamber where the giant boilers and heating units chugged. Two workers were walking around with notebooks, marking down readings.

"Hey, watch out!" one of them barked as Sofia darted by.

"Sofia!" Nick called.

She went straight to his supervisor, Beto. He had lost his arm as a teenager trying to clear a jammed conveyor belt.

"Always assume the machine is on," he had told Nick when he was first brought to the shop and given his living quarters.

"Beto, can I have a moment of your precious time?" Sofia asked.

Beto looked up from the table where he was cleaning slag from a weld.

"This is no place for little kids," Beto said.

"Good thing I'm not a little kid."

Nick moved in front of her. "I told her not to come in here."

Beto peered at him through thick glasses. He had almost lost an eye in a welding accident years ago.

"Can Nick please come with me to arrive early for the Rangers' send-off?" Sofia asked. "It would mean a lot to us."

"He can go when the rest of us go," Beto replied.

"We need to arrive early for a good view. Otherwise, bigger folks will block us."

Beto stared at Sofia, then looked over to Nick before his gaze went to a pad of paper on his desk. He moved his dirty finger down the ledger. "Yeah," he said with a grunt. "But I need you back right after."

"No problem, boss," Nick said.

Sofia looked over, grinning.

He sighed.

"Go, before I change my mind," Beto said.

Nick threw his backpack on and followed Sofia out of the shop. More workers slogged to their stations, stacked with crates of goods from the higher floors. Things that needed fixing: a vacuum, a broken broom, an eggbeater.

Sofia led the way to the stairs across the room. They heard ratcheting as they crossed the workshop. Nick knew the source of the noise, just as he knew the source of *every* noise. This one came from an elevator shaft that had long since stopped operating. They had removed the car and installed a cart on a rope-and-pulley system.

The bottom of the shaft was right next to the open stairwell that led to the top of the bunker. On each wide landing, a door next to the open shaft was gated off to prevent anyone from taking a catastrophic fall.

At the third floor up, they came across a cart being cranked down using the archaic pulley system. On it were eight crates of freshly harvested cabbages and carrots, and six jugs of fresh water. A Ranger in blue-and-white fatigues guarded the shipment with a shotgun in the dimly lit shaft. He raised a hand when he saw Sofia, and right away Nick knew this was Mac, one of the nicer Rangers, and funny too. The guy always joked with the kids.

The other Rangers were rougher. Guys like Hugh, who hardly talked, and Glock, who cursed too much and always carried two of the ancient handguns he was nicknamed after.

But that was what the job did to them. The Rangers didn't just protect the bunker. They went to the surface from time to time. Someday Nick was going to be one of those lawmen.

He lingered in front of the gate, noticing two caches of unmarked supply crates, plus a television with a disc player. Nick had seen a few of those over the years.

"Yeah, that's right," Mac said. "We got a disc story. Heading down to Beto for a bit more fixin' up."

"Wow, and it might work?" Sofia asked.

"They wouldn't give me this if it didn't," Mac said. He waved his shotgun as the cart lowered him into the dark shaft. "Don't get any ideas now and try to steal nothin'. I don't want to have to give any of you a whuppin'."

"Gotta catch me before you can whup me!" Sofia shouted as she took off up the stairs, two at a time.

"That's a real sassy little friend you got there," Mac said. "Better watch her, and watch your amigos too. Don't want them borrowing anything that ain't theirs."

Nick looked through the gate at the disc player. "Don't worry. I don't care about that crap. I care about what's *up there*." He pointed up the shaft. "Think about all the treasure we could bring back from the wastes."

Mac glanced up with hardened eyes. "Nothin' good comes to anyone who goes out there. They don't bring back treasures. Some don't come back at all."

And then he was gone, descending into the black.

Nick stood up and stepped back from the edge.

"Hey, you comin' or what?" Sofia called down from the stairs.

Nick pondered Mac's words another minute before following her up to the fourth level. A faint cackle echoed out of the semi-darkness. At the entrance to the room, a desk with a computer terminal sat empty. The salvage chief—a man who went by "Hyena" for his high, giggling laugh—was already out among the mounds of carefully organized junk that took up this entire floor and the two floors below them.

He walked with a cane, tapping it and tittering as he talked to himself—something he did most of the day. He had some disorder that Nick couldn't pronounce, but he was brilliant at fabricating parts.

They went up two more levels, past the generator plant, water treatment, and laboratories now converted to farms. Normally, they would stop to look at the pigs, chickens, and dairy cows, but not today. The wide stairs weren't busy yet, since most people were still sleeping, and they breezed right up, past the crops, then past the communal spaces that included the library and school.

Next, they reached the living quarters, where people were just starting to move around. But others were already gathering in the mess hall. The usual scents of coffee and garlic were mixed with bacon this morning—a delicacy reserved for the semiannual surface mission. The Rangers would get a hardy breakfast with oats and eggs too—a tradition for the men who sometimes didn't return.

Nick hesitated outside the mess hall, his stomach growling. He had tasted bacon once—just a bite—back when he crawled inside a machine a year ago to replace a panel that had become lodged inside. Beto gave it to him for the risky work.

"Hurry, and we'll beat everyone," Sofia said.

They kept going to the next level, which served as a command-and-control center. This was the one door that was kept locked at all times. Inside, someone manned the station that showed monitor feeds from the surface and from each level of the bunker.

"Man, I wish I knew what they see in there," Nick said.

Sofia stopped on the landing outside the door to catch her breath. "A whole lot of nothin's my guess," she said.

"You don't think they're talking to people from other bunkers or places on the surface?"

She shook her head. "You know we're—"

"Come on. We *can't* be the only ones left. The world is huge."

"That's what my auntie says, that we're it."

"Well, your auntie's wrong."

Sofia shrugged and kept going, and Nick followed, thinking of what Mac had said about people who went out and never came back. He shook his questions away as he arrived at the vehicle depot entrance. The door was propped open, and a small group of fifteen had already arrived. Gus, Chubs, and Ron were all there. They were some of the youngest kids in the bunker besides Sofia and Nick.

"Hey, fellas," Sofia said.

The group of youngsters turned from the railing overlooking the bay—the best seat in the house. Ron nudged Nick as he moved up for a view of the five rusted ancient vehicles in various stages of maintenance.

"Nice to see you up early," Ron said.

"Yeah," Chubs said. "How's life down in the nether regions?"

"He's been working out," Sofia said.

Nick felt his face getting warm. He looked down at the faded green military Humvee, two pickup trucks—one red and one white—and a car that was beaten all to hell. The pride of their small fleet was a military CBRN reconnaissance truck called a Stryker.

The vehicle was about the most famous asset the bunker possessed. It was the Stryker that had saved many of the original residents here during the war, protecting them from the nuclear fallout and toxins that made the surface uninhabitable.

Over the next hour, hundreds of people gathered, including all but one of the dozen Rangers, who were probably on security detail inside the bunker.

Glock, Hugh, and Mac stood at the front of the group.

Nick scanned the surrounding faces. He knew everyone and always wondered who among them was his father. It could be any of several men.

"Your mother was a whore," Tyshon had said to Nick two years ago.

The eighteen-year-old was in the crowd now. Nick clenched the fist that had popped the older boy in the mouth back then. That was the first time Nick ever threw a punch. Also, the first time he ever lost a tooth.

Sofia had been there to pick him up. "Don't worry," she said. "It's a baby tooth. You'll grow another one."

The gathering people chattered among themselves, some whispering about today being special—perhaps even the day they could all go to the surface. Others said that day would never come. Nick thought it was all bullshit. In his mind, they could go out right now in their fancy suits if they wanted. They could explore the Old World. There had to be more survivors. This couldn't be the only place.

"Greetings to you all, the saved souls of ITC Star Station," boomed a voice.

The crowd turned to face a man they all respected and feared: Creed, the minister of the bunker.

The sixty-year-old dark-skinned man with salt-and-pepper hair walked onto a mezzanine overlooking the assemblage. He wore a navy-blue robe. He held up his arm over his flock.

"Another day has arrived to send two of our brave Rangers to the poisoned surface far above us," he said. "We have gathered to wish them well and to say a prayer they will return with positive readings."

"It is not yet time! The gods will curse us!" shrieked a crackly old voice that Nick knew all too well. It was Valkia, the witchwoman his mother had asked for when he was born.

"Silence, or I will have you strapped to the truck and sent into the wastes," Creed ordered.

Valkia's eyes narrowed, but she said nothing. They glared at each other for a long moment before Creed finally turned his stern countenance back to the Rangers. Then he reached into his pocket and pulled out a printed note.

"Today the council has chosen the following Rangers to embark on this mission," he said.

After a brief pause, he read three names.

"Glock is assigned as mission lead, with Mac and Luigi accompanying him."

Luigi's bearded jaw dropped. After all, this was his first mission topside. Glock, on the other hand, appeared excited.

"Time to fuckin' ride, ya ugly bastards," he said with a grin. He slapped Luigi and Mac on the back as they broke off from the other Rangers. The three walked toward the crowd, carrying their helmets. Civilians parted to let the armored men through. They went to the weapons crate, where Mac selected the same shotgun he had carried in the elevator. Luigi took an assault rifle, and Glock grabbed a scoped rifle. Everyone watched as they checked and double-checked their gear.

Someday Nick would be like them. A Ranger. Big, strong, and trained to deal with what was out there. He would lead these people to a new life aboveground—to a place where the sun shone.

As the Rangers climbed into the vehicle, the crowd bowed their heads. Nick glanced up to see their leader still holding his arms up. He glared down at Nick, and Nick lowered his head as Creed recited the prayer passed down through the generations.

"Eternal Guardian of the depths and silences, in the shadow of our world's ruin, we gather in this sanctuary of steel and stone. We, the remnants of humanity, offer our prayer, not from beneath the open sky but from within our ark, that you, Blessed Keeper, guide us through the darkness that has fallen upon our world. Give us the courage and strength to endure the trials of this existence, until the day we may emerge from our isolation. And forgive us the follies that led to the world's destruction by our ancestors, so that we may rebuild a civilization in balance with the nature that once sustained us."

Nick finished whispering the words with the rest of the crowd—all but Valkia. She flapped her arms like a demented bird, following the two Rangers. Mac reached out, gently pushing her away. She grabbed Glock next.

"Get out of our way, ya crazy old bat," he grumbled, shoving her not so gently to the floor.

A Ranger on standby grabbed her and pulled her away.

"It's not yet time!" she shrieked. "We must prepare for the demons!"

Creed glared angrily as she was removed from the chamber. On her way out, her eyes met Nick's.

"You will see," she hissed. "You, Nick Baker—you have the fire inside you."

The rumble of the Stryker's engine drowned out her words, but he had heard them loud and clear.

"May the gods watch over you!" Creed said in his deep, resonating baritone.

The crowd milled and shuffled to look at the vehicle. The tires squealed as they turned, rolling over the smooth concrete as Mac drove toward the bunker doors. They slid open to reveal a sloping tunnel that led to the surface. Headlights flipped on, illuminating the roadway.

The doors closed behind it, sealing the view with a loud clank that echoed throughout the chamber. A few hushed voices wished them luck.

"Do you think they'll find monsters today?" Chubs asked.

"There are no monsters," Sofia whispered.

"Sure there are," said Ron.

"Yeah, big ones with fangs," Chubs said. "They can fly, and they will eat us."

"Not Nick though—way too skinny." Ron laughed. "They would definitely go for you first."

"Which is why I'll never leave this place." Chubs sighed, then grinned. He looked over at Nick. "Do you believe in monsters?"

Nick raised his chin, no longer caring if people made fun of him.

"Yeah," he replied. "Monsters are real, and someday, when I'm a Ranger, I'll kill them."

CHAPTER 2

The Stryker rolled to a stop in front of the blast door. Mac took the wheel, Glock rode shotgun, and Luigi sat in the back, visibly shaking as he cinched the harness straps over his chest.

"It's gonna be okay, man," Mac told him. "We're just going for some readings. You can even stay inside if you want."

Glock looked over. "I'm mission lead. I give the orders, not you."

"You're right," Mac said without apologizing.

"Damn straight I'm right, and this isn't just for readings. We're here for some new tests, and that means we're leaving the vehicle." He twisted in his seat to look at Luigi. "You're a Ranger, kid. That means going outside."

"Yes sir."

Glock looked at him a long moment before turning back to the front. Mac took that time to consider what "new tests" meant. Something was definitely up.

"A'ight, Command, we're ready to roll out," Glock said into the radio handset.

In the back seat, Luigi bowed his head, quietly reciting a prayer. Mac didn't know him all that well, partly because the kid was quiet. Just twenty-two, he had served for three years. He wasn't their best fighter, but he was smart and obeyed orders.

A green light flashed on the dashboard. Minister Creed's voice crackled over the comms. "All clear. Doors opening in five, four, three, two…"

With a low whine, the blast doors parted, letting in the blue flash of electrical storms above the bunker.

"Good luck, Rangers," Creed said.

Mac put the Stryker in gear and pulled out into the darkness. His gut tightened, as it did every time he thought of what prowled among the ruins—the same creatures that had taken his father from him when he was a boy. It was during a mission outside, before Creed's reign and before his predecessor's, when twice as many people lived at Star Station. But then the plague had hit, wiping out the old and the young—among them his mother.

Each time Mac was deployed out here, he relived those traumatic moments of his youth. He could still picture his mother coming to get him out of school the day his father deployed to the surface.

"Did Daddy find something out there?" Mac had asked.

But he remembered the look in her eyes. And the tears that welled up.

"I'm sorry, Mac, but your father had an accident," she had said. "He isn't coming home."

Mac never learned exactly what happened, only that the Rangers had stumbled upon some sort of mutant creature that moved like the wind, snatching his father and dragging him into the rubble. The other Rangers hadn't gotten a good look, but one of them described a wail that sounded like an audio oscillator, and a face without eyes.

On that day, Mac decided to become a Ranger, to protect ITC Star Station, and to hunt the monsters that had taken his dad.

That was three decades ago, and Mac had fulfilled that promise to himself.

The beams from the Stryker blazed through the darkness of a poisoned, alien world as Mac drove over broken asphalt. All three Rangers peered out the reinforced windows at a cityscape they had never known but had seen on story discs and in books. It was hard to believe this place once had color beyond the palette of sooty gray and black. That the sky had once been blue, and the sun had shone over fields and forests and vibrant cities. Now those magnificent buildings had crumbled to piles of rubble, and those that still stood had lost their exteriors, like skin and flesh peeling away from bones of steel.

Charred hulls of vehicles littered the road. Mac navigated around them, careful not to nudge or bump anything. It was one of the first things he learned as a Ranger: Leave the topside as you found it. Any faint trace could lead enemies back to ITC Star Station.

But this was not so easy in practice.

The rugged tires crunched over broken glass and twisted metal—the sounds of a civilization ground to dust. A half mile into the drive, a Geiger counter clicked rapidly—a grim reminder of the invisible threat that pervaded the air and land. The readings flashed across the screen, downloading to a drive that would go straight to the command center.

Mac turned through an intersection, veering around a truck on its side. He knew what lay beyond each blockage, having memorized the route over the years. On the next block, two apartment complexes had collapsed into rubble. Between them, miraculously, a dilapidated playground remained mostly unscathed.

As they passed, a swing rocked ominously in the breeze over the cracked dirt. Mac always wondered how the playground had survived over the years.

Soft mumbling behind him drew his gaze to Luigi. The young man prayed, his voice barely audible over the Stryker's engine.

"Almost there," Mac said.

The next street was the oddest on the route, with four row houses still standing amid the destruction. The two-story brick buildings had been blasted by the shock wave of the nuclear explosion, blowing out every window and door. But the buildings had withstood it, shielded partly by bigger structures that had all fallen in the blast, creating a cushion of rubble.

Mac pictured a family of four living inside the first row house he drove past. Eating dinner at a table behind a broken window, watching a disc story on their television. Christmas lights hanging from the awnings.

Whoever had lived here was now nothing, not even a memory. Life had been wiped out, and for what? Mac still had no idea what had caused the war.

He turned down another street, snapped from his thoughts by the peculiar red luminosity that always greeted them at this location. Today it was far brighter, burning in the darkness with an eerie glow.

He slowed the vehicle but didn't stop. The nuclear aftermath gave way to an unusual spectacle of nature's relentless adaptation to the devastation. From the husk of a collapsed building, thick red vines spilled forth, sprawling across the broken concrete like the tendrils of some giant, otherworldly octopus. The bioluminescent red glow wasn't just coming from above the street. It was also coming from below.

"Holy shitstorms, it's grown!" Glock breathed.

Mac swallowed hard at the realization. The strange thicket of vines hadn't just grown; it had overtaken a huge section of the city block, spreading from the initial building to several adjacent structures. A portion of the street had given way, collapsing into a massive sinkhole. Behind that hole, red rims of light pulsated from two visible manholes.

"It's spreading underground too," Mac whispered.

Mac brought the Stryker to a full stop a hundred feet from the sinkhole. Luigi squeezed up between him and Glock, and all three Rangers gazed in horrified awe.

"How can anything survive out here?" Luigi asked. "These rads are sky-high."

And yet, at the edge of the radioactive abyss, life clawed and probed and crept its way through the ruin. The red vines swayed slightly in the breeze—a rare splash of color in the monochrome wasteland, both beautiful and grotesque in the stark contrast to the devastation all around.

"Time to figure that out," Glock said after staring for a moment.

He looked away and tapped the dashboard with his security code. It came to life with a list of orders.

"Our main objective is to take samples of that flora and get it back to the labs," he explained. "The council wants to research how the plants metabolize the radioactive material, and whether this is just a manifestation of nature's resilience or a new hazard."

"Ugh. Pretty damn obvious—it's both," Mac said.

"Are you a scientist?"

"No."

"Yeah, I didn't think so."

"Let's get this over with, then," Mac said. "I'll do the tests on my own."

Glock shook his head. "Luigi's going with. He needs the experience."

Mac resisted the urge to shake his head in disagreement. Considering this was the kid's first mission, Mac felt Luigi should be the one to stay with the Stryker. One Ranger was always required to remain in the vehicle. It was protocol. But apparently Glock wanted to be that man.

"Got it," Mac said. He unstrapped his harness and climbed into the back. Luigi was already at the back hatch.

"You good?" Mac asked.

Luigi gave a nod. "I'm ready."

"Okay, open it," Mac ordered.

The younger Ranger flipped the lever, then another, and pushed the hatch open. Mac went first, dropping lightly to the dirt with his shotgun up. Luigi came next, holding the field-testing kit. He followed Mac away from the Stryker, both Rangers halting about fifteen feet from the closest vine. Mac shined his flashlight on the tip and noticed strands reaching out from the thick hide.

This strange flora hadn't just adapted down here. It was thriving, spreading like a fire above- and belowground. This must be what the council feared: that eventually the vines might reach the bunker and find a way inside.

Luigi pulled a pair of shears from the test kit. He went up to a cluster of vines, light casting a ghostly red hue on his suit as he crouched. Mac played his beam over the structures and saw ivy-like tendrils clinging to the bricks. The thickest branches weren't from the original building. They were coming from the gaping scar in the ground. The sinkhole seemed to serve as a cradle for the eerie life form, its seeds germinating and sprouting belowground.

He heard a loud cracking as he stepped up closer to the sinkhole.

"Careful," Glock said over the comms.

Mac stood at the edge, staring down below street level with his flashlight off. Each pulsating burst captured the network of vines, glowing down deep in the earth, where they connected to a root system surrounding what looked like a giant heart.

He crouched for a better look into the abyss. It was obvious that the flora had started down there. Then it had expanded, braiding and twisting outward in all directions. If the limbs could break through concrete, then the bunker was indeed at risk.

"Oh, wow," Luigi said.

Mac turned to see that the young Ranger had cut through one of the tendrils on the street. The limb retracted across the concrete, squirting out purple sap. Rattling and crunching echoed in the distance.

"What the heck is that…" Mac whispered.

As if in answer, the skein of vines across the street pulsated with a darker red glow. It seemed to be reacting to Luigi's snipping of that small strand. But the vine wasn't just turning colors. The entire cluster began to move.

Strands snaked out from the rubble. A vine squirmed past Mac's leg, and he hopped away and hurried back toward the Stryker. Luigi, however, had stopped to stare.

"Get back!" Mac said.

Finally, the kid turned, just as a vine wrapped around his ankle. It yanked him off his feet, knocking him to the ground so hard his helmet cracked.

"Luigi!" Mac shouted. He unsheathed the machete on his belt and started to move as more of the vines curled out of the sinkhole, casting their malevolent glow across the road. He hacked one that reached for his boot. Sap spattered the road. He slashed another, severing it. But a flood of the branches flowed out of the sinkhole. Thick limbs tunneled out of the dirt and burst from the collapsed structures framing the road. In seconds, Luigi had been wrapped up in a web.

"Help…" he choked before a limb tightened around his neck.

Mac couldn't help but wonder if this was how his old man had died.

"Get back to the truck now, Mac!" Glock shouted out the open door.

Mac swung at the limbs coming at him, but with each passing second, Luigi was pulled farther away. The web dragged him steadily toward the sinkhole.

"You can't save him!" Glock yelled.

But Mac had to keep trying. He couldn't leave him the way the Rangers had left his father. He fought harder and was making some progress, but Luigi was now fully cocooned. As Mac slashed, he spotted something moving in the glow at the end of the street, beyond the manhole covers, one of which was now removed. The light captured muscular limbs pulling a gaunt white body from the sewer. It darted into the rubble, vanishing.

Were his eyes playing tricks on him?

Mac hacked and kicked at the vines, making another foot of progress toward the sinkhole.

"Hold on!" he shouted.

But it was already too late. The vines dragged Luigi into the glowing abyss. His muffled screams receded.

"Luigi!" Mac shouted.

An electronic tone answered.

Mac froze, his heart leaping. The ethereal call seemed to be coming from down the street, where he thought he had seen the strange bipedal creature. He remembered the story about how his father had died, and what the Rangers had described hearing.

A steady electronic tone, like that from an oscillator.

They had also described a pale, muscular figure that moved like the wind.

He looked at the rubble where the beast had vanished earlier. And there it was again, an eyeless humanoid beast perched on a slab of concrete. Hanging from its mouth were vines that it chewed like spaghetti. It hunched down, sniffing the air with slotted nostrils, raising and lowering a mane of spikes running up its neck to the crest of its deformed skull.

Mac had assumed he would be brave in this moment—that he would raise his shotgun and shoot the abomination. That was why he had become a Ranger.

But instead sheer terror took hold at the sight of this horrific alien creature.

A vine wrapped around his leg, pulling him to the ground and dragging him. Mac slashed at it, but this limb was thicker and stronger than the others. Barbs bristled from the dense flesh. He swung wildly, missed, and hit the concrete hard enough to chip the blade.

The Stryker roared forward, and Glock popped the passenger door open.

"Get in!" he shouted.

Mac reached back for the rusted running board. The limb around his leg pulled him closer to the sinkhole, but he managed to grab the running board.

"Go!" Mac screamed.

Glock reversed the vehicle, pulling Mac back from the sinkhole. The vine tightened, stretching him in a painful tug-of-war. Glancing over his shoulder, he saw dozens more of the vines rushing out of the hole, coming for him.

A violent boom sounded, and the limb holding Mac's leg exploded. The weight loosened on his leg as the vine snapped apart. He collapsed to the concrete and looked inside the Stryker as Glock jacked another round in his shotgun.

"Get in," he said as he lowered the weapon.

Mac pushed himself up and climbed into the vehicle, the severed section of vine still attached to his leg. Shutting the door, he heard the haunting call of the beast rising like an emergency siren.

CHAPTER 3

"The reports are here!" Beto shouted in an uncharacteristically excited voice.

Nick hurried over for a look at the single computer screen in the machine bay. Workers clustered around it for a view of the data the Rangers brought back yesterday. Rumors had already started to spread about what they had found up there. Some people were saying not all the Rangers had even come back. So far, nothing was confirmed.

Nick knew better than to buy into any rumors. He also knew better than to get excited about any of the data changing since the last time they deployed. Still, he found himself anxiously reading the data as it scrolled down the screen.

AIR QUALITY
CONTAMINANT: *Radioactive particles*
LEVEL: *Elevated*

WATER QUALITY
CONTAMINANT: *Radioactive isotopes such as cesium 137 and iodine 131*
LEVEL: *High*

With each line, his heart sank a little. There was no change in any of the data. The other workers around him sighed, sharing his sentiment.

SOIL QUALITY

CONTAMINANT: *Strontium 90, plutonium*

LEVEL: *Very high*

CONCLUSION: *No changes have been detected aboveground to indicate safer conditions. Prolonged exposure will cause breakdown of cells and cancer in biological entities. At this time, the council suggests the same semiannual monitoring and updated tests to monitor for significant changes on the surface.*

Nick knew he shouldn't be surprised, but he still lowered his head in despair. Another six months had passed without any noticeable changes topside.

"Okay, that's that," Beto announced. "Still poisonous, still dark, still hell. Time to get back to work."

He shifted to the chalkboard displaying their work assignments.

Nick shook off his disappointment and searched for his name and the tasks set out for him. This morning he was assigned to the grindstone. One of the most boring jobs possible.

With a sigh, he moved along with the other workers.

"Don't worry, Nick," Smitty said. "We must have faith our situation will change. Someday things will be different."

Grunts and muttering came in reply. "Bullshit," one man said. "We're gonna live down here forever. Don't try to give the kid hope."

Nick blocked out all the noise as he headed to the scrap chamber. Hyena was standing in front of a pile of scrap metal that dwarfed his stooped and twisted body.

"Six bolts, six bolts, six bolts, ha-hah!" He cackled.

"Hyena," Nick said.

The frail man whirled toward him, and Nick told him his assignment. Hyena limped over, gesturing with filthy black fingernails.

"This way, this way, ha-hah," he said.

The salvage chief scurried over to the gate of the fenced-off storage room and swung it open. Pushing his spectacles up, he went inside to the shelved boxes, grabbing one.

"Knives, lots of knives. Don't cut yourself, boy, ha-hah!" Hyena said. He shoved a plastic crate across the desk to Nick.

"Thanks."

"Wait, not done, little fella, ha-hah!"

"My name's Nick."

"Don't care. Nope, don't care. Nick or not, don't care."

Hyena brought a long steel rod over with some sort of club on the end. He placed it on the desk, then put a broken broom shaft beside it.

Nick took them both. Then he carried the crate of knives back to the hallway, struggling to balance everything with the rod and broom under his arm.

Sounds of welding and grinding guided him to the shop. The grindstone was in the middle of the room. He situated the box by the grinding wheel, then set the club and broom down. He held up the rod, remembering that it was for some sort of ancient sport, to hit balls.

He thought it odd.

He cut off the club with a hacksaw and drilled a hole in the end. Next, he removed the broom head and fastened it to the end of the rod where the club had been. A few minutes later, he had a functioning broom.

Nick worked quickly, hoping that if he finished his tasks for the morning Beto might let him go play with Sofia and the other kids before school started in the afternoon. The classes lasted just two hours; then Nick would come back here and work a second shift until eight o'clock.

He examined the grinding wheel to check that the axle was secured and lubricated.

For the next hour, he sharpened dull blades of various kinds. The first two were chef's knives; the third was a trident attachment used to hunt rats, the tips still covered in dried blood. When he unsheathed the long fourth blade with a duct-taped handle, he recognized Mac's machete.

There was something on the end of it too. He held the weapon up to the dim lights and studied the red substance. Blood, maybe? But no—it looked like some sort of fungus, or maybe it was flesh.

The blade had several chips along its edge. His mind swam as he considered what Mac might have used it on out there.

Had they encountered a monster? Had he killed something?

Nick looked up at the ceiling, picturing the surface. His heart pounded, not from fear but from excitement.

"Hey, get your ass to work, Baker," Beto said.

Pushing down his face mask, Nick moved back to the machine. The wheel turned, and he held the blade to the stone. Sparks danced from the end as he polished off the dried red substance.

Nick tried to focus, but his mind was on the surface. He tried to imagine what the Rangers had encountered topside. A huge, scaly lizard, or a mutant dog, or perhaps it was flora—some sort of tree or plant that had adapted to live in the inhospitable radio-active terrain.

His excitement grew with each possibility.

After shutting down the grindstone, Nick took the sharpened blades back to Beto, placing them on his desk as the man read a report on the computer terminal, his back to Nick.

"I'm all done," Nick said.

Beto pointed to the chalkboard without turning. Nick frowned when he saw a new task. There would be no playing with Sofia today. He would be replacing a broken heat shield in an oven.

"Be careful," Beto said.

Nick crossed the shop to the ovens they used to make glass. He was the only one who could fit inside. First, he made sure the power was off before going in. As he crawled into the oven, he heard a muffled announcement over the PA system.

Nick decided to keep at it until he was finished, not wanting to stay in the oven a moment longer than necessary. But as he started replacing the broken component, he noticed the sounds of industry out in the shop—the tapping of slag hammers and the popping of arc welders—had stopped. Turning, he looked out the grimy glass door at what appeared to be an empty shop. Every workstation he could see was abandoned.

Where had everyone gone?

Reaching out, he pushed the oven door open and climbed out. The other workers were across the room, huddled around the monitor again with Beto.

"What's going on?" Nick asked.

"Creed just made an announcement," Beto said. "Ranger Luigi was lost on the mission yesterday."

"Lost?"

"Killed," someone clarified.

Nick didn't even turn to see who had spoken. The news shocked him to his core. And while this wasn't the first time a Ranger had died on the surface, it was the first Ranger to die in the line of duty during Nick's lifetime.

The monitor turned on, displaying Minister Creed's face.

"Today we honor our brave fallen brother Luigi, who tragically lost his life protecting our sanctuary when he fell into a sinkhole." Creed looked out, as if he were staring into the soul of every single person inside the bunker.

Where most people saw a strong leader, Nick saw the face of a liar. A man who told everyone what they wanted to hear so that they felt safe underground. But Nick didn't buy that they were safe—or that Luigi had fallen into a sinkhole. He had evidence to the contrary. The team had discovered something on their mission, and it had killed the young Ranger.

"Let us pray for our brother Luigi now and remember him for the quiet, kindhearted young man he was," Creed said.

Nick bowed his head with the rest of the machinists and mechanics.

"We ask the Great Creator to care for the soul of our brother and to help him pass to the next life," Creed said.

Nick looked up during the same moment that Creed's gaze returned to the screen. The minister gave a final nod, and with that, the feed ended. The mechanics shuffled back to their work, heads down, all saddened by the news but accepting it.

Not Nick. As he flipped on his headlamp and climbed back into the oven, his mind returned to the machete. Whatever was on that blade had killed Luigi.

Mac knew the truth, and so did Glock, but they were sworn to secrecy, to keep the lies of the council and the minister from being exposed. But the truth was also inside the Stryker, on the database, and Nick knew a way in through the vent system. The ductwork wasn't much narrower than the oven he was in now. If anyone could get in, it was him.

Nick came up with a plan as he worked on the oven. By the time he finished, he had made up his mind: He would break into the vehicle bay, find a way into the Stryker, and see what the Rangers had found out there—what had killed Luigi.

They were lying, and he wanted to know why.

*　*　*　*　*

"What do you think happened to Luigi?" Chubs asked.

"He fell into a sinkhole," Ron said. "You heard Minister Creed."

"Yeah," Gus chirped. "Sinkhole."

Nick and Sofia exchanged a look across the mess hall table where they sat eating their supper of soup and corn bread. She was young, but she clearly had her suspicions too. Still, he couldn't tell her what he had found. Not that he didn't trust her, but he didn't want to put her at risk.

"All I know is, I'm never trying out to be a Ranger," Chubs said.

"Fear not—they'd never take you," Ron said. "Don't think you'll have to worry about working in the farm either. No way the council would assign you there, 'cause you'd eat everything, like Peter Rabbit."

"Frek off."

"What's *frek* mean?" Gus asked. Just seven years old, he was the youngest of the lot.

"I'm going to be a doctor." Chubs took a bite of corn bread. "Me and Sofia. Right, Sofia?"

"If by *doctor*, you mean *chef*, then yes."

The kids all chuckled, except for Nick. He was busy looking over the sea of people eating at the metal tables in the room. Many of these residents seemed to have already moved on from news of Luigi's death, accepting it as normal. But that just made Nick more determined to find out the truth.

"Nick, you okay?" Sofia asked.

He turned back to his friends and nodded.

"You're being really quiet," she said.

"Tired from work. Gotta get back to it," Nick lied.

"Come on, I can tell something's bothering you. It's the Rangers, right?"

"Wait. Do you think Luigi got killed by a monster or something?" Chubs asked.

Nick paused as he picked up his tray.

"No," he lied again.

Then he left his friends, starting the long journey to the bottom of the bunker. All those steps gave him time to consider his plan.

*   *   *   *   *

At eight thirty in the evening, Nick lay on top of his sleeping bag, watching Timmy Tam. The mouse nibbled on the piece of corn bread Nick had brought back from dinner. As his tiny friend ate, Nick planned how he would get to the top floor of the bunker without being seen.

He already knew the routes like clockwork. The engineering room would be empty at this time unless there was an emergency. The last automatic check would have been done at eight o'clock, with the next worker not showing up until ten o'clock.

At nine, supplies came down to the workshops, along with any items tagged "urgent," which needed to be fixed as soon as possible. That was the last planned delivery of the day, and then the cart would return up the shaft. He would follow it up, using an internal ladder to avoid being seen on the stairs after curfew.

He got off his sleeping bag and sat on the floor, stretching his legs out all the way to the door of his tiny living space. At this time of night, he would usually feel exhausted after a busy day of work, school, dinner, and then a few more hours of work. But his excitement had given him a second wind.

Timmy Tam watched him curiously while nibbling on his corn bread crumb. Maybe the little critter was concerned because his provider was about to do something very dangerous.

"Don't worry. I won't get into trouble," he said.

He slid open the door to his closet and pulled out a black

outfit that was a bit too big for him. The elevator shaft was dark, but he would need the disguise to keep himself hidden.

Nick looked at his furry friend, who had retreated into his home and was peering up with his tiny eyes as if to say, *Be careful.*

"I will," Nick whispered.

He stuffed his gear into his pack and slung it over his black outfit. Stepping up to the door, he listened for anyone who might be in the hall. Hearing nothing, he opened it, then checked both directions.

Empty.

Nick pulled a balaclava over his face and set off, keeping to the shadows. A bare bulb flickered ahead, illuminating the closed doors of the workers, who were all inside their rooms, most of them probably already asleep, except for Tomás, who was on night shift.

He made it past all the closed doors without disturbing anyone. Just as he had expected, no one was currently working in the cavernous space filled with boilers, heating and cooling units, and other equipment. He ran across the dark space until he got to the entrance of the workshop, where he encountered his first problem.

Across the room, Beto was still at his desk, facing the corridor where Nick now stood. A lamp illuminated the paperwork the boss was reading. A few workstations down, Tomás was also reading something, but with his back turned to Nick.

Rows of machines separated Nick from his coworkers and the elevator shaft and stairs. Keeping low, Nick darted into the workspace. It was dark here, too, but he knew the room by heart and easily avoided bumping into anything.

Hunching behind the sharpener he had used on Mac's machete just this morning, he stopped to check on Beto, who was still going over paperwork. Tomás, however, stood up with his book and let out a loud yawn.

"Hope we don't have anything major tonight," he said.

Beto glanced up, looking right in Nick's direction.

Heart pounding, Nick crouched back down, expecting his name to be shouted across the room. He prepared to run, but nothing happened. A look at his wristwatch confirmed that it was five minutes to nine.

Slowly, he peeked up over the machine again. Beto was back to reading, but now Tomás was starting to walk toward the corridor that led to the elevator shaft. Nick had to get into the stairwell first and hide there, then wait for his moment after the cart returned to the upper levels.

He darted to the next station, a workspace where they kept most of their tools. In his haste, Nick knocked something loose. He reached back, fumbling but somehow catching a screwdriver someone had left on the edge of the station.

Instead of putting it back, he stuck it in his pocket and let out a quiet exhalation. The sound of Tomás's shoes clicked across the concrete. Nick tried to walk in step with him as he moved to the final station separating him from the elevator and the stairs.

"Hey, Tomás," Beto said.

The footsteps stopped. Nick looked out. Tomás halted and was looking away. This was his chance.

Keeping low, Nick ran out of the workshop and into the stairwell. The shaft was empty, but he could hear the cart cranking down.

He hurried up to the second level to hide. This was the tricky part of his plan. Ideally, he would have taken the ladder on the bottom level, after the cart went back up. But that would put him within view of Tomás and Beto.

Nick kept going to the third floor just to listen for anyone who might be coming down. Hearing a choking noise, he halted. As he listened, he realized the sound wasn't choking; it was snoring. He looked cautiously across the open floor to the computer terminal, where Hyena slept with his head on the desk.

Perfect.

He sneaked back down a few stairs, keeping between the third and second levels. The cranking got louder—right on time.

A loud snort rang out above him.

Nick froze at the sound of shuffling feet, punctuated by the tap of Hyena's cane. He was awake, and he was moving. Nick considered retreating back down the stairs, but instead he hunched down, eyeing the top landing and listening.

The *tap, tap* of the cane was drowned out by the lowering elevator cart.

"Got anything good for me, ha-hah?" Hyena said.

"Not tonight," came the rough reply from Hugh, the Ranger on duty.

Nick stayed put for the next few minutes while Hugh dropped off the supplies to Beto below. The cart started to rise, and Nick moved into position, back up a few stairs until he had a view inside the doorway by the elevator shaft. Hyena was back at his desk, head down.

Moving fast, Nick darted to the left of the elevator shaft, remaining in the shadows. He would access the ladder here. The cart cranked higher, and he glanced into the shaft, spotting the metal rungs attached to the wall across from the open door. It was a long drop, and he would have to jump across.

You got this, he thought.

As the cart rose up, he didn't stop to dwell on what he was going to do. He backed up and then ran, leaping the five-foot gap and hopping onto the ladder with a *clunk*. His left boot hit the rung, but his right slipped. He tried to hold on with his hands, but they slid a little.

He heard grumbling above, and the cranking stopped abruptly

just as his hands found purchase, gripping the rails. He brought his right boot back up on the rung, placing it down softly beside his left.

A radio crackled above.

"Mac, you copy?" Hugh asked.

"Yeah," answered a tired-sounding Mac from the control room. "What's up?"

"Heard a noise."

Nick's heart was in his throat.

"What kind of noise?" Mac asked.

"Nothing. Must've been this old cart. I'll ask Beto to take a look tomorrow."

"Copy that."

The cranking resumed, and Nick continued his climb.

He resisted the urge to look down during the ascent. On the tenth floor up, he forgot himself and glanced down into the darkness. His stomach fluttered.

Keep going, and keep looking up.

He continued the climb, sweat beading on his face. His bony arms began to tire. He climbed past the farm, water treatment plant, mess hall, school, and living quarters. All silent.

Sofia and his friends were there, sleeping in their warm beds.

And Nick was doing the craziest thing of his life. He smiled, trying to ignore his burning muscles and the sweat stinging his eyes. The cart stopped two floors from the top, where Hugh disembarked and went inside the command center.

Nick waited a few more agonizing minutes, and his left leg began twitching up and down like a sewing machine. Finally, certain that Hugh was gone, he climbed up the ladder, squeezing between the cart and the wall of the shaft. Then he took his right boot off the rungs and set it down on the safety railing built around the cart. Using it as a step stool, he eased himself down onto the wooden cart. From there, he went through the open door of the shaft, into the stairwell, where he found the ventilation unit access. He unscrewed the bolts and pulled the grate away.

After climbing inside, he turned and replaced the grate. Next, he crawled through the ventilation shaft to the end, which looked over the vehicle depot shrouded in darkness.

Nick quickly unscrewed the final grate. He laid it carefully down, then pulled a flashlight from his bag. The beam played over the parked vehicles until it picked up the Stryker.

He jumped down six feet to the floor, landing with a soft thud. He ran over to the vehicle, going around the back, where the Rangers climbed in each time they left the bunker.

The door was unlocked—protocol for all the vehicles. He climbed inside and shut the door. He swept the beam over the installed equipment and found the monitor he was looking for. He took a seat in the worn leather. Nick wasn't all that familiar with computers, but he understood the basics. After a few attempts, he activated the terminal. The screen glowed to life, spreading over the interior of the vehicle. He scrolled through the thumbnails of video footage from the mission, clicking Play once the Rangers had gotten topside.

Nick watched the monitor in awe as the Stryker drove out of the tunnel to the surface. A skyline of ruined structures broke the horizon, lit by the nearly constant flash of lightning. The vehicle motored down a ruined road, veering around rubble, guided by its bright beams.

But there was another light out there—red and flickering. The light spread over rubble piles covered in a tapestry of vegetation that reminded him of blood vessels. The truck stopped, and Mac got out with his shotgun. Luigi went next, carrying a testing kit up to the glowing vegetation. As he bent down with a pair of shears, Mac walked closer toward what appeared to be a gaping hole in the road. He shined his light down.

The red glow suddenly darkened, and Nick noticed the vines across the street... *moving*.

"What the bloody hell?" he whispered.

Glock cursed in the audio, but Nick couldn't hear it over his own voice. The vines came to life across the screen, snatching Luigi and pulling him to the street.

Hearing a noise outside, Nick turned as the hatch opened. Mac stood there with his shotgun aimed into the Stryker.

"What the hell are you doing, kid?" he asked.

Nick raised his hands above his head. "I... I was looking—"

"You dumb little shit," Mac said. He lowered his shotgun and climbed inside. Then he shut off the terminal.

"I'm sorry," Nick said. "I wanted to know what you got on your machete out there. I figured you killed a monster."

"My machete?"

"Yeah."

"I thought I had it all cleaned off." He shook his head and motioned for Nick to get out. "Come on, let's go."

Nick climbed out of the truck and stood outside.

"How much did you see?" Mac asked.

"I saw the vines. I saw them take Luigi."

"And you will tell no one."

"What?"

"No one can know."

Nick was the one to shake his head. "You're just going to lie about what's out there?"

Mac grabbed him by the shoulder, rattling him.

"If the council finds out you know, they could punish you severely—maybe even kill you," Mac said. "Do you understand?"

"Kill me for finding out the truth?"

Mac snorted. "You're young and dumb, just like I was at your age. When I had hope that there were good people out there. But I learned years ago that's a pipe dream."

"There has to be."

"Oh yeah?" Mac moved closer to Nick, his breath hot. "There ain't nothin' good out there. Only monsters—monsters you didn't see in that video, but I did with my own eyes. The same kind that killed my old man."

He gave an angry snort.

"And not all monsters are beasts, Nick," Mac said. "Some are disguised as men."

CHAPTER 4

Mac woke in a sweat from a nightmare about monsters. In that dream, he had been back at the sinkhole, trying to save Luigi from the vines.

Three years had passed since that tragic mission. Not a day went by that Mac didn't think of what had happened out there. He could still hear the kid's muffled screams and the ethereal wail of the monster. The same type of creature that had likely killed his father. And, like a damn coward, Mac had frozen up when he saw it.

That creature haunted his dreams most nights, like tonight, waking him up in a sweat. But it was always on the eve of a new deployment that the dreams got worse with the prospect that he might have to go back out there. Of the five missions since the one Luigi died on, Mac had been back out there only once. Two deployments ago, almost a year now. Each time the Rangers went, they would observe the vines, keeping their distance to avoid the fate that befell the young Ranger. And each time, those vines had spread to a new city block. Closer and closer to the bunker.

Today three Rangers would be heading back out there to document the mutant flora. Perhaps soon they would deploy to destroy it. At least, that was what several of the councillors had proposed. Others argued to leave it alone. Mac wasn't sure what the right answer was, only that if the order came to try to kill it, he would.

He sat up in bed and saw that it was almost six o'clock. Deciding it was useless to go back to sleep, he went to the sink in his small room and splashed cold water on his face. Then he looked at the mirror, studying the face that looked back at him. He was thirty-eight, and it was starting to show. Gray had begun a slow spread throughout his thinning hair. Crow's-feet had formed around his eyes, and three deep grooves had quietly, mysteriously implanted themselves on his forehead.

He scratched the shadow of beard and decided to let it grow out for the day.

"You're getting old," he told himself.

He stepped back, threw on his uniform, and went to run the steps, as he did every morning. It kept him *feeling* young, at least. And this morning it kept his mind from focusing too much on the mission.

He kicked off his run up the stairs, twenty floors to the top, on the landing outside the command center. When he arrived, he immediately wondered if the council was there now, deciding who would be going topside.

Mac heaved a breath, turned around, and began the descent. By now, other early risers were using the wide stairs to get to their jobs: Rhonda to the farm, to check the irrigation and water whatever needed it. Then Jason to replace the night worker at the water treatment plant. Finally, Ted, who was on his way to the kitchen to start breakfast with two other workers.

Mac greeted each of them with a nod. When he got to the bottom of the bunker, the machines in the shop were already whining and grinding. Standing at one of the stations was Nick Baker, sanding the wooden handle of a saw.

From the shadows, Mac watched the kid, sweat beading on his pimply forehead, eyes intent on his work. When Nick wasn't here or in school, he was running the stairs, too, or working out in his little closet of a room. Everyone knew the kid wanted to be a Ranger.

He reminded Mac of himself at that age, wanting to make a difference by becoming a lawman. It wouldn't be long now before Nick volunteered. But that didn't mean he would get on the force. Ultimately, the council determined who ended up wearing the badge.

And if they ever found out that Nick knew what had happened to Luigi, he would end up topside without a suit, left to die in the wastes. Mac, too, would likely meet the same fate for not ratting the boy out.

Mac's radio crackled, and he reached down to his belt to pull it. When he looked back up again, he felt Nick staring at him from across the room. With a nod, Mac acknowledged the kid, then stepped back into the stairwell.

"Mac, you copy?" came Glock's voice over the radio.

"Yeah, copy. I'm in the machine shop."

"Shit, all the way down there? I need you at the community center."

"What for?"

"Got a situation with Barney again. He's wasted."

"Copy that."

Mac groaned as he clipped the radio back on his belt. Barney was a fifty-year-old maintenance worker who had failed to launch in every way. He spent most of his days sneaking booze on the job and his nights bingeing, when he could get a hold of moonshine. When Mac arrived at the community center, he could tell it had been one of those nights.

Barney stumbled over by the cafeteria window, where Ted

was setting up the coffeepots for breakfast. The aroma of brewed coffee drifted across the room, along with the scent of booze.

"Give me a mug, ya sod," Barney shouted. "I said *now*, goddamn it!"

"Get out of here!" Ted yelled back.

Mac hurried over, holding up his hand. "Barney, calm down, man."

The drunk turned so fast he almost fell over.

"Teddy Freddy won't give me a damn mug," Barney grumbled.

"'Cause it's not time—you know the rules," Mac said.

"I know the dumb rules, but I need coffee."

Ted stepped back from the window as Barney turned around. He clambered up on the windowsill, one leg up, the other kicking for purchase.

"Son of a…" Mac muttered. This was the part of his job he hated: being a cop, or rather, more like a babysitter. He ran over to grab Barney, plucking him off the ledge.

"You're gonna sober up in the brig," Mac said. He wrestled him to his feet, twisting his arm in a hammerlock until Barney yelped.

"Hey, that hurts!" he protested.

"That's the point, genius," Mac said. "Come on, let's go."

He released the hammerlock and pushed Barney toward the exit, wanting to get him out of the mess hall before the first people came for their breakfast.

"Carry on, Ted," Mac said over his shoulder.

"Thanks, champ," Ted called back.

Mac led Barney into the hallway, then to the stairs.

"I just wanted coffee," Barney said in a low tone.

The old Mac might have felt bad for the guy, but not anymore. As he got older, he stopped having empathy for people who wouldn't make changes. Barney was a drag on the bunker, and if he didn't make some improvements, he might be the first resident in a decade to be exiled to the wastes.

"You want to get shipped outside?" Mac asked him.

"Fuck off, man."

Mac turned him around, wanting to tell him what was out there. About the vines and the eyeless beasts. But he decided instead to just slap him in the face so hard that it echoed.

"Get your shit together, or you'll soon be puking your guts out from radiation poisoning and crying like a baby."

Mac pushed him again. When they arrived at the brig—a single cell retrofitted from a storage area—his radio buzzed again.

Mac pulled it off, but this time it wasn't Glock. It was Creed.

"Ranger Mac, you're needed in the control room," said the minister. "Report immediately."

"Copy that."

Mac nudged Barney inside the cell, then locked it.

"Sober up. I'll be back later," he said.

"Bring me some coffee when you do."

Mac scoffed and then shut the door. He ran to the stairwell, loping up the steps, his heart skipping. Deep down, he knew he had been selected for today's deployment. But why have him go to the command room? He couldn't remember the last time he was summoned there.

He broke into a run, moving as fast as he could to the very top of the bunker. At the top landing, he stopped to catch his breath. Then he knocked on the thick door. Hugh opened it, and Mac stepped into a small room furnished with a single long table and a dozen chairs. Maps of Houston hung on the concrete walls. Four working monitors hung from mounts, displaying surface data and images of the wastes. Terminals faced those screens, each serving a different purpose. Facing the radio station was Creed, his back turned.

Mac walked inside and saw Glock to the right of the door, chewing on a toothpick. He gave Mac a subtle nod. It was difficult not to ask what the hell was going on, but Mac had a feeling he already knew when he saw the screen showing the sinkhole and the mutant flora growing out of it.

"Minister Creed," Mac said as the man turned.

Creed nodded and motioned to the table.

"Have a seat, all of you," he said.

The Rangers all went to the table and took a chair. Creed stood at the far end, sucking in a short breath through his nostrils. And then he did something Mac hadn't seen before. He smiled.

"At midnight, Hugh received a transmission," Creed said.

"A transmission?" Mac asked. "From who?"

Creed looked up at the ceiling and then spread his arms out.

"The sky," he said. His gaze returned to Mac. "The angels have arrived to take us home."

Mac narrowed his eyes as he met the minister's gaze.

"We don't have to worry about the vines anymore," he said. "Our days living in ITC Star Station are coming to an end."

*   *   *   *   *

"I hate this one," Sofia said.

Nick sat in the library with his friends, waiting for a disc story to start, though his mind was elsewhere. Today the Rangers would deploy back to the wastes. Probably to the same site where Luigi had died. Nick had never told anyone what he saw with his own eyes when he was in the Stryker. Not even Sofia. She was eleven, and he was sixteen now, just twenty-one months shy of being eligible to volunteer as a Ranger. But Nick had a lot of work to do if he wanted to be considered. While he had grown taller by a few inches, he was still thin as a rail—gaunt, even. The doctor said he had a deficiency of this and that. Things that didn't matter, because he couldn't get them anyway.

"Here we go," Chubs said.

The screen blinked on, and the credits of the story rolled across. Nick sat between Sofia and Ron, with Gus and Chubs beside them. The boys were all excited about watching the ancient movie that they had seen several times on the disc story player. But each time, the killer machine that hunted down the woman scared the crap out of them all.

"I love it. The robot is crazy cool," Ron said.

"I can't believe all the different food they used to have up there."

"Is that all you think about?" Gus asked.

Chubs shook his head. "No."

Sofia laughed.

Today, as the movie started, Nick wasn't thinking about the killer robot or the food, but rather about the city that was once called Los Angeles. Ever since he saw what was really up there, he had a hard time understanding how humans could have destroyed such a marvelous place, burning down the green forests and reducing towering cities of glass and metal to rubble. And worst of all, blotting out the bright sun to plunge the world into darkness.

But maybe it wasn't *all* like that up there. Nick remained hopeful that there was a place beyond the devastation. That it wasn't all monsters, as Mac had said. That there were people like those in ITC Star Station, just out there trying to survive.

Sofia nudged him as they watched.

"What?" he asked.

"I like the new look," she said.

He reached up and stroked his chin. Though he wasn't growing much, he was starting to get some fuzz on his face.

"Shh," Ron said. "This is one of my favorite parts."

Nick watched the naked muscular robot disguised as a man as he took a sawed-off shotgun from a bearded guy in leather.

Ron chuckled.

The screen suddenly shut off.

"Hey!" Ron cried.

Disappointed voices rang out from the tables and chairs where dozens of people had been watching. Nick got up, prepared to help fix the disc player, when a deep voice called out from the back of the room.

"A gathering has been called by Minister Creed."

Nick looked back to see Hugh standing in the open door.

"Everyone is to head to the vehicle depot as soon as possible," said the Ranger.

Hushed voices broke out as the room began to empty. Nick followed the group with his friends, wondering if this was it— the day the secret he kept would be shared with the rest of the bunker. Maybe they were finally announcing what really happened to Luigi.

"An announcement," Sofia said. "What do you think it is?"

"No idea," Ron said.

"Me either," said Chubs.

Each of them looked to Nick, but he remained quiet.

They marched into the corridor and up the stairs. Feet pounded up the worn tread over the concrete, up flight after flight to the vehicle bay. The line surged inside, forming a crowd in front of the empty platform where each bunker minister in turn had addressed them all, ever since the world ended.

Creed was already there, gripping the rusted iron bars, dark eyes glaring down over his flock.

"Tonight I have remarkable news," he announced in his deep, commanding baritone.

Nick felt Sofia nudge up against him.

"We are *not* alone," Creed boomed. "Our comms have picked up a message from an airship."

"An airship?" someone called out.

Loud voices rang out across the crowd. Some rejoiced, holding their hands up in prayer as if they had all just been saved. Others trembled at the news.

Nick wasn't sure what to think.

"Silence!" Creed shouted.

The noise slowly subsided as he gazed out over the faces of his flock.

"Captain Alfonzo sent out a message in search of survivors," Creed said. "We have yet to answer this call, but I am sharing it with you all so you understand. There are others out there, people like us."

Nick felt a chill up his back. He was right. There *were* others.

"How do you know they are like us?" someone asked.

"Listen," Creed said. He nodded at Hugh, who stood to his right.

The speakers crackled, and a voice with a heavy accent spoke.

"Attention to anyone out there. This is the airship *Angel*, broadcasting on all available frequencies in search of any remaining souls. We have navigated the skies in our quest to rebuild the shattered remnants of civilization. Our airship is a sanctuary equipped with resources and medical aid, and with a community of survivors united in the cause of renewal. However, our sanctuary has been adrift for far too long, and we must put down soon before we crash to the surface.

"I implore anyone hearing this message to respond with your location. If you provide us coordinates to land, we will share our resources. We have charted maps of safe zones and a network of other survivors. Whether you are alone or with a group, whether in desolation or in a haven of your own, you are important.

"To those in hiding, to those who believe they are the last humans on earth, let this message be a beacon of hope. We are here, we are searching, and we can help each other. Together we will rise. We will rebuild. *Angel* out."

Immediately, the room erupted with answers to the transmission. Of all the voices, one was loudest. Valkia made her way to the front, standing directly under Creed.

"These are demons, not angels!" she said. "They will bring death and destruction to our home!"

Creed wasted no time giving the order to have her removed. Glock grabbed her by the back of the neck.

"No, stop!" she wailed. "You will doom us all!"

She kicked him in the shin.

"You dumb bitch!" Glock yelled. He shoved her to the ground, then pulled out one of his pistols. "I should blast your face off!"

"Stop!" Mac shouted. He ran over and moved in front of the old woman, holding up his hand to Glock. "Put the gun away, Colin."

That was the first time Nick had heard anyone call Glock by his real name. Hell, Nick hadn't even known he *had* a real name.

"Do not desecrate this place with blood," Creed called down sternly. "Take her away."

Valkia pushed up and backed away, glaring at Glock and then up at Creed.

"Remove her!" he shouted.

Another Ranger came over and escorted Valkia out, the door clanking shut behind them.

"That's right, you ugly old biddy," Glock said, holstering his pistol. "You're lucky Mac saved your wretched ass."

Mac shook his head, then stiffened as Creed grabbed the railing. He swept his commanding gaze over the crowd.

"I have shared this message with you because you all deserve to know we are not alone, that there are others out there like us. We must not let heretics like Valkia distract us from this fact."

He raised his chin, striking a confident pose.

"To survive the future, we must embrace it, and in that effort, I will be sending out a delegation that includes Rangers Mac, Hugh, and Glock, to meet the crew of this ship at an undisclosed location."

Nick felt Sofia brushing his hand with her fingers. She had done this a few times in the past, when she was worried or scared. He took her hand, squeezing it to let her know it was okay, that he would protect her.

But deep down, Nick wasn't sure that was true. He thought back to what Mac had told him about the monsters outside—beasts and men.

Were these people the monsters that Mac had described?

They would soon know.

CHAPTER 5

Mac held the framed picture of his mother and father that he kept inside his locker. This was the only image he had of them. It was taken when she was six months pregnant with Mac, her hand over her growing belly. His father had a broad smile of pure joy on his face. From what Mac remembered, he was always cracking jokes and teasing his mom. That was his old man, and where Mac had gotten his own sense of humor.

But Mac hadn't done much smiling lately—not until today. As much as he found himself suspicious of the transmission, he couldn't help but feel excitement at the knowledge they weren't alone down here. That there were people living topside, in the sky.

Mac shook it all away, reminding himself they knew exactly nothing yet. That this mission could be a trap. For Mac knew all too well that men could be just as bad as any clawed and fanged predator in the wastes. He recalled the classified stories he was told when he joined the Rangers. Stories about raiders.

There were people out there, but none of them had ever been good. And that was why he was surprised to see Creed inform the bunker about this airship. They could end up just as evil as the raiders and cannibals his ancestors had encountered over the past two centuries following the war.

Mac had to keep his guard up. He placed the picture back in his locker and resumed cleaning his shotgun. When he finished, he began the long process of checking his suit, then his armor. Two hours later, he felt as prepared as he could be. He took a lukewarm shower, dressed, and left the locker room for the vehicle depot. Glock was already there, cursing about something or other. Mac ignored him. After that stunt with Valkia, Mac wanted to avoid the unhinged Ranger altogether.

Hugh arrived thirty minutes later, and by then Creed had joined them.

They gathered by the Stryker.

"Today is the most significant day in our modern history," Creed said. "For today, I believe we will make contact with the first survivors who are in the same situation as us. I've spoken to this Captain Alfonzo, and I believe him to be a good man. Of course, he could be a liar, but my gut tells me otherwise. We have agreed on a meeting place I've provided based on maps Rangers put together from years ago."

He reached into his robe and pulled out a map, which he handed over to Mac.

"I've never been out that far, sir, not even close," he said.

"No matter, I trust you will get us there."

"*Us?*"

Creed looked at Mac and Hugh in turn.

"I believe in this mission so much that I will be joining you today to ensure its success," Creed said. "That means, Glock, you will stay behind."

Mac glanced over, expecting Glock to curse and put up a fight, but he merely shrugged. Happy not to be going, it seemed.

"Minister, all due respect, but I'm not sure you coming with us is a good idea," Mac said. He didn't like the idea of Glock coming either, but he liked the idea of Creed coming even less.

"It's not an idea, Ranger; it's an order." Creed turned away. "Once I get suited up, we head out. Prepare the Stryker."

He left Mac, Glock, and Hugh.

"I got a bad feeling about this," Hugh said.

"You guys get to be glorified babysitters—lucky you," Glock said with a grin.

"That's my concern. Creed's never been topside."

"It'll be all right," Mac said. But he wasn't sure that was true as he considered the implications of their leader going with them. Without proper training, a thousand things could happen out there—a tear in his suit, a malfunction with his HUD. Not to mention that he didn't even know how their HUDs and systems worked.

It put them all at risk.

Glock was right. It was like babysitting a kid on their first field trip to a place where everything wanted to kill you. Shit, even Nick had a better chance of surviving than Creed.

"Damn it," Mac said.

He buried his frustration and went to the truck to start going over the systems. By the time he finished the first round of checks, Creed had arrived. He wore a padded black hazard suit, the nicest Mac had ever seen. But Mac was more focused on the pistol holstered on his belt.

"Good luck," Glock said, saluting. He stepped away with a sly grin on his face.

Mac refocused on the minister. "You ever fired one of those, sir?" he asked.

"Don't patronize me," Creed said.

"Not trying to, sir. I'm just interested in keeping you alive."

"I can take care of myself. I have the gods watching over me."

Mac wanted to roll his eyes.

"If you'd like me to go over the suit with you, I can show you how everything works," Hugh said.

Mac fully expected Creed to say he would figure it out, but the minister surprised him by agreeing. While Hugh went over everything, Mac climbed into the front of the truck and sat behind the wheel. He pulled up the digital map and plotted the route based on the hard-copy map Creed had provided.

"I'm ready," said the minister.

Mac took a deep breath and fired up the engine. He did a final check, then steered toward the opening doors. The headlight beams shot through, and he steered inside the tunnel, climbing all the way to the final blast doors. They parted to the perpetual blue glow of the storms that ravaged the world above.

As they started off, Creed held up a hand.

"Let us pray first." He bowed his head and whispered, "Eternal Guardian of the depths and silences, today I offer our prayer under the open sky. Blessed Keeper, guide us through the darkness that has fallen upon our world. Give us the courage and strength to survive our journey from isolation and to meet with these survivors. Bless them, and us, as we set off to rebuild a civilization in balance with the nature that once sustained us."

He looked up and said, "Proceed."

Mac drove out into the wastes. Flicking off the headlights, he switched to night-vision optics. The blast doors behind them shut, disguised by the half-collapsed building above.

Mac normally took a long moment to look out over the road, but today his eyes went to the skyline, far above the jagged teeth of broken structures, for the shape of an airship. He could see no sign of anything up in the swollen clouds. These people also likely went to great extremes to stay hidden.

Pushing down the pedal, he started up the cracked street.

He weaved easily between the burned shells of vehicles and the mounds of rubble, knowing the terrain from his previous deployments. Creed hovered behind him, watching through the slotted viewport for his first-ever glimpse of the surface. He remained quiet, probably a bit in shock, like everyone else the first time they saw the decay of the outside world.

Mac had gazed upon the new, apocalyptic world with excitement on his virgin trip, until he saw what they were about to see now. The first red hues pulsated against the rim of rubble on the horizon. He could tell right away that the killer flora had spread significantly since Luigi's death.

He didn't even get to the turn before encountering the first tendrils of vines that curled out along the street and up into the mounds of collapsed structures. Bringing the vehicle to a stop, Mac searched the terrain for the eyeless beasts.

"Gods," Creed said.

Seeing nothing, Mac maneuvered around a truck turned on its side. Beyond the wreck, he had a better view of what they were dealing with. The bioluminescent glow of the vines winked up from the deep gorge carving through city blocks, where the sinkhole had now swallowed multiple structures along with the road.

"We'll have to take a detour," Mac said.

Creed gave a nod.

Mac backed the rig up to the intersection behind them, took a left, and started down the unfamiliar path. The road eventually sloped upward, cresting a hill that gave them a view of the flora's sprawl to the east. Webs of the veiny limbs had spread in all directions, covering everything. The exterior of a four-story building was completely covered in a maroon cascade of the dangling vines.

Mac spotted movement amid the living ropes that swarmed over the concrete slabs and steel columns. But what he saw wasn't flora; it was a human-shaped, muscular animal. He jerked the vehicle to a stop as the creature turned its eyeless face in their direction.

"What's wrong?" Creed asked.

By the time Mac pointed the beast out, it had darted away, moving swiftly.

He kept driving, grateful to be inside an armored vehicle, where it was safe. For the next half hour, they advanced slowly and cautiously toward the coordinates. Mac had been this far only once, and he still remembered the shock he had felt at the sight before them. Once again, he stopped the Stryker.

"Incredible," Creed said.

The impact crater formed a bowl on the horizon, stretching so deep that the lightning flashes couldn't illuminate the bottom. All around the edges, buildings had been swept away in a tidal wave of fire that erased everything for miles. Houston had been a sprawling, vibrant city in its prime.

The ocean was only twenty-five miles to the south. As a kid, Mac had always wanted to see it. And today, for the first time in his adult life, he wondered if that might be possible. But as much as he wanted to hope the survivors on this airship were the saviors they claimed to be, he had to be prepared for evil. To believe anything else would be to let his guard down.

Mac threw on the brakes when he noticed movement in the street. The bumper came to a stop just a few feet away from a black-shelled creature the size of a large dog. Some sort of cockroach hybrid with antennae the length of a rifle barrel. It was so dark he had almost missed it.

"Sorry," he grunted.

"What in heaven's name is that thing?" Creed asked.

"Mutant insect," Hugh said. "Lots of 'em out here."

Mac steered around the creature. When he was clear, he

checked the digital map display. The coordinates were less than a mile away now.

"Almost there," he said.

"Good. I'll go with you to meet the envoy," Creed said. "Hugh, you stay in the Stryker."

"And if it's an ambush?" Mac asked.

"Then Hugh is to drive away." Creed turned toward him. "You do not, under any circumstances, lead them back to the bunker if that should happen. Got it?"

"Understood, sir," Hugh said.

Mac resisted the urge to ask Creed what would happen if they got captured. There were a lot of things men could do to get information out of someone. He thought back to the bug they had just come across. If it were him trying to get intel, he would tie someone down and let the giant insect feed on them until they gave up whatever information he wanted.

As he drove closer, Mac decided that if worse came to worst, and he had the chance, he wouldn't let himself or Creed be taken alive. He would shoot Creed and then turn the gun on himself.

The road sloped up again, providing another long view of the demolished city. And of something else—something in the sky.

Hovering just below the clouds was an airship that had to be the size of a small city. It was a monstrous airship two hundred feet across, kept aloft by bladders of some lighter-than-air gas— helium, he supposed.

"Angels are real," Creed said. He turned to Mac. "Park here. Hugh, take over. We're heading in."

Mac went to the back of the vehicle to grab his shotgun. Again he found himself excited. The airship wasn't a lie. It was up there. But that didn't mean the people aboard were good. He pumped in shells and went over his gear one last time. Creed met him at the back hatch.

"Ready, sir?" Mac asked.

"I've been ready my entire life," Creed answered.

Mac nodded at Hugh and opened the hatch. He stepped out, his boots sinking an inch into the radioactive mud from a recent toxic rain. Bringing up his weapon, he led Creed through a maze of stagnant pools across a sprawling field of debris. Creed walked upright, looking as if he were just going for a stroll in the bunker. Believing, Mac supposed, that the gods would protect him.

Mac would rather put his faith in his shotgun.

Lightning flashed over the blasted city, the gap between thunderclaps never lasting more than a few seconds. Mac guided Creed across the muddy field to a hill covered in burned debris and slick from rain.

"Stay here a minute," Mac said.

He trekked up the hill cautiously. From the low summit, he scanned the area beyond. Seeing nothing unusual, he waved Creed up.

"Careful," he called down to the minister.

He reached out and helped Creed at the crest. Together they started down the other side to a street forming a ravine half filled with rubble. An insect hissed somewhere in the darkness, but Creed didn't seem to fear it.

Mac crossed a fallen riser that formed a bridge over the ravine, taking them over a moat of murky water. On the other side, they passed down another leveled city block. At the end of it, two thousand feet away, he saw the buildings where they had agreed to meet.

"That's it," he said, pointing.

The structures were mostly still intact, their stone facades cracked but upright. Mac noticed something metallic in front of them, but before he could get out his binoculars, Creed started off on his own.

"Sir, hold on, goddamn it," Mac said, grabbing him by the arm. "Let me check things out first."

Creed pulled free from his grip and hunkered down. Mac centered his binos on an ancient machine with a rotor. A helicopter, he realized.

Three people stood near the cockpit, two of them gripping rifles and wearing black hazard suits. The person in the center had on a navy blue hazard suit and a pistol holstered across the chest.

"What do you see?" the minister asked.

Mac handed the binos over.

"That must be Captain Alfonzo," Creed said excitedly. "Come, let's meet our brethren from the sky."

Creed handed the binos back, and Mac hurried to keep up with him. As they approached across the rubble-strewn terrain, the two armed sky soldiers stepped away from the helicopter, their gun barrels angling up slightly in defensive readiness.

The man in the dark-blue hazard suit took a step forward.

"Minister Creed?" he said in a heavily accented voice.

"Yes, and you must be—"

"Captain Alfonzo." He extended a gloved hand as Creed stepped up.

Mac stopped a few feet back, eyes flitting from these mysterious sky people to their helicopter.

"It's a great honor to meet you," Creed said.

"The honor is mine, Minister," Alfonzo said.

A flash of lightning captured their handshake.

"We have so much to discuss," Alfonzo said. "After all this time, to find more survivors is a miracle!"

A crunching sound in the broken concrete distracted Mac. He turned slightly to see a beetle the size of his boot skittering out of the debris. The two guards flanking Alfonzo had noticed it too. One of them looked out at the skirt of rubble around a collapsed building.

Another beetle scrambled out of the mound. Followed by two more, pulling their hard-shelled bodies out of holes in the dirt and scuttling away on long, stilt-like limbs. The hissing creatures clambered away as if fleeing something, while Creed and Alfonso spoke excitedly.

But Mac had gone from excited to nervous about the insects. He had been out here enough to know that bugs didn't show themselves unless they were hungry, or there was something in the area they were trying to escape.

Maybe it's us, he thought. *We're the predators.*

Mac suddenly felt the ground vibrate under his boots. He crouched, putting a hand to the earth. Both sky guards looked at him curiously.

"What is it?" one of them asked.

"I don't know," Mac said. It almost felt as if a vehicle was coming. Had Hugh driven the Stryker closer? He turned to look the way they had come.

A soft whistling came over the wind—a noise that seemed familiar to Mac but one he couldn't place. Choking and a guttural cry pulled his attention back to the guards, one of whom reached up to a bolt sticking out of his throat—the source of the noise.

The sky guard dropped his rifle and fell to his knees with both hands on the arrow shaft.

"Ambush!" shouted the other guard.

Creed turned, right into an arrow to his midsection. He fell backward, pulling Captain Alfonzo to the ground with him. The second guard pointed his rifle at Mac, probably thinking he was behind the attack. Mac aimed his shotgun at that man just as an arrow hit him in the side of the helmet.

Lightning flashed over the rubble behind the helicopter, and in the glow, Mac saw on the mound's crest a squad of six armored figures holding crossbows and rifles.

Mac went to grab Creed as a bright orange fire burst forth. Its glow illuminated a hulking figure wearing a flamethrower pack. The flames raked over Creed and Alfonzo, who writhed in agony.

Another wave of insects fled the flames, squeezing out of the ground and skittering into the darkness. Mac tried to flee, too, but he stumbled and fell to the ground as arrows zipped overhead. He pushed up and sprinted back the way he had come. Creed's anguished cries followed him, but he didn't look back until he heard a raucous thumping, loud as thunder. The moment's lapse cost him his footing. He slid down a mound of loose scree, tumbling into a ravine as a distant explosion boomed far overhead.

Mac glanced up at the clouds, which vented flames as if they were on fire from within. But this wasn't lightning. It was coming from the airship that had been hiding in the storm.

The raiders had shot the airship.

Looking frantically about for a place to hide, he found refuge under a slab of concrete. Tucked underneath, he peered out and watched the airship burning as it fell from the heavens.

CHAPTER 6

The elevator stopped with a loud clank at the bottom of the bunker. Nick went over to collect whatever parts and implements had been sent down for repairs. Mac greeted him with a nod. But this wasn't the friendly, joking Ranger Nick had known his entire life.

"Got two loads," Mac grumbled.

He held out a plastic crate of heat pumps and transformers in need of repair. Nick noticed Mac's tired eyes. He had a three-day beard and smelled of body odor—not the typical presentation for a man who wore the uniform. But something had changed in Mac since he deployed topside with Minister Creed seven months ago. No one knew what had happened out there—only that Creed never came back. Since then, Mac had changed. So had Hugh.

They had been attacked, no doubt, but by what? The council remained secretive, of course, so Nick could only guess. He wasn't sure there ever had been an airship. If he had to guess, it was all a ruse by the raiders to lure them outside.

Whatever had happened out there, it was severe enough that the council scrubbed the next scheduled test topside. The Rangers were staying back.

All Nick could do was keep training each day, trying to put on weight so he could volunteer when an opening to the Rangers presented itself. The last slot had already been filled after Luigi's death, and there was no telling when another would open.

Nick returned to his work of repairing electronic circuit boards, soldering a blown capacitor, finding the break in an open circuit. The work was tedious and long, taking him over an hour just for the troubleshooting. As he approached the finish line, he noticed other workers at the adjacent stations stopping. He propped his ear protection up to hear the PA system.

"Shut off the equipment!" Beto shouted.

All across the room, the buzzing and grinding of machines faded. Nick raised his goggles and waited for the announcement. It came a moment later, from a councillor named Silvio.

"All residents are to gather in the mess hall at eight this morning," he said.

Nick checked his watch. That was an hour from now.

"Get back to work. You can leave ten minutes before the gathering," Beto said.

Slave driver, Nick thought. That wasn't enough time for most of them to get up the stairs. Not even close. But they had their quotas, and Beto got his orders from above.

He touched the hot iron to the wire end and sweated the solder into the connector, his mind already bouncing around ideas on what the council would announce tonight. He doubted they would shed any light on what had happened to Creed.

Nick finished the circuit board and took it over to the finished-projects table. He marked it as complete and then went back to his room to change clothes. Timmy Tam poked out his white-whiskered face. The little mouse was getting old, and Nick was beginning to dread the day his little pal would no longer greet him.

He wasn't sure how much time he had left, but he would treasure these remaining moments.

"Hey, buddy," he murmured. He smiled and bent down, holding out his hand. Timmy Tam moved gingerly over to the morsel in Nick's palm. He stroked the mouse's bony back with his fingertip as its cheek pouches filled with corn bread. At least the little guy's appetite hadn't changed.

Nick gently placed his friend back at his hole and said goodbye.

By the time he got to the mess hall, it was packed. It appeared that he was one of the last people to arrive. Only Beto and Hyena filtered in after him. He sidled through the crowd until he saw Sofia. She waved him over, and he stood beside her.

"Thought you were going to miss it," she said.

"Miss what, exactly?" he asked.

"Not sure yet."

The crowd spoke in a low buzz that filled the large room. As soon as the clock struck eight, the normally locked doors on the other side clicked apart. In came all five councillors. But one led the group—the same man who had called the gathering: Silvio, a middle-aged man with slicked-back black hair and a thick beard. Instead of standing in front of the crowd, he walked into it until it formed a circle around him.

"I called this gathering for two reasons," he said. "The council has voted, and I am the new minister of ITC Star Station."

Nick wasn't surprised to hear this. A lot of people had assumed Silvio would be the next minister. But not everyone liked him. Many thought him a dangerous leader because he tended to favor extreme punishments for residents who committed even minor offenses. Barney, the bunker's resident drunk, would probably be heading topside soon.

Silvio raised his chin, sweeping his gaze over everyone.

"I will start my service as minister by sharing something with you that has been withheld," he said. The minister paused for a moment.

Nick narrowed his eyes, suspicious of whatever was coming next. *More lies*, he thought.

"Seven months ago, Minister Creed was killed by hostile forces when he went to meet with an envoy of the airship *Angel*," Silvio said. "That airship was shot down by raiders during an ambush of the airship and our people."

He raised a hand to ward off the flurry of questions.

"My first action as minister is to put together a security force that will protect our home from the danger out there," he explained. "Creed was soft and believed that the gods would protect us. I can tell you, there are no angels, only demons. His death proves that evil is alive and well out there. My promise to you is to protect you from it, and to do that, we need more Rangers."

Nick hadn't held a strong opinion on Silvio one way or the other—until now. He already liked the guy.

"In the past, we have accepted only volunteers, and we've always had enough," Silvio explained. "No more."

Stepping forward, he leveled his commanding gaze on the gathering.

"All males between the ages of eighteen and thirty will be considered for this service and will be conscripted by the council if deemed fit."

Concerned voices filled the hall, and loved ones reached out to their young men. There weren't many—only about twenty-five who fit the criteria. Everyone appeared to be anxious about this news, except for Nick. He couldn't be more eager.

"Our future requires vigilance and sacrifice," Silvio said. "As soon as we have a force capable of mounting an offensive, I will deploy them to the surface to learn more about our enemy. For the only way we can protect ourselves is by knowing what evil is out there. In the meantime, all scheduled trips to the surface for testing are canceled."

He nodded at the crowd.

"All men who fit the conscription parameters, stay in this room. Everyone else, you are dismissed."

Ron, Chubs, and Gus hurried off with the others, all too young to be considered.

Sofia looked at Nick, who held back a smile. This was it, this was his moment to finally step up. He swelled with pride inside. Despite not quite being of age, he was going to volunteer—he was ready.

Fifteen minutes later, he stood in line with twenty-four other young men and the only teenager, Tyshon. The same kid who had knocked Nick's baby tooth out after he called Nick's mom a whore.

He didn't look so big now. Tyshon visibly shook where he stood.

Mac, Hugh, Glock, and the other Rangers formed a line in front of them.

"Well, I can already tell you who won't make the cut." Glock snickered. "This skinny runt can leave."

Nick looked over and realized that the Ranger was referring to him.

"I can serve. I *want* to serve," Nick said.

Silvio walked over. "He's right, Nick; go back to the shop," said the minister.

Nick stepped out from the line, standing as tall as he could, chest puffed out.

"I'm a hard worker, and strong," he said. "And I can fight—"

Glock laughed.

"Shut your stupid mouth," Nick snapped.

The Ranger walked out of the line with his hand cocked, but Mac reached out and grabbed his wrist. "You're testing my patience," Mac said.

"I don't give a f—" Glock started to say when Silvio turned.

"You're a loose cannon, Colin," he said. "Any more outbursts, and I'll be replacing you."

Glock stared back and then seemed to settle down as he fell back in line. Nick felt some satisfaction at that, but he wasn't done arguing.

"I'm fast. I can get in and out of tight places," he said. "I'll be good in the wastes. I'm not scared of anything."

Silvio flicked a finger as if to shoo Nick away as he kept walking down the line. Glock, red-faced and seething, looked as if he might explode. That anger appeared to be centered on Nick as Mac led him out of the room and into the hallway.

"You don't want this," Mac said. "Trust me. Half those young men out there will be dead in a year if Silvio gets his way. Maybe more than half."

Nick's eyes narrowed. "What do you mean, 'gets his way'?"

"I already told you about monsters, and Creed found out the hard way what I meant. I don't want to see the same thing happen to you."

Mac stepped away without another word, the conversation over for him.

Nick wanted to storm back in and plead his case. He had more heart than anyone in that room, and he wasn't scared of monsters—human or animal.

But he knew now that the only way to become a Ranger was to prove himself. And that was exactly what he would do.

*　　*　　*　　*　　*

A year ago today, Minister Silvio conscripted twelve new Rangers. Nick had turned seventeen, though he didn't look it. Five feet eight and only 130 pounds, with hardly any facial hair and plenty of acne.

But that didn't stop him from trying to bulk up. He had spent the past year training on his own for the Rangers. And today all that effort would pay off, because a team was heading to the surface.

Nick would be going with them, sneaking out there to prove he had what it took. He would show them.

He returned to his small room, covered in grease after a long day at work. He shrugged off his backpack and pulled out the old motorcycle visor he had liberated from Hyena's junk pile. He spread out the various parts to the suit he had assembled. A full black underlayer would insulate him from toxins and the cold. Over this went kneepads, elbow guards, and a steel chest plate under a black work vest. The exterior pockets and pouches normally used for shop tools would hold weapons and survival gear.

He clipped a flashlight on his duty belt, then the sheath with the butcher knife he had pulled from the scrap heap last month. Pulling the blade from the sheath, he admired the new bone hilt he had given it.

"Come out, Timmy Tam," he whispered. "Look at what I made."

When the mouse didn't come out to investigate, Nick bent down to the hole, angling the flashlight beam inside. His heart sank at the sight of his furry pal lying curled in a fetal position. Reaching inside, he gently picked up the limp, cold mouse.

"No," he whispered. "Timmy…"

Warm tears blurred his eyes, but Nick didn't let himself cry. He had never been easily moved to tears, and he wasn't going to start now. He wanted to be strong for his friend.

Sitting cross-legged on the floor, he held the little creature in the palm of his hand.

"I'm sorry," Nick whispered. "I won't ever forget you, Timmy Tam."

He wrapped the mouse up in a cloth, holding it for a few moments before placing it back just inside its hole in the wall.

Then he sat on his sleeping bag, uneasy. Maybe tonight wasn't the right time to sneak outside and prove himself.

Or maybe it was the perfect night.

He would turn his sadness into strength and prove he had what it took to become a Ranger. To protect the bunker from the monsters, whether man or beast.

Nick got into his suit, then used a roll of tape to seal off any exposed areas. The knee and elbow pads went on next.

In a few hours, the Rangers would head out in the Stryker. He needed to beat them into the vehicle depot and hide.

Helmet in hand, he went over and said a final goodbye to Timmy Tam. Picking up the mouse, he decided what better send-off than to take him to the surface, where he could finally be free of this concrete tomb.

Nick tucked the tiny remains in a vest pocket and left his little room. Sneaking through the engineering room and workshop was even easier than last time. Just after nine o'clock, he was climbing the ladder up the levels of the bunker, thinking of all the souls he was passing by. Especially Sofia.

After he swung off the bottom of the cart, he returned to the utility shaft. This time it was a lot tighter than his last visit. He had grown a bit since then, and his suit and helmet added bulk.

Careful not to make any noise, he squirmed to the final grate. The vehicle depot was just below. He unscrewed the bolts to the grate, then dropped to the concrete floor. After a quick sweep of the dark room, he ran over to the blast doors, where he crouched behind two oil drums and waited.

An hour later, four Rangers entered the room carrying their helmets and gear duffels. To Nick's surprise, Glock wasn't with them. He saw Hugh, Mac, a man named Brando, and—another surprise—Tyshon.

It was no secret Tyshon had done well in the training. News

had raced through the bunker, as it always did. What surprised Nick was that they would put their greenest recruit on the first mission topside.

All the better. Tyshon would likely mess up, and Nick could come in and save the day.

He ducked back down, barely able to contain his excitement.

"Okay, heads up," Mac announced. "We're headed back to the ambush site for recon. This is a four-mile journey, mostly driving."

Nick tensed at that. Four miles was a long way for him to go on foot, but he had trained for this by running the stairs every day.

"Our job is to recon and return without leaving a trace, understand?" Mac said.

"Yes sir," Brando replied.

"Got it," Hugh said.

"What if we encounter hostiles?" Tyshon asked. "The raiders who killed Creed and shot down the airship?"

Nick was still shocked about the confirmation back at the gathering. Not at the confirmation that it was raiders who had indeed killed Creed but at the mention of the airship being shot down. Why would someone do that? Why would someone destroy such a valuable piece of technology that could keep hundreds, if not thousands, of people alive?

Whoever this enemy was, if they could destroy an airship, they were more than capable of destroying this bunker.

"I'll decide what we do if that happens," Mac said. "Do not fire unless I give the order."

"Okay," Tyshon replied.

Nick hesitated, suddenly feeling grossly underprepared. He had the butcher knife, but that was it. He started to consider that he might not be coming back. And he hadn't even said goodbye to Sofia.

What if he died out there? No one would even know.

The Stryker growled to life. Time to decide.

Nick shook away the confliction. He would finally prove every-one wrong.

The blast doors began to part, and the truck headlights swept his hideout. He froze, his heart thumping faster as the vehicle passed his location. After two more beats, he crept out from his hiding spot.

Keeping low, he followed the Stryker up the long tunnel. The vehicle stopped at the top, and the thick blast doors creaked open, letting in the blue light of the storms. Nick realized he had been holding his breath, which came out in a huff as the Stryker drove outside.

Thunder boomed as he gazed at the strange world outside the bunker. Mounds of rubble stretched across the horizon from collapsed buildings and bridges. He had known darkness his entire life, but nothing like this. Sporadic flashes of lightning cleaved through the blackness, backlighting skeletons of tall buildings—jagged husks of steel rising toward the storms.

The doors started to close, obliging him to hurry out after the vehicle as it rolled ahead on its all-terrain tires. It was already picking up speed, and he had to run to keep up.

A few steps out, he tripped on a rock, stumbled, and almost fell in the darkness. What he needed was his flashlight, but that would give him away. To make things worse, his visor obstructed some of the view.

He trotted ahead, trying to catch up with the truck. A single mistake could be his last if he fell and tore his suit. And there were a hundred other ways things could go badly. A broken leg, a twisted ankle, or simply losing the truck and becoming stranded out here would mean certain death.

He ran until he was twenty feet behind the Stryker, then slowed to a jog, keeping out of view and trying to conserve energy.

He briefly considered climbing onto the vehicle, but the Rangers inside might hear that or see him.

Over the next fifteen minutes, he followed the Stryker up a winding road, managing to keep pace. But then he saw the glowing bioluminescent vines curling out of a trench ahead. The rustling of the alien ecosystem sounded like eerie whispering voices.

For the first time, Nick felt pure terror, knowing that Luigi was down there somewhere, his body consumed by flesh-eating vines. He kept to the middle of the road, knife at the ready.

The truck turned down another road, and he ran to catch up. The engine noise, along with the sporadic flashes of lightning, guided him up the debris-covered street as the Stryker climbed a low hill, struggling over the terrain.

Nick decided this was a good time to give Timmy Tam his send-off. He bent down, pulled out the cloth-wrapped mouse, and tucked him between some rocks.

"Goodbye, my friend," he whispered. "You are free now."

The rumble of the truck grew distant, and he looked up to see the vehicle moving faster. Nick got up and ran after it in a panic, afraid he was falling behind. Near the top, a piece of metal snagged his boot, sending him sprawling. He hit the ground and slid right over the edge of the hill, into a ravine. The last thing he saw was the chunk of concrete looming up at him. Then his world went dark.

When Nick woke, he found himself back in the darkness. He felt something wet dripping down his face. A clap of thunder made him flinch. Then he remembered where he was.

Reaching up, he felt the helmet that had likely saved his life from the fall. He pushed off the ash-covered ground and looked up at the bulging storm clouds. Lightning forked down, thunder booming shortly after.

Panicked from being left behind, Nick scrambled up the embankment of dirt and rock to look for the Stryker. He searched the road as it led farther out into the wastes, but the vehicle was long gone. He turned back the way he had come and saw the pulsating red glow of the mutant flora. Rattling came from across the street.

His hand went to his knife, and he drew it from the sheath. With his other hand, he shined the flashlight into the darkness. Shadows darted away from the weak beam, which felt like a candlewick that might blow out at any moment.

Heart pounding in his ears, he scanned and listened. There was no denying the feeling—he was gripped with fear.

The rattling sound came again, like the tail of a snake he had seen on a disc story. He swept his beam over the rubble behind him and saw red tendrils protruding from fissures in the ground. The plants curled out onto the road as if they could sense him.

Nick retreated to the side of the hill he had fallen down. He stood there trying to calm his heart, knowing he had a decision to make right here, right now: head back to the bunker or try to find the Stryker.

He turned back the way the truck would have driven.

You didn't come this way for nothing.

Nick took off up the road, using his light to guide him. It announced his position to any and all that could see, but it was his only option. To make up some of the lost time, he broke into a fast trot.

For the next half hour, Nick didn't stop until he had to after trekking up a brutal hill. Struggling for air, he looked out over... nothing.

Sprawling in front of him was the crater left by the bomb that destroyed this city. He had known it was out here, but seeing it with his own eyes sent a chill through him. He imagined the force of the weapon that had created the vast circular depression and the curtain of fire that had spread out to obliterate everything around him.

Nick glanced over his shoulder to make sure nothing had followed him. Seeing only darkness, he ran toward a hill. On the way up, he heard a faint growling noise. It grew louder as he advanced. He shut off his flashlight and crouched at the hilltop.

Distant lightning flashed over a valley, and he saw the Stryker sitting idly in the road two hundred feet away. Buildings lay reduced to cracked foundations, their stone cladding littering the ground, their steel beams pointing skyward like rusted spears.

A closer flash of lightning illuminated a colorful bit of debris that didn't match the rest of the gray-and-brown wasteland. A shiny swatch of aluminum protruded from the dirt. Nick waited for the next blast of lightning. When it came, he beheld a downed airship, its charred pieces scattered over several city blocks.

The airship had been gigantic. The bow was crushed and destroyed, but the stern had mostly survived the crash. He got up on a partially collapsed brick wall for a better view. He noticed movement near the stern of the ship. In the next flash of lightning, he saw it was Mac with his shotgun, looking down at something in the dirt.

Moving closer, he saw what appeared to be equipment and supplies from the airship, placed in a neat path, as if someone had…

Beat us here, he thought.

Another moment of fear gripped him. He shook it off as Mac started back to the truck. Nick checked the Stryker but didn't see any of the other Rangers outside.

He watched Mac's progress across the field. Along the way, the Ranger crouched to look at something. Nick could make out what looked like a hand. Mac went down on one knee and began covering the body.

Nick respected that about Mac. He was strong, but he had a kind heart.

Thunder boomed as Nick got up to move. Then came a sharp, echoing crack.

He swallowed. This wasn't thunder—it was a gunshot.

Screams came from the Stryker. Nick twisted for a view, seeing muzzle flashes on the other side of the vehicle. He scrambled for a better view when he heard Hugh shout, "Raiders!"

Nick hopped off the foundation and ran over to a mound of broken concrete. Knife in hand, he crept around the side, and there was the Stryker.

A flurry of gunshots cracked, making Nick pause. When they ended, he heard a muffled scream. He went around the edge of the mound and saw a helmet roll in the dirt and stop. A large shadow moved away from a headless body sprawled on the ground.

Hugh was suddenly flung away from the truck, hitting a wall of concrete with a crunch. A long pole through his chest pinned him there. He squirmed and held up one hand, making a throaty, gurgling noise.

"Help!" screamed Tyshon.

Nick followed the voice to the back of the Stryker. The young Ranger was on the ground behind the truck. He raised his hands as if to shield himself.

"No, please, *no!*" he shouted.

A blade came down, splitting his helmet like a melon. The blade rose, held in the hands of a massive metal beast that lumbered away on two legs.

Nick froze at the sight of what looked like one of the machines from the disc story. Any fantasies of bravery fled his mind like leaves in the wind.

The giant robot plucked the spear from Hugh, then turned as Nick stepped out with the knife in his shaking hand. The domed helmet turned to him. Tubes hung down, connecting to a pack on the creature's back.

It was then Nick realized this wasn't a robotic monster like those in the movie he had watched with his friends. Machines didn't need breathing masks. Under that armor was a man.

He raised his knife, ready to fight. The armored behemoth let out a muffled laugh and strode forward, raising the axe to cut Nick in half.

A gunshot cracked the air, and the figure went down.

"¡Mátalos!"

The voice came from a second armored raider, who stood on a pile of debris holding two swords. He jumped down, screaming.

Another boom rang out, and this time Nick saw that the shooter was Mac. He moved out from cover behind the Stryker, pumping in another shell and firing it into the chest of the charging raider. The buckshot hit him square in the armor, stopping him like a brick wall in a spray of blood.

Mac turned the shotgun at Nick. The trigger clicked before Nick could say anything—out of ammo. The Ranger reached for a holstered pistol.

"Wait! Mac, it's me!" Nick managed to stammer.

Mac hesitated with the raised handgun, then grabbed him by the arm. "You dumb shit, come with me if you want to see tomorrow."

CHAPTER 7

Nick had run and run, not stopping until Mac told him to stop. They had fled into the wastes looking for a place to hide. Mac had selected the inside of an old store of some sort. Rows of display shelves lay scattered, their contents long since pilfered or decayed.

"We can't lead them back to the bunker," Mac whispered. "Stay here, and if something happens to me, hide."

Nick got up from a crouch. "I want to help. I can fight—"

"You stupid little…" Mac grabbed Nick and shook him, then lifted him off the ground and held him up to his face. "Do you understand what just happened? Do you understand what will happen if those raiders find our home?"

Nick squirmed, but Mac tightened his grip.

"I just want to help," Nick said. "I'm not afraid."

Mac held him another moment, then dropped him to the ground.

"Well, you should be," Mac said. "If not for yourself, for your friend Sofia—"

An electronic tone floated over the wastes, and Mac drew

back. He crouched down in a swift motion, clearly frightened of whatever made the noise. Was this the monster he had warned Nick about?

They both looked out the broken doors of the store, listening to the alien call.

"Should we move?" Nick whispered.

Mac put a finger up to his helmet, then motioned for Nick to get behind a collapsed shelf with him. The wailing rose again like an emergency siren, then faded away to new sounds, of human engineering: a rumbling motor.

Lights speared outside—beams from a vehicle.

Nick kept low but glanced over the shelf with Mac.

A four-wheeled truck moved slowly down the road adjacent to their hideout. In the back, a cage held the source of the wailing they had heard: a humanoid figure with pale, wrinkled skin, domed head, and spiked back.

It grabbed at the bars with clawed hands and pressed an eyeless face against them. Two men in the same massive armored suits followed the truck, using electric prods to shock the beast into submission. Each jolt sent it screeching and biting at the metal.

Behind the two men came a second truck—also a pickup with a cage, this one empty. Then came a pair of pack mules wearing protective suits and helmets. Draped over the back of one was the raider Mac had killed.

The third truck was larger, with a bed full of scrap metal salvaged from the airship—apparent from the red paint on several pieces. There were other salvaged items, too, including a dozen stacked crates.

Two more raiders followed the slow-moving convoy on foot. One of them wore some sort of curved, bulky backpack with a tube connecting to a long wand that he carried in his hand. At the end of the wand rose a small blue flame. Nick remembered seeing one of these flamethrowing weapons in an old war book. He could only imagine the kind of damage that would inflict if the raider got inside the bunker.

"Mac," Nick whispered as soon as they passed.

Mac kept looking at the road, then glanced down.

"Do you think they know where our home is?" Nick asked.

"I don't know, but that is the route we took with the Stryker."

"Did you leave tracks?"

Mac shook his head but then hesitated. "Maybe we did. I don't know."

Standing, he looked out the doors again.

"I can't risk them finding the bunker," he said. "I'll distract them and lead them out into the wastes. You stay here. Understand?"

"But—"

"I don't have time for this. If I'm watching over you, I can't do what I need to do to save our home. Think of your friends."

Nick considered Sofia, Chubs, Ron, Gus, and everyone else.

"Tell me you understand, Nick. That you'll stay here."

"I understand. I'll stay here."

"If I don't come back in two hours, you go back to the bunker. If it's clear, get back inside and tell Silvio what happened. Tell him not to send anyone else up here—that everyone else is dead."

"Okay."

Mac got up to move, but Nick grabbed his arm.

"Be careful," Nick said.

"You too. Stay here and stay quiet, and you'll be okay." Mac hesitated another second. "You're strong, kid. I believe in you."

The Ranger took off after the convoy, running with his shotgun cradled across his chest. Nick watched him go, then slouched against the shelf. In that moment, everything came crashing down over him. He had seen monsters, both human and animal, and he had seen them kill the other Rangers, including Tyshon. And now they were going to kill Mac.

And then, if they found a way inside, they would kill Sofia and everyone else in his home.

Nick knew that leaving here would likely mean his death too. But staying also meant death. He had to help Mac, damn it.

Exhaling, Nick buried his fear and got up. Then he started off down the road. Mac was out of sight, but the convoy lights were still visible. They were indeed following the Stryker's path.

Too afraid to turn on his light, Nick used lightning flashes to guide him across the dangerous terrain. He slipped several times but managed to keep from falling. It wasn't long before he saw the pulsating glow of the flora that had overtaken block after city block. But now he didn't stop to look out in awe.

He ran hard, following the raiders' tracks in the glow of the lightning. A mile later, he picked up the electronic wail of the monster.

But this seemed close…

Nick crouched when he realized it wasn't coming from in front of him—it was coming from above.

A winged monster flapped a dozen yards above him, shrieking in its electronic-like voice as it flew toward the convoy. The lights ahead stopped, and Nick saw a new light—flames shooting up into the sky.

The eyeless beast flapped higher, away from the jet of fire.

Nick ran ahead, using the distraction to make up some ground. He came to a ridge overlooking the road. The bunker was close now. He could see the slabs of concrete over the partially disguised bunker door. On top of the slab, he noticed a figure lying prone.

Mac, with his shotgun, preparing his one-man ambush.

The convoy had stopped, and the raiders on the ground spread out with their weapons as the monster circled above them like a wheeling vulture. It came screaming down in a dive, right into a column of liquid fire that enveloped it. A horrible shriek of agony rose up into the sky as it flapped its burning wings once, twice. Smoke trailed the beast until it went limp and plummeted to the ground.

Nick stalked the convoy as it inched toward the bunker door—right toward Mac. He held his shotgun, ready to fire. But Nick knew there was no way Mac could stop all these raiders, not even with Nick's help.

His heart thumped as the raiders drew closer. There was no doubt now: They knew the location of ITC Star Station. Of home.

A flash and boom came from above the blast door, breaking through the windshield of the front truck. The two raiders behind it went down for cover. Mac fired a second shot into the windshield, then took off.

Shouting in the foreign language echoed.

Another man jumped out of the second truck, firing an assault rifle at the top of the bunker where Mac had been. But Mac had already flanked them. He fired a shot from the side of the road, right into the helmet of the confused raider. Gore spattered out the other side.

Nick ran forward with his knife in hand, watching as Mac moved like a demon in the shadows, firing and moving, firing and moving. The raider with the flamethrower torched the street while the other two men moved from behind the first truck.

One of them went down from a shot to the back, losing his weapon. Nick noted where the pistol flew into the dirt. He crouched behind a rock along the road, waiting for his chance. But four raiders on the ground were still moving into position, including the one with the flamethrower. And there were still the men in the trucks.

But Nick couldn't just sit back. This was his chance not just to prove himself but also to do something to protect his home and people.

A boom from Mac's shotgun came from farther up the convoy, followed by return fire. This time, the scream of pain wasn't from one of the raiders, it was from Mac.

"No," Nick said in a voice shy of a shout.

He got up and saw the raiders moving in over Mac's writhing body, including the man with the flamethrower. Nick burst away from his position and scooped up the pistol.

He aimed it at the guy with the flamethrower and pulled the trigger. Nothing happened. He pulled it again and it clicked. One of the raiders turned toward him, and Nick ran right for him, leaping up to his chest and thrusting the knife into his neck.

"I'll kill you all!" Nick screamed.

Someone grabbed him and plucked him off, tossing him to the ground next to Mac. Blood oozed from a hole in Mac's chest armor.

Nick got back up only to get smacked in the head by a spear shaft. He hit the ground hard, his vision going red. Frantic, he rolled over, slashing blindly with his knife and knocking the spear back.

The raider with the flamethrower strode over, aiming the barrel at Nick and Mac.

"No," boomed a voice.

Nick glanced up at the biggest member of the group. He held a large axe with a curved bit. The same man Mac had shot in the side. The thick plates of armor had stopped most of the blast, but Nick noticed bloody bandages covering the wounds.

He crouched in front of Nick, tilting his head like a scientist studying a strange rodent. Then he got up and swung his axe at the bunker door. The raiders advanced.

"No," Nick muttered. He squirmed, trying to get up, when something hard hit him in the helmet.

*　　*　　*　　*　　*

Nick woke to light. A light he had never seen before.

Sunlight.

He raised a hand to his eyes to shield them from the blinding glow.

This couldn't be real. It had to be a dream. It occurred to him that he might be dead.

But this sure felt real. He could feel his aching head and smell a salty breeze. Moving his hand to his skull, he felt a sticky patch that burned at the touch. Something hot and metallic touched his arm and back, but he was too exhausted to move.

He was thirsty, too, more parched than ever. He licked his dry, cracked lips.

The lap of water echoed in the distance.

Squinting, he blinked at the bright yellow light high above him. But the blazing orb was so intense it hurt his eyes, forcing him to look away. His vision slowly cleared to a gridded view of a sprawling pale blue sky over a sea of teal.

The ocean.

I am dead, he thought. *Dead and gone to paradise.*

A scream came from somewhere nearby.

Nick managed to turn slightly against the hard metal touching his back. It was then he saw the reason for the gridded view. He was inside a large cage of rusted steel. Across from him were familiar faces. Most were beaten and bloody. Some were sleeping. He looked for Sofia but didn't see her in his cage. In total, there were four of the twelve-by-twelve-foot metal prisons on the deck of a boat.

No, a ship.

Shielding his eyes from the sun, he took in the view. He confirmed that he was on a large, rusted ship sailing on open ocean. On the bow was a single command structure, where multiple figures stood behind cracked glass windows. Their distant voices spoke in the same odd language he had heard back in the wastes.

Smoke chugged out of stacks, the plumes rising into the blue sky and trailing behind them. He spotted two men covered in grime. Goggles covered their eyes under matted hair.

None of these people appeared to have any weapons and were instead equipped with tools. They appeared to be mechanics or engineers.

Nick shifted his gaze to the masts that rose over the deck. He noticed something attached to one of the towering metal posts.

Squinting again, he made out what looked like a man strung up—a man he recognized.

"Mac," he breathed.

The Ranger was tied to one of the masts, about eight feet up, wearing nothing but a cloth around his groin. His head drooped, chin against his chest, sweaty hair clinging to his face. Nick wasn't sure if he was still alive but thought he saw his chest moving.

Nick looked to the adjacent mast, where a second prisoner was bound. This one had slicked-back hair.

Silvio.

But there was no doubt—the minister was dead. His legs had been cut off below the knee. Not far in front of him stood a massive warrior wearing brown fatigues. Bandages clung to his torso, blood seeping through. In a sheath over his back was the large axe with a curved bit. Nick could never erase the mental image of it splitting Tyshon's head in half after the young man had begged for mercy.

The hulking warrior was just one of many on the vessel. Across the deck were dozens of them. Far more than the raiding party that Nick had seen back on land. But there were other people too. Some were frail and thin and were working on machinery in the stern. Slaves, perhaps. Two others were roasting meat over a grill behind the central masts.

"Nick," whispered a familiar voice.

He turned to see Ron and the other prisoners. Six were huddled in the cage behind Nick. Smitty was there, his tattered shirt hanging off his humped back. Next to him was a muscular man with matted hair and a crooked, broken nose. Puffy, bruised eyes glanced up at Nick. The last time they had, they were filled with rage, but now they conveyed only fear.

"Glock," Nick said quietly. He crawled over to the others, huddling up next to Ron. His friend whimpered, the tears cutting pale lines through the dirt on his face.

"Sofia—where's Sofia?" Nick whispered.

"They took her," Ron sobbed. "And they got Chubs."

"He's dead?"

Smitty nodded. "I saw him die. He begged, and they still killed him. Then they took my Ginger."

"What about Gus?"

"I don't know."

"He's dead. Now shut up," Glock hissed. "Shut your fucking mouths before you attract attention."

"You could've helped." Smitty glared at Glock. "You could have fought—"

"And I would've died, ya dumb shit."

Nick stared at the Ranger as realization passed over him: Glock had surrendered without a fight when the raiders entered the bunker.

"You're no Ranger," Nick said.

"What?" Glock said, turning. "What did you say, bird shit?"

"I said you're no Ranger. You're a coward."

Nick prepared for the man to lash out. To hit or choke him, but his furious gaze flitted behind Nick. They felt the rap of heavy boots through the cage. Glock lowered his head as a warrior approached. He wore black boots, tan fatigues, and a sleeveless shirt that showed off his tattooed arms. He slapped a whip against the bars of their cage and grumbled in his foreign tongue.

Ron whimpered, but Smitty hushed him.

Scooting away from the bars, Nick kept his gaze low, checking out the other cages as the warrior patrolled. He didn't need a panoramic view to see that the other prisoners were all men. Not a single woman in sight.

"Where did they take Sofia?" Nick whispered.

"I don't know," Ron said.

"How long have we been on this ship?"

Ron shook his head.

"Ron, think," Nick said.

"I don't know. I—"

"One night and one full sun," came a voice. "Ha-hah!"

Nick saw Hyena's face grinning out from behind the other prisoners. The man was at the back of their cage, rubbing his hands together nervously as if he were trying to build a fire with a stick.

"Where did they take the women and girls?" Nick asked.

"Did you see?" Smitty asked.

"Not sure, ha-hah!" Hyena said.

"Shut up," Glock said. "You're going to—"

"*¡Silencio!*" shouted a gruff voice.

The prisoners all bowed their heads as the warrior with the axe walked over, joined by the man with the whip. Smitty and Ron both cowered away, but Nick looked up at the man holding that curved axe that had split Tyshon's head.

The other warrior jammed a rod through the bars. The tip sparked blue light. Nick pulled back, but it was too late. An electrical current zapped him in the arm. He yelped in pain and slumped over, his vision dimming.

Eyes blurry and half open, he watched the warrior with the axe draw the weapon from its sheath. He waved the blade, motioning for the other raider to open the gate. The metal cranked open, and the giant warrior stepped inside. He stepped over to Nick, but instead of grabbing him, he took Hyena, dragging him out of the cage.

"No, no, no!" Hyena squawked.

Nick tried to stay conscious, but the adrenaline was gone, replaced by a burning pain across his entire body. His vision faded to red.

He didn't see what they did to Hyena, but he heard his wails.

"No, stop, no, ha-hah! No, not my—"

His panicked voice rose into a scream. Nick didn't need to witness what they were doing to him to know they had cut out his tongue.

Hyena would never cackle again.

Darkness again gripped Nick, and he embraced it.

*　　*　　*　　*　　*

A hand shook Nick awake. The first thing he saw was a bird flapping overhead. It was the first bird he had ever seen.

Pushing himself off the warm deck, he saw more ships in the distance. Or that was what they looked like at first. But as his vision returned in the bright light, he realized they were towers of metal. A city on the water—*cities*, rather.

The bird flapped down, landing on Mac and pecking at his neck. The Ranger screamed and squirmed, biting at the bird.

Laughter echoed across the deck, where three warriors stood watching.

Mac looked down at them, blood drooling out of his mouth. He spat and grumbled, "Go to hell, you bunch of pukes!"

The man with the axe laughed, then turned to the other two men, neither of whom seemed amused. They were holding strips of cooked meat, eating and looking up at Mac where he hung from the mast.

A Klaxon screeched in the distance, pulling Nick's gaze out to the approaching towers on the sea. One stood out, larger than the others, looming on the horizon. Another ship had already arrived, and as the ship he was on got closer, he saw cages on the deck of the other vessel. The figures in the cages had long hair. These were the women from the bunker.

An animal howl of agony drew his gaze across the deck to the mast where Hyena had been roped up alongside Silvio. But it wasn't Hyena screaming.

The warrior with the axe held Silvio's severed arm. One of the slaves took it away while another used a glowing iron to cauterize the wound. He pulled it away, smoke curling up from the charred flesh.

Tears fell from Silvio's eyes, mixing with the blood pooled on the deck under his stumps.

Nick blinked, praying this wasn't real—that Silvio was indeed dead—and he was just seeing things. But his chest was definitely moving up and down. One of the warriors inserted a syringe into a cord dangling from his other arm.

The horrific view nauseated Nick. He dry-heaved as he watched a slave take the severed arm to the fire barrel where they were grilling meat. Silvio's head slumped as he went unconscious. It was then that Nick realized they were keeping him alive with some painkiller in his tubes. They would take him apart limb by limb, his body still alive so the meat wouldn't spoil.

No, no, no, Nick thought.

The soldiers went over to Hyena next. He squirmed and struggled, but he couldn't have screamed if he wanted to.

Nick retreated from the horrific sight. Behind him, Ron hyperventilated and Smitty sobbed. Glock remained silent, his head cupped in his hands.

Looking away, Nick watched the tower grow as their ship sailed closer. He focused on the ship that had already arrived outside the exterior marina. In one of the cages, he spotted a figure smaller than the others.

"Sofia," he whispered. She was at the bars, gripping them, looking out defiantly while the rest of the women cowered in the shadows of their cages.

They had arrived in paradise for those who called this place home. But the screams and sobs of the prisoners, combined with their captors' maniacal laughter, told Nick that he and the other survivors hadn't gone to heaven—they had been condemned to hell.

Those who had died back at the bunker seemed to be the lucky ones.

PART 2:
THE CAZADORES

CHAPTER 8

Nick turned eighteen as a prisoner. He knew because he had kept track of each day since he was captured by scratching a mark in the deck of his cell. This was day sixty, and it started like all the others.

A bell rang, and the other twenty prisoners jumped in their cages. Nick pushed off the deck with his lean, sinewy arms. Veins protruded from his sun-bronzed skin. While the other prisoners were wasting away around him, he was growing strong from the sunlight, the fresh fish they fed him, and the scraps of other meat he got from time to time.

From what Nick could tell, he had actually gained some weight, maybe even grown a little taller too. Maybe it was the vitamins or the sun, but whatever it was, he seemed to be thriving.

A guard walked down the aisle with a rusted cutlass in hand. A helmet covered his face, while stringy, oily hair hung down his back. He wore light armor over his chest, his bare arms showing tattoos and scars.

Nick stuck his hands through the bars of his cell as the slave who always brought them morning chow showed up with a dirty bucket. The man wore a tattered brown shirt and ragged shorts. His sandal straps were held together by string.

Every day, Nick tried to make contact, but this guy never spoke or even looked up from his work of handing out food. This morning it was half a nearly spoiled banana, some dried fish, and a big strip of the mystery meat. He plucked it out, though it was far too thick to be human.

He tore off a chunk of the gamy meat as he looked out of his cell. Down the dim corridor, grimy hands reached through the bars. Nick counted those hands each morning and usually found fewer of them. It seemed they lost another member of their group almost every day.

They had lost over half the original group who survived the attack on the bunker. Three of them had been eaten on the journey from Texas to this place, which Nick heard being called the *Islas Metálicas*.

A few cells down, Ron stuck his little hands out. Nick felt relief at that, because the kid was starting to fade away.

Next, he identified Glock. The cowardly Ranger kept to himself, becoming more and more withdrawn, and talking to himself at times.

Smitty was still alive, too, and hanging on, hopeful that his wife, Ginger, had survived. Their captors had taken the women somewhere else, including Sofia, who Nick hadn't seen since the day they arrived.

He hadn't seen Mac either, but he knew that if anyone could survive out there, it was the brave, tough Ranger. Thinking of him and Sofia helped Nick get through the long workdays in the darkness of the lower decks with the other male captives. They had all been put to work by the crew based on their engineering knowledge. Nick had explained that he was a mechanic. That got him work in the narrow passageways of the engine room. Aside from the heat, it wasn't much worse than the work he had done in the bunker.

Most days, he was crawling through the greasy confines of the engine room, where he navigated a labyrinth of pipes, wires, and machinery. He dealt with oil leaks and changed out filters caked with grime. A few times he had to replace worn-out belts and gaskets or faulty hoses.

The worst part was cleaning the bilge pumps that removed the foul water that collected in the bottom of the hull. He still hadn't gotten used to the horrible smell that clung to him. And no matter how much he tried to scrub it off, he had a perpetual layer of grime on his skin.

But not all his time was spent in the dark. Each day, they let the prisoners out on the deck of the ship to bask in the sunlight. Most of his comrades from the bunker kept to the shade of the towers, but Nick enjoyed the sun.

The slave and guard left the corridor, and Nick stuck his head up against the bars to look for Ron. The fourteen-year-old sat in his cell, chewing on fish, eyes cast down.

"Hey," Nick whispered.

Ron glanced over at him.

"Did you get some sleep last night?" Nick asked.

Hearing a clank at the far end of the corridor, Ron cowered back into the shadows of his cell. The guard returned, barking orders in his foreign tongue.

"¡Arriba, levántense!"

Nick and Ron both understood those commands by now and stood behind their cage doors. The man walked down the rows, unlocking them one by one. The prisoners fell in line, heads down. Normally, they went down to the engine compartments, but today the guard led them up a stairwell.

Nick could see Ron shaking ahead. Smitty turned his humped back and whispered, "Have faith, Ron. We're gonna make it."

That was Smitty—always positive, even now, after they had watched three of their friends butchered alive to feed these psychotic, savage warriors. One of those bastards pushed open a hatch ahead of the group, yelling, "*¡Vámonos!*"

The prisoners were taken up the ladder into the sunlight. Gruff voices echoed across the deck. Nick made out four muscular warriors, their leathery skin covered in tattoos.

The guard shoved several of the captives, including Smitty, who hit the deck hard. He got up and moved into the single rank now forming. Most of them stood there cowering; some, like Ron, were visibly shaking. Nick did his best to stand tall in the face of these barbaric cannibals. He didn't fear them. Someday he would kill them.

As his eyes adjusted to the sunlight, the largest of the warriors stepped forward. He wore tan camo pants, a duty belt of weapons, and a leather vest over his thick chest muscles. Metal armguards covered his wrists, and tattoos seemed to move whenever his biceps flexed.

He strode over, and Nick got a look at his shaved head, gleaming with sweat, and the image of an octopus on his forehead. Two dark eyes above a crooked, bulbous nose swept over the prisoners, stopping on Nick. It was then he saw the giant axe resting on the man's shoulder. This was the warrior who had led the attack on their home, murdering Tyshon without a shred of mercy.

A dark-skinned, bearded man in a tan tunic came across the deck. This worker seemed to be higher on the totem pole of jobs—not quite a slave. Clutching a clipboard with paper, he joined the group of warriors.

"Greetings again," he said to them in English. "I am scribe, Ernesto."

He flipped a page on his clipboard.

"Two months you have spent at the Metal Islands, working in your assigned roles," he said. "As you now see, all islanders participate to keep the gears of our great civilization turning. Some of you have proved your worth and are destined for great things. To join the ranks of the fierce, brave forces of the greatest navy and army left in the world, under the legendary King Mayac, Lord Portatormentas, the Stormbringer. To become a Cazador. A *hunter*."

He gestured to the warrior with the axe.

"You have all met Captain Maximus, also known by his comrades as el Pulpo," Ernesto said. "He's here to select the best stock to replenish his ranks."

El Pulpo lumbered over, drawing his axe. He smacked the haft against his palm as he eyed the line of prisoners up and down. Ernesto followed with his clipboard.

Nick was fourth in line. He puffed his chest out, not sure if he wanted to be picked but also not wanting to look weak.

El Pulpo stopped to look at him, snorted, and kept going. He walked to the end of the row, then moved in front and halted. He snorted again as he looked at one of the prisoners, clearly unimpressed.

Nick glanced over and saw that it was Ron, head down, sniffling. A puddle grew on the deck beneath his feet.

Smitty whispered something, then braced himself as a spear shaft hit him from behind, knocking him to his knees. El Pulpo moved away from Ron and over to Smitty, glancing down at him. Then he nodded at the scribe.

"You. Your name is Smitty, yes?" asked Ernesto.

Smitty nodded.

"Stand up. You have been selected."

"What? No, I—" He held up his arm to deflect another spear

shaft, which crunched against his wrist. He groaned in pain, holding his forearm. The guard shoved him out in front of the others.

"Take *him*. He's a fighter," Smitty said. He jerked his chin at Glock. "He's a *Ranger*."

"Fuck you, you lying piece of shit!" Glock yelled.

Smitty backed away as Glock reached out for him before turning to plead his case.

"I'm not a Ranger," Glock said. "I'm a mechanic, like I said. I didn't fight when you came, remember? I didn't—"

A spear shaft whacked him across the diaphragm, knocking the air from his lungs. Glock went down, gasping for air.

El Pulpo went to Ernesto, grunting and saying something Nick didn't understand.

"He wants to know who is telling the truth," said the scribe.

"I'm telling the truth," Glock wheezed. "I—"

El Pulpo angled the axe's curved blade under Glock's throat.

"*¡Silencio!*" he said. His eye flitted to Nick as he spoke in his own language to the scribe.

"El Pulpo wants to know if this man was a Ranger," said Ernesto.

Nick looked to Glock, who glared back, terror in his eyes.

As much as Nick wanted to sell him out and see him skewered like a bug, he couldn't lie, and the truth was, Glock *wasn't* a Ranger. He had given up that honor by being a coward when the raiders came.

"Is this man one of your Rangers?" Ernesto asked.

Nick shook his head. "No, he is not. He is the furthest thing from a Ranger."

Glock let out an audible sigh of relief, but el Pulpo kept his blade there. He crouched down, snarling through his sharpened teeth.

For a second, Nick thought he had just signed Glock's death

warrant—possibly even put him on the barbecue menu—but it seemed the Cazadores had enough meat for now. El Pulpo stood and kicked Glock onto his back against the deck. Then he gave a nod. Two guards hurried over with shackles, which they placed on the hands of Smitty and Glock. Both men squirmed but didn't protest, apparently accepting their new and unknown fate.

The same guard herded the other prisoners back through the open hatch. Nick looked over his shoulder to see Smitty with tears streaking down his face. He met Nick's gaze for a single moment before he was pushed away.

The prisoners were led back down to the engine room, where they stood around in silence, too afraid to speak to one another. While they waited for their jobs, a slave handed out water. They drank sparingly, knowing to conserve. Judging by how cloudy and yellow Ron's piss was, Nick knew his friend was dehydrated. He drank half his water and then gave Ron the rest.

"Drink it," he whispered.

Ron shook his head. "It's no use."

"What do you mean?"

Nick could tell then by the blank stare that Ron had already checked out. He was giving up, the fight inside him gone.

"It's going to be okay. You just have to be strong," Nick said. "Smitty's right, you have to keep faith. We will get through this. You just have to—"

"I'm not strong, Nick. Not like you. I'm going to die here."

*   *   *   *   *

Six months later, Ron was gone.

Nick had known the day was coming, but it was hard to watch him suffer to the end. One morning, when Ron didn't stick his hands through the bars, Nick knew his friend had died in the night. An hour later, the guard showed up with two slaves to take Ron away.

A tear welled in Nick's eye as he watched them take the gaunt little body, which had wasted away to almost nothing.

By contrast, Nick continued to put on weight. And he wasn't just gaining weight; he was bulking up. The rigorous exercise routines he had developed back at the bunker were finally showing results, thanks in part to all the sunshine, fresh fish, and unknown meat.

The Cazadores had stopped giving him the real shit jobs, like crawling through the cramped corridors in the engineering room. Now he was given other jobs that required not just skills but also strength. Jobs that most of the other prisoners couldn't handle anymore, for many were starting to fade. Most of the prisoners who seemed to be floundering were men who had easy jobs back at the bunker—watering and weeding on the farm or doing equipment maintenance for a few hours a day—nothing to prepare them for toiling away in the hot, stinking guts of a ship. It led to disease, and half of them were sick from dysentery. Some said it was the mystery meat making them sick.

Nick had endured a few bouts of illness himself but had come out stronger. His immune system seemed to have adapted, protecting him from the worst ailments. But today it would be tested again with another shit job.

"We'll be working on the bilge pump," said the scribe in charge of assignments.

After eight months of captivity, Nick was already starting to pick up some of the Spanish, and he quickly got the hang of things by watching and listening. It would take strength, though, wrenching bolts that were rusted or stuck.

"Franco," the scribe called out.

Nick looked his partner over. The fifty-year-old man with

weathered skin stepped forward from the crowd. He wore ragged brown coveralls and a floppy hat over his graying hair. As they set off with their assignment, Franco handed Nick a canvas bag of tools.

"*¿Cuál es tu nombre?*" the slave said.

"*Me llamo Nick. Yo* speak *poco español.*"

Nick could understand a fair amount, but some of the foreign sounds were hard to replicate.

The man pointed at his own ear. "Listen."

"*Sí*, okay," Nick replied.

Franco held out a tool bag.

"*Toma la linterna,*" the man said.

Nick looked inside, fished out the headlamp, and strapped it on his forehead. They went two levels down, then took one more ladder down a shaft to the lowest deck on the ship. At the bottom, Nick found himself alone with the slave in a dark, foul-smelling corridor. They both turned on their headlamps.

Franco opened a hatch and shined the beam into a passage. The space was cramped and narrow and gave off an acrid smell of gear oil, stagnant water, and sewage.

Franco guided Nick down the narrow access ways to the bilge pump—a critical system for keeping this lower area from gradually filling with water. They took a heavy wrench and breaker bar and began dismantling the pump's housing. Using hand signals and a mix of words they both understood, they found they could effectively diagnose the issue.

As they worked, Nick debated whether to engage Franco in conversation. He saw it as an opportunity to get to know someone outside his own group from the bunker.

"How long you live here?" Nick asked.

Franco stopped wrenching and looked at him.

"*¿Cuántos años… tú* live *aquí?*"

"Toda mi vida."

The answer surprised Nick. This man had lived here his entire life?

It struck him that Franco was born here on the Metal Islands. Maybe he wasn't a slave. Maybe he got paid for doing this job and then could return to the rigs and his family after a long day.

Franco turned back to his work, breaking loose a rusted nut from the pipe fitting, but he kept talking. Nick was able to piece together that the man's wife and two kids lived on one of the rigs, and he worked here on this ship. As Nick processed that, he felt a wave of dizziness and a growing headache.

He pushed through it by focusing on his work and getting lost in it, just as he used to do in the machine shop of ITC Star Station. And after an hour working together, the two men managed to remove the corroded bilge pipe. Franco leaned down for a tool, then wobbled.

"You okay?" Nick asked.

Franco turned, then collapsed in the muck on the deck.

Nick bent down as another wave of dizziness hit him. His vision dimmed, and he realized they were being overcome by toxic fumes. Knowing he had very little time to get them out of there, he grabbed Franco under the shoulders, lifting him up slightly. Normally, Nick could have picked him up with all that newly built muscle, but whatever they were breathing made him dizzy.

He stumbled, banging his head painfully on a pipe.

Nick shot his light back at the closed hatch. It was close enough that he could escape through it. But if he left Franco behind, the man's wife and kids would be without a husband and dad.

Bending down, he grabbed Franco's ankles and began to drag him. A few feet in, Nick nearly collapsed again. He took his partner by his ankles a second time. Head pounding, Nick fought off the vertigo and pulled the older man all the way to the hatch. He turned, opened it, and got them both out into the corridor, where he gently dropped Franco. He pushed the hatch closed with his shoulder. He collapsed against the hatch, greedily sucking down the sweet, fresh air. But something was making his headache worse. His vision wobbled, the bulkheads around him shifting. He tried to fight, to stay awake, but his body grew numb. He couldn't feel it as he slumped forward, but he saw the deck rise up to meet him before he slipped into darkness.

A cold jet of water shocked him awake. He shot up in the bright glare of the sun, gasping for air.

"Hey!" he shouted.

He held out his open hands, trying to block the powerful spray of water hitting his naked body. The pressure flipped him onto his side, then his back. It hit him in the face with the force of a hard slap, stinging his ears and scalp.

Nick shielded his eyes with his wrist and pushed off the deck.

The water suddenly stopped.

His long, wet hair hung over his eyes. He whipped it back to see Franco standing with the aid of another worker. Another man held the hose that had sprayed Nick.

Behind them, two Cazador soldiers lumbered up with spears, speaking in raised voices. Nick, still dizzy, tried to make out what they were saying. He picked up the scent of something grilling. Meat.

His heart thumped with fear as the warriors lumbered over, looking mean and hungry.

Was he next on the menu?

Nick scooted back, when he heard a voice behind him shout, *"¡El perro pequeño es valiente!"*

Heavy footfalls thumped closer as Nick turned, his face inches from the tree trunk–size calves of el Pulpo. The cannibal captain's sharpened teeth grinned at Nick.

"*¿Cómo te llamas?*" he asked.

Nick looked up and met the murderous gaze.

"Nick," he said, trying not to stammer. "Nick Baker."

"No," el Pulpo said.

The captain called for his scribe, and Ernesto hurried over.

"*El Perrito,*" Ernesto said. "He says that is your name now—Small Dog. El Pulpo sees something in you," said the scribe. "He says you have the heart of a lion but were trapped in the body of a rat until you arrived. Now you are a bit bigger, more like a little dog—bigger than a puppy."

The Cazador captain studied Nick during the translation, eyes flitting over his muscles as if sizing him up.

"He saw you fight for your people, and now you have risked your life to save one who is not your own," Ernesto continued.

Franco looked at Nick and nodded. "*Gracias, Perrito,*" he whispered.

El Pulpo motioned in the other direction to someone who Nick couldn't see. He got up, dripping wet, squinting from the sun's glare as he looked out at a warship, connected by a gangway to their barge. On the decks stood armored men wearing helmets with tubes like the limbs of the octopus tattooed on el Pulpo's forehead. Some of the warriors stood outside containers where prisoners were being yanked out by cables.

New prisoners? Nick wondered.

Prisoners, yes, but not *human* prisoners. These were the same type of beasts el Pulpo had captured when raiding ITC Star Station. Only now there were dozens of them, maybe more.

As the wind shifted, Nick picked up a heavier scent of barbecuing meat. The monsters were being carved up and cooked on grills.

The warrior el Pulpo had waved at hurried across the gang-way, carrying a crate in his strong arms.

"The Black Order is leaving tonight to hunt on that ship under the leadership of Colonel Vargas and Colonel Santiago," Ernesto said. "To celebrate, we are offering a sacrifice to the Octopus Lords in the Sky Arena. El Pulpo says it's your time. Tonight you will fight. But first you must eat."

The Cazador carrying the crate set it down and lifted the lid off steaming steaks of thick meat—the same cuts that Nick had been eating since his arrival. This was what he had been eating?

He looked at the monsters, suddenly queasy. Maybe that was why the others had languished, from some sort of toxin in the meat. But how was that possible if the same meat had the opposite effect on Nick, making him stronger?

He swallowed hard, wondering if he was somehow mutating, but there was no time to speculate.

El Pulpo drew a knife from his belt and impaled a slab of monster flesh. He lifted it from the crate and tossed it to the deck in front of Nick, as if throwing a bone to a dog.

And knowing he had no choice, Nick got down and ate.

CHAPTER 9

At dusk, Nick boarded a sleek, torpedo-shaped boat clad in plates of armor. A machine-gun turret protruded from the bow, with belts of ammunition draped over a barrel.

El Pulpo slid behind the wheel and fired up the three big outboard engines. Vertical exhaust stacks belched smoke into the sky. Three Cazador warriors boarded behind Nick and the other two prisoners they had taken along.

"Where are you taking us?" asked one of the slaves.

None of the Cazadores answered, but Nick remembered what Ernesto had said on the barge about fighting. He felt his heart lurch with the boat as it sped away from the ship. Looking back, he saw *Elysium* painted in white on the rusted hull.

El Pulpo pushed down on the throttle, engines roaring, salty spray hitting them with each jounce over a wavetop. Nick had spent most of his young life around machinery, but he had never felt a surge of power like this.

"Yeehaaaawwwww!" shouted el Pulpo.

Nick turned back around to see two towering rigs silhouetted against a blazing orange sunset.

El Pulpo steered the boat toward the largest tower. At the top, Nick noticed the oddly shaped dome. He hadn't seen it earlier. It reminded him of the hull of an airship—a smaller version of the vessel the Cazadores had shot down back in Texas.

As the boat raced closer, Nick realized that was exactly what this object was, retrofitted to the top of the rig. Palm trees rose from the crest like spiked hair on a balding head.

El Pulpo pushed the throttle down all the way, jerking them back in their seats. Nick hit his head on the seat with a thud, much to his captors' amusement.

"*El Perrito*," el Pulpo said, laughing. He motioned for Nick, then shoved the warrior out of the seat next to the wheel.

When Nick didn't move, el Pulpo pushed his helmet up and growled. "*¡Vámonos!*"

"He wants you to sit with him," Ernesto explained.

Nick got up and staggered over, falling to the deck and inspiring more laughter. He pushed up and grabbed the seat, sliding into it. Much to his surprise, el Pulpo slapped him on the back hard, almost knocking him down.

Adrenaline surged through Nick as they raced across the waves. He wasn't sure whether he should be excited or terrified.

The ride came to an end a few minutes later as they pulled up to a marina outside the huge domed tower. Small fishing boats with mounted poles and stacked nets were docked at the many slips. Fishermen moved about the docks, loading supplies while soldiers patrolled. Another armored boat was backed into a stall, its engines chugging. Two men in black armor got out with an entourage of four Cazadores.

"*El coronel Vargas y el coronel Santiago*," remarked Ernesto.

El Pulpo pulled the war boat into a stall, climbed out, and saluted the two higher-ranked officers. They hardly acknowledged him. He grunted as he tied up the boat.

Nick climbed out, gawking at the balconies protruding from hundreds of dwellings built across the enclosed decks. On some, people looked down. Their flesh was tanned and tattooed, but these weren't like the others he had met, such as Franco. These people wore colorful clothing and jewelry that sparkled in the sun.

El Pulpo and his guards escorted Nick and the other prisoners down the long slip, passing dockhands who didn't bother to look up from their work.

A chorus of shouts and what sounded like cheers caught Nick's ear as he neared the end of the marina. He glanced up to the bowl-shaped roof, where the noise seemed to originate.

The Sky Arena, he realized. They were being taken there. To fight.

Nick felt seasick. He resisted the urge to vomit.

One of the Cazadores pushed him hard from behind, nearly knocking him to the deck. Nick turned, rage building inside him.

The hulking, half-naked Cazador shouted, *"¡Muévete!"*

Nick kept walking, his anger replaced by a sense of awe. Not just at the rigs but also at the people, their homes, the boats. As much as he hated the raiders, he couldn't help but feel a glimmer of hope that maybe this place could become a home for him.

No, not unless…

He glared at el Pulpo, knowing he would have to kill him and many more of the cannibalistic barbarians if there was to be any hope of making this place a home for Nick and what remained of his people. One thing was certain: He would be fighting sooner rather than later.

He took a deep breath, trying to calm his nerves. Keeping calm was the only way he would survive. And surviving was the only way to help Sofia.

El Pulpo stopped at an elevator car hanging from a cable pulley system, not unlike the car they had in their elevator shaft back at ITC Star Station. The sergeant of the guards told Nick to go inside with the other prisoners and Ernesto.

They piled in, and the cart rose. Nick found himself again in awe. The last streaks of sunlight glinted off the towers strewn across the sparkling sea. He counted eight of them in all directions, and ships—a dozen giant ships. He was beginning to realize how vast this place really was and how many people were out there.

Fighting them all seemed impossible. Surviving did too.

Shouting voices caught his ear again, but this wasn't cheering. It was booing. This soon gave way to shouts of anger. Nick looked up as the cart clanked to the top. El Pulpo opened the gate.

Nick froze at the most mesmerizing sight yet—a jungle of trees and plants growing out of the rooftop. Healthy branches drooped from the weight of oranges and lemons growing on them.

El Pulpo plucked an orange, using his sharp teeth to rip the skin away. Juice ran down his square jaw as he led the way around the forest to a railing that appeared to surround a recessed area in the rooftop. The din of shouting issued from the large open area the size of an Old World football field he recalled from a disc story.

This was the Sky Arena.

Two warriors stood with crossed spears before a gate. They opened it as el Pulpo approached. The little group of Cazadores and prisoners emerged at the top level of a stadium with many rows of seats. There hundreds of people stood, fists raised, snarling and shouting. Some of them held sticks of jerky that they tore at with sharpened yellow teeth.

Nick got his first glimpse of what they were cheering and jeering at down on the sandy bottom of the arena. Two men battled with swords on the blood-soaked sand.

"Welcome to the Sky Arena," Ernesto said. "Soon you will fight for glory, honor, and your lives."

"No, please. I don't know how to fight," said one of the other two prisoners.

Nick simply stared in shock as the two men hacked at each other with cutlasses. It was obvious that one of them was experienced. He wore armor shielding vital parts, and a spiked helmet. His scrawny opponent wore only a loincloth—clearly a slave.

Blood ran from cuts on his arms and torso. He swung wildly with his sword while the more experienced fighter easily parried the blows and sliced him across the thigh, toying with the poor bastard.

Nick was pushed again. He started down the stairs, which formed an aisle through the seats. The group passed hundreds of onlookers, some of whom noticed Nick. Fingers pointed at him, and laughter broke out.

"*Niño muerto*," someone said.

Nick didn't know what *niño* meant, but he understood *muerto* to mean "dead." Easy enough to understand—they were calling him a dead man, or boy, walking.

The rest of the crowd cheered out of bloodlust as the gladiator played with his opponent like a cat with an injured mouse. The panicked man swung his sword out in desperation, his momentum turning him too far. The gladiator stepped back and kicked the man in the rear, knocking him to the ground.

The arena erupted with gleeful shouts as he kicked the fallen slave. Scrambling in the dirt, the bleeding man tried to escape, only to be skewered through the back by the sword. The gladiator withdrew the blade and held it in the air, dripping blood, to great applause.

A horn blared, cuing every person in the arena to rotate toward an elevated booth. In it stood a gigantic man wearing black armor. While most of the warriors were big and muscular, this man clearly spent more time eating than fighting.

At the moment, he was inhaling a chicken wing covered in brown sauce, ripping the flesh away with gold teeth. His double chin jiggled as he chewed. Next to him, a robed servant pointed to the arena, then reached out to help him stand. The huge man waved the servant away and instead grabbed a rail, pulling himself up from his throne to stand in front of the crowd. He tossed the bones of his snack away behind him.

Waning sunlight glinted off his ornate armor decorated with gold lightning bolts on the chest plates and gilt shoulder plates. His long dark hair streaked with silver fluttered in the breeze.

"That is King Mayac, or Lord Portatormentas," Ernesto explained. "Which translates to 'stormbringer.' Before that, he was known as the Golden General, or *el General Dorado.*"

The king dragged a gold cuff across his graying goatee to wipe the sauce dripping from his chin. Then he raised a fat hand, each finger displaying a shiny gold ring. He dragged one of those fingers across a golden collar around his neck, mimicking slitting his throat.

His lips opened to reveal gold-crowned teeth. *"¡Muerte!"* he bellowed.

The crowd went wild as the gladiator hacked the head off the dying slave.

"Oh God, oh God," said the prisoner behind Nick. "I can't fight. I don't know how."

Nick didn't know either, but he would use his fingernails if that was what it took to survive.

El Pulpo led them into a vestibule and down the stairs into the depths of the arena. In the gloom were cages holding more slaves. The stench of raw sewage and the far worse scent of rotting flesh drifted down the corridors. Nick held his breath as he passed a concrete slab where pieces of the dead were discarded. Some had been stripped of meat.

Suddenly, he understood what those sharpened teeth were chewing on.

This wasn't just a gladiator arena. It was a slaughterhouse where gladiators provided the entertainment, and victims became food for the patrons in the crowd. It wasn't just the fighters, Nick realized. It was all these people. They were all cannibals.

Nick retched with an empty stomach.

El Pulpo shoved the first two prisoners into a cage but then motioned for Nick as he stood back up, wiping his mouth. He was guided to another section of the dungeon—to a rack of weapons mounted on a stone wall. Rows of helmets and armor were arrayed on tables. A guardsman saluted el Pulpo as he approached the equipment. He looked at it all, then selected a helmet, which he handed to Nick.

Then he chose a sword, holding it up and placing it back on the rack. He picked an axe next, running a finger across the blade.

"*Fuerte*," he said, handing the hilt to Nick.

Nick took it, feeling as if his heart might thump its way right out of his rib cage. Ever since he was a kid, he had wanted to prove himself. But this? He couldn't hold back the waves of fear that shook his body.

A pair of guards brought more prisoners out of their cells. Nick could hardly see through the grid of his helmet visor as he was led into a corridor. He heard retching and sobs behind him, but he didn't turn.

The crowd shouted and screamed as he was led down a shadowed corridor, out toward the last rays of sunlight that shone through the closed iron gate.

Outside, massive lights clicked on, spreading a bright white glow across the arena as the gates opened. Nick stepped out barefoot into the sand.

In the center of the arena, a man with a red mohawk and

white-painted face held a microphone. He wore bright-red baggy pants and a colorful shirt with sleeves that hung down like feathered wings. Bells jingled on his black boots as he tapped them in the dirt.

Ernesto stepped out with the prisoners and el Pulpo, who had the blade of his own axe propped against his shoulder armor.

"*¡Todo el mundo alaba al Portatormentas!*" shouted the man with the mic.

"All hail the Stormbringer," Ernesto translated. "You best repeat that."

Nick did as ordered with his best accent. "*¡Todo el mundo alaba al Portatormentas!*"

El Pulpo pumped his axe in the air, repeating the words with the crowd. They chanted it over and over until the hulking lord moved back up to the railing. Sweat dripped down his forehead as he took a slug of something from a gold goblet. He raised his other hand, and the arena fell silent. Both Colonel Vargas and Colonel Santiago moved into view inside the booth. They were two of the highest-ranking officers of the infamous Black Order.

Then came four women, who stepped up to the lord on his sides. They each wore a white dress, with flowers entwined in their hair and turquoise jewelry hanging over their breasts. Nick was close enough to see that they were all beautiful and young.

The jester clicked his boots together, the bells tinkling as he spoke.

Ernesto translated rapidly.

"Tonight, as we prepare to send our Barracudas back into the darkness, we gift the people with a fight between our newest additions to the Metal Islands—a pack of rats plucked from a nest in the ground."

The crowd clapped and cheered.

Spinning with a little dance move, the jester then whirled

toward Nick. He came over and draped an arm around him. Raising the mic, he said something about a *perrito*.

"For your enjoyment, we have selected Small Dog—a fierce little heathen who tried to kill a Cazador during the attack on his former home," Ernesto translated.

The jester pulled him tight and grinned the yellowest grin Nick had seen yet. Then he released Nick, pushing him away.

El Pulpo came up from behind Nick and pushed him again, knocking him to the sand. The crowd erupted in laughter.

Nick spat grit from his mouth and pushed himself up in front of a fresh bloodstain. The axe el Pulpo had selected arced over, landing beside him. Bending down to pick it up, Nick noticed a new figure being pushed out from a gate across the arena.

Squinting in the glow of the torches, Nick saw a thin man with a humped back.

"Smitty," he mumbled.

The mechanic who had helped bring him into the world eighteen years ago staggered to his feet. A cutlass was tossed to the ground. He looked at it, then picked it up.

"Nick," Smitty called. He turned to a Cazador guard and said, "I can't. I won't!"

Two arrows smacked into the sand on either side of Smitty's feet. Nick watched as the two archers nocked fresh arrows to their bowstrings.

"If you don't fight, you die," said Ernesto. "If you fight and win, you live. Your choice, but make it fast."

Nick glanced at the other prisoners, who cowered in fear. Several had dark, wet stains on their pants. He gripped the axe in his hand, feeling like he was going to puke again. Or pass out.

Wobbling on his feet, he breathed in, filling his lungs.

The jester with the mic ran off the field, clicking his boots together several more times to gales of laughter. El Pulpo grunted and smacked Smitty in the side of his head, knocking him down.

Smitty got back up with his cutlass, his enraged eyes staring not at el Pulpo but at Nick.

"I'm sorry," Smitty said.

He slashed before Nick could dart backward. The blade cut his arm open, drawing blood. All around the arena, people screamed in delight. Nick stumbled backward, still hoping he might wake up from this nightmare.

In what seemed like slow motion, he took in the sights around him. Mouths full of sharpened teeth screamed and snarled alongside others with toothless gums. Tattered clothing hung off suntanned, tattooed flesh. Women with tangled hair, and breasts casually exposed, pointed at him, sneering.

These people reminded Nick of wild animals.

But over all the raucous voices, he thought he heard a softer, kind female voice shouting his name.

"Nick, watch out!"

He backed away as Smitty charged with the cutlass, holding it up above his head. Terror filled his teared-up eyes.

Nick jumped away from his next swing, then darted around Smitty. The older man turned, slicing at Nick in an attack that nearly cut his neck.

"Nick!"

That female voice came again, and this time he knew it was real. He dashed away from Smitty, much to the dismay of el Pulpo, who barked, *"¡Lucha!"*

As Nick retreated, he noticed a small figure among the three taller women in the booth, trying to look down. A servant appeared to be gesturing for this person to get back. Due to the shadows, he couldn't be sure, but he thought he glimpsed Sofia's freckled face.

Smitty chased Nick, hacking again and again as Nick avoided the blows. With a long swipe, Smitty changed his tactic and almost succeeded in taking off Nick's chin. In that moment, as the blade whooshed past his face, the lights shifted, and Nick saw Sofia's freckled features in the booth looking down at him.

"Nick!" she yelled down.

Gripping the axe in a shaky hand, he stared back at her, not quite believing his eyes at first. Smitty slashed out, cutting Nick across the arm again.

The crowd roared, but Nick drowned out all the noise to look at Sofia's horrified gaze. Her lips moved, but he couldn't make out the words.

Dripping blood from his arm, he backed away to get more distance from the crazed Smitty. The humpbacked man screamed as he chased Nick with the sword over his head.

Nick looked back to Sofia, and this time, he read her lips.

"Fight, Nick. Fight!"

He surrendered to the violence. If this was a step toward saving her, then he would kill a thousand Smittys. No matter what it took, he would rescue her someday, and they would leave this horrid place.

He turned back to Smitty, who swung harder and with too much momentum. Nick sidestepped the blow, throwing out a foot. Smitty didn't see it coming and went down hard, face-first.

Rolling on his back, he looked up—right into the axe that Nick brought down on his head with a wet crunch. Warm blood peppered Nick across his face, getting in his eyes.

He wiped it away, looking back up to the booth for Sofia, horrified at what she would think. Maybe now she would see him as a monster.

Deep down, that was what he felt as Smitty jerked on the ground in front of him.

Nick saw Sofia again, their eyes meeting.

He wanted to scream up that he would save her, that he would set her free, but he knew that would only make things worse for them both.

Heart pounding, he watched his closest friend. But instead of looking down in horror, she gave him a slight nod. Lord Portatormentas leaned down to her, and Nick took a step forward, terrified that the king was about to punish her for yelling.

But instead he handed her an apple from a plate of fruit that a servant held.

The giant lord then looked down at Nick like a god gazing upon an insect, before raising his goblet again. El Pulpo strode out and grabbed Nick by an arm, lifting it up and shouting, "*¡El Perrito!*"

CHAPTER 10

Nick was almost twenty now, although he wasn't quite sure of today's date. Months had passed since he split Smitty's skull open. Maybe more—he had lost track of time in his new cage. When the adrenaline wore off after the brutal arena fight, shock set in, along with remorse at having killed a good man. Everything after that was a blur, from being escorted and transferred to the *Elysium*, to the journey that followed. He recalled the ship suddenly rocking and groaning as if they had passed through an invisible force field, leaving the calm and entering a wicked storm.

Even now he could hear the storm outside. Thunder boomed, rattling the hull and overhead. Faint blue traces of lightning flashed at the end of the corridor in the brig, illuminating a rusted wall.

He stood at the bars, searching for a guard or prisoners who might be in other cages he couldn't see throughout the brig. The only person he had seen since he came here was a single slave who brought him a pail of dried fish each day, night, or morning—he had no idea which.

The flashing glow of lightning never changed regardless of the time of day. Not once did he see the glow of sunshine.

Where the hell had they taken him?

Nick sat back on the metal slab that was covered in a tattered blanket. He rested his back against the hull, his mind reverting back to the Sky Arena. He could hear the sound of his axe cracking through bone, and Smitty jerking in the sand.

He had killed the man just as el Pulpo had killed Tyshon.

There were plenty of reasons Nick could use to justify his actions, but none of them relieved the anguish he had felt in those final moments of combat.

He banged his head on the back of the hull, the sound echoing in the cavernous space. If there were other prisoners in the cages, none answered. And it was too dimly lit for him to see anything.

"Let me out!" he shouted. "Let me the hell out!"

He thought of Sofia. She was out there, and he couldn't let himself go crazy. That wouldn't help either of them.

He exhaled, relaxed his body, and went down on the deck. Then he started push-ups to kick off his workout routine. Whatever else happened, getting soft wasn't an option. He had to stay strong, had to stay ready. He had proved he could fight.

Against Smitty, he thought. Not against a Cazador.

An hour later, drenched in sweat, Nick curled up on a blanket and closed his eyes in exhaustion. Dreams of his youth and the bunker filled his mind. He dreamed of his friends. Of working in the machine shop. And of his mother, whom he never met.

At some point, he awoke to a clanking noise. He shot up, his stomach growling from hunger. Standing, he went to the bars, eager for the meal that he hoped was coming.

But the clanking wasn't from the chained slave bringing his fish and water.

A Cazador walked down the corridor holding a key. He unlocked the cage as Nick stepped up. Drawing his cutlass, the warrior then pointed to his right. Nick went that way, trying not to stagger toward the intermittent flashing blue light.

They went down another corridor, and Nick saw two prisoners in cells.

"No, fuck you, fuck you," grumbled one of the prisoners.

Nick couldn't see the man's face, but he knew the voice. It was Glock.

The guard opened his cage, yanked him out, and smacked him in the head. Glock fell back, and the Cazador grabbed the second prisoner, who Nick recognized from their bunker as Jaden, a fortysomething farmer with long black hair.

Jaden swept the hair back from his sunken eyes and acknowledged Nick with a slight nod. They exited from the brig, heading up another level to a corridor with a row of portholes that lit up with the lightning flashes outside.

"*Alto*," growled the Cazador.

He climbed a ladder to a hatch, which he pushed open. Howling wind rushed inside with a spray of the rain. The warrior lumbered out onto the slick deck, motioning for the slaves to follow him over to a skiff hanging from davits above the rail. A second Cazador waited there with a spear.

Multiple lightning flashes lit up the silhouettes of ships off the *Elysium*'s port side. Nick counted four of them in the lightning's afterglow, each bristling with barrels of cannons and machine guns. The raging storm swirled over the fleet, capturing the sheer monstrous size of the ancient warships, their hulls covered in scars from bygone wars.

Two Cazadores cranked the skiff down until it was flush with the gangway. After boarding, it was lowered into the choppy water.

"Where are you taking us?" Glock asked.

"*Silencio, puto*," said one of the guards.

Nick looked at Glock, who glared back. Jaden kept his head down, his long black hair hiding his face.

Cold water splashed inside the boat, shocking Nick to full alertness. He shivered in his wet clothes as the skiff thumped over the waves. Every few seconds, he would glance up, expecting to see the ships towering over him, but the skiff wasn't heading for those ships.

In the residual glow from a brilliant flash of lightning, he saw their destination looming on the horizon: a giant mountain rising over an island—a *real* island. He looked out over the mutant jungle.

The boat rolled up over a wave, then down the other side, knocking him backward into Glock. Instead of helping Nick up, he pushed him away.

"Fucking runt," he said.

Nick got up from the deck and sat back down just in time to be launched again into the air. He braced himself against the hull as the boat hit the surf and caught a wave, then slid up onto the sand.

The Cazador at the bow hopped off, shouting for everyone to get out. Nick jumped off into the water, which came up to his waist. Jaden fell in and flailed when the next wave hit. Nick grabbed him and helped pull him onto the sand, where Glock watched, snickering.

The Cazadores pulled the skiff up, away from the reach of the tide, leaving it next to a row of dozens of similarly sized crafts. Boot tracks led away to a cleared section of jungle where torches burned.

Both warriors set off up the beach, going up a hill. Below lay a sprawling camp of tents, shipping containers, and shacks. Gathered together were a group of at least a hundred warriors in bulky metal armor. No, more than that.

Again Nick felt the sheer overwhelming sense of dread at the military force the Cazadores had built. How could he ever save Sofia and escape this war machine?

The enemy wasn't just the legion of cannibalistic barbarians themselves. They also had a fleet of warships and a massive army. Over two hundred soldiers in armor faced an elevated platform. The two guards led Nick, Glock, and Jaden closer. On the platform stood a behemoth of a man wearing the same gold-adorned black armor Nick had seen back in the Sky Arena.

King Mayac, Lord Portatormentas, the Golden General.

Lightning flashed, illuminating the chubby jowls and double chin beneath the wispy goatee. He shifted his mountainous body as two more warriors in black armor climbed the ladder to the elevated platform. They were Colonel Vargas and Colonel Santiago of the Black Order. Ernesto joined them up there.

The guards took Nick, Jaden, and Glock to a row of cages. Inside were other prisoners, huddled in small groups. He didn't recognize these people. They numbered twenty-five—mostly middle-aged men, but a few females. All of them wore green fatigues and hats that shadowed their filthy, frightened faces.

Nick and his two fellow prisoners were shoved into an empty cage that reeked of feces and urine. But Nick was soaked and glad to be out of the rain for now. He went to the bars to watch as the crowd of warriors parted to let through a giant man with an axe over his back.

"El Pulpo," Nick whispered.

He bowed and then went down on one knee in front of the platform.

Lord Portatormentas motioned for him to rise. Then he snatched the mic from Ernesto and began to speak in a deep, sonorous voice.

Nick gleaned bits and pieces of conversations. The Black

Order had led a successful raid hunting monsters, and el Pulpo had once again returned with flesh offerings, along with something about fuel. The gathered warriors raised their fists, pumping them at the storm clouds.

Portatormentas pointed a sword at the cages full of slaves, saying something about fuel again and how el Pulpo could have his pick. The captain bowed and then headed toward the prisoners with two guards. They stopped at the cage next to the one Nick had been tossed inside. The captives screamed as they were pulled out into the cold rain and mud. Three additional Cazadores came to help, using electric prods to shock any who tried to scramble away.

El Pulpo surveyed the new prisoners as he had once surveyed Nick and the men from his bunker. They were all on their knees now, heads down, shaking, many of them sobbing. The warrior selected two women from the batch and a single man. They were led away with el Pulpo, but most were whisked back into the cages. All except four, who were taken toward a row of three large steel drums with hinged doors cut into them.

Rumbling sounded, and Nick saw the beams from an approaching vehicle. Not just any—this was the Stryker from the bunker, and it was pulling a trailer with a shipping container. Over the chug of the motor, he heard the same eerie electronic-sounding wail from outside the bunker.

Glock and Jaden both joined Nick at the bars to watch.

"What the hell is making that sound?" Glock asked.

The truck stopped, and two Cazadores went to the back of the container hatch. The shrieks grew louder, followed by thuds and banging. The warriors raised electric prods as a third man came over to unlock the cage.

He pulled it open, then jumped back.

A guttural roar came from the darkness inside.

Nick flinched as a pale, muscular beast with a spiked back lunged out with clawed hands. An eyeless face flitted back and forth, its crooked mouth snarling. Chains around its neck jerked it back when it lunged, pulling it to the mud. Muck splashed out, the beast slashing and screeching in those strange oscillator tones.

"What in all holy hell is that?" Glock whispered.

Nick knew exactly what it was: one of the same creatures they had been eating since they arrived. But he also knew this beast would just as quickly eat them if given the chance.

El Pulpo went over and punched the slashing beast in the face. It crashed to the ground, and he grabbed one of the chains, dragging it away. For several minutes, everyone watched the warrior pull it all the way to a fence on the border of the camp, where a guard opened a gate. Then el Pulpo tossed the creature out into the mud beyond.

Perhaps this monster wasn't going to suffer the same fate as the others.

But why let it go?

Not a moment after el Pulpo got back inside the gate, the creature staggered up and slammed against the steel bars. Raising his arms above his head, the captain roared and kicked the gate.

El Pulpo screamed louder, his voice sounding almost nonhuman.

"Guy's a fucking psychopath," Glock said.

After another kick to the gate, el Pulpo sent the beast darting off into the jungle. He returned to the camp and went right to the platform, bowing again below his superiors. Portatormentas shouted what Nick understood to mean, *Before the hunt, we will feast!*

The king licked his sharpened gold-studded teeth.

Panicked voices called out as the four prisoners were pushed toward the drums. Their doors had been opened, and fires burned inside.

Nick swallowed with realization when he remembered something from the speech about the fuel. The fuel the king had been talking about had nothing to do with petroleum; it was food in the form of people. And those people seemed to understand their fate.

Nick tried to drown out their screams as the prisoners were hauled away.

The warriors in front of the platform moved off, heading into the camp, where they would await their next meal, it seemed. Raising his head, Nick noticed one of them deviated and walked over, lifting his helmet slightly to look at Nick.

To his shock, he stared into the hardened eyes of Mac. Whatever softness his heart once had, it was gone now. His gaze went to Glock and Jaden.

"Do what they say, and you might survive," Mac said quietly. "Refuse, and you'll end up in one of those stoves."

And then he was gone, marching away with the rest of the army.

Nick stood there, his heart thumping.

Over the screaming slaves, the electronic wail of the monster rang out from deep in the jungle. Two more answered the call. Then a fourth and a fifth.

It was then that Nick understood something else. The Cazadores hadn't freed the monsters. They had simply given them a head start for the next hunt.

*   *   *   *   *

Almost a week had passed since Mac saw Nick, Jaden, and Glock alive in the cage. He wasn't surprised to see Glock, a bit more so to see Jaden, and downright shocked to see the kid. It was a miracle Nick had survived this long.

Truth was, he looked healthier than ever before, muscular and energetic. Maybe even taller. Hard to believe that he was doing so well when most men from the bunker had died from disease, violence, or being eaten by their captors.

But that didn't mean Nick would make it much longer. He had a lot of heart, but heart alone couldn't keep him alive out there. To survive where they were sending him, he needed fighting skills and killer instinct.

Dozens of new recruits like Nick were heading into the Quill, the dormant volcano on Sint Eustatius—what Mac had heard the Cazadores call the "Man Maker." This infamous place was once used as a fortress during a civil war between a king and a faction that rose up to dethrone him. Now it was used to train warriors.

But the cannibalistic warriors had other plans for Mac. He had joined a group of fifty warriors on the warship *Dragon*, heading back out to sea under el Pulpo's command for another raid.

Mac remained in a cage with the other non-Cazador fighters. They were all slaves from other raids where survivors deemed worthy of fighting had been conscripted into this brutal war machine. Fighting back was the best chance of surviving, it seemed. For Mac had met several others like him who had defended their homes, killing Cazadores before they themselves were captured.

Mac remembered when el Pulpo had given him that chance, almost a year ago now. Pinned down with a knife to his throat, he had joined, with the hope of someday escaping.

But now he knew there was no escaping. The only way out of the Cazador army was death. And even after seeing how horrible this life could be, Mac wasn't ready to die. He rested his head on the bunk inside the cage, trying to drown out the laughter, shouting, and general racket coming from the raiders across the deck. A dozen men sat on crates, playing some sort of drinking game with jugs of their homemade liquor.

Rock music in English crackled from an ancient stereo. They might not understand the words, but they sure enjoyed the music.

Mac shot up in his bunk at the crack of a whip. Holding the leather whip was el Pulpo, a demented grin on his scarred face. In his other hand, he raised a jug. He turned back to the others, stumbling slightly as he took a slug.

"Mac," he said. "*Vámonos*. Come, driiinnnk tequila."

Mac stood and went to the cage door, which el Pulpo had unlocked. He stepped back as Mac walked out into the dimly lit open space. The Cazadores all stood, glaring at him under a dangling light that illuminated their muscular, tattooed bodies. One of them was wearing only a loincloth that barely covered his parts. His chest bore the tattoo of a hammerhead shark, with the bizarrely shaped head branching out over his bulging pectoral muscles. His face was bright red, and his words came out slurred.

"*Vámonos,*" el Pulpo said again. He whipped Mac on the butt with a stroke that made him wince in pain. The other Cazadores broke out in howling laughter.

Mac whirled about, clenching his fists.

El Pulpo noticed, his drunken gaze going down to Mac's fists. He walked over, staggering slightly, then halting right in front of Mac. He exhaled a hot breath that stank of the potent tequila.

"*Tú* big *hombre,*" he growled. "*Muy fuerte.*"

Mac had picked up enough of the language to know that the Cazador was calling him a big, strong man. Or taunting him, rather.

Hammerhead belched, then glared at Mac, mumbling something about a *puta*. He, too, appeared intent on getting Mac to fight. And then there was Vampire, a pure brute of a man with a thick beard and a mustache that curled at the tips directly over his two sharpened canines, which happened to be the only teeth left in his mouth. And the reason for his name.

Vampire flashed the dagger tips of his teeth and licked his

lips like a hungry wild carnivore. In Mac's view, the guy wasn't much more than that. Mentally, he wasn't all there, which made him dangerous and unpredictable.

Mac relaxed his fists and took a breath, trying not to take the bait. He forced a smile.

El Pulpo grinned back, satisfied. He held out the jug, and Mac took it, knowing that to decline would be worse than throwing a fist.

The disgusting warm fluid ran down his throat, burning into his guts. He couldn't hold back the cringe.

El Pulpo chuckled and clapped him on his back as Mac coughed. More laughter. Then it suddenly ceased.

When Mac looked back up, he saw that el Pulpo was no longer grinning. He stepped closer until their faces were just inches apart.

"*El Perrito es muy fuerte,*" he said.

"What?" Mac asked.

"The small dog," translated one of the other Cazadores, named Izan. "El Pulpo says the small dog is very strong."

"Small dog?"

"*Nick,*" el Pulpo said.

Mac raised a brow. "Yes, he is strong. Always has been."

"*El Perrito rompió la cabeza de tu camarada como un demonio.*"

"I … don't understand."

Mac looked back to Izan. The dark-skinned Cazador with blue eyes came closer, but el Pulpo grabbed Mac and pulled him back.

"*¡El Perrito es un demonio!*" he shouted.

"He says the small dog split the head of your comrade like a demon," Izan said.

This time, Mac didn't look away. He was trying to understand what el Pulpo was saying, and it seemed he was telling Mac that Nick had killed one of their own.

That couldn't be right. Maybe Nick had killed one of the Cazadores.

El Pulpo took another drink from the jug, then gestured for Mac. He went to the group of Cazadores. Izan shook a can of clattering dice. The other warriors crouched along a runway on the deck. The strip was marked by chalk with hastily sketched symbols of an octopus, some sort of long-jawed fish, and burning skulls.

Izan shook the four dice out of the can, into his palm. Hammerhead pounded his chest like drums as the dice were tossed.

Shouting erupted from all the warriors bordering the white chalk marks. The dice rolled across the deck.

Mac had no idea how the game worked, but he could tell who the winner of the roll was when Vampire shot up and flexed his tattooed arms and chest. He let out a roar, eyes bulging as saliva dripped from his sharpened canines.

Hammerhead picked up the jug of homemade tequila and took three large gulps. El Pulpo snatched it away and took another slug as his men picked up the dice. Wiping his lips, he snarled something in Spanish.

Izan took the can and gave it to Mac.

"El Pulpo says maybe you are better luck," he explained.

"And if I'm not?" Mac asked.

"Then maybe your head roll next."

"I figured as much."

El Pulpo ran a finger across his neck, confirming the stakes. Hammerhead barked, and Vampire hissed like a snake.

Mac had no illusions about his prospects. The Cazador army did not value life, because they replaced it easily enough on their raids. And with the *Dragon* heading out on another raid, his life was worth less than whatever these bastards were betting.

Mac held out the can as Izan dropped the dice back inside.

"Good luck, gringo," he said. "Maybe you will have good luck like the boy did when he split the humpback's head."

"Humpback," Mac whispered.

Could he be referring to Smitty?

No, no way Nick killed him. Right?

"*¡Apúrate!*" el Pulpo shouted.

Mac shook the can of dice, trying to focus on not getting his head cut off. He looked at the markings on the deck as el Pulpo and the others placed coins on the different symbols. That gave him an idea of how the game worked—simple enough, but he lost track of where the coins were as the men spread out.

All Mac could think about was Nick killing Smitty. A theory began to develop as he thought back to how badly Nick wanted to be a Ranger. That theory grew stronger when he pictured seeing the kid at the Cazador island camp, thriving while so many others wasted away.

Had Nick found his calling at the Metal Islands, among these bloodthirsty cannibals?

Had he killed Smitty for a chance to become what he always wanted—a soldier?

Mac shook away the thought.

He wouldn't believe it. The kid wasn't evil like Vampire, el Pulpo, or Hammerhead. The opposite, actually. He had a *good* heart.

"*¡Tira los malditos dados!*" el Pulpo yelled.

Mac didn't need Izan to translate that. Removing his palm from the can, he pulled out the dice and tossed them toward the coins he remembered el Pulpo placing. In what felt like slow motion, the dice rolled over the deck until they came to a stop.

El Pulpo had his back to Mac, but he whirled about, glaring at him. Then he charged, screaming. Mac backed away, raising his fists, but it was too late. He had let his guard down thinking about Nick. Lowering his head, el Pulpo slammed into Mac, hoisting him up with his arms wrapped around his back.

"¡YO GANO!" el Pulpo shouted.

Mac tried to squirm free of the powerful warrior's grip. He noticed the other Cazadores growling and pushing each other. Hammerhead launched Vampire against the hull with a thud. The smaller of the two brutes got right back up and charged with another man, trying to wrestle Hammerhead to the deck—but all in good fun, it seemed.

In the five heartbeats that passed since the dice came to a stop, the brawl was over, and el Pulpo released Mac, who crumpled to the deck. He pushed up on one knee, gasping.

"¡Excelente, Mac Suertudo!" he said.

Mac massaged his throat as the other men grumbled.

"He says your name is now Lucky Mac," said Izan.

"Mac Suertudo!" el Pulpo shouted with his arm in the air.

A Klaxon wailed, silencing them all.

El Pulpo's smile turned to a scowl, his ears perking like a dog's.

All trace of jocularity vanished. The men all rushed to their suits hanging on racks—everyone except Hammerhead, who took off with only a sword.

Within minutes, the rest of the warriors had donned their armor. Mac and the other prisoners were already in their hazard suits but were not given armor or weapons.

Slipping his helmet on, Mac followed the squad up a ladder toward the sound of rolling thunder. Flashing blue lit up the outline of an open hatch at the top landing. El Pulpo went out onto the slick deck under a raging storm, where two more squads of Cazador raiders waited.

Hammerhead stood there with his two swords, wearing only his loincloth and sandals. He scanned the darkness.

"What's going on?" Mac asked.

No one answered.

Water sprayed over the railing, sliding across the deck. The creaking and cranking of the ship echoed as the bow cleaved through thick fog drifting over the turbulent seas.

El Pulpo spoke in a hushed voice to his men. Vampire went to a mounted flamethrower while a team of six riflemen spread out. Mac and the other prisoners remained near the hatch.

Thunder boomed. Then came a wink of light, but this wasn't lightning.

On the horizon, a faint red glow came, then went. Mac lost sight of it as the ship tilted on a massive storm wave. Water exploded up and over the razor wire–wrapped rail. Voices called out from the command tower behind him, where two sailors in hazard suits looked out through night-vision goggles.

Something was out there, but what?

Mac searched for the red light again while three sailors brought up a chest of weapons. Hammerhead pulled out a spear, then waved it, signaling Mac and the other prisoners to come over. Just as Mac bent down to grab a sword, he saw the red spark through the fog.

Someone standing in the superstructure shouted down in Spanish, "*¡Cuidado!*"

A deep whistle sounded just before an explosion burst across the deck, knocking three Cazadores down in a flash of fire. Shrapnel whizzed the fifty feet over to Mac before he could take cover. A piece of flying wood hit him in the back, knocking him to the deck. Pain jolted up and down his body. The prisoner beside him screamed out, his voice dimming before shutting off abruptly. Mac got up to see that the man had gone overboard.

Another explosion burst against their ship. Two more prisoners vanished in the blast.

Vampire screamed as he released a jet of flames, raking it back and forth. In the glow, Mac saw the silhouette of a vessel cutting through the fog, its figurehead a steel horse. Lights burned like flames in the eye sockets of the demonic-looking beast, perhaps used as a beacon for friendly vessels, or to intimidate foes on the seas.

Those glowing eyes did nothing to scare el Pulpo. He screamed and waved his forces forward to fire on the enemy ship.

Ears ringing, Mac listened to the responses from the other warriors across the deck. These weren't the excited voices of bloodthirsty cannibals he was used to hearing. These were men in pain.

Mac scrambled for cover, passing the scattered bodies of the three Cazadores hit by the first impact—or what remained of them. Only a single warrior was still alive, and not for long. His legs were gone, and one arm. Blood ran from his mangled armor.

Another explosion burst against the bow, flinging two Cazadores back.

"¡Vira el barco!" el Pulpo shouted, waving at the command center.

Mac stumbled over to a dead Cazador and picked up his assault rifle. The only survivor raised a shaky hand to him, begging for mercy.

A spear suddenly punched into the captive soldier's chest.

Flinching, Mac turned, pointing the rifle at the half-naked figure of Hammerhead. He stepped right up to the muzzle pushing against his shark tattoo. Snarling, he snatched the gun from Mac, then took off running to the bow.

Gunfire cracked, muzzle flashes lighting up the armored figures of el Pulpo and his comrades as they blasted away at an enemy ship that fired cannons back at them. Another blast detonated across the *Dragon*'s deck, nearly knocking Mac down again.

He dove for cover behind a mast, where he found another rifle. He picked it up and checked the magazine, then got up and aimed at the burning eyes of the steel horse mounted to the prow of the attacking ship. The figurehead made it look as if it had time-traveled from the fifteenth century. But this ship was much more modern. Advanced weapons from the enemy craft fired projectiles that blasted against the hull. Tracer rounds streaked over the deck, cutting through any Cazador unfortunate enough to be in their path.

Mac fired a burst at a figure manning a turret on the enemy ship. El Pulpo moved into his line of fire, and for a second, Mac considered killing him. But that thought quickly passed since it was el Pulpo, and only el Pulpo, who could get them out of this battle alive.

CHAPTER II

Nick had spent most of the past week in his cage with Jaden and Glock, coming out only to train with a rusted cutlass and throw an axe at targets set up in the training camp. Jaden, a simple farmer in his past life, was giving it his all, but he was weak and sick from dehydration. The rain made everything worse.

It hadn't stopped raining during their entire time on the island, and they were all drenched to the bone. The padded black suits might have kept them warm but for the water. Nick was constantly cold. The only thing that helped was moving around, but half the time he was too exhausted.

Shivering, he returned to his cage, where he poked through the bucket of swill for scraps to eat. There wasn't much today, just some dried fish and a rib from one of the monsters, which was mostly gristle. As usual, Nick had to vie with Glock for every scrap.

"That's mine, you little shit," Glock said, swiping with his hand.

Nick pulled the bone back, growling like a feral animal as he sucked the fat. Glock cursed and reached back into the bucket.

Jaden lay curled up on the cage floor. Nick wanted to help

him, but it would just be a waste of food. There wasn't enough for all of them.

Glock pulled out a stringy piece of meat about four inches long, held it up, then tore off a piece with his teeth.

Nick noticed something odd about the strip. There was tattoo ink on it. This was one of the prisoners. He almost gagged at the realization as Glock wolfed it down.

But Nick had bigger problems than cannibalism.

The distant wails of the monsters echoed from the jungle, where Cazador trainees had been heading all week. Nick knew he would be going there soon enough. He had to be ready, and that meant conserving his energy, eating everything he could, drinking enough water to stay hydrated, and trying to keep warm.

The short break lasted a few minutes, and he used every second to wiggle his cold toes and fingers and rest his eyes.

A Cazador came and opened the gate. "*Levántate,*" he grunted.

Jaden sat up with a groan.

Another guard came over and spoke with the first. Nick knew then that it was over for the farmer, saying something about how Jaden was a waste of food.

"No, stop," Jaden said, trying to stand as one of the guards grabbed his feet.

The second Cazador drew a sword from a sheath.

"No, I can still fight," Jaden cried, struggling with the last of his strength. "Please, don't—"

Nick had seen so much death since he arrived, the execution hardly bothered him. In a way, it was a relief knowing that Jaden wouldn't suffer anymore after the sharp blade pierced his heart. The guards dragged the dead body to the barrels, where they would cook him. Perhaps the next bucket would contain pieces of Jaden. Nothing went to waste here.

In the end, he would become fuel for the army.

When the two Cazadores returned, they took Nick and Glock from where they normally trained to the now-empty shipping containers where the monsters had been kept before being released into the wild. Just beyond the razor-wire fence was the jungle, alive with the droning of insects and the howls of beasts.

Three more Cazadores stood in front of the iron gate. Headlights shot out of the jungle as a truck came banging down a dirt road under the dense canopy.

The gate opened, and the truck drove inside. Two Cazadores in the back jumped down and opened the lift gate as Nick and Glock were led over to an area of tarps spread out on the ground. In the glow of the truck lights, Nick noticed that some of the tarps were stained with blood.

A guard pulled back a corner to reveal the bruised face of a man, his lifeless eyes looking up at the sky.

Two more corpses were brought over, uncovered. A scribe who didn't introduce himself slogged through the mud with a clipboard.

"Names?"

Nick and Glock both answered.

"Take whatever gear fits, and prepare for the hunt," the scribe said without emotion. "You will be assigned a squad shortly. Those of you who survive the hunt will join the Cazador army."

One of the Cazadores barked at them and clapped his hands.

"He says hurry, before the bodies go bad," explained the scribe.

Nick realized then that these men would be going to the cook fires, just like Jaden. Their bodies would feed the army. He pulled back a tarp from a man who had deep gashes from claws and teeth. His legs were mangled, but the chest armor looked like a fit. Nick worked fast to scavenge the gear, and in a few minutes, he had what he needed.

Next, the scribe took him and Glock to a rack of weapons. For his primary weapon, Nick selected a long-bladed cutlass that went in a scabbard over his back. For his secondary piece, he picked a dagger and threaded the sheath onto his belt.

The scribe led them back through the camp to where three prisoners stood in front of another gate. They were all darker-skinned and tattooed—not prisoners but Cazador youths. They didn't look much older than Nick. They eyed him and Glock as they were brought over.

"I'm supposed to go with a bunch of kids into the jungle to fight those eyeless beasts?" Glock scoffed. "You got to be fucking kidding me."

"This is not a joke," said the scribe. He removed his helmet. Creases formed around his dark eyes as he squinted to read his notes. Then he glanced up. "I am Imulah, the scribe assigned to document your hunt at the Quill," he said. "These natural-born Cazadores will join you."

Imulah pointed to the three warriors.

"This is Fuego, Whale, and Zorro," he said.

Nick nodded at them, but Glock muttered something under his breath.

Whale lumbered over, holding a large wooden club with a spiked head. Then came Fuego, carrying a flamethrower pack. Zorro was armed with an assault rifle. After looking Nick and Glock up and down, they started over to the gate.

Imulah hurried after them, clearly anxious about something.

Nick's heart pounded with fear. His entire life he had wanted to prove he could fight. He had fought the Cazadores at the bunker, or tried to, and he had fought Smitty. But killing a humpbacked civilian didn't really prove anything.

This hunt would show whether Nick had what it took to become a warrior. And the stakes were clear: Kill the monsters or be eaten by those who did.

He swallowed as the gate opened and the guards motioned them forward. Whale led the way, flicking on the flashlight affixed to his helmet. Zorro and Fuego followed suit.

Glock hung back with Nick, suddenly acting odd. They hadn't spoken much at all in their cage, but Glock always seemed to be looking around. Maybe he was plotting an escape. If he wanted to try, so be it; Nick couldn't care less.

The group marched up the muddy trail, following the boot prints of trainees who had taken this very path for days now. Some had returned, but many had not.

Nick thought of Sofia, using the memory of her to bury his fear. He remained determined to see her again—to *save* her somehow.

They walked for a half hour in silence, amid the chirr of insects resonating throughout the jungle. The Quill loomed in the distance, its peak shrouded in clouds.

Whale halted at a distant howl. Nick drew his cutlass from the sheath. This noise was different from the calls of the eyeless beasts they had unleashed, and it seemed to be coming from the canopy. Peering into the darkness, he spotted red eyes glowing on a branch.

"There," Nick said, pointing.

Fuego raised his flamethrower barrel in that direction, squirting out a line of flame at a branch. A small monkey with huge eyes squawked and leaped away. Other animals called out, howling.

They went silent as a horrific scream answered. This was man, not beast.

Lights flickered across the path ahead, and Whale went to meet a Cazador trainee. He halted in the mud, out of breath, saying something about *un demonio.*

Two more trainees emerged ahead, carrying a comrade with a mauled leg. All three were bleeding from long gashes in their suits. Imulah hiked over, asking about their scribe. One of the men shook his head. It seemed the other scribe hadn't made it out of the Quill.

Glock pulled Nick back as the Cazadores spoke.

"When I tell you, go for the fool with the rifle," he whispered. "I'll take it and kill these barbarian fucks. Then you follow me to a boat. Get out of this hell for—"

An ethereal shriek cut him off.

Nick held his cutlass up as he scanned the jungle for the source of the alien noise. The Cazadores from the Quill scurried away, taking cover while the new squad came together in a defensive position.

The high-pitched shriek rose and fell like an alarm siren. Glock put his hands over his ears and crouched behind a tree.

Nick ducked as the screech sounded right over him. He glanced up at a winged beast sailing over the jungle canopy. Its massive wings flapped hard enough to sway the upper branches.

This was something new, something bigger—a *real* demon.

*   *   *   *   *

Another round from the enemy warship shook the *Dragon*. Mac could see the steel hull clearly now, all six hundred feet from stern to sharply angled prow mounted with the horse figurehead. It was larger than the *Dragon* but also slower.

Mac could hear el Pulpo shouting orders from the superstructure. There was no way to outgun them, so he had decided on a different tactic: ramming them and boarding. The problem with that, as Mac saw it, was they wouldn't get the chance before they sank.

Alarms sounded in the lower decks, where he heard someone shout that they were taking on water. He looked down the iron sights of his assault rifle at the enemy ship's superstructure, bristling with advanced sensors and communications arrays. Much of that technology probably no longer worked, like much of the gear on their own ship, but the various weapons systems seemed to be tracking and guiding fire to the *Dragon* accurately enough.

Two flashes came again from missile launchers on the deck of the enemy ship. Two more explosions burst against the *Dragon*'s hull. They couldn't take much more of this punishment.

Mac grabbed a rail to steady himself. He looked up at the *Dragon*'s superstructure, where el Pulpo was surrounded by five of his loyal warriors, including a half-naked Hammerhead almost entirely covered in blood. Vampire was also there, now wearing armor. They continued to fire at the distant warship, now only a thousand feet away.

The *Dragon* closed in, its pilot pulling some expert maneuvers to confuse the enemy gunners.

"*¡Mas rápido!*" el Pulpo shouted.

The machine-gun turrets in the stern of the enemy warship blazed again, spraying the portside deck. Mac scrambled away from the rail, bullets zipping past the spot where he had been standing a second earlier. A round clipped his shoulder plate, knocking him to the deck.

He scrambled for cover behind the superstructure. Safe for now, he ejected his magazine to check the load—only seven rounds left. He palmed it back into the weapon.

He took a ladder up three levels to the command center. From this vantage point, he could see the destruction to the bow. Multiple impacts from missiles had blown open the hull above the waterline. A dozen Cazadores lay scattered across the blood-spattered deck. Four were still firing rifles, and one remained on a mounted machine gun while a sailor kept the belt-fed ammo coming.

Mac made his way up to el Pulpo and Hammerhead. They fished out magazines from a crate and loaded them into weapons as the *Dragon* pursued the larger vessel. A shell streaked overhead and smashed into the deck behind Mac. When he turned, the mounted machine gun was a mangled wreck, the gunner gone. Mac winced from the ringing in his ears.

When it passed, he heard shouting from the command center. He picked up bits and pieces, but the gist was that they were taking on water.

"No!" el Pulpo shouted. He stood, shoulder-firing his rifle at the distant ship.

Two of his men grabbed him, pulling him away from the railing, but he fought free, knocking one man down. Two more shells burst against the *Dragon*. Mac went down hard. His vision dimming, he saw Cazadores pulling el Pulpo back from the rail.

Mac tried to get up but fell back down with a jolt of pain up his back. He groaned in agony, feeling something hot between his shoulders. As he looked out over the water, he saw that the enemy vessel was no longer running—it was turning.

Coming in for the kill.

Someone picked Mac up under his arm, helping him to his feet. A blast from above knocked them both down. Above, the viewports in the command center exploded outward, fires raging inside. A screaming sailor climbed out and jumped down to the bottom deck, telescoping his legs. His arms flailed as flames consumed him.

Mac pulled himself up by the rail and looked down at the Cazador who had helped him moments earlier. A length of the deck rail had impaled him through his chest.

The *Dragon* tilted to the port side, and Mac realized no one was at the wheel. They were going to sink. He had to get to a lifeboat. He made his way to a ladder above four Cazadores who were dragging a kicking and screaming el Pulpo in that direction.

Another salvo of blasts hit the ship with enough force to shake Mac off the ladder. He fell to the next deck, hitting it hard.

Groaning, he sat up. The enemy ship was closing in, but they were holding their fire now. On the deck, he saw humanoid figures with odd, pointy helmets.

They were preparing to board the *Dragon.*

Mac got up and hurried over to the fleeing crew. Cazador sailors and warriors climbed into the lifeboats.

"No!" el Pulpo roared. He went on with something about an Octopus Lord being with them. Then the captain broke free from his men. Hammerhead, Izan, and Vampire ran after him, along with three other surviving Barracudas.

Mac felt conflicted as he staggered over to a lifeboat packed full of sailors and injured warriors. Two Cazadores cranked the lifeboat down into the choppy sea. The small vessel had limited gas and water, and no food aboard. Even if they did somehow escape the enemy warship, they would just be trading one terrible fate for another.

But Mac decided he would take his chances.

He hopped over the railing of the ship, dropping down into the lifeboat as it began its descent to the surface. The hull splashed into the water, and a sailor started the engine, chugging away from the *Dragon.* From sea level, they all had a grim view of the damage to the warship.

Flames vented out through gaping holes in the ancient hull, licking upward. The command center billowed smoke out of shattered viewports.

El Pulpo still would not abandon ship.

Two more lifeboats made it off, pulling away as the bow

of the *Dragon* dipped below the surface. The enemy warship came closer, and Mac got a better view of the warriors who had attacked them. They wore lighter armor than the Cazadores and had long hair draping back from the crests of their armets.

Holding his ever-present axe in the air, el Pulpo taunted these alien-looking sailors on the warship as they coasted closer to the disabled *Dragon*. The Barracuda soldiers stood with him, prepared to defend the vessel and their captain to their last drop of blood.

The enemy ship slammed against the *Dragon*, and a gangway slid across to connect the decks. El Pulpo lowered his axe and pulled something out from his pocket that Mac couldn't see. But he could hear the high-pitched whistle.

The soldiers around Mac suddenly got up. Even the injured men managed to move for a better view. At the back of the boat, the man gripping the motor eased off the throttle.

"¡El señor Pulpo está con nosotros!" el Pulpo shouted.

Mac tried to interpret on the fly—something about Mr. Octopus being on our side—just as bubbles boiled up around the *Dragon*. At first he thought it was just from the sinking ship, but something was moving under the surface, toward the enemy vessel.

Hammerhead moved in front of el Pulpo, screaming in Spanish, a cutlass in either hand. Vampire, now wearing a flamethrower, stepped up but held his fire from the phalanx of enemy warriors charging across the ramp.

Instead, massive brick-red arms unfurled out of the bubbly water, smacking four of the attackers off in different directions and coiling around another.

"What in the name of all that is unholy…" Mac muttered.

Three more arms exploded out of the ocean, plucking soldiers off the enemy ship as el Pulpo blew again into his whistle. When he stopped, he raised his axe at the ramp, and the Barracudas stormed across, with Vampire leading the way, a plank of liquid fire jetting from his flamethrower.

The lifeboat Mac rode on was already thumping over the waves back toward the battle—or massacre, rather. By the time he got back aboard the *Dragon*, the fight was over, and el Pulpo held an enemy armet with a horsetail draping from the crown. Blood dripped from the severed head inside.

"*¡Todos alaben a los señores pulpos!*" he shouted.

"All hail the Octopus Lords," Mac said.

CHAPTER 12

Two hours from the encampment, Zorro had guided them off the trail into the jungle at the foot of the Quill. The high-pitched wails of the hideous flying abomination echoed from deep within the mountain. More than rock stood between the hunters and their prey. Not long after taking them off the main path used by the other trainees, they had reached a seemingly impassable thicket of forest. A curtain-like webwork of vines blocked the way.

"*¿Qué?*" Whale asked. He shook his head and muttered, "*Haremos nuestro propio camino.*"

Imulah translated: "We will make our own path."

Turning, Zorro gave a nod to Fuego, who unleashed a salvo from his flamethrower, blasting a doorway through the jungle. The burning vines curled back, providing a path forward. All around them, bushes pulsated an angry red. Nick thought back to that sinkhole in Houston and the vines that the council believed would eventually threaten ITC Star Station. Now, with no one to hold them back, he had no doubt they had already overrun the bunker. Not that it mattered, now that everyone was gone.

The trainees trekked forward over the scorched dirt. Nick

watched the Cazadores working together, pointing out venomous plants and other hazards. He paid close attention, knowing those weren't the only threats. Snakes and giant insects also prowled in the darkness of this thriving mutant ecosystem.

Imulah hung back with Nick and Glock while Whale held rear guard.

As the group passed along the newly burned path, more vines wormed back into position behind them. One snatched at Imulah's arm. Nick reached out to help, but the scribe wasn't helpless. He drew a curved blade from his suit and sawed through it. Behind them, Whale swung his spiked bat, severing any vine that ventured too close.

Nick felt something wrap around his ankle and swung his cutlass down as a thick tendril yanked him toward a glowing bush. He missed, hitting only dirt as he went down on his back. Slashing outward, he cut a chunk from the vine, freeing himself. He felt someone lifting him up to his feet. He expected it to be Glock, but it was Zorro. Glock had been watching, doing nothing.

"Thank you ... *gracias*," Nick said.

He fell back into formation, and the squad tightened into a huddle, striking at the ropy limbs curling out toward them as Fuego blasted a path forward. Thunder boomed in a sky that Nick could no longer see through the dense canopy. He relied on the flames and flashlights, but even those didn't push back the darkness.

"*¡Empieza a pelear!*" Whale growled at Glock. "*Tú* ... fight!"

The former Ranger had yet to lift a hand.

"Do something!" Nick shouted.

Glock stalled another few seconds before Nick finally saw him swing his blade at a vine that uncurled from a branch above them.

The jungle had activated a defense mechanism, reacting to their assault. Nick feared that Fuego would run out of fuel before they got clear of this area. But all he could do was keep swinging his cutlass, which grew heavier with every stroke.

Think of this as practice for the real battle, he thought.

Nick lost himself in the rhythm of swings and slashes. Together the motley squad fought its way through the thicket, up a slope. At the crest, Fuego raked a line of flames back and forth, scorching the pulsating net that blocked their way. The spiked branches burned, then broke away, crumbling to ash.

A final blast of flames opened a doorway out of the jungle. Beyond, a rocky field with scattered trees separated them from the mountainside. Zorro broke from the group and went ahead, standing on a rock for a better view before signaling the others to advance.

Nick checked back the way they had come. A blackened path cut through the dense jungle still beating with the furious glow of the spiky plants. From the elevated vantage point, he could see the flickering of torches back at the encampment. And past that, the shore, lined with the beached skiffs that had brought him and so many others here. Past the surf, out in the bay, the fleet of six ships sat watching.

"*Ven*," Zorro said to Nick.

He understood this to mean "come," and he hurried after the squad as it started the trek up the rocky slope. Zorro remained on point, clambering over boulders with the agility of a mountain goat.

Whale stopped several times to catch his breath, prompting a few jokes and some laughs from Zorro and Fuego. Nick picked up a few words, primarily *gordo*, which he knew from context to mean "fat."

During the short break, Nick studied the face of the mountain, searching for the winged monster. Lightning flashes captured the jagged peak, but nothing moved up there.

Imulah wiped the plant sap off his knife and tucked it away. "They say we're almost to the tunnels," he said.

"Tunnels?" Glock asked.

"Where the monsters dwell. To return to the camp victorious, you must kill one and place it at the sacrificial chamber inside the volcano."

"Fucking gods," said Glock.

Zorro motioned for the group to continue.

"Better start helping," Nick said to Glock.

"Don't forget what I said," he whispered.

Nick looked to see if Imulah had heard, but the scribe was already following the other Cazadores. The group pushed on, trekking into a stretch of drainage that looked like mud but was fine silt.

Zorro went up on another rock for a look, then waved them on.

He jumped down, and as Nick followed, a scream of pain rang out. He rushed up with the Cazadores to find Zorro plucking orange insects the size of Timmy Tam off his body. The creatures surged out of a mound.

Fire ants.

Fuego moved into position with his flamethrower, shouting in Spanish for Zorro to get clear. But Zorro was too busy pulling the insects off his body. They surged up his leg, and several had made it to his torso, neck, and even under his helmet. He finally flipped, rolling over and sliding downhill.

A jet from the flamethrower hit the mound where the ants kept boiling up out of a hole.

Nick slid down the other side of the boulder, away from the fire. He clambered over to the young Cazador scout, who wailed in agony as the little creatures bit and stung him. Nick used his knife and gloved hand to scrape and slap the insects away from Zorro's legs. Whale picked his way down the boulder and began smashing the creatures.

Above them, Fuego yelled something, and Nick glanced up

to see the flame jet weakening. He was running low on gas or was already out.

"Shit!" Nick shouted. "Help me get him out of here."

Whale seemed to understand, and they dragged Zorro back up to the rocky ledge overlooking the basin. Chest heaving, Nick caught his breath and looked out over a little mountain range of anthills. Just beyond, not two hundred feet from their position, lay a dark opening—an entrance into the mountain.

But they could not keep going this way, especially now, with their scout injured. Zorro writhed on the ground in pain, moaning. Whale crouched with a med kit while Fuego held security, saying something about being too exposed.

Whale grunted a response that Nick didn't understand, then leaned back down and started to apply some sort of herbal gunk from a tube onto Zorro's wounds.

A whistle pulled Nick's eyes to Glock, who was eyeing the rifle the wounded scout had left on the ground. With Fuego turned toward the mountain, and Whale occupied by Zorro, it seemed like the best opportunity they were likely to get.

But Zorro had helped Nick, and these young men were just doing what they must to survive. Could he really help Glock kill them? And even if they should succeed, where would they go?

He glanced back to the camp and the warships beyond.

The words Mac had offered when Nick saw him back there echoed in his mind.

Do what they say, and you will survive.

Glock began to move, and Nick knew he had seconds to make a decision. In the end, it came down to one person: Sofia, and the best way he could help her.

Killing these men without a plan in place wasn't going to accomplish that.

Nick waved his hand, signaling Glock to stand down, but it

was already too late. The former Ranger drew his sword and smacked Whale in the helmet with it, resulting in a cry of pain. Then he scooped up the rifle and aimed it at Fuego as the husky Cazador spun with the flamethrower.

An ethereal shriek came from the cliffs far above, and Nick spotted the winged shadow of the monster swooping down toward them. In what felt like slow motion, Glock fired the rifle, hitting Fuego in the shoulder and knocking him away.

Zorro tried to get up, but Glock hit him with the rifle butt. Then he went to shoot Whale, who had one bloody hand on his cracked helmet and was reaching out with the other.

Nick swung his cutlass, and a horrific scream filled the jungle as Glock twirled, a geyser of blood shooting from the stump where Nick had severed his arm.

The hand, still holding the gun, fell to the dirt. Nick bent down and grabbed the weapon as Glock staggered backward, scream-ing in horror and staring at his hand on the ground.

From the sky, the monster swooped down, clawed legs extend-ing. Nick shouldered the rifle as he had seen Mac do before. Then he closed one eye, lined up the iron sights on the beast, and fired.

Glock turned—right into the claws that plucked him effort-lessly off the ground. The beast flapped back into the air, gripping him with its curved talons.

"Help me!" Glock wailed.

Nick aimed the rifle again at the beast as it sank its teeth into Glock's neck. He kept it steady, holding a breath in his chest but keeping both eyes open. He led the creature with the barrel, then fired right at Glock.

The man didn't deserve mercy, but Nick decided to grant it to him anyway. The three-round burst killed Glock instantly. The creature shrieked as it carried his now limp body.

Nick sighted up the beast and fired another burst. Bullets

cut through the wings, forcing it into a dive. He pulled the trigger and heard a click—out of ammo. Dropping the weapon to the ground, he took off running back downhill, toward the jungle, cutlass in hand.

He leaped over spiky plants and severed vines. A web blocked his way, but he could see where the monster had fallen into a barbed net.

Nick hacked a path through. The beast had almost broken free when he arrived. Squealing like a wounded hog, it thrashed outward with a broken limb through the collapsed web. A pale, bony head centered on Nick as he approached. There were no eyes—just a slot for a nose and a wide, tooth-filled maw dripping with blood.

Nick hacked at an arm as it slashed outward. Then he jumped onto a shot-up wing, crushing it. Standing on the creature, he raised his cutlass in both hands and brought it down on the neck. Blood trickled from the narrow, crooked lips.

He swung again, harder, crunching through bone. A guttural sigh came from the dying beast. On the third swing, the head finally fell away.

Gasping for air, chest heaving, Nick took a moment to look at his kill. Then he leaned down and picked up the head.

"*El Perrito mató el demonio*," said Whale.

He turned to see the husky Cazador had removed his helmet and held a bandage to his bleeding head. Fuego was helping Zorro while Imulah stood nearby with his clipboard, documenting what had happened.

Nick lifted the deformed head, partially in shock from slaying the beast.

Whale spoke louder. "*El Perrito mató el demonio.*"

Fuego helped Zorro stand and started toward Nick. He tossed the head in front of the Cazadores. "You can take it to the sacrificial chamber," he said.

Whale picked it up and threw it back to Nick. "*No, no, Perrito,*" he said.

"That honor is yours," explained Imulah.

Fuego nodded and spoke rapidly in Spanish as Nick turned to look for Glock's body.

"He says they are grateful for what you did to your comrade," Imulah said.

Nick walked back over and grabbed the head. "Glock wasn't my comrade," he said. "Write that down too, Imulah."

*   *   *   *   *

Mac dreamed of a monstrous octopus hurling sailors like bean-bags and tearing them apart as easily as a child playing with an insect. Thick, suction cup–lined arms broke through the water, whipping back and forth before snatching the enemy soldiers off the deck of their ship. In this nightmare, he was sprawled on the lifeboat, paralyzed and unable to move as the creature turned on him.

Those limbs whipped down, spiked barbs crunching through his armor and lifting him off the lifeboat. Laughter rang out from el Pulpo, who watched joyously. In Spanish, he yelled, "You ran, Lucky Mac. Coward!" Wrapped in the massive arm, he felt it pull him out of the boat, then slap him down into the water.

The darkness gave way as he awoke in a dimly lit space that smelled of chemicals. Footsteps clanked over, and he sat up, groaning in pain. More pain gripped his back as he reached to a bandage over his shoulder. Touching it brought back the memory of having the shrapnel surgically removed before he passed out.

He also remembered what had happened before that.

The giant mutant octopus was real.

Mac looked over for the Cazador who had told him the story

from the adjacent bed. The man was gone now, but Mac recalled what he had said about el Pulpo bringing the monster along in a cage beneath the *Dragon*. When all had seemed lost, he used his "magic" whistle to turn the beast loose on the enemy.

One of those enemies walked over to Mac's bedside and looked down at him. *Not really an enemy now*, he thought. Like him, she was a slave to el Pulpo.

Mac sat up as the nurse in a gray uniform stood in front of his bed. She looked about thirty, with good teeth and hygiene, which told him these people were fairly civilized.

"How do you feel?" she asked in heavily accented English.

"I'm fine," he replied.

"You are a very long way from *fine*."

He tried to look in her eyes, but she avoided his gaze.

"I need to check your wound," she said. "Turn around."

A thought ran through his head that maybe she would try to kill him, just as he had considered murdering his captors, especially el Pulpo. But he doubted she would try here, in a room full of injured Cazadores and with the guard just outside.

He turned to give her a look at the bandage on his back, but even that hurt from the injury he sustained on the ship. Gently, she removed the dressing over the wound.

"No sign of infection in the cut," she said. "That is good."

She reapplied the bandage with the same gentle care. When she turned away, Mac reached out. "What's your name?" he asked.

"What does that matter?"

"I want to thank you."

"I am doing this to keep those people ... those *animals* ..." Her face tightened, and Mac knew what threats she had heard.

"They aren't my people." He kept his voice low.

"And yet you fight with them?"

She narrowed her eyes at him, meeting his gaze for the first time.

"You are a prisoner, like me?" she asked.

"Yes."

She looked at him again, snorted, and walked away to check the next patient. Mac rested his head back on the bed, exhausted and ready for sleep.

Just as he was drifting off, the hatch burst open and el Pulpo stumbled inside with a jug of liquor in his hand. He took a swig and then gazed out over the room.

The injured who could get up did, including Mac. He swung his legs over the side of the bed in a sign of respect, but also because he remembered his dream—how el Pulpo had called him a coward and laughed at his demise in the arms of the octopus.

The captain made his way through the medical bay, offering the jug to his men. The nurse stood with her head down, stiffly submissive. Seeing her, he grinned and strode over, sniffing her as a dog might sniff another dog.

She reared away, prompting a laugh.

"You no think I *guapo*?" He turned to Mac. "*¿Cómo se dice 'guapo' en inglés?*"

"Handsome," Mac said.

"*Sí, sí.*" El Pulpo chuckled. "You no think I handsome?"

He circled her, sniffing again, then licked her cheek.

Mac watched, feeling sick to his stomach. He stepped barefoot onto the cold deck, wincing. That caught el Pulpo's eye. He walked over, his smile vanishing into a snarl.

"*¿Cómo se dice 'cobarde' en inglés?*"

Mac also knew that word: *coward*. His bad dream, it seemed, was about to become reality.

El Pulpo glared with rage in his eyes.

"He was hurt very badly," came the voice of the nurse, which was no longer soft.

El Pulpo turned to the woman. A wide grin returned to his demented face.

"Maybe she think *you* handsome."

The woman appeared to understand this and scoffed.

A Cazador appeared in the open hatch. He removed his helmet, revealing the hardened face of Hammerhead. It was odd seeing the burly warrior with clothes and battle gear on. Hammerhead relayed a message from the captain—something about approaching the harbor.

They were nearing land.

El Pulpo nodded and turned back to Mac, eyeing him like a rat, as he had that day back at the bunker raid.

"I can fight," Mac said. *"Lucharé."*

"Muy bien."

El Pulpo left, and Mac limped across the room, pain jolting up and down his back. Just as he was about to leave, the nurse said, "My name's Elena."

"Mac," he said. "Thank you again."

A moment passed between them, a bond forming from their similar plights. Mac nodded and then left the medical bay, joining el Pulpo and Hammerhead outside. They took him to their retrofitted armory, where they had transferred salvaged gear, armor, and weapons from the *Dragon* before it sank.

Four Cazadores were gearing up inside. Mac found his hazard suit and armor, which had been patched up after shrapnel tore through the back and into his flesh. By the time he was dressed, he was all alone. He went to a rack of swords and hefted the best-looking one. With a twirl and slash, he tested the blade, finding it both strong and sharp.

After grabbing a spear, he left the armory and headed to a ladder. Dim lights guided him through the foreign ship, past closed hatches and others that were open. The belongings of the ship's former occupants lay scattered about.

The Cazadores had likely searched the vessel top to bottom for supplies, food, and weapons—things they would need to replace what was lost on the *Dragon*.

Curious, he stepped into a small space, formerly personal quarters for one of the ship's officers. A colorful quilt was draped over the end of the bunk. The material was fairly new, from the looks of it. Two hardcover books lay upside down. He picked one up—*Shōgun*, printed in English.

He placed it down on the small table beside the bunk, by a necklace of blue and red beads—also fairly new. Next to it was a small wood carving of a horse and rider wearing the same helmets he had seen during the attack.

Horsehair, he realized.

A distant shriek of pain resonated through the vessel. Mac stepped out. The noise came from the upper deck. The scream grew louder. And a second, different voice followed.

Mac moved as fast as he could with his limp. Pain shot up his aching back. The screaming transformed into an animal howl near the top landing. A discarded helmet lay on the landing. The braid at the crest of that helmet was definitely horsehair, and it was coated with blood. Spatters covered the hull and overhead.

Someone had died here, and it sounded as though someone was dying outside.

Mac opened a hatch to find a human torch on the deck. The prisoner writhed, screaming as flames consumed his naked body.

The rest of the captured crew were on their knees: eleven sailors in gray uniforms and five soldiers in light armor with the logo of a horse and rider, much like the figurehead on the ship's bow.

Sobs and shouts came from the group as their comrade burned.

El Pulpo paced in front of them, with Ernesto at his side.

"I know where your port is!" the scribe translated. "You will tell the captain how many more of you there are."

Barracudas and Cazador warriors stood across the deck, holding a variety of weapons. In total, fifteen of the original twenty-five were still in fighting condition.

Hammerhead went to the burning prisoner, who was still twitching. He used his cutlass to slice off a piece of flesh. Then he popped his helmet and blew on the morsel of meat, which he then chewed with sharpened teeth.

"I will tell you," said a man.

El Pulpo eyed the grime-covered sailor. Probably one of the mechanics they had left alive to keep the ship running after losing so many of their own.

Ernesto crouched in front of the slave.

"My master wants to know how many of you there are and what kind of defenses," he said. "If you share this information, you will be spared."

The prisoner looked at the others. One of them glared at him, lipping something before his face suddenly distorted as an axe split it. Blood spurted away from the blow, hitting the sailor who had offered to talk. He stumbled backward and fell on his bum.

El Pulpo pried his axe from the dead prisoner's skull and grinned.

"Tell, or I break *tu cabeza*," he said in broken English.

Mac suddenly felt lightheaded. He stumbled slightly, then rushed over to the railing, tipping his helmet to vomit over the side.

Laughter came from behind him, but he could hardly hear. The prisoner started to talk as Mac dry-heaved. Stars danced before his eyes. Shaking them away, he noticed something on the horizon.

Mac wiped his mouth, straightened, and turned back to the

conversation. The prisoner was spilling his guts now. "This is the Iron Reef, where we have a great source of fuel," he explained. "There are men here who will die to protect it. Many men."

Ernesto relayed the information to el Pulpo.

El Pulpo turned back to the Cazadores on the deck, looking at them in turn, his gaze stopping on Mac. He walked over to him and pulled a sword from his sheath.

Mac studied the blade, half expecting it to come down on his own head. But instead el Pulpo handed the hilt over. He growled something about Mac caring or having *corazón*.

Heart.

Then he pointed at the sailor who had spoken.

"*Enemigo*," el Pulpo said, pointing the sword at the man.

Mac understood then. The captain wanted him to kill this sailor, this enemy.

The man understood, too, and shook his head, sobbing. "No, please, I beg you."

As the other Cazadores went to partake of the cooked prisoner, Mac stood there holding the blade and shaking, knowing that if he wanted to survive, he must become what he had warned Nick of years ago: a monster.

He walked over to the sailor and said, "I'm sorry," before thrusting the sword into his chest. It was over fast, and Mac held the man's dying gaze.

El Pulpo walked over with Ernesto, who documented the kill and translated what the captain said next about the Iron Reef.

Mac, trying not to throw up again, looked away from the dead prisoner and out at the distant shore.

"El Pulpo says if you help us take the enemy fortress, you can have the medicine woman," explained the scribe. "She will be your flesh trophy."

CHAPTER 13

Nick held his trophy in his hand, in front of the sacrificial chamber Zorro had guided them to inside the Quill. The three Cazadores and Imulah stood behind him, watching him hold up the skull. He looked down at the eyeless face of a predator that could have torn him in half. By killing it, he had proved himself and finally accomplished what he always wanted.

But at what cost? he wondered. This wasn't the first thing he had killed. Smitty and Glock were now dead because of him too. People from his own bunker—his people!

Nick tried to tell himself he had no choice, but was it true?

He held up the bloody head, understanding the implications. Hunting this beast down made him a Cazador, a warrior part of the cannibalistic army that followed their obese Lord Portatormentas.

Still, Nick couldn't deny the swell of pride he felt as he tossed the head of the creature into the pool of water. Nor could he deny his pride as the three Cazador trainees shouted his name.

"*¡El Perrito!*" Whale boomed.

Zorro limped away from Fuego, who held him up upright, and reached out to Nick.

"Muy bien, Perrito," Zorro said.

"Gracias," Nick replied, shaking his new comrade's hand.

He looped his arm around Zorro, helping him out of the chamber the way they had come.

Two hours later, the four warriors emerged at base camp with their scribe. Guards at the gate opened it and ushered them inside. Imulah raised his newly bloodstained clipboard, explaining they had killed the demon.

The two guards both looked at Nick, and while he fully expected them to laugh, as people always did, they nodded.

"This way," Imulah said. He led them down the muddy terrain to a processing station, where he again handed over his documentation. Then he went up to Nick. "You will be granted a night of leave before your first training assignment," he said. "Return to the Metal Islands with Zorro, Whale, and Fuego."

And just like that, Nick was leaving the island, no longer in chains or a cage. Zorro went to a medic to get bandaged up. Then they boarded a boat with four other trainees who had survived their own mission and killed one of the beasts.

Most of them fell asleep right away, but Nick was still riding high on adrenaline. And Whale's snoring didn't help. Finally, from pure exhaustion, Nick drifted off to sleep.

He awoke in sunlight. A bird flapped overhead as the boat skimmed over the calm waters of the Metal Islands. On the horizon, the largest tower rose up like an Old World skyscraper. Nick thought of Sofia, his heart hurting at the thought of her in captivity.

I will save you someday.

He had just come a step closer, he told himself.

The boat curved away, heading for a pair of rigs linked by bridges over the water. Each level was parceled into many living quarters, from shacks and tents to solid metal structures with real glass windows.

Nick had seen this rig a few times and knew it was where a significant portion of the Cazador population lived.

Whale had woken up and stood on the boat, saying something about how his mom would be happy to see him alive. Fuego laughed, joking about how she wouldn't be happy to feed him again.

They motored into a marina alive with the midafternoon activities of fishermen and people from other rigs ferrying things back and forth. Boats of scrap material, jugs of water, and homemade items waited to be unloaded while scribes walked up and down the piers, documenting everything.

Their boat coasted into the last slip. Waiting there on the dock was a lean man, arms folded over his leather armor. Hair as dark as squid ink was slicked back on his head.

He pushed sunglasses up over brown eyes to look at the warriors as they piled out of the boat onto the deck. The trainees all stiffened like boards in front of the middle-aged warrior, who wore the rank of lieutenant on his breast. Joining him was a scribe.

The lieutenant stepped forward and spoke in a gruff voice.

"Congratulations on the hunt," translated the scribe. "This is Lieutenant Forge, who will oversee the next phase of your training. For now, you have a day's leave and may see your families. Tonight you will report to the top of the rig for your official induction."

The other trainees saluted, and Nick followed suit.

Forge turned away, hurrying off to the next group of survivors. Fuego, Whale, and Zorro started down the piers, leaving Nick alone.

For the first time in his captivity, he could move freely. But now he had nowhere to go.

An odd sensation passed over him as he looked up at the levels of the rig. He felt so strangely free that it frightened him. He had been used to a regimented schedule, orders, and fearing his captors. As he scanned the levels, he thought of Sofia again. Was it possible she was here, among the Cazador people? He considered looking or trying to get a boat to go search for her at the capitol tower. But he had no money and no means, only his boots and the clothes on his back.

"Nick," Zorro called out.

Whale waved at him. "*Ven.*"

Nick hurried after the men, finding himself suddenly excited. They led him up into the rig, using an interior stairwell that took them to the second level, which was full of industrial machinery that clattered and groaned noisily. The third level was a long, dimly lit space of pens with livestock. The stench of manure drifted through the sprawling space, which was supported by pillars every twenty feet or so.

This place was vast, like an open-air version of the bunker.

The fourth level was a machine shop that reminded Nick of the place where he had spent so much of his youth. He had always wanted to escape that place, and now he had, but it meant fighting. *Killing.*

He tried to blot out that thought.

On the fifth level, he got his first close-up view of the people who lived here. And again he saw similarities to the bunker where he was born—this time, with the people themselves. Although many had tattoos and sharpened teeth, and all of them spoke another language, they weren't all that different from the people of ITC Star Station. He peeked inside living quarters along a passage where families lived inside the small rooms. Kids played with toys on the deck, and women stirred pots or cut vegetables. Others knitted or repaired clothes. There weren't many men though. That was one major difference.

He followed his squad to the sixth floor, brimming with tents and shacks. Whale went to his home first.

"*Mamá.*"

A short, stout woman pulled back a tarp and gazed out. She gave a nearly toothless grin and hugged him. Then she looked to Fuego, Zorro, and finally Nick, narrowing her gaze at him.

"*¿Cómo te llamas?*" she asked.

"Ni—"

"*El Perrito,*" Whale said, cutting him off.

She looked Nick up and down, then asked if he liked fish.

"Oh, *sí,*" Nick said with an eager nod.

She grinned, then told them to return later for a meal.

The group pushed on, with Fuego stopping by to see his younger brother and the aunt who cared for him. Zorro stopped by his grandmother's, the only living relative he had left. It struck Nick that maybe these people weren't the blood-thirsty ghouls he had thought. They were people wanting only to survive.

Of course, there were plenty who had taken extreme measures in that effort. Eating other people wasn't something Nick would ever get used to or condone, but the civilization was alive and well. They had built it around a warrior soci-ety that valued the sword to take what was necessary to live.

An hour later, the three young Cazadores and Nick returned to Whale's home, where his mother worked a large paddle in a pot of simmering stew. Hearty chunks of fish and potatoes simmered, giving off a mouthwatering aroma.

She pointed to the bowls. Nick took a cracked piece of pottery with a faded flower stenciled on the side. He got in line behind the others, but she waved him forward and filled his bowl to the top.

"*Gracias,*" he said.

"*De nada,*" she replied.

Nick went to a cluster of plastic crates arranged in front of a rail overlooking the ocean. Whale, Fuego, and Zorro joined him there, taking a seat on the crates.

Chewing with his mouth open, Whale said something about being glad to be back. Fuego replied he was surprised they all made it—especially Zorro, who, he said, was most fortunate not to lose his penis.

Nick laughed even harder when Whale joked that the ants spared it because they couldn't find it—too small. He tipped his bowl up and drank down the broth.

Zorro kicked Whale in the shin with a snort, saying something about it taking a million fire ants to lift up Whale's belly in search of *his* dick.

Whale eyed Nick, a brow raised. Then he stood up, towering over the group.

Nick stopped laughing and swallowed, realizing his mistake. Just because he had fought with them didn't mean he could disrespect them by laughing.

Whale's mother walked over, breaking the tension.

"*¿Cómo es la sopa?*" she asked.

Nick smiled. "*Excelente*," he replied.

Whale held out his bowl, which was almost empty.

She clicked her tongue and went back to the pot to fetch him more.

Zorro held up his bowl, too, but it was still full. This wasn't a request for more; it was a toast. "*Gracias a Nick Baker*," he said, explaining that Nick had saved his life.

Fuego raised his bowl, and Whale nodded, grunting, "*Gracias.*"

They sat there enjoying their soup and the blazing purple sunset on the horizon. Then they got up and headed to the top deck for the ceremony.

Hundreds of Cazadores had gathered, forming a wide circle

around a rusted barrel venting flames. Lieutenant Forge stood with six Cazadores in full armor, armed with spears.

Nick, Fuego, Whale, and Zorro joined sixteen trainees in front of the group.

Imulah the scribe walked over to document and translate. When he was in position, Forge went to the barrel. With a heavy glove, he drew out an iron rod with a red-hot symbol on the end that looked like some sort of sea creature.

Holding it up, he faced the recruits, Imulah translating in English.

"We gather here tonight to induct a new generation of warriors into the courageous ranks of the Cazadores," he said. "Loyal to Lord Portatormentas, living god and general of our legions."

Nick scanned the crowd, feeling eyes on him. He noticed a group of pale, thin women standing in a cluster a few rows deep. They were dressed in light blue.

He shifted slightly to get a better view.

"Step forward," Imulah commanded.

Nick followed the line as they moved toward the burning barrel. His heart skipped when his new position provided a view of a familiar face. There was no mistaking the curly orange hair of Smitty's wife, Ginger. She glared at Nick with anger in her eyes, and he felt it to his core. Despair ate through him like a hungry parasite. All sense of pride vanquished.

A pained grunt snapped him back to the ceremony.

Whale held up his arm, simmering where Forge had branded it with the stylized image of an octopus. Nick stepped up, pulling back his sleeve. As Forge lowered the glowing iron, Nick didn't move, even as the heat scorched his flesh.

He found a second familiar set of eyes—Sofia.

She watched with wide eyes as if she couldn't believe what she was seeing.

The searing metal stung his flesh, and yet Nick stood stoical, unflinching, staring right back at his friend. He wanted to yell out to her, to say he wasn't like them.

But he knew her, and she wouldn't believe that lie. He had killed men out of self-preservation, including the husband of the widow standing beside Sofia.

Nick was one of them now. A Cazador.

*   *   *   *   *

The four skiffs moved silently away from the captured enemy vessel, toward the harbor. Each boat was packed with four or five Cazador soldiers. Mac crouched in one, holding his cutlass. All around him, el Pulpo and his warriors prepared to raid the home of the enemy that called themselves the Horse Lords.

According to the captive sailor Mac had executed, there would be a considerable force guarding this place located in a bay of the former country of Belize.

Mac had spent time looking at the map, but this long after the apocalypse, Old World maps meant very little. The terrain had changed considerably from the bombs and the tsunamis. To know what was really out there, they would need to see their target with their own eyes.

The skiffs carved through the fog, rowed by the strongest Cazador on each boat to avoid engine noise. Hammerhead, Izan, and Vampire all sat around Mac. He could hear the crash of waves on the shore.

They weren't far from land now.

Mac rose up slightly, using the sporadic lightning from the storms to spot land. The first looming silhouette of a facility came into focus in the blue light reflecting off the steel surfaces of massive storage tanks that stood like silent sentinels.

As they paddled closer, Mac saw an intricate maze of pipe-lines under the storm-lit clouds. They stretched from the storage tanks, over a rocky shoreline, down to a docked container ship that cast a long shadow over the harbor.

El Pulpo pointed out a pair of guards on the deck of the ship. Then he pointed at a guard tower twenty feet from the surf, watching over the rocky shoreline.

Using hand signals, el Pulpo directed his men to take out the threats. In each skiff, a Cazador aimed a crossbow as they glided closer into the harbor. Mac groaned as they thumped over a wave, his sore back complaining.

Thunder boomed, and the crossbowmen used the distraction to fire their all-but-silent bolts. On the ship, both enemy guards crumpled with a bolt to the chest. The lookout in the tower also slumped out of view.

The fourth Cazador shooter waited, then fired at a fourth enemy guard who rushed out on the deck of the ship to look out over the water. This bolt missed, however. He raised his rifle into the air but didn't get a chance to pull the trigger.

Hammerhead's axe flew from almost twenty feet away, hitting the guard square in the helmet. He fell backward, twitching on the deck as the skiffs closed the gap. El Pulpo directed two of the boats to the container ship, where a Cazador threw a grappling hook up to the top. While those eight warriors boarded, el Pulpo led the other two skiffs to shore.

Mac got up to jump into the water, then hesitated at the sight of the rocky beach. The giant slabs weren't rocks but pieces of broken concrete from a partially collapsed seawall. The facility on the other side had mostly survived, shielded beyond a secondary wall that Mac hadn't seen earlier—a wall they would have to get themselves over. And that was after moving up the hundred feet of rubble covering the shore.

El Pulpo was first out into the water. They pulled the skiffs up and secured them out of view between four large slabs of shattered concrete. The hunters used the giant sloped shards to climb up the shoreline, hopping from slab to slab to the top. With each jolt, Mac's back screamed in protest.

He hurried over to the guard tower, where el Pulpo ordered Hammerhead to climb up and check inside. The hulking Cazador returned a few minutes later with the severed head of the guard, a slung enemy rifle, and a flare gun.

Mac focused on the secondary wall, now only about thirty feet away. The Cazadores pushed up the sloped shore. On approach, el Pulpo took a grappling hook on a rope and slung it up, knocking back razor wire. He pulled it taut and then started climbing up the fifteen-foot wall.

At the top, he used his axe to knock the razor wire away. Then he dropped over the other side. Hammerhead went next, and by the time Mac was up and over, the warriors deployed to the container ship had come ashore.

The entire twenty-trooper force made it over the secondary wall. Crouching behind el Pulpo, they looked out over an oil facility that appeared to be operational. The humming of machinery from the rows of buildings confirmed that his eyes weren't playing tricks on him.

Protected behind the second seawall were a dozen giant tankers and a network of maintained pipes connecting to three processing units. Towering stacks released steam and emissions into the sky. Mac noticed a single control building, with boarded-up windows but light coming through the cracks. An access road led from that structure to a gated fence in the distance. A flash of lightning captured the rubble of a city beyond.

El Pulpo turned to his hunters, no doubt grinning behind his helmet. He split them up again, sending half to hunt for patrols and guards while the other half headed for the control building. Mac went with el Pulpo, moving toward the building's double metal doors.

Hammerhead went to it and tried the lever, then shook his head to confirm it was locked. Mac and the other six Cazadores got behind el Pulpo. He flipped his axe-head over to the hammer face. Then he strode up to the doors, cocked the axe back, and slammed it against the levers with enough force to shatter them both.

Roaring, Hammerhead led the charge inside. Mac hurried after them, raising his cutlass. As his eyes adjusted to the lighting of the command room, they fell on five men and two women in black coveralls, all staring in terror at the Cazadores.

One of the men took off running for a side exit, only to be skewered by a spear that a Cazador launched, pinning him to the wall. The other warriors stormed ahead, slashing and stabbing at the horrified workers.

"¡No, para!" el Pulpo commanded.

But for three of these people, it was too late. They lay on the ground, bleeding out from severed limbs and deep gashes. Hammerhead grabbed a squirming female worker, who screamed and then fainted.

Gunshots cracked outside, and Mac turned. El Pulpo waved for some of the fighters to head back there, including Mac. He rushed out the broken doors with Hammerhead, Vampire, Izan, and el Pulpo. They ran toward the gates, where a huge four-legged beast lay in the dirt, leaking blood from several bullet holes. A man lay crushed under the massive creature.

"He's getting away!" someone yelled.

Mac looked out past the gates, down a road where another enemy rode the same type of beast that lay dead on the ground—a horse.

Hammerhead unslung his rifle and handed it to el Pulpo. He shouldered the weapon, aimed, and fired a shot that cracked like thunder.

The horse and rider kept going and vanished into the darkness.

El Pulpo grunted an oath and handed the rifle back to Hammerhead, then turned to the outpost. He took off his helmet to look with his own eyes.

Mac also took a long look at the fortress they had just breached. This wasn't the home of these people but a fuel production facility. A working one, to boot, where they refined the liquid gold.

El Pulpo raised his axe toward the sky and let out a roar, which his men took up with gusto. Even Mac held up his sword, caked with the blood of the man he had murdered.

A hard clap on his back from el Pulpo made him stagger.

"Medicine woman *es tuya* . . . yours, Mac *Suertudo*," the captain said.

CHAPTER 14

Nick rested in his hammock, trying to block out the snoring from his comrades and get some sleep in the open-air barracks on the Cazador rig. He turned to look out over the ship's rail protecting them from the ten-story drop to the ocean. It wasn't the snoring or the beautiful star-studded sky that kept him awake; it was thoughts of Sofia. He couldn't stop thinking about her horrified gaze as Lieutenant Forge branded him with the Cazador logo.

He glanced down at the painful new scar that symbolized his transformation. On the one hand, it meant he had finally proved himself as a warrior. On the other, it would forever be a reminder that he had thrown in his lot with the Cazador empire.

Over the past year, he had fought for survival with one goal in mind: saving Sofia, promising himself he would do whatever it took. He had thought that becoming a Cazador would bring him closer to that goal. Now he realized it only put him further away, because now Sofia saw him as the enemy.

But there was no going back from what he had done to secure his place in this war machine.

All around him slept the new cogs in the machine. Of all these

strong, hard young men, he was the only one not born a Cazador—the only traitor to his own people.

Anger ate at him as he lay there staring up at the bejeweled
sky, feeling like a monster, a sellout. He closed his eyes and tried
to let the anger subside.

Something stung his head, jolting him awake. Sitting up in
his hammock, he saw the moon high in the sky, glowing and then
dimming as clouds rolled in.

A familiar female voice whispered behind him.

"Nick."

This had to be a dream. It couldn't be… Sofia, could it?

He turned to see a robed figure holding on to the guardrail
bordering the barracks. A loud snore made the mystery person
let go of the rail and drop to the deck below.

Nick slipped out of his hammock and made his way over to
the railing. The robed figure climbed down to a raised platform
with lemons, limes, and oranges growing in planters. Heart thumping, he followed quietly to the lower level, where she pulled her
hood down. It was her…

"Sofia, I—"

She put a finger to his lips.

"We don't have much time," she said. "If I'm caught, he will
kill us both."

"Who?"

"Lord Portatormentas."

Nick froze, his fears realized.

"They say I must marry him," Sofia said. "But I won't. I'd
rather die."

"I will save you."

She stared into his eyes, then looked down at the burn on
his arm.

"I'm not like them, Sofia," he said. "I've done what I had to do—"

"I know."

He didn't breathe as her lips moved.

"You killed because you had to, and that doesn't make you one of them—not yet. But you will become one of them if you continue to fight with them. That, or you will die."

"I'll die if I don't. Fighting with them is the only way to save you."

"Save me?" She scoffed. "Nick, you can't save me."

"I'll find a way."

"A way? Look around." She swept her arm, indicating the rigs. Lightning forked on the horizon, the storm rolling across the water miles away. "The Cazadores are everywhere, and they are evil."

Nick thought of Fuego, Whale, and Zorro. He had started to look at them differently, almost as friends. But they weren't like his old friends, not like Gus, Chubs, and Ron. They were all gone now, dead because of el Pulpo and Lord Portatormentas.

"You can't save me, Nick," Sofia said. "But you can save yourself. When you're on your first raid, *run*. You run and you don't come back. Ever."

"No, I won't do that. I will find a way."

Sofia smiled and then gave Nick a hug.

"I love you, Nick, but you have to forget about me. I'll survive. I'll be okay."

She pulled away and melted into the shadows.

"Sofia, I will save you—"

His words were drowned out by someone shouting in his sleep. Looking down at Sofia one last time, he caught her gaze as she looked back up at him. And then she was gone.

Nick returned to his hammock as the shouting drew near.

"*¡Levántate!*" commanded a deep voice in Spanish.

The thud of heavy boots drew closer. In the torchlight, four Cazadores in full combat array marched through the outdoor barracks.

Lieutenant Forge shouted for everyone to stand at attention.

The newly minted soldiers stood, most of them shirtless like Nick. Whale fell off his hammock to the deck with a thud, prompting laughter.

"¡Silencio!" Forge yelled.

The Cazadores went quiet as they rushed to get ready. Nick put on his new uniform and leather armor, watching the weather change rapidly outside. Swollen clouds blocked out the moon, and lightning cleaved the horizon as a storm rolled toward the Metal Islands.

Whale, Fuego, and Zorro fell into line with Nick as they made their way to a ladder. The rungs extended all the way down to the marina at the bottom of the rig, where six skiffs waited in the choppy water.

Lightning captured the silhouette of a warship farther out. A scribe joined Lieutenant Forge on the docks, translating for the English speakers. But Nick understood much of the Spanish, too, and felt a chill at the message.

The trainees had survived the monsters on land. Now they must face the monsters in the ocean. Forge pointed to the ship.

"Your next test is to swim there and survive," said the scribe. "Do so, and you will deploy on your first raid."

The twenty-five new Cazadores around Nick exchanged glances. Some whispered, but none seemed too worried. They all had grown up on the sea, swimming since they were small.

Nick had spent his first seventeen years in a bunker, never seeing much more than a bathtub of water at any one time. He had learned how to swim over the past three years, but it wasn't his strength.

Forge walked over to a large assortment of swim masks, snorkels, and fins. Behind these was a rack of spearguns. One by one, the new recruits stepped forward. When it was Nick's turn, he picked goggles and fins but decided to skip the snorkel. He always had a problem with water getting in, and with today's choppy seas, he didn't want to mess with it.

Next, he grabbed a speargun before heading down the pier. At the end, a pair of fishermen stood with buckets. Nick halted when he smelled the rotting fish from a distance.

My God, it's bait, he thought. *I'm bait.*

The predators were already here. The elongated bodies of sharks darted between the piers, their fins slicing the dark surface as more chunks of rotting, bloody chum were tossed in.

"Swim hard and stay together!" shouted the scribe, translating Forge's orders.

Whale was the first one into the water, sending up a splash that might have made Nick laugh if they were not jumping into shark-infested waters.

The other Cazadores all ran and jumped in, giving loud war whoops. Nick leaped in with them and started kicking. All around him he saw a chaos of bubbles and churning limbs.

Nick slung the strap of the speargun over his back, then started off in a freestyle crawl after the main pack of warriors heading out into the open sea. A heel caught him in the head, and then another kicked his neck.

Treading water, he saw the dock twenty feet behind him, and Forge holding a torch, screaming at the last recruit on the dock. At last, the reluctant Cazador jumped off. Nick turned, eyeing the fins that circled them. But they weren't alone. The skiffs from the marina motored out, the pilots tossing out more chum to distract the sharks. Apparently, Forge didn't want too many of his greenhorns to die.

Nick pushed ahead, continuing the long swim to the ship. Something big and rough scraped his right leg. He glimpsed a fin as he pulled into the main pack of swimming warriors. Most of them were doing a standard crawl stroke, but some were so frightened of the sharks that they stayed in a breaststroke so they could see around them. Panicked voices shouted as a fin carved through the center of the pack.

A *thwack* sounded from a speargun. The projectile narrowly missed a shark that had abandoned the rotting fish for a chance at something bigger. That fin weaved this way and that, as if browsing the prey for the weakest target.

Nick realized the shark had decided on him. The head broke the surface, jaws preparing to snap. He unslung his speargun just as someone grabbed him and yanked him hard to the right.

The jaws closed where his head had been a moment earlier. "*¡Cuidado!*" yelled the warrior who had pulled him to safety. It was Zorro.

Slinging the weapon again, Nick pulled through the water. With every flutter kick, he anticipated those jaws clamping down.

The knot of swimmers pushed forward, keeping together as the sharks fed on the chum still being thrown from the skiffs behind them. But that would hold them only for so long before they began attacking the group.

Nick saw red in the water and knew the sharks would swarm to the spot. He kept close to Zorro and saw Fuego not far ahead. Whale had fallen back from the front of the pack and was breaststroking to catch his breath. They caught up to him a few moments later.

"*¡Juntos!*" Fuego shouted. Stay together.

Whale nodded, coughing.

They were over halfway to the ship. Nick could see the lead swimmer now—a slender, agile warrior cutting through the chop in a front crawl. It was Wendig, the lone female among the new trainees.

Nick turned into a quick backstroke to catch a glimpse of

those behind him. He couldn't tell for sure, but it looked as though they had lost someone, or maybe two.

Pull, pull, breathe, pull . . . Nick kept his rhythm, sticking with the group even as feet kicked him from ahead and bodies slammed into him.

One of the skiffs motored just five feet to his right. A warrior stood with a long spear, which he thrust into the water, skewering a shark as it darted toward the swimmers. Nick kicked forward as the speared shark flailed. It jumped, slamming into the boat hard enough to knock the spearman overboard. Luckily, he wasn't wearing full armor, or he would have sunk like an anchor.

As Nick went under, he saw the warrior struggling to kick back up to the boat. Another shark darted over, drawn to the blood from the skewered creature, which was starting to sink. But instead of going for it, the second shark snapped at the spearman as he grabbed the side of the boat. Maybe armor could have saved him, but without it, the jaws took his leg below the knee.

Nick kicked back up and kept his mantra going. *Breathe, pull, pull, breathe…*

All around him, the other Cazadores swam like madmen—and, in Wendig's case, madwomen. She was still in the lead, and they were closing in on the warship now.

Nick could hear a rumbling sound and noticed a new boat motoring over. The long, sleek craft had a mounted machine gun manned by a warrior wearing a horned helmet—el Pulpo's son, Horn.

The barrel blazed as Horn fired into the water. The fins darted away, but Nick didn't let up. He kept pushing all the way to the warship. Two skiffs waited there, with sailors shouting orders to the exhausted swimmers. Nick couldn't hear over the growl of engines, but he saw Wendig and two other Cazadores already climbing a rope ladder that hung over the side of the warship.

Nick kicked over, grabbed it, and began climbing. He didn't

look down until he climbed over the rail and flopped onto the deck. Coughing, he turned onto his side.

Nick gazed out across the water, seeing the long path back to the Cazador rigs. Sofia was up there, maybe even watching him now. He thought of what she had said.

On your first raid, run. You run and you don't come back. Ever.

He shook his head, determined never to run.

I will come back for you, Sofia.

*   *   *   *   *

The Horse Lords' ship pulled away from the slip in the harbor at the Iron Reef. El Pulpo stood on the deck of the captured vessel, holding up his axe. He was heading home, back to the Metal Islands.

"Defend the liquid treasure with every drop of your blood!" he shouted in Spanish. "When I return, we will hunt the Horse Lords and destroy them all!"

From the steel wall of the outpost, Mac watched the ship vanish into heavy fog, wondering if he would ever see the sun again. He had been left behind with eleven other Cazador warriors, including Hammerhead, who was in charge of defending the fuel outpost. Izan and Vampire were also holding position on the fortified walls.

Mac took in the elevated fortifications surrounding him. Four machine-gun turrets and three flamethrowers were mounted on the fifteen-foot blockhouses overlooking each corner, and a metal fence topped with razor wire surrounded the outpost. Beyond that was five hundred feet of muddy terrain that provided a clear field of fire for the defenders' weapons. Jungle encroached on the other side of the sloppy stretch, growing up through mounds of rubble in the destroyed city.

It wasn't just the Horse Lords that Mac worried about. Distant howling resonated from the giant mutant trees and snaking red vines that had overtaken the city. Hammerhead unslung his rifle mounted with an infrared scope.

The howls were unlike those of the eyeless creatures the Cazadores hunted for food and to train their youth. This was more of a catlike growl.

Hammerhead handed the rifle to Izan, the best sharpshooter of the remaining troops. He aimed into the jungle, panning slowly, watching for movement.

They waited another few minutes for the noise to come again but heard nothing.

Hammerhead stepped away, motioning for Mac. They took the ladder back down to the muddy ground. Four of the warriors remained on the walls as lookouts while two more went on patrol.

Hammerhead said something in Spanish about hoping Mac was still feeling lucky. He didn't understand what that meant until he got to the front gate with three other warriors, two of whom carried a salvaged crate marked as explosives. The other man held two shovels.

A howl pierced the quiet, resonating out of the distant city. Undeterred, Hammerhead led the group to the dual front gates, which stood fifteen feet tall.

The two men set the crate down and lifted the lid to reveal saucer-shaped bombs, or what Mac had seen referred to in books as land mines. After a quick inspection, they closed the lid again.

Izan called down from the wall above, giving the all clear.

Stepping up to the gate, Hammerhead grabbed the wheel handle and began turning it. The doors cranked open to a muddy road still marked by the hoofprints of the Horse Lord who had escaped during the invasion.

Mac searched the rubble of the city about two thousand feet

away for hostiles. Red vines curled out from the destruction, looking from a distance like insulated electrical wires. They were the same type of vines that had snatched Luigi all those years ago. Mac buried the unwelcome memory.

Hammerhead gave the order for Mac to help place the mines. The two warriors with the crate started walking ahead, and he took a shovel.

Izan covered them with the rifle.

Mac set off with the group outside the perimeter of the outpost. A slope took them down to the muddy terrain, and they made their way across, boots sinking in the muck until they reached firmer ground. Mac heard a crunch with his next step and looked down to find half-exposed bones. He lifted his boot over them, nearly coming down on skeletal fingers that protruded from the dirt.

A few more strides, and the Cazadores found themselves in the middle of a graveyard of human remains. The soldiers carrying the crate set it down. Mac followed them, digging holes where they carefully placed the mines before ever so gently covering them with mud.

Hammerhead watched for a few minutes, then headed back into the outpost. For the next hour, Mac worked with the men laying the mines around the road and along the edges.

A scream rang out as Mac dug a hole. He looked out over the rubble, but this was coming from the outpost.

Some of the prisoners were being tortured again. Last Mac heard, none of them had given up the location of their real home, but he knew that eventually one of them would talk. Then their home would be raided, just as Mac's had been.

The cries of pain pulled on his heart. These people were just like his own.

No, there's a difference.

Elena, maybe, and some of the staff working in the command center seemed like decent sorts. But the Horse Lord warriors had attacked the *Dragon*. They had brought this hell on themselves when they decided to go to war with el Pulpo.

At least, that was what Mac told himself. It made justifying his role a bit easier to swallow.

Still, as he planted his mines, he had a hard time drowning out those screams. At least none of them were Elena. She had been spared through the promise that el Pulpo made to Mac.

She was Mac's now—a "flesh trophy," el Pulpo had called her before departing on the newly acquired ship.

Mac shook off the distant noise and focused instead on not getting his legs blown off as they continued the tedious, dangerous work.

Once they finished, Mac returned to the command center and entered the clean room. A chemical shower washed his armor down. When it finished, he twisted off his helmet, taking in a breath of filtered air. After shedding his armor and hazard suit, he went to a secondary shower, where he rinsed off his sweaty skin. Parched from being outside, he drank some of the water. Then he changed into fresh clothes, grabbed his sword, and went through the building to the lower level. Hammerhead and Vampire were waiting for him and motioned him to a door. It opened to a walkway overlooking a giant chamber with mezzanines over the tunnels that supported the pipes.

A single Cazador guard named Cortez stood on the lower level, watching over the Horse Lord prisoners, who were now packed inside the tunnel beneath Mac's boots.

Hammerhead went to the rail and asked if any of them had spoken.

Cortez shook his head. He turned to a cart full of bloody tools as Mac, Vampire, and Hammerhead made their way down a skeletal stairwell rank with the stench of feces and urine. The conditions in the tunnel were horrid, with only filthy blankets to sleep on and buckets for waste. Mac walked over the mezzanine, looking down at the frightened faces below him. There were ten— eight men and two women, including Elena.

She was huddled in a corner and glanced up at Mac with weakened but still determined brown eyes. He stopped when he noticed a cut across her face and a black eye.

Apparently, el Pulpo had not explained to the other Cazadores about his promise to Mac.

He went over to Cortez, who was looking through his tools.

"She … no hurt," Mac said.

Cortez stared at him, clearly not understanding.

"*No la lastimes*," Mac said.

Cortez looked at Elena, then back to Mac, a smile on his face. He understood now. The Cazador turned to his tools and pulled out a pair of bolt cutters. He opened a hatch and reached down to grab Elena by the hair.

"No!" Mac shouted. He grabbed Cortez, who released Elena and shoved Mac away.

Hammerhead and two other warriors came closer, but none intervened.

Snarling, Cortez pointed at Mac, calling him a mutt, among other Spanish profanities. He pointed the bolt cutters back at Elena and continued talking fast. Mac understood the gist of what he was saying: There was no scribe, and he could do what he wanted, including taking Elena's hair, fingers, and whatever else he desired.

Fuck that.

Mac's hand went to the hilt of his sword, drawing Cortez's gaze. He reached down to a curved knife on his belt. As he pulled it out, he suddenly swung the bolt cutters at Mac, then slashed with the knife.

The tip shaved Mac across the chin. It stung. He punched Cortez in the face with his cutlass hilt, cracking open his nose in an explosion of blood. As he fell backward, Mac pounced, pummeling him with his fists.

Hammerhead shouted for Mac to get off, but Mac threw another punch. He managed three before a firm hand grabbed him by the shoulder. Vampire pulled him backward, but Mac ripped free and headbutted Cortez's bloodied face. His dazed eyes stared up at Mac as Vampire finally pried Mac off.

"Let me fuckin' go!" he shouted. "I'm gonna kill him!"

Vampire shoved Mac, knocking him to the mezzanine. He tensed, ready to fight, but a soothing voice from below the walkway said, "Stop. They will kill you."

Blood dripped from his chin as he looked down at Elena, who stared up at him.

Hammerhead walked over to check on Cortez. The injured warrior lay on his back, twitching. Vampire also crouched down, saying something in Spanish. A red pool spread out from behind Cortez's head. Mac realized the Cazador was seriously injured with a cracked-open skull.

Reaching up, Mac wiped blood from his dripping chin. It was a deep cut. He was going to need stitches.

Hammerhead turned away from Cortez and glared first at Mac, then down at Elena. Footsteps came from the platform above them, and a figure emerged with a rifle. It was Izan, breathing heavily. "*¡Enemigos!*" he gasped. "*¡Ven!*"

Hammerhead snorted, pushed Mac away, and stormed off with Vampire.

For a moment, Mac stood there, glad for the distraction, until he realized what this meant. The other Cazadores rushed away, leaving him alone.

"Go," Elena said.

Mac looked at her. She paused, then added, "Go while you still can."

"What do you mean?"

"When my people return, they will kill you all, and they won't do it slowly either. They will do worse to you."

He clamped his hand over his bleeding chin.

"You may not be one of them, but it won't matter," she said.

In the back of his mind, Mac had considered escaping with this woman, maybe even joining the Horse Lords. But from what he was hearing, these people were just as bad as the Cazadores.

A gunshot cracked in the distance.

Mac picked up his sword. There would be no running, no escaping. Only fighting.

PART 3:
THE HORSE LORDS

CHAPTER 15

The storm had passed, and the sun blazed high in the sky, baking the warriors on the deck of the warship. The other young men and one woman were spread out across the area, training with wooden weapons. Nick held a cutlass, waiting his turn to enter a chalked-off circle.

Every sweat-drenched trainee looked out over the ocean at two ships approaching in the distance. One was an oil tanker. The second was a warship unlike any that Nick had seen in the Cazador fleet.

The growl of engines pulled his gaze over to the marina of the capitol tower, where a war boat fired away. Metal glinted in the bright sunlight as the armored boat raced toward the warship and tanker.

Nick saw the source of that golden glint. "Lord Portatormentas, the Stormbringer," he said to no one.

The leader of the Cazadores rode with three of his Praetorian guards, their boat traveling at a high speed. The newly branded Cazadores spoke in hushed voices as the two ships drew closer. They were close enough now that Nick could see a horse figurehead jutting from the bow.

"*Pirata*," Whale said.

"*Es possible*," Zorro replied.

"*¡Regresen al trabajo!*" shouted an angry voice.

Lieutenant Forge strode over to the trainees, who broke apart and headed back to the rings. But Forge didn't follow them. He, too, stopped to look out at the new vessels, then at the war boat carrying Lord Portatormentas.

"*¡El Perrito!*"

Nick turned to see that he was up next, against Wendig. She held a long pole and licked her lips, reminding him of a hungry predator.

Something told Nick this wasn't going to be an easy match. He walked up to the chalked-off circle. A dozen of the twenty-three warriors surrounded them as another duel was being readied at the bow of the ship.

Whale tossed Nick a pole, which he caught in midair. A scar creased his broad forehead from the blow that Glock gave him back on the island.

Defending the Cazadores from the former Ranger and the beast had gotten Nick some respect from his squad. That was obvious in the way they all nodded at him as he twirled the wooden shaft. But not everyone felt the same way.

Wendig spat on the deck. "*No eres uno de nosotros*," she said.

"Damn right I'm not one of you," Nick said.

She stared at him, rage in her eyes.

It was clear she had a lot to prove as a female in a military of almost all men. Nick, too, had a lot to prove. This fight would be brutal, and his strategy was to use his agility and speed to wear down Wendig, who would strike fast and hard.

He was right. She jabbed with the pole while rushing him at the same time. Nick swiped with his own pole, knocking hers aside. But she was already on him, shoulder-barging him in the side and knocking him back slightly. He held his ground.

Nick looked up, right into a blow that hit his eyebrow. The impact stunned him, and he blinked as blood seeped from the cut into his eye. In the second that followed, he forced himself to roll away, to get some distance and perhaps another few stolen seconds to recover.

He swung low with his shaft to keep Wendig back, and to his surprise, it struck her with a thud. With his good eye, he saw that it had caught her just below the ribs with enough force to knock the wind out of her.

Now was his chance.

He strode over to strike, but she saw the move coming and swung upward with her shaft, nearly hitting him in the face a second time. He stepped away and wiped blood from his eye.

Wendig also retreated slightly, twirling her pole expertly through the air in whooshes. She was a master of the damn weapon—just his luck.

"Rah!" she shouted as she came again, jabbing with the end. He leaned back, evading the blow, but then she kicked him in the back, knocking him forward. He staggered, almost falling. Desperate, he swung backward, hoping to catch one of her legs. The wood connected with bone, cracking audibly.

Wendig bellowed in pain and fell to her back.

Nick had gotten lucky, but he would take it.

A whistle blew as he went to finish her off.

Forge walked over, and Wendig pushed up on one foot. She hopped, her face red with anger and perhaps embarrassment. Her eyes went back to Nick, showing rage when Forge motioned for her to step out.

Nick heaved a breath, then hesitated when Forge motioned for him to stay. Then he gestured for Whale to join Nick in the ring.

"Oh, shit," Nick muttered.

He didn't want to fight the big guy, and Whale didn't look

overly enthused either. He lumbered over, holding two wooden axes.

The whistle blew again, kicking off the match.

Whale charged, hurling one of the axes, which Nick side-stepped. He swung upward with the staff, trying to knock the other axe from his grip. The end of the thick pole hit Whale in the arm and didn't even slow him down.

He grabbed the staff with his other hand and pulled Nick forward. All Nick could do was dive onto the deck, sliding under Whale's wide stance. Nick let go of the staff and scrambled to his feet. As the giant warrior turned, Nick jumped, throwing a round-house kick right into Whale's face.

Blood exploded from Whale's mouth as the steel-toed boot connected. Nick snatched his pole off the ground, but Whale reached out and grabbed him before he could escape. He let go of his axe while lifting Nick off the deck, crushing him against his massive upper body.

Nick was already starting to feel his body going limp. He couldn't get air, and his vision began to dim. He glared down at Whale's bloody grin.

Unable to move anything but his head, Nick used it as a weapon, bringing the forehead down on Whale's nose. Bone cracked, and more blood flowed down Whale's face as he relaxed his powerful grip.

Nick dropped to the deck, falling on his backside and trying to scoot back. His vision returned, but he was so dizzy he fell when he tried to get up.

The squad of trainees cheered, yelling and egging them both on in Spanish.

"Crush him, Whale!"

"Bite him, Small Dog!"

Whale let out a howl of anger and lumbered forward, his

fists up. He swung at Nick, who rolled away. Then Nick scrambled on all fours to his spear shaft. As he turned, he swung, the pole hitting something hard.

Nick turned to see Whale drop to his knees, holding his face. Cautiously, Nick went over, still gripping the pole.

"*¡Sométete!*" he shouted.

Whale threw a haymaker, unwilling to submit.

This wasn't over.

Nick twirled the shaft, waiting for Whale to get up. As he did, Nick kicked one of the axes over to him. Whale looked out with his good eye, his hand still covering the other one.

He picked up the axe and stood, wobbling slightly.

Nick reached out, then beckoned Whale with his fingers. The big man charged, but it was just a fake-out—a good move. He waited for Nick to make a mistake.

Whale surely understood by now that sheer force wasn't going to achieve victory. He had to be smart, and that meant Nick must adjust his own strategy.

The group around them shouted louder, taunting them both to fight. Nick decided to be the first. He lunged with his staff, thrusting it toward Whale's head. Whale tried to grab it again, and at the last second, Nick decided to let him.

Whale pulled so hard he lost his balance, and Nick used his forward momentum to jump up and kick Whale square in the chest with enough power to knock him on his back. Before he could recover, Nick was on him, throwing a punch right into his head as he lifted it. Another punch to the jaw, then a third to the injured eye. Through the blows, Whale managed to grab Nick by the throat, squeezing it. But Nick elbowed down on his wrist before he could do any major damage, freeing his neck. Then he swung again and again, screaming. Rage took over, and blood-lust set in.

"*¡Alto!*" Fuego yelled.

He felt arms on his shoulders, jerked free of them, and landed another blow on Whale, who hardly responded. Someone finally tackled Nick, knocking him off and holding him down. Knees went down on his side, and someone stomped on his legs.

"Back off, *Perrito*!" someone shouted.

Nick recognized that gruff, heavily accented voice. He took several deep breaths, trying to calm himself. The weight eased off him, and he stood up in front of el Pulpo, who held his axe in one hand and a jug in the other.

Behind the captain stood the shadowed figures of Cazador veterans in armor, holding their helmets by the cords. Their breastplates displayed the infamous Barracuda logo.

They had returned from their raid.

Nick realized one of the faces was missing. Where was Mac?

He looked past the group. The new warship and the tanker had stopped a bare half mile from their own ship.

It all made sense. El Pulpo had not returned empty-handed, and Mac had not come back at all.

Whale slowly recovered on the deck. Blood dripped from his broken nose, his mouth, and cuts on his face. Nick reached down and offered his help. Whale glanced up with a bloodshot eye, and for a moment, Nick thought he was going to attack again. But then he muttered something about Nick beating him, using the word *justo*, which Nick thought meant "fair."

Whale took Nick's hand, and Nick heaved him up.

El Pulpo held the jug out.

Parched, Nick took a big gulp, expecting water.

The warm, potent liquid burned his throat. He retched and spat it out. Laughter rang out across the deck, but it quickly died down. The wall of armored bodies parted, the scarred faces bowing before the golden armor of the massive Lord

Portatormentas. He waddled over to gaze upon the Barracudas and then the trainees. Colonels Vargas and Santiago arrived behind him, jogging over in their black armor.

Ernesto, the scribe, scurried along with them, clipboard in hand, preparing to document every word. Portatormentas shouted his first words, which Nick tried to translate on the fly. The king wasn't happy, that much was certain.

El Pulpo bowed, saying he had brought the lord either gold or perhaps "liquid gold." The captain confirmed Nick's guess when he pointed at the tanker.

Lord Portatormentas looked in that direction but quickly turned back.

"*¿Dónde está el* Dragón?" he shouted.

El Pulpo looked up ruefully, explaining that it had been lost but that he had captured the enemy vessel. He went on about some sort of outpost and something about "Horse Lords."

Slowly, the king began to calm down. El Pulpo continued to relate what his troops had encountered on their raiding mission when they were attacked by this other civilization. Nick didn't understand everything they said, but he got the last part.

El Pulpo requested a larger army—to return and conquer these Horse Lords.

For a moment, Lord Portatormentas seemed to consider this request. He turned to Colonel Vargas and Colonel Santiago. "*Preparen mi barco,*" he said.

"*Sí, su majestad,*" Vargas said.

Both colonels bowed, then retreated with the king.

El Pulpo remained behind with the Barracudas. As soon as the king and two officers were gone, he grumbled under his breath, "*Poto gordo.*"

He turned to the trainees and walked over with his jug. When he got to them, he raised the jug to Nick.

"*A tu primer asalto, Perrito,*" el Pulpo said.

Nick took it, toasting his first raid.

*   *   *   *   *

Mac hunkered behind the wall of the fortress as an arrow streaked overhead. Sporadic sniper shots cracked at odd moments. It had been like this for days now. Three long days of not knowing much about the enemy—how many there were or when they might attack in force.

He thought back to what Elena had said about the Horse Lords doing "worse to you" when they did break through the Cazador defenses. He wasn't sure how things could get much worse, but he took her word for it. There was only one option: hold his ground and fight.

But they were running low on everything, from sleep to ammunition. Since el Pulpo departed for reinforcements, the skeleton crew of Cazadores holding down the walls had lost two of their own to enemy snipers. Two more men were injured, and with Cortez out of commission with a cracked skull, they were spread thin over the outer walls. It was just a matter of time before the Horse Lords decided to attack them head-on.

Vampire stood behind a shielded flamethrower, and Izan held a sniper position on an adjacent north wall. A single Cazador watched over the eastern wall, and another watched the water on the western flank. Hammerhead stood at the gates below Mac's position. The remaining two warriors were back at the command center, one watching the prisoners while the other slept.

Mac had a few hours' shut-eye scheduled soon, and it couldn't come fast enough. He was starting to feel lightheaded. The constant anxiety of not knowing when a bullet might blow out his brain had kept him jumpy with adrenaline. But even that was subsiding. Part of him wondered if a bullet might indeed be merciful—a sweet release from this hellish world.

But another part of him wanted to live—some stubborn aspect of human DNA that had kept his species going throughout time.

"*Alerta, hostil a caballo,*" Izan called out.

Mac peered through a wide bullet hole in the wall, at a cloud of smoke swirling away from the rubble of the city. The smoke seemed to grow as the enemy covered their movements. Within the cloud, he could see a soldier on a black horse wearing armor plates. The beast kicked up, the rider holding firm in the saddle while raising a horn.

The blare echoed like one of the howling monsters.

Was this it? The real attack?

Hammerhead clambered up the ladder behind Mac, crouching beside him.

Dozens of arrows and bullets shot out of the smoke screen, crossing over the minefields and slamming into the walls of the outpost. Izan stood, aimed his rifle, and fired at the mounted warrior, but the long shot missed, and the rider reined his horse back into the shadows.

Another volley of arrows flew. One of the bolts hit Hammerhead in a shoulder plate, knocking him slightly to the side. He laughed and then raised his spear in the air, exposing his entire body.

"*¿Eso es todo lo que tienen, malditos cabrones?*" he shouted in Spanish. Then he looked to Mac and told him to translate.

"Is that all you got, you damn bastards?" he yelled.

Hammerhead laughed.

Izan took another shot, and a Cazador on the eastern wall laid down a burst of fire from a mounted machine gun. More arrows zipped overhead, followed by a return shot that whizzed past Hammerhead's helmet. He finally hunkered back down.

Silence swept over the outpost. The other Cazadores remained behind the walls, waiting for the next wave.

Mac looked through the hole again to see the smoke cloud dissipating and the Horse Lord gone. The attack or test, it seemed, was over.

Sitting down, Mac waited for his relief, who came a few minutes later. The fresh Cazador trooper climbed up, and Mac took the ladder down. He went to the command center, past hundreds of arrows sticking out of the dirt.

Once inside, he started the cleaning protocols. Exhausted, he made his way into the area of the facility the Cazadores were using as a bunker and medical room. One of the injured lay unconscious in a bed, hooked up to a saline drip. Elena attended to him while the other injured warrior with a neck wound watched.

She looked up at Mac, who nodded at her.

"Everything okay?" he asked.

She glanced over to a shadowy corner, where Cortez sat up in a chair, his head wrapped in a bandage, one eye swollen shut. His other eye went to Mac, but his cracked lips didn't move.

Hammerhead had ordered Cortez not to harm Elena, saying they needed her to take care of their injured, but Mac didn't trust the man to obey. The only comfort he had when out on the walls was that the soldier with the neck wound could watch him.

Still, that man had to sleep too.

Mac went over to a bed and sat down. Exhausted, he knew that the moment he closed his eyes, he would likely drift off. He forced his heavy eyelids open.

Elena made her way over. "Turn around. Let me check your back."

He turned on his side.

"I heard the shots," she whispered. "They will come soon. Now is your last chance to escape."

"And go where?"

"Anywhere but here. I can speak to my husband. He is a Horse Lord."

Husband, Mac thought to himself.

"I can ask him to spare you," she said. "Tell him you helped save me."

"If I run, Hammerhead will kill me. Looks like I'm doomed either way."

A loud grunt came from across the room, and she pulled back. Cortez was standing now and staring at them. He pulled his pants down and began to piss in a bucket. When he finished, he held the bucket out to Elena.

Mac began to get up, but Elena shook her head and whispered, "Let me."

She walked over, gasping when Cortez splashed some of the piss on her shoe before handing the bucket over. Mac stood, but a distant gunshot cut the tension with a reminder that the real enemy was out there, closing in.

He sat back down, knowing he needed rest. With Elena gone, he decided to close his eyes. Sleep took him in its soft embrace, and he dreamed of ITC Star Station and then of the Metal Islands, of the sunshine and the fruit he could get from time to time. But those happy thoughts turned to nightmares as he sank into deeper slumbers.

Shouting woke him up abruptly.

Groggy, he looked around the room, but Elena was gone.

His eyes went to Cortez, who was slumped in his chair. Mac got up and walked over. Sliding on something slick, he very nearly fell but managed to catch his balance. To his right, a pool of blood extended under the bed of the warrior with the neck wound. That wound was now much larger—a gaping smile carved into his throat.

The unconscious warrior was also dead, a scalpel sticking out of his eye. Mac moved over to Cortez and found a cord wrapped around his neck. He rushed back to his bed to find a note tucked under his cutlass.

Hide and then go home. Don't ever come back.

Two gunshots boomed in the distance, followed by more of the shouting that had woken him. It didn't take long to figure out who had killed these Cazadores or what was happening topside.

He grabbed his blade and hurried out of the room, heading outside in just his hazard suit and boots. Rain sheeted down from dark, swollen clouds.

Lightning sizzled across the sky, suddenly illuminating the outpost. To the north, he saw that the gate was wide open, and a slender figure had escaped.

"Elena," Mac whispered. "Stop!"

He started running out toward the gates. After a few steps, he stopped at a scream coming from the wall to the west. He processed the fact that it came from the border of the outpost facing the water. When he saw a figure on the eastern wall stagger and fall, his brain further processed what was happening.

The Horse Lords were attacking, and Elena had opened the gate for them.

Bullets and arrows slammed into the north wall where Hammerhead, Izan, and Vampire held positions, too busy firing back to notice the open gate. Through it came a dozen mounted warriors.

Elena ran toward them.

"No!" Mac yelled. He kept running in the mud, sliding and slipping. He lost his balance and went down hard in the muck. When he looked up, Elena was looking down at her boot. His heart skipped at the realization.

"Don't move!" he shouted.

Elena shifted her gaze in his direction, locking eyes with him for a beat. And then she was gone, obliterated in a poof of black smoke and red mist.

CHAPTER 16

"All contact... lost."

Nick translated the words from the sailor talking to Lieutenant Forge and el Pulpo across the barracks. A thunderclap obliterated their words, the din filling the compartment as the brutal storm lashed the warship *Golden Sentinel*, under the command of the Stormbringer himself, Lord Portatormentas.

Two days had passed since they set sail from the Metal Islands. For most of that time, Nick had remained in the barracks belowdecks, sick from the ship's constant roll and sway. Thoughts of Sofia and Mac kept him going.

Nick tried to eavesdrop further as the sailor debriefed el Pulpo and Lieutenant Forge, but the thunder, combined with snores from the other twenty-two Cazador trainees sleeping around him, made it impossible.

Judging from the furious reaction and cursing that followed, the Barracuda captain was not happy about this report. The sailor left the barracks, and el Pulpo said something to Forge about the "new cockroaches" before he stormed off.

Nick felt cold dread grip him. Did this mean Mac was dead, along with the Barracudas left behind at the Iron Reef?

"*¡Levántense!*" Forge commanded.

Groaning, Nick climbed down from his hammock and put his feet on the shaky, cold deck. Seasick but managing to keep his stomach down, he stood between Whale and Zorro. In his peripheral vision, he could see Wendig glaring at him. She had been doing that since the moment he put her on her ass.

Forge faced the trainees and laid out what the sailor had told him and el Pulpo. He spoke loudly, and Nick, whose Spanish had improved remarkably, got the gist of it.

All contact with the forward operating base the Barracudas had established at the Iron Reef was lost. The enemy had likely attacked them.

Nick thought of Mac. Suddenly, he felt more alone than ever before in his life. Mac had been a friend and the closest thing to a mentor, and he was one of the last survivors of their people.

Nick gagged, trying to hold back the puke. Smirking, Wendig held up a bucket to him.

With a brave face, he pushed it away. This wasn't good. His first raid, and he could barely hold himself upright.

Nick staggered and put a hand to his groggy head while the young warriors were getting into their gear. Shaking away the fog in his brain, he bent down to the footlocker under his hammock. In it were his meager belongings and the patched-up hazard suit. He hardly checked it as he threw it on, not wanting to be the last one out of the barracks. As he double-timed it to the ladder, Zorro turned to him in the enclosed space, eyeing him sightly.

"I'm good," Nick said in correct Spanish. "I can fight."

Zorro nodded, apparently satisfied.

Whale said something about how they would drive these Horse Lords into the sea.

"Don't get cocky," Fuego said in Spanish. "You'll end up like Wendig."

"Fuck off, fire-shitter," she snapped back.

Thunder boomed as they walked out on the weather deck. The sleek warship sliced through the dark sea. Unlike the *Dragon*, this vessel had advanced weapons systems, including large cannons and rocket launchers.

A shout came from the command tower. Nick looked up at the third level, where an awning shielded Lord Portatormentas from the rain. El Pulpo was on one knee, bowing as the Golden General yelled at him in Spanish.

Nick listened from the deck below as the king chastised el Pulpo for abandoning the outpost and returning to the Metal Islands before he had fully secured it. This was the most docile Nick had ever seen the captain, who remained on one knee, head bowed, saying nothing. Portatormentas continued to verbally abuse him, shouting in Spanish, "I should have your head and toss it to your precious Octopus Lords."

El Pulpo finally rose up. "I will take the base back or die trying," he replied. "Or, if it pleases you, I will sacrifice myself to the Octopus Lords now, to bring you the gold you worship."

Nick felt fairly sure he understood el Pulpo's meaning.

"And waste valuable resources? You're lucky I need you alive." Portatormentas dismissed him with a contemptuous wave, and el Pulpo retreated from sight. In his place, a servant brought a silver platter laden with fresh fish and shrimp. Another servant held out a mug of ale, which the king tipped back at once, gulping it down. Ale dripped down his goatee as he looked at the warriors on the deck below him.

"Bow," Zorro whispered.

Nick did so just as the lord gazed at him.

Lieutenant Forge shouted orders for everyone to ready

their weapons. Nick and Zorro were taken to the upper deck, not far from where Lord Portatormentas was stuffing himself. Nick looked at the tables covered with bowls of nuts and fruit, and plates of fresh fish—not jerky but real fillets. He had never seen so much food in one place.

And ice. Real ice.

Zorro guided him up to a machine-gun turret mounted on the observation deck. They cleaned the barrel and checked the ammo belts. One of the first things Nick had learned about weapons systems was how much maintenance they required. It wasn't all that different from his first job in the bunker. Things broke, wore out, lost their edge. They had to be constantly maintained in the wastes.

For the next few hours, the two young men cleaned and oiled the weapons across the ship. By this time tomorrow, the guns must be ready to blaze away against an enemy that Nick knew only as the Horse Lords.

It wasn't just cannons and artillery that were being prepared. A whistle called the warriors back to the lower decks, where Nick joined the others in the armory. He heard grinding already from one of the workstations. El Pulpo sat at a grindstone that he turned with a foot treadle, sending sparks flying from the bit of his curved battle-axe.

Nick took his assigned cutlass over to the machine next to el Pulpo, who remained focused on his work. The other warriors busied themselves cleaning and sharpening their weapons, then went to inspect their armor. A row of thirty units hung from steel hooks overhead.

He looked at his reflection in the slotted eyepieces of his helmet. It seemed so long ago that he had seen one just like this outside his bunker.

He stepped up to the tough, lightweight armor. The back of each rig was open, ready to mount.

Nick stepped into the boots, and a padded underlayer pressed on his arms as he pushed them into the unit. Next to him, Whale squirmed to get into the underlayer.

Wendig sneered. "Whale's too fat, and the *perrito* is too small," she said in Spanish.

Neither statement was precisely true. While Nick wasn't the tallest Cazador, he was already one of the strongest as his body continued to fill out.

A technician snapped the shoulder plates in place over his back. Nick raised his arms, feeling the weight of the armor over his flesh and bones. He felt *strong*.

The tech held a helmet up to Nick, and he took it in his armored fingers. Then he slipped it over his face. The heads-up display, or HUD, flickered to life. A translucent window provided an overlay of readings: *Oxygen, Radiation, Power.*

There was no tutorial, no manual to explain how to operate the suit—just Lieutenant Forge telling them to lift their arms, move their feet, and walk. The warriors moved out of the large open space and went up a ladder to get back topside.

El Pulpo and three Barracudas, also armored up, were unwrapping tarps from a four-barreled weapon that Nick had never seen. Someone shouted something, and he bowed low as Lord Portatormentas made his way across the deck, his golden armor gleaming in artificial light. An entourage of four Praetorian guards moved in stride with him, red capes whipping in the stiff breeze. Colonel Vargas and Colonel Santiago followed in their black armor, carrying their helmets. Then came Ernesto the scribe, with someone Nick had seen but a handful of times.

Dressed in a black robe and wearing a fearsome-looking composite mask over his face, this man was some sort of spiritual person called a *mage*. He looked through gold-rimmed eye sockets on the otherwise featureless mask.

The gathered warriors backed away, and the king and his entourage marched up to the gigantic weapon. Four barrels protruded off a turret. The barrels telescoped slowly outward, from six feet to double that when they finally clanked into position. Then the turret rotated, raising its four barrels toward the storm clouds at the same time.

Chains clattered somewhere behind Nick. A chill shot up his spine at the sight of two females in white dresses shuffling across the deck, led by a single Cazador holding the chains.

Nick moved out of line for a better look, heart thumping at the thought that one of these women might be Sofia. Had she somehow been spotted with him back on the Cazador rig? Was she being punished for—

He stepped completely out of position, which got him a disapproving grunt from Whale.

"*Perrito!*" Zorro hissed.

Nick ignored them and took another step, trying to see out through the fort of armor surrounding him as the two women were led toward Lord Portatormentas.

A horn blared, and the warriors all went down on one knee—except for Nick. He stood there staring at the women, ruling out one immediately. The other prisoner glanced in his direction, and he saw blue eyes. Not Sofia.

Nick stepped back into formation.

The sound of soft chanting pulled his gaze back up to the scene at the bow of the ship, where Lord Portatormentas approached the two women. Towering over them, he reached down and lifted each chin to gaze at them. The mage stepped up, holding a golden ewer. A scribe handed each woman a glass of water. Then he spoke to them softly and nodded at a soldier, who wrapped blindfolds around their eyes.

Neither woman seemed to fight what was happening.

The mage twisted the lid off the vessel as Colonel Santiago and Colonel Vargas drew their swords. They came up behind the two unsuspecting women.

Nick understood, and it was easy to translate the mage's words. "We sacrifice these two souls to the lords of the sky, providing our king with the power he will need to destroy the Horse Lords!"

In a swift stroke, Santiago stepped forward from behind and drew his sword across the first woman's throat. Blood splashed over the white dress. The mage angled the ewer under the spurting blood, collecting it while the second prisoner screamed, falling to her side and trying to scoot away. Lord Portatormentas stomped on her neck while Vargas cut her open.

Nick looked away, unable to watch these innocent souls suffer any longer. Anger built inside him at the thought that Sofia could easily have been one of them. And he felt powerless to stop it.

The final muffled screams were silenced by the crunching of bones. When Nick looked up again a minute later, Lord Portatormentas held a heart in each hand. He raised them toward the strange four-barreled weapon in front of him, blood dripping off his golden cuffs.

Three prongs, reminding Nick of a grounded electrical plug, telescoped out of each barrel and began to glow with a flickering blue light. Nick felt the hair on his arms and legs stand up from the static charge. Brilliant blue arcs snaked out from the three prongs into the sky, forming a dazzling round patch. It was as if the sun had burst through.

All sorts of theories collided in Nick's mind as he watched in awe—everything from strange, newly unlocked Old World technologies to magic. He wondered if they had used this device to clear the storms from the Metal Islands.

But that theory quickly faded as thunder boomed and

lightning split the sky. The ocean swirled up in huge waves in front of the ship.

He wasn't clearing the storms. He was making them.

The Stormbringer.

*　　*　　*　　*　　*

Hoofbeats pounded above the ancient storm drain. Mac hunched down in the waist-deep water next to Hammerhead and Vampire. The men all gripped their swords, ready to fight hand to hand if they must. A collapsed wall blocked the way to the left. The only possible exit was the same way they dropped in, through the collapsed street. Izan stood back from the opening, his rifle trained upward.

They could hear the snorting and whickering of large beasts on the street above.

Minutes after Elena had stepped on the land mine, the enraged Horse Lords had broken into the outpost, killing everyone but Mac and the other three Cazadores. It was only due to a brilliant plan that Mac knew nothing of that they managed to escape.

A huge fuel tank, rigged with Cazador explosives, had burst into a fireball, producing a massive wave of heat that incinerated the enemy forces in front and kept the rest at bay. The smoke curtain that followed had masked the surviving Cazadores' escape into an old oil pipe that emptied into a pool of water. From there, the four men had evaded the enemy patrols and made it here, somewhere a few miles into the city.

But Hammerhead had led them underground with no way out. The Horse Lords were closing in, and it wouldn't be long before they found the Cazadores hiding in this antique shit pipe. Mac had spent the past year on raids where Cazadores were the hunters—fearless barbarians who took what they wanted wherever they went.

But now they were the hunted.

The irony might have made him smile if it didn't mean his own death.

Maybe he deserved it for everything he had done over the past few years. For not saving Elena or his own people. Instead, he had thrown in with the Cazadores, helped them spread more pain and suffering.

He had done it to survive, especially after seeing the Metal Islands and the sunshine, eating the food, listening to the waves. Mac wanted that again. He had to hope that maybe someday he could live out his life in peace after all the killing. But that hope was fading with every passing moment.

A rat squirmed out of a hole in the wall and plopped into the water next to Mac. It flailed and clawed its way up his armor. He didn't dare move, afraid to make a sound and draw the horsemen's attention.

One of the beasts seemed to have stopped. The rider called out something in English.

Hammerhead raised his axe and nodded to get ready. The only way out was to fight.

As Mac gripped his cutlass, he thought again of what Elena had said about being captured. He may have to turn the blade on himself.

Up ahead, Izan suddenly backed away, retreating into the shadows and wading back to the other men. A beam of light shot down the sloping shaft, raking over the area where he had stood just moments earlier. Hammerhead motioned for the Cazadores to hunker down. But unlike the others, Mac had no place to hide. The next flashlight beam would catch him.

He ducked under the dark water. Now he was not only blind

but also deaf to whatever was happening above. The thought of ending his life crept over him. If the Horse Lords didn't kill him, the germs and radiation he was being exposed to down here would eventually do their job for them.

His lungs burned as he held his breath.

A strong arm heaved him out of the muck. Mac drew in a deep breath, filling his lungs and blinking in the darkness. The flashlight beams at the end of the storm drain were gone, and the hoofbeats were receding in the distance.

They had somehow evaded the enemy.

An eerie howl echoed through the city above. Maybe there was another hunter out there that even these Horse Lords feared…

Hammerhead waited a few more minutes before giving the order to leave the tunnel. Mac followed the men through the darkness, feeling his way. Izan climbed out of the tunnel and momentarily vanished.

A rope dropped down to them—a vine, actually.

Smart, Mac thought.

He grasped the thick liana. After first testing it with his body weight, he climbed out of the shaft to the street. He stood there blinking and using the flash of lightning to make out his surroundings—a sea of rubble mounds.

Hoofprints led in all directions except for a patch of thick jungle. Spindly trees rose out of the poisoned dirt, their branches sinking with the weight of spiky fruits. Vines curled around beams of concrete and rusted iron that once supported the structures now reduced to scattered mounds of rubble. Lightning illuminated a building's ivied facade. The vines would soon obscure the ancient mural showing kids playing with an inflated white ball.

For as far as Mac could see, trees had taken over the ruins until there was only the canopy of mutant flora. It was here, in the postapocalyptic jungle, that the howls of beasts seemed to be concentrated.

And that was exactly where Hammerhead motioned them to—the one place that not even the Horse Lords would go.

Cutlass in hand, Mac followed the Cazadores through devastation much like the ruined city surrounding the bunker where he had lived most of his life.

Another howl drifted out of the jungle, silenced by a boom of thunder.

Hammerhead motioned everyone down. As Mac turned, he saw why. A quarter mile to the east, a horse and rider stood on a slab of concrete from an old parking ramp. The warrior in the saddle held on as the startled beast reared, kicking both front legs up at the sky.

The rider regained control of the horse, then used binoculars to scan the debris below. Izan lifted his rifle, but Hammerhead waved him to stand down. The shot might kill the rider, but it would draw the others out to this location.

Mac watched the Horse Lord lower his binos, turn his horse, and ride away. Hammerhead gave them the order to move as soon as the enemy was gone. He continued toward the jungle that had grown over the remnants of the old civilization.

A waterfall cascaded down a collapsed rooftop, pooling where the street had fallen into a giant sinkhole.

Hammerhead guided them to the other side of the pool, then up a two-story rubble pile. Without his helmet, Mac couldn't see much even from the elevated vantage point. But he could see a clear route to the jungle below them, where a street cut through an area of buildings that were still mostly upright. Burned-out vehicles lay scattered, some of them little more than shells of ruined plastic and metal.

Hammerhead skirted the crumpled brick-and-stone wall. Mac

followed, moving carefully in the storm light down to the fractured roadway below. They passed a truck that Mac recognized as military. The tires were long since gone and the armored doors removed, but the plates of reinforced glass remained. Through the passenger window, he noticed a skeletal figure slumped against the dashboard, its helmet and most of the gear long since looted.

A centipede scurried across Mac's path, and he jumped, very nearly crying out in surprise. Hearing a crunch sound behind him, he turned to find Vampire holding the skewered bug on his spear. Chuckling, he held the shaft out to Mac, who reared back.

Vampire grunted and jerked in front of him. Hot fluid splashed Mac's face. He wiped it away as Vampire grunted a second time.

A flash of lightning spilled over the street, and Mac saw two arrows sticking out of the Cazador's chest. Vampire stumbled around toward the building, where two Horse Lords were nocking fresh arrows to their bowstrings. Despite the bolts protruding from his armor, he hurled a spear into the gut of a man standing about fifteen feet away.

Izan aimed his scoped rifle and shot the other man in the head. But before Izan could chamber another round, he took an arrow to his helmet.

"Run!" Hammerhead shouted.

A horse came charging up the mound they had just clambered down. Then two more started trotting down from above, dislodging bricks and stones. Vampire snapped off the arrows with a howl. Then he plucked a five-foot-long piece of rusted rebar from a pile of concrete.

The first Horse Lord charged down the mound, thrusting his lance at Vampire. Vampire managed to dodge the thrust and jammed the rebar into the rider's neck, dropping him from the saddle.

Mac ducked an arrow, then started for cover when someone

or something pushed him forward. Somehow keeping his balance, he turned to see Hammerhead, waving for him to keep going.

They ran through the gauntlet of arrows and gunshots. Using the destroyed vehicles for cover, the two men kept low and moved fast. Mac tripped and hit the ground hard, his knee screaming in pain. He looked back at Vampire, who was flanked by two horses now, the riders hacking through his armor with swords. Blood sprayed from his many wounds.

Vampire screamed as he thrust the rebar he still held into the breast of a horse, using his strength to push it over. The beast fell into the other, knocking both riders to the ground.

Staggering, Vampire raised his spear up into the air in victory for a single moment before his body was riddled with arrows and bullets. He looked at Hammerhead and Mac one last time before collapsing.

Hammerhead let out a war cry and pulled Mac to his feet.

A whinny came from the shadow of a building. Another horseman came charging with his lance leveled. Hammerhead threw his axe right into the warrior's chest plate, knocking him back in the saddle. As Mac passed by, another Horse Lord jumped onto the roof of a rusted-out vehicle, aiming a rifle at Hammerhead.

Mac came up behind the man and swung his cutlass below the back of the knee, hacking through flesh and bone with enough force that the blade stuck. The warrior howled and fell to his back, dropping his rifle.

Hammerhead turned, nodding at Mac, who went for the rifle. An arrow punched into the car before he could grab it. Abandoning the attempt, he kept running, weaponless now. They made it to the end of the road and turned the corner to a nearly pitch-black view of the jungle looming before them.

Hammerhead waved Mac toward the black hole. But Mac hesitated, for he was now unarmed and without a helmet or any armor. He pictured hideous monsters dwelling in the darkness: jaguars covered in spikes, insects the size of dogs, snakes that could swallow a man, armor and all.

Once again the choice: Mutant beasts or the human kind?

Either way, he must face the monsters.

Mac decided his odds were best with Hammerhead, and he darted into the jungle.

CHAPTER 17

Thunder boomed from the sky like an enraged god. As if in answer, a Cazador horn blared, summoning a war party to the top deck of the *Golden Sentinel* as it approached the Iron Reef. Nick had overheard it was located on a harbor at the northern tip of the former country of Belize.

He tried to slow his elevated heart rate as he marched out with the other Cazador troops, a pair of scribes, and the mage, who was here to bless the troops with holy blood from the sacrifice Lord Portatormentas had overseen.

The Golden General now sat back on his throne, drinking ale and chewing on a slab of ham. Nick felt his stomach growl at the sight. He had mostly recovered from the seasickness and now was hungry for something other than the slop they had been fed on the long leg of the trip. It was day six now, and in minutes, they would have a view of the Iron Reef.

The raiding platoon gathered in the sheeting rain. Nick held a spear, and over his shoulder he had a sheathed cutlass. The weapon was sharp, strong, and lightweight, and he preferred it over the axes or heavier double-edged swords that many of the other Cazadores used.

Lieutenant Forge stood in front of Nick and the other green-horns while el Pulpo moved in front of his Barracudas. The groups of warriors spread out across the deck in front of the mage. He wore a black suit with a cape that seemed to flow around his body as he held his arms up toward the sky. The ghoulish metal mask with golden eye sockets covered his features as he chanted, "Portatormentas!"

Colonel Santiago double-thumped the butt of his spear on the deck. Every warrior came to attention.

Nick felt his heart pound faster. It wasn't from excitement exactly, or from fear, but rather from something in between. The adrenaline made him jittery.

The mage dipped a small ladle into the golden ewer, then pulled it out and flicked the handle, sprinkling blood on the warriors. Droplets spattered across Nick's helmet.

Striding up and down the rows of warriors, the mage dappled each of them with the dark red blood. When he finished, he returned to the front of the group. Colonels Vargas and Santiago bowed, while everyone else went down to their knees.

Slow and heavy footfalls heralded the approach of Lord Portatormentas as he made his way down to the main deck. Nick glanced up as the massive man waddled to the weather-modification device. With his back turned, Portatormentas raised his arms. But Nick, standing on the edge of the formation, could see something he hadn't noticed the first time the lord used it. He flipped up one of the golden arm cuffs over a glowing screen, which he tapped with a finger.

This wasn't magic. It was technology disguised as magic.

All four barrels began to glow in their electric-blue hue. They rotated back toward the sky and released a blast of energy into the belly of the storm clouds.

The mage raised his hands skyward, speaking in Spanish.

"Hail the Stormbringer in all his glory, for he has brought us to this plentiful new land with a tremendous discovery of oil," he said. "We, the disciples of storms, will follow the Golden General and lord of the Metal Islands to victory against the Horse Lords who call this dominion home. Let us pray they are worthy opponents for our lord's righteous sword."

Nick noticed el Pulpo looking up in what seemed a show of disrespect.

Of course, the man had to be enraged at what was being documented, with Lord Portatormentas taking credit for the engagement.

"Rise, raise your blades, and prepare to cleanse this land of heretics," said the mage. "All hail Lord Portatormentas!"

Another Klaxon sounded, and the warriors rose to their feet, chanting their lord's name as they faced the bow of the ship. Nick thought he saw shapes on the horizon after a flash of lightning, but he wasn't sure. Moving to the side, he strained to see over Whale's shoulder.

Nick began to notice a flickering beam on the horizon. Whale shifted his feet slightly, and Nick moved for a better view of what appeared to be a raging fire. The flames were a beacon guiding the ship to shore, through the cloak of darkness under the storm clouds. Augmented by the sporadic flash of lightning from the storms, the blaze gave the Cazadores a sprawling view of the ancient city left in ruins by the war. But not everything had been destroyed by the bombs or the tsunamis that followed.

Lord Portatormentas again raised his golden cuffs, no doubt pressing buttons on the same hidden screen, and fired more bolts into the sky. The wind howled in response, and waterspouts spun down to the surface. Waves like mountains rolled under the ship, making it pitch and roll.

As they rode up a giant wave, Nick got his first glimpse of the outpost called the Iron Reef. A fortress of walls surrounded an intricate network of pipes and six tall silos, one of which billowed with flames.

"Some of your souls will be consumed on this great hunt to locate the home of these Horse Lords," said Portatormentas in Spanish. "For those who make it through the inferno, you will be rewarded with treasure—gold and flesh beyond your wildest dreams."

The warriors all raised their fists and weapons, cheering wildly. Portatormentas retreated from the deck as the warship cruised toward the harbor. Glowing flames from the burning silo flickered brighter on the horizon. Did the Barracudas who el Pulpo left to defend this place set it ablaze? Or was the fire from an attack by the Horse Lords?

But Nick feared the worst for Mac.

He could still be alive…

As much as Nick wanted to believe that, he didn't see how it was possible. Smoke rose into the violent storm clouds. But the heavy rain from the weather-modification tech was already starting to douse those flames. Lord Portatormentas stood on the upper deck of the command center, fidgeting with his golden cuffs and controlling the very storms that raged above them.

Zorro huddled with Nick, Fuego, and Whale. As the leader of their squad, he offered a few words in Spanish. "We watch out for one another, and we never surrender. We fight to the end."

Nick nodded back at the young man who had become a friend. The squad walked over to the skiffs hanging in their davits, waiting their turn to board. The first boat was already lowering, with el Pulpo standing at the bow and six of his warriors behind him. The skiff hit the waves, two men unhooked the cables at the bow and stern, and it motored away. Three more of the small boats were lowered in short order with five- and six-person squads aboard, and they followed the leader into the harbor. Nick boarded with Wendig, Fuego, Zorro, and Whale. The boat creaked with their weight.

"Gonna sink us, you fat fuck," Fuego joked in Spanish.

"Learn to swim better, then," Whale replied.

"You all blow at swimming," Wendig said.

"Doesn't matter how good a swimmer you are. In these suits, nothing's gonna float," Zorro said. "So don't get cocky."

The skiff thumped over a wave and came back down with a splash, spraying them all. Nick shifted his attention to the fast-approaching shore. Images from his life surfaced and faded away, from his years of toiling in the bottom of the bunker to his capture just outside it. From that first journey to the Metal Islands, where Silvio and Hyena were butchered and eaten, and where Ron wasted away.

The terror over the past three years had made Nick stronger, but it had taken pieces of him. He had survived imprisonment, the lower decks of that dark and filthy ship, the Sky Arena, the island known as the Man Maker, and the training that followed. He was twenty-one years old now—a man by all indications, but not yet a warrior.

Looking out over the wastes, Nick prepared for another test. There was no denying the fear he felt thinking of what awaited him out there and what he might have to do.

Nick focused on the view. Fires still raged inside a section of the outpost, sending up a plume of thick black smoke. He couldn't see much of the infrastructure—just a few silos, and pipes bundled and leading in every direction. El Pulpo's skiff beached, and the squad of seven warriors disembarked, hurrying up toward the walls they had already taken once.

Rain sluiced down the warriors' armor as they charged up

the beach, weapons at the ready. Nick saw no sign of the enemy up on the walls, but he knew they could be waiting to ambush the Cazadores.

El Pulpo tossed up a grappling hook. After setting it with a hard yank on the rope, he put his feet to the wall and started hauling himself up. Reaching the top, he looked out, then down, and waved the others forward.

A dozen grappling hooks went up, and Nick soon found it was his turn to climb. Despite the weight of his armor, he mounted the fifteen-foot wall with adrenaline-fueled ease. At the top, he clambered over to join twenty warriors making their way into the outpost. Smoke curled away from the burning silo ahead, the flames still so hot they blocked the main gate.

The patrols set off across the walls. They marveled in silence at the former Cazador firing positions riddled with bullet holes and arrows. It was obvious the Barracudas stationed here had held their own for a long time before they were overrun.

El Pulpo hurried across the walls toward the front gate, where he peered down. The other veterans crowded up around him, all focused on something beyond the base.

Nick wormed his way through the knot of warriors and felt a chill at the sight of the field bordering the walls. Framing the dirt road were ten stakes topped with Cazador heads. The eyes had been removed.

El Pulpo scaled the wall down to the dirt. His men shouldered their rifles, covering his advance to the piked heads. When he got there, he hefted his axe up onto his shoulder. Then he bowed his head in the first real display of emotion that Nick had ever seen from him. From his vantage, Nick could make out the face of Vampire, one of el Pulpo's greatest warriors.

He searched the other heads for Mac but didn't see him out

there. For now, he could only cling to the hope that somehow his friend was still alive.

*　*　*　*　*

Mac tried to hold back a cough as he trudged over the moist jungle soil. Three days out here, and he was getting sicker by the hour. Freezing cold, drenched from head to toe, and itching and burning from a dozen bugbites.

He blinked his tired eyes, trying to peer through the darkness of the jungle. In one hand, he gripped the knife Hammerhead had given him. The hulking Cazador was just ahead of him, crouched behind a thick tree at the crest of a hill.

Mac choked on the scent of rancid air. He tried to stifle his cough but failed, his lungs crackling, prompting Hammerhead to turn toward him.

A chilling howl answered.

They had evaded the Horse Lords but were being hunted by a demon in the jungle. The beast prowled somewhere in the thicket, drawing closer. Mac searched the darkness, trying to pick the predator out from among the thorn bushes and gnarled tree trunks.

He heard a loud growl, and a branch snapped.

"*¡Corran!*" Hammerhead commanded.

And Mac ran, following him away from the tree to the top of a slope Mac hadn't seen in the darkness. He went over the edge, sliding in slick mud toward the source of the foul air: a swamp twenty feet below. It reflected the glow of lightning sizzling across the swollen sky.

The concrete shell of a building rose from the middle of the stagnant water, and two more structures loomed just across the swamp—potential areas where Mac and Hammerhead might seek shelter if they could make it there.

A root snared Mac's boot, slowing his descent down the slope, but Hammerhead kept going due to the smoothness of his armor. Mac slid, then rolled, mud caking his armor. His spear went flying when he hit thick roots protruding from the bottom of the bank. He cried out right before hitting the water with a muddy, stinking splash. Spray kicked all the way up to Mac ten feet above him, where he had managed to thrust his knife into the mud, arresting his slide.

Using his other hand, he wiped the muck from his face and looked to the top of the slope, where two, then four red eyes sparked to life. Lightning captured not two beasts but the snarling maw of a single jaguar. The mutant beast had the powerful, muscular body, but the sleek coat with its distinctive rosettes appeared coarse and patchy.

It prowled closer to the edge of the slope, angling its four eyes down on Mac, then at the water. A fin of bony spikes that grew out of the mutant vertebrae rose along its back, and the jaw unhinged, drooling into the mud.

Mac gripped the knife and rotated his body as the jaguar crouched down, growling low. The eyes shot to the water, where Hammerhead was floundering, fighting his way up the bank. But thick roots had tangled around his legs.

"¡Auxilio!" he shouted as he struggled back up to the bank.

As Mac began to scoot down the muddy bank, the "roots" moved, and he realized they were the mottled flesh of a huge snake. The tail rose out of the water, wrapping around Hammerhead and yanking him back. He landed with a plop in the mud at the edge of the swamp.

Horrified, Mac flinched as two more snake heads, both of them eyeless and rimmed with barbs, broke through the surface. They wriggled up the hill at amazing speed, making him flinch as they stretched closer and closer.

When Mac turned, the jaguar was gone. He flattened his back in the mud as the two snakes squirmed away, back down to the water to search for prey.

Hammerhead writhed on the bank, rolling over as the snake wrapped him up and began to drag him into the swamp. His feet went in, then his legs. Now three of the strange, eyeless barbed heads snaked up, hissing as they wriggled toward the flailing Hammerhead.

"Mac…" he choked out.

Mac started down toward him, knife in shaking hand, as the water rippled behind the swimming snakes, then exploded upward as something massive rose up from the mire. Only then did he realize: These weren't all separate snakes but rather component parts of this abomination that had camouflaged itself in the muddy bank.

Bioluminescent gills glowed down the torso of the behemoth rising up on sinewy back legs. Blobs of cloudy, deformed eyes protruded off horns topping the bony head of the creature.

"*¡Mi lanza!*" Hammerhead managed to shout as he was jerked toward the wide mouth.

Mac glanced around him for Hammerhead's dropped spear as the two snakes on the hill squirmed upward, their blind faces hissing closer. The beast they were connected to didn't seem able to see either. Maybe if he just stood still, they would…

Writhing, muscled flesh wrapped around his leg, pulling him down. He slapped into the mud, still flailing for something to hold on to. Rolling to his back, he began stabbing the mottled skin with his knife. The body whipped, releasing him, but two more of the eyeless serpentine appendages shot out of the mouth.

"*¡Mi lanza!*" Hammerhead said in a muffled voice.

Mac looked around him again, and this time he saw the spear the warrior had dropped. It was just a few feet away. He scrambled over and grabbed it just as one of the snakes wrapped around his other arm. With surprising strength, it pulled him face down. He slid forward, right toward the cavernous mouth, which had already swallowed Hammerhead's legs. He struggled as it slowly engulfed him down to his waist.

Another snake squirmed around Mac's neck and squeezed. Still holding the spear, he thrust it backward, finding the thick flesh. But that seemed only to make it squeeze his neck harder. Red encroached his vision as his brain starved for blood. He hacked as hard as he could with the blade. On the third blow, it let him go.

Mac sucked in air, gasping, his vision slowly returning. Stars bounced around his field of vision as he pushed up, swinging the spear wildly to keep the other snakes away. Now, just six or seven feet from the giant monster, he had his chance.

Spear in both hands, he swung at the eyes on the horns. The cloudy lenses exploded at the first blow. He hit it again, breaking the horn and the eyes off the head.

A hideous roar issued from the gaping mouth. The snakes whipped outward, knocking him onto his back. It felt like getting hit with a steel cable. He scooted back a few feet as the creature reared back, reaching up with a webbed paw to cover the wound where the horn had been broken off.

Mac pushed himself up with the spear shaft. He slashed a snake head, severing it from the neck. Then he jabbed the blade right into the open gullet, just to the right side of Hammerhead's half-swallowed body. Mac thrust the spear deeper, digging his boots into the muck and pushing until he himself was nearly inside the mouth.

Then he yanked backward, pulling the spear free with so much force he fell on his back again and was stuck in the gluey mud. The monster rose up, exposing the bioluminescent gills.

Mac worked frantically and managed to get up on one knee in the sticky mire. He slashed, opening a horizontal gash in the gills. Back and forth he worked the spearhead until the wide wound in the creature's throat reminded him of a jagged smile.

The monstrous serpent collapsed onto the bank, its two smaller "snakes" flopping like dying fish as it let out a gaseous groan. Hammerhead practically exploded out of the mouth to land in the mud, where he lay still.

Using the spear shaft, Mac got to his feet, prepared to strike again. He nudged the beast with the point, but nothing moved. After giving it a harder nudge, he slogged through thick mud over to Hammerhead. As he checked the throat for a pulse, Hammerhead slapped his hand away and pushed up off the ground.

Mac shot up when he heard a loud zip noise. Still high on adrenaline, he whirled, expecting to see the jaguar. Instead, four figures stood in the shadows with bows drawn. Behind them, a hulking warrior sat in the saddle of a huge four-legged beast. It let out a neigh.

Hammerhead sprang up and scrambled away. Mac moved, too, but froze as arrows smacked into the mud around him in a circle. The Horse Lords fired more bolts at Hammerhead as he fled. Shouts came from the jungle, where more of the warriors had hidden. He wouldn't get far.

Mac stood there, too exhausted to run.

He had squared off against the beasts of the jungle, and now he would face his fate with men. If they cut him up into pieces and fed him to the snake-headed freak, so be it.

The Horse Lords on foot took off after Hammerhead as the mounted warrior let his towering brown steed pick its way down the muddy slope. At the bottom, he looked down as his horse circled Mac. When it finished the pass, the rider shifted in his saddle for a look at the dead beast in the swamp.

Mac thought he saw some measure of respect in the man's posture, but then he kicked his horse in the flank. It reared up in front of Mac on its hind legs. A front hoof came down, kicking Mac in the chest. He flew back into the water with a splash, too stunned to move as he sank below the murky surface.

CHAPTER 18

Four hours after arriving at the Iron Reef, the *Golden Sentinel* was anchored in the harbor, off-loading equipment and support crews. But inside the outpost, the Cazador warriors were still fighting the fire in the burning silo. Despite the heavy rains triggered by Lord Portatormentas's weather-modification weapon, the oil continued to burn, fed from an underground pipe that they needed to shut off.

For now, Nick and the other greenhorn warriors worked on digging trenches around the other silos to prevent the flames from spreading. They had to protect the liquid gold.

Whale heaved huge scoops of dirt with his shovel, all the while grumbling about the filthy job.

"I came here to hunt," he said.

"You'll get your chance," Zorro replied.

"I'm ready," Fuego said.

Nick looked at the battle-scarred terrain around them, wondering what had happened here. There were theories among the young warriors. Some believed the Horse Lords had intentionally set the silo on fire rather than let the enemy have it. Others believed it had occurred during a fight. An even more important question Nick pondered was what had happened to Mac and Hammerhead. Theirs were the only heads not on spikes.

"Get back to work!" Wendig shouted in Spanish.

Nick saw that she was talking to him.

"You ever gonna get past the fact that he kicked your ass?" Fuego sneered.

"He got lucky, and luck only gets you so far," Wendig grumped.

Nick scooped up another shovel of dirt and tossed it aside. She was definitely getting on his nerves, but she was also the last thing he cared about right now. This was his first raid, and he had a hundred other more important things to focus on.

Engines rumbled on the other side of the smoke screen. Four trucks broke through the billowing wall of black, one by one, followed by a trailer with four dirt bikes. Nick moved out of the way with the rest of his squad to let the vehicles pass. They drove up to the central building a few hundred feet away, where the warriors piled out. There was still no sign of the Golden General or any of his guards.

Colonel Santiago climbed down from the last truck and approached el Pulpo, slouched against a wall. The colonel shouted up to him, commanding him to come down. El Pulpo took his sweet time, and Nick watched as he continued working on the trench.

Santiago put a hand on the hilt of his sword as el Pulpo walked over. Ernesto, dressed in a hazard suit, rushed over to document the exchange as Nick listened in, trying to make out what he could of the Spanish.

"Lord Portatormentas wants to know why the oil line still burns," Santiago said.

"We're working on it," el Pulpo replied.

Four of the black-armored warriors closed in around the

captain. His own men shifted in the rising tension. Forge walked over, motioning for Nick and the others to continue their work on the trench.

As Nick scooped up dirt, he noticed Santiago go right up to el Pulpo, their helmets nearly touching.

"You failed to secure this outpost, leaving it without the forces needed to keep it out of enemy hands," Santiago said in Spanish. "Now the precious fuel you promised our lord is burning. Every minute that passes we—"

El Pulpo turned and strode off, straight toward the burning silo. The troops with Colonel Santiago followed.

Santiago shouted at him to stop, but el Pulpo kept going, right into the smoke.

"*¿Qué demonios está haciendo?*" Whale asked.

Nick wanted to know the same thing, because heading into the inferno would be suicide. Even in their hazard suits and protective armor, they couldn't survive that kind of heat. El Pulpo wouldn't last a minute inside before he succumbed to the blaze.

Still, his chances might be better there than staying here after disobeying a direct command from the Black Order.

Nick stood and watched, along with everyone else, even Lieutenant Forge. Santiago and his own men, along with Barracudas, walked over to see.

Thirty seconds passed.

Then a minute.

At two minutes, Nick shook his head. He had seen the last of the cannibalistic barbarian warrior who had invaded his bunker three years ago. A hint of pity rose in his heart. No, that wasn't the right word. Maybe it was respect for his bravery or for his warrior ethos. But neither of those things came close to absolving him of his crimes.

El Pulpo was a monster who deserved to burn for his sins.

Santiago turned to Ernesto and ordered him to document the time that Captain el Pulpo perished. Before the scribe could finish writing, a loud popping sound rang out, followed by what sounded like sucking air. The flames dwindled, then ceased altogether.

"¡Qué milagros!" Whale bellowed.

"He did it. He really did it," Nick whispered.

But he wasn't so sure that el Pulpo had survived his audacious stunt. Another fifteen seconds passed. Then thirty seconds. At one minute, a figure strode through the smoke.

Shouts of astonishment came from all around the outpost where troops had gathered to watch. El Pulpo staggered out of the smoke, black with soot. He twisted his helmet off, sucking in air.

Santiago and his men stood silent as he walked through the crowd of cheering soldiers. El Pulpo stopped a few feet from Colonel Santiago, smoking rising off his scorched armor.

"Tell Lord Portatormentas his precious fuel is now secure," he said in Spanish. "Soon I'll start tracking down these Horse Lords, and if the Octopus Lords will it, I will deliver their leader's head to our lord and bring to him the location of their territory, to add to his dominions."

El Pulpo paused to cough hard, his chest rattling. He spat blood onto the dirt, then looked back up.

The colonel jerked his head, and his troops followed him back to the truck.

El Pulpo twisted his helmet back on and turned to Nick and the other youngsters. "Put those *pinches* shovels down and pull out your steel!" he commanded, to more cheers. The warrior had single-handedly energized the Cazadores and saved his own hide after disobeying Santiago.

Lord Portatormentas needed el Pulpo for his bravery and his unpredictable battle strategies. That was obvious.

Nick tossed the shovel and drew the cutlass from over his back. He followed the rest of the warriors over to the vehicles to help unload gear. The next step would be to fortify the outpost. Veteran warriors were already up on the firing positions Hammerhead had lost. New machine guns were unloaded from crates, along with belts of ammo, which Nick helped carry up a ladder.

Whale grabbed an eighty-four-pound .50-caliber machine gun and hoisted it onto his shoulder, heading for a ladder. Nick draped the ammo belts over his shoulder, then followed Whale to the top of the wall. From this vantage point, they could see the *Golden Sentinel* at anchor in the harbor. A skiff raced across the dark water to the ship, ferrying Colonel Santiago and his forces back to Lord Portatormentas.

Nick undraped the ammo from himself while Whale locked the machine gun onto a turret. He swung the barrel out toward the road, where the spiked heads had been removed. Craters remained from land mines that had detonated during the attack. Forming a halo around one of those blackened holes were bloody bits where someone met a grisly end.

As Nick fed the belt into the machine gun, he noticed movement beyond the road. Standing, he watched a figure trudging away from the rubble across the field.

"Someone's out there," he said.

Whale looked up, and Nick pointed to the figure.

"*¡Contacto!*" Whale boomed.

In a mad dash, they worked together to finish setting up the machine gun while guards on the wall took up position. Nick watched the figure advance slowly, pulling something with a rope.

Not something, Nick realized. A body. Spotlights blazed from the walls, illuminating the walker, who stopped, raising one arm to his helmet—the helmet of a Cazador. A spotlight beam hit the person being dragged.

Was this Hammerhead and Mac?

The spotlights lanced out into the rubble, raking back and forth for more contacts. Nick held the ammo belt in anticipation, his heart racing.

Chains clattered below as the gates opened. El Pulpo double-timed it down the road with two of his men following. Nick alternated his gaze between the two approaching figures and the bombed-out terrain, using the spotlights to scan for hostiles. But from what he could tell, it was just the lone Cazador and whomever he was dragging.

El Pulpo ran out, shouting, "Hammerhead!"

Nick let go of the ammo belt and looked down at the second person, who wore a faded green hazard suit and a rope around the ankles. At first glance, he thought it was Mac due to his light skin and matted brown hair, but then he saw the symbol of a horse head on the shirt.

Once they were safely inside the outpost with the gates closed, el Pulpo crouched in front of the prisoner.

"What do we have here?" he asked in Spanish. "Imulah, over here."

The scribe assigned to the captain walked over with his clipboard protected under a plastic cover. He bowed slightly, then nodded after el Pulpo explained what he wanted translated.

"This is Captain el Pulpo of the Barracudas," Imulah said. "He wants to know where your people are located. You all will have a chance to assimilate and to see the great sunshine of the Metal Islands."

The prisoner laughed. "I take you to my people, and you will slaughter us all. I know your people. You are barbarians, cannibals. You know nothing of mercy. Only evil."

Imulah translated, and el Pulpo grunted. He glanced up at Nick, then waved him down.

Nick joined him on the ground, and el Pulpo motioned him closer—so close, in fact, that he put an arm around Nick as he spoke to Imulah.

"He says you and this young warrior have something in common," Imulah translated. "Small Dog came from a distant land and earned a spot in our society. You can too. All of you can enjoy the sun, food, and women of our lands."

The prisoner looked at Nick, then shook his head. "Serving in this war machine is a fate worse than death. You have taken his soul. I will never fight, and I will never show you our home."

El Pulpo took his arm off Nick, then nodded to a warrior wearing a flamethrower. He activated the flame and angled it down at the man.

Still the prisoner did not yield.

"Go ahead—do what you must," he said. "My soul will find salvation in the next life."

"So be it," Imulah said after relaying his words to el Pulpo.

Hammerhead stripped the man down as another soldier brought an earthen jug over from the trucks. The prisoner wailed as they dribbled honey over his naked body. It took only a few seconds before the bugs started coming. First giant flies, then wasps the size of Timmy Tam.

A truck engine rumbled over, and Lord Portatormentas climbed down from the back with the support of two men. Colonels Vargas and Santiago followed him with a phalanx of six Praetorian guards.

An hour later, the naked, writhing prisoner was covered in red welts and begging for mercy. El Pulpo pinched a wasp off his sticky, bleeding neck.

"I will tell you," the man wailed.

El Pulpo nodded and crushed the insect on his palm. Then he commanded Imulah to bring over a map.

"Put a finger where your home is," said the scribe.

The man blinked his swollen eyelids, then raised a finger, which el Pulpo grabbed and broke with a quick snap. He let out a shrill cry of agony.

"My captain says if you give us the wrong place, resulting in the waste of precious fuel, it will only get worse for you," Imulah said. "Your honey bath will seem refreshing by comparison."

Whimpering, the man used a different finger to point at a location west of their current position, on a riverbank.

"Here," he groaned. "Xunantunich."

"Xunantunich," el Pulpo repeated. He studied the location for a few seconds.

Lord Portatormentas heaved his mass over, and el Pulpo bowed slightly.

"Perhaps you may redeem yourself at last," said the lord in Spanish.

Nick watched as el Pulpo slowly raised his helmet. "I will find these Horse Lords, and I will crush them," he said. "You have my word."

"We shall see." Lord Portatormentas returned to the truck and climbed into the comfortable back seat, where Nick could see a platter of food waiting.

El Pulpo grumbled under his breath, then turned to Hammerhead.

"Mount up," he said. "We have some Horse Lords to hunt."

*   *   *   *   *

Mac jerked awake. He tried to open his eyelids and see his current surroundings, but there was only darkness. Groggy and confused, he tried to remember where he was and how he had gotten here.

His body jolted up and down as he sat up, bumping his head. He hurt—his skull, nose, and mouth. Pain on top of pain. He groaned as he brought a hand up to feel a giant welt on his forehead.

Whinnying made him freeze for a long moment.

He cautiously forced an eyelid open. He was in some sort of cage in the back of a cart that was being pulled by a horse. At the sight of the beast, everything came crashing back to him.

Two more riders trotted alongside his moving prison. One of them looked over and said, "The infidel is awake."

A whistle sounded up ahead, and the horse pulling the cart halted. There were two more carts directly ahead of his, each packed full of equipment and supplies. Two carts behind his held fifty-five-gallon drums of gasoline. Mac counted eight mounted warriors, all armed with bows or rifles.

Mac scooted back from the bars as the rider to his left swung a boot out of the stirrup. It was the same man whose horse kicked Mac in the chest back at the swamp.

The warrior swung down onto the dirt. He wore leather boots, green camo pants with plastic knee guards, and holsters on both thighs: one with a pistol, the other with a sheathed knife. Covering his upper body was a thick green camo tactical shirt and an armored vest that appeared to have bulletproof plates. Extra magazines for his pistol protruded from pouches on the vest, along with two fragmentation grenades. A helmet with a prominent nose guard covered much of the face, connected on the sides by cheek plates that swept back to provide substantial protection. Two mirrored visors covered the eyes of this warrior, which were locked on Mac. At the crown of the helmet, the long hair from a horsetail hung back, draping over the man's shoulders.

He removed his helmet, and Mac saw that this wasn't a man

at all. Looking back at him were the brown eyes of a boy perhaps thirteen years old. Far younger than Nick had been when he became a Cazador.

"I am Prince Rin of House Leon," said the youngster. "What is your name?"

Mac took in the two soldiers who stepped up behind their prince, towering a good foot over the kid.

"Prince Rin asked you a question," one of them growled.

"Mac," he replied.

"And where is your home?" Rin asked.

"Place called Texas—a long way from here."

Rin raised a brow. "You are not dressed like the others, but you fought like them."

"I was a Ranger in a past life. Then the Cazadores came. They will do to you what they did to my people."

Both soldiers drew their swords and angled them down at Mac. Rin stepped up closer to the bars. His men moved with him, keeping their blades up.

"This is not the first time you have seen the inside of a cage," Rin said.

He was smart for his age. And polite, unlike the barbarians Mac had spent the past three years serving on these brutal conquests. He thought of Elena and her kindness to him before she was blown to smithereens. Perhaps showing him some courtesy would not go amiss.

"No, this is not my first cage," Mac said.

"You are not one of these Cazadores?" Rin asked.

Mac hesitated, knowing his answer could be the most important thing he ever said in his life. "No," he replied. "I was forced to fight with them. To come here."

"Tell me, then . . ." Rin took a step even closer, just outside the bars. "Why do you fight with the demons who slaughtered your people? You could have let the beast in the swamp eat the man who escaped."

Mac sighed internally. The kid was right. He should have let Hammerhead die.

"Answer him," said one of the warriors, gesturing with his sword.

Rin held up a hand for his guard to stand down. Part of Mac wanted to lie that he had some grand plan to kill the Cazadores or escape. But this kid seemed far too smart to believe that, and he had seen Mac save Hammerhead's life.

"If I hadn't killed that beast, it would have killed me too," Mac said. "I didn't do it to save the Cazador. I would gladly have slit his throat if I had the chance."

He shook his head. "Thing is, ever since those barbarians showed up, everything has been trying to kill me," Mac said. "I have a hard time giving up. I've been fighting my entire life, trying to scrape by, and when I saw the sunshine of the Cazador—"

Commotion came from behind the cage. A horse trotted up, lathered in sweat. The rider swung out of the saddle, breathing hard as if he had been doing the running. He bowed to the prince.

"Your Highness, we just got word from our scouts the fire is out," he said. "More enemy forces have arrived. One hundred on the ground, plus a warship in the bay. They have vehicles, too, and guns."

"Pick up the pace," Rin ordered. "We must travel faster. Dump some of the supplies if we must."

His soldiers fanned out, working fast. One of the carts was emptied altogether and pushed to the side of the road, the horse unharnessed and tethered to the cart pulling Mac's cage. Two of the Horse Lords dismounted and went over to the abandoned cart. After heaving the barrels off the back, Rin reined his horse to knock them down. They fell over, pouring gasoline across the road.

Mac understood then: By setting the jungle ablaze, they were making sure they weren't followed.

Using his heels, the young prince moved his horse back to the cart. He looked down at Mac as one of the warriors behind them tossed a torch, sending the fuel up in a whooshing blaze. Flames roared across the ground as the men ran from the barrels. They exploded a beat later, lifting into the sky and falling to earth somewhere in the jungle.

Prince Rin's horse let out a whinny as he came up beside the cart.

"So, Mac," he said. "Tell me more about this sunshine you speak of."

CHAPTER 19

El Pulpo bent down to look at the road. Nick could see the hoof-prints from where he stood next to a parked truck. The Horse Lords had taken this route; there was no doubt. Even without the prisoner, it was likely the Cazadores would be able to track them back to their city, but the challenge would be in getting there.

The jungles rustled with stalking beasts, mutant insects, and poisonous plants, and the potential was always there for an ambush against the small convoy of Cazadores. There were twenty-three new boots after one had fallen ill on the journey and another died on the training swim through shark-infested waters.

Marching with the group were el Pulpo and his fifteen Barracuda soldiers, who now included Hammerhead. From what the survivor had told them all, the Horse Lords had over fifty riders in their attacking forces. But their biggest advantage was that they knew the terrain.

The Cazador vehicles hadn't fared well on the trek so far. They were not two full days into the journey, and three of the four trucks had broken down. Old parts jerry-rigged together, combined with the muddy, rocky roads, plagued the ancient vehicles. Now the convoy was stopped for a truck that had gotten stuck in the mud while trying to push rocks off the road with the plow blade.

Whale was part of the team trying to get it dislodged. Nick spent the time helping two mechanics replace a broken alternator belt on another truck. At the moment, he had his head under the hood and was just finishing up his work when he heard a laugh and a deep voice speaking Spanish behind him.

"I knew I kept you around for a reason, Small Dog," he said.

Nick backed out and faced el Pulpo, who clapped him hard on the shoulder before he went to help Whale and the others pull out the stuck vehicle. With his own work done, Nick walked down the side of the road, past the third truck, which had the prisoner tied to the grille guard. The man was clothed again, but bugs were still buzzing around his head.

El Pulpo had kept him alive, barely—just enough to get them where they were going. As Nick passed, the prisoner glanced up at him.

"Please," he said. "Water, I beg you."

Nick wanted to ignore the man, knowing that any sign of mercy might get him shit from Wendig or some other Cazador. But as he looked through his visor into this poor bastard's eyes, he saw something that reminded him of Smitty. Empathy tugged at his heart.

Reaching down, Nick pulled his water bottle from his belt. He twisted off the cap and lifted the man's chin to help him drink. The prisoner sucked down water, using his tongue to lap up every drop. Nick pulled the bottle back from him after a few long chugs.

"Thank you," the man groaned. "You are not like the others. You can still find salvation. But you must leave these lands."

A whip cracked against the bottle that Nick held, knocking it into the mud. El Pulpo stormed over, shoving Nick to the ground on his backside. Silence descended over the entire convoy. Helmets turned in their direction, watching as el Pulpo picked up the bottle.

"*¿No quieres agua?*" He shrugged and then tossed the water into the jungle, where it landed in a thorn bush. El Pulpo pointed, then huffed like a dog.

"*Busca, Perrito*," he said.

Nick got up to fetch his bottle back, only to be shoved back to the ground in front of the ditch. He rose to his feet again, anger burning in his veins. Reaching over his back, he pulled his cutlass.

El Pulpo laughed, towering over Nick. But Nick turned and slid down the ditch. He made his way over to the bush, hacking its branches to free his bottle. The vines curled away, pulsating an angry red. Nick heard a soft rustling and looked up, seeing movement among the trees. It appeared to be a long-bodied creature with the sinuous movements of a cat. Four red eyes watched him.

The engines of the convoy growled to life, and the eyes switched off like a light.

Nick snatched his bottle and then made his way back up the bank. El Pulpo had climbed back into the bed of a truck and tapped the top cab.

Nick hurried over to Fuego and Zorro.

"Mercy will get you killed out here," Fuego said in Spanish.

Zorro looked at Nick but said nothing. It was obvious he had made a mistake giving the precious resource to the prisoner. But he himself had been a prisoner not long ago, and he hadn't forgotten.

Whale lumbered back from the front of the convoy, covered in mud. He shook it off his armor, then climbed into the back of the truck. And on they drove, through the mutated jungle.

Nick rested his helmet against the cab window. Then he closed his eyes, hoping for some rest. He drifted off to sleep and into a nightmare about their bunker. He was with Ron, Chubs, Gus, and Sofia, hiding under a table in the library. Banging came from the closed door. It flew off the hinges, and in came a hulking Cazador warrior.

A jet of flame lanced into the library, torching bookshelves and two people hidden behind them. The soldier blasted a table away, spraying the flames in all directions. In the glow, Nick saw the face of the helmetless warrior. It was his own face.

The jolting vehicle jerked him out of the dream. Blinking, he saw they were still deep in the jungle. Shouts came from the lead truck.

"How long was I sleeping?" Nick asked groggily in Spanish.

"Three hours, maybe more," Zorro answered. "Passed through a lot of small cities."

He hopped out of the side of the bed with his squad and followed them up the sloped road. The Barracudas had spread out on both sides of the road. They had come across a lighter area of jungle bordering an ancient city. Crumbling walls framed the ancient two-way road. A bus lay on its side, hardly recognizable.

An off-road motorcycle whined as a scout returned to the convoy. He stopped in front of el Pulpo to give a report.

The convoy stayed put while el Pulpo sent three four-person squads out for recon, including Nick's squad. Zorro led the way, with Whale, Fuego, and Nick falling in behind. Nick saw Hammerhead heading off with the Barracudas in the opposite direction and lost sight of them as they rounded a pile of rubble.

A row of crooked light poles hung over the road ahead. Four cinder-block buildings stood in various stages of decay. A concrete sign with a pyramid-shaped top still stood on the shoulder of the road, some of the words just legible: *Hotel Paradise*.

On the other side of the broken asphalt was a large brown cross, leaning to one side. Nick knew that it symbolized an old religion, and he found himself wondering what life had been like here before the war.

He heard the low, steady roar of the convoy behind them. El Pulpo was in the back of the lead pickup, signaling to advance up the road, where Nick and his squad had gone. It appeared that the rest of the squads had already finished their search.

Nick kept walking on the road. Dense jungle had retaken much of it. But it wasn't just vines and trees choking the path ahead. Zorro was on his way to a blocked-off section covered in rubble. Almost there, he stopped to look at something along the ditch. Nick was close enough to see roundish chunks of some sort of scat.

As he walked over, he heard a twig snap. It stopped him midstride. The sound came from the left of the road, where a towering stand of mutant trees rose toward the sky.

He held his spear ready as he scanned the base, where thick buttress roots rose like walls, some the height of a man. Then he started toward the thicket, motioning to Fuego, who pointed his flamethrower at the area.

Nick got to the edge of the road when he heard the noise again—not from the ground but above him. A branch sagged down, swinging toward him. He brought his spear up to knock it away when he again saw four red eyes. The creature he had seen back in the ditch had been stalking him this entire time. And it was massive—a sleek, muscular jaguar. A patchy coat of black fur clung to its scarred body.

It gave a soft purr as it tensed and then sprang at Nick, taloned claws extended. He dove away as Fuego shouted for him to get down. An arc of fire caught the beast in midair, and it gave a scream of agony.

Fuego fired another wave of flames, chasing it into the jungle. It rolled on the ground, screeching and kicking up debris, then bolted away into the shadows.

In the flickering glow of the retreating monster, Nick saw what appeared to be a humanoid figure standing next to the base of a tree not twenty feet from him. Zorro came over and helped Nick up to his feet, and in that instant, he lost sight of the figure. When he looked again, it was gone.

Fuego sent another burst of flames into the jungle, and Whale lumbered over, laughing.

"Almost lost your head, Small Dog," he bellowed in Spanish.

Nick remained serious, scanning the jungle.

"We're not alone," he said. "The Horse Lords are watching us."

*　　*　　*　　*　　*

Mac took a drink of water from the canteen Prince Rin had given him. He was too thirsty to worry about being poisoned. As he swallowed, he considered what Elena had told him about the Horse Lords doing worse to him than the Cazadores had done to them.

So far, though, his treatment by the Horse Lords had been anything but brutal since his capture. They had given him extra clothes to keep warm, and even some scraps of food. Of course, he had vomited all of it back up, and a terrible headache had set in. He recognized the symptoms of radiation poisoning and knew he wouldn't last long without treatment.

He handed the water back through the cage, nodding his thanks.

"The sun," Prince Rin said, "it shines on these Metal Islands every day?"

There it is, Mac thought to himself. The reason they were keeping him alive. And perhaps his one bartering tool.

God*damn*, he wished he could just go back to his simple life as a Ranger at the bunker, where the only real thing he had to worry about was whether Barney would cause another drunken scene, or Glock would piss him off.

"Yes, every day I was there," Mac finally replied to the prince.

"The houses—they are built right on the water? Out in the ocean?"

"On former oil rigs."

"How many people live on these Metal Islands?"

"Ten thousand, give or take a few hundred. They like to kill each other."

The rapid thudding of hooves on mud drew Rin away from the cage. He twisted in his saddle as another mounted warrior trotted up. He spoke in hushed tones about some sort of creature hunting in the jungle.

Mac looked out at the three carts ahead of him, each piled high with supplies and one filled with more drums of gasoline from the outpost. The tires thumped over the broken asphalt, the horses struggling to pull the heavy loads.

The scout talking to Rin pulled away, heading back to the front of the caravan.

"The ocean," said the prince as he moved back next to Mac.

"What about it?"

"Is the water really as clear as glass?"

"Yes, on some days."

Mac freely gave the information to his captor because he wanted him to know the truth. Any thought of attacking the Metal Islands was likely a terrible idea that would result in the obliteration of the Horse Lords.

Unless, of course, they had far greater numbers than he thought. So far, everything he had seen, aside from their warship, suggested they were scraping by out here—a far cry from the empire he had seen unravel under the Cazador banners.

"And you can eat the fish right out of the water?" Rin asked.

With a nod, Mac looked at the young prince, who seemed mesmerized by what he was hearing. "Fish is their primary diet, but they have livestock, and they also eat…"

He stopped himself from finishing his sentence.

"Also eat what?" Rin asked.

"The Cazadores also eat men. I saw it happen to my own people."

Rin didn't react as Mac had thought he might. The youngster nodded.

Were they cannibals too?

Mac had spent most of his life underground, living with a system of laws and rules, and a farm that produced enough food for everyone to go to bed at night with something in their stomach. But up here, there were different laws. Up here, it was the state of nature, where the sword dictated who was fed and who was food.

Rin reined his horse away to meet with a soldier who had ridden over.

Mac's headache grew into a deep, pulsating pain. All the jolting and jouncing on the road didn't help. Mac coughed, and his lungs rattled like the tires rolling over the cracked asphalt.

He carefully sat back down, trying to relax, hoping maybe even to sleep. But something was happening. He heard bits and pieces of the conversation—trucks spotted, men with rifles and flamethrowers.

The Cazadores were on the hunt.

El Pulpo had wasted no time after retaking the outpost.

Rin put a whistle to his mouth and blew it. Four riders reined their horses away from the caravan and charged down the road in the opposite direction. Mac looked that way but couldn't see much in the darkness.

Rin came back to the side of the cart. "How many reinforcements will the Cazadores bring?"

Mac honestly wasn't sure about that. He coughed again and probably appeared to be stalling. But the rattle in his chest was real, and so was the pain. He spat a gob of brown phlegm out and tasted the coppery hint of blood.

"How many?" Rin asked.

Mac heard rising anger in his youthful voice.

"One hundred, like your scout said. Maybe a bit more." Mac kept coughing, suddenly struggling to breathe. He hacked up a ball of sticky red phlegm onto the bottom of the cart. Rin looked down, then turned away without another word.

Throat clear now, Mac managed a deep breath. He watched the prince ride off ahead of the caravan, unlike the four horsemen who had just galloped back the way they came. Mac rose up to look in that direction and noticed light on the horizon. He tried to make it out in the dark jungle, but the radiation poisoning was also starting to affect his vision. It occurred to him that he might be hallucinating the glowing orbs that flickered up in the canopy. They reminded him of the main chamber of ITC Star Station, when people had strung up lights across artificial tree branches.

He closed his eyes and took several deep, slow breaths, giving himself a short reprieve from the nausea. The cart climbed a hill, rising for almost a minute before the ride evened out again. When he opened his eyes, the orbs were no longer just sparkles in the distance. They weren't just lights either. They were flames—torches burning high in the branches on platforms built onto the giant trees.

Mac grabbed one of the vertical bars of his cage to pull himself up. On his feet now, he hunched over in the cage and got a sprawling view of a valley carved out of the jungle. His jaw hung open at the sight before him as he beheld yet another community of humans living aboveground.

This was it. They had arrived at the home of the Horse Lords.

The torches and lights illuminated multilevel structures built in the branches of the towering trees. But there were also dwellings on the ground, including a massive stone pyramid that jutted steeply from the jungle.

Fires burned in pits around the colossal building, silhouetting the people who stood guard outside the entrances. The caravan started down the hill, leaving the asphalt road, which ended, for a dirt track at the bottom. Down at this level, stone walls blocked off most of the view. On those walls, Mac could see guard posts and a tall steel gate adorned with a wrought-iron horse head.

The gates parted as the lead horses and riders approached. Rin was the first inside. A violent fit of coughing brought Mac down to his knees. Lungs burning, he hacked up bloody phlegm.

He slumped over and curled up on the straw-covered floor of the cage.

A horn blared. It was not a Cazador horn.

Mac tried to sit up as the caravan passed through the gate. Too weak to sit up on his own, he slid over against the bars. His vision continued to deteriorate. He struggled to look out beyond his prison. Tiny figures ran up toward the cart—children, he realized. They followed the procession, shouting and laughing.

Two soldiers on foot shooed them away.

The gate closed behind the procession, sealing off the walls. Mac shifted his body, coming up on his knees and gripping the bars in a short burst of energy. The horses approached the pyramid, where fires burned in stone hearths on the various levels.

At the very top, Mac could vaguely make out robed figures. They faced the caravan as it came to a stop at the base of the pyramid. A group of perhaps thirty people flooded out of a stone entrance, some carrying spears, others dressed in colorful attire. Torches illuminated the group, which included a woman in a flowing red dress, with a jeweled necklace that sparkled in the glow.

Rin dismounted and walked over to the people who had emerged from the pyramid and knelt in front of the woman. She raised her hand, and Rin stood. He ushered her over to the cart, which was surrounded by warriors. One of them came to the cage door and unlocked it, gesturing for Mac to get out.

He nearly fell. Staggering, he brought a hand up to cover his cough. Mustering what little strength he had, he tried to stand straight. He bowed his head, not daring to look at the woman's eyes.

"You have entered the dominion of the Horse Lords," she said.

Rin walked over. "This is Queen Latuh Leon," he said. "My mother."

"I am honored," Mac said, keeping his gaze on the ground.

"You are one of the barbarians?" she asked.

"He claims to be their prisoner," Rin said.

The woman walked closer until he could see her boots. The cold edge of a spearhead went to his neck, forcing his chin up, and Mac looked upon one of the most beautiful faces he had ever seen.

"Who are you?" she asked.

"My name is Mac. I am from an underground community outside what was once Houston, Texas, in the former United States. I did not come here of my own accord. The Cazadores killed my people, enslaved me, and forced me to fight."

"Where is their home?"

"A place called the Metal Islands."

"The sun shines there, Mother," Rin said.

She turned to the youth. "The sun, you say?"

Mac nodded. "Yes. In the middle of the ocean. I don't know where, exactly."

She stared back at him with an intensity that sent a chill up his spine.

Then she looked back to the robed man carrying the metal pole with the horse emblem. He raised his standard into the air, and a horn blared once, then again.

Mac felt a tremor beneath his feet.

"The Cazadores made a grave mistake coming to the dominion of the Horse Lords," she said. "Now they will meet their fate."

In that moment, a massive black horse wearing armor plates over its broad chest rounded the side of the pyramid. The rider was also wearing armor. He held a pole with a banner sporting the horse-head logo in one hand, and a torch in the other hand. Two more horses with riders in full battle array followed. Then five more. Those eight turned to twenty.

Prince Rin slipped his helmet on and went to his horse.

"Crush them," she commanded.

"We will erase them from these lands."

"They have guns and flamethrowers," Mac said before breaking into another coughing fit.

"Then those weapons will soon be ours," Rin said. "We have pushed back every invader from these lands. This will be no different."

He bowed to his mother again, then swung up into the saddle and rode out to lead his cavalry.

In the wall that surrounded the pyramid, the towering steel gate began to open. Guards patrolling the walkways above looked down as the Horse Lords on their beasts trotted out through the gate and back into the jungle.

Mac watched them go, wondering if one of them was Elena's husband. And if he would avenge her.

Twenty horsemen against the hundred Cazador reinforcements the scout on the road had seen was not an even match, especially with el Pulpo in command. But then again, the Cazador captain didn't know these jungles.

Mac coughed hard, bleeding from his cracked lips. He watched the gates close behind the horsemen as they sallied forth to face el Pulpo. Deep down, he found himself rooting for the young prince, hoping he would indeed crush the cannibalistic bastard who had pillaged Mac's home.

A deep, burning cough ignited in Mac's chest again. He brought up a hand to cover his mouth as he broke into another violent fit. Queen Latuh motioned to the entourage that had gathered around them. Out stepped a woman wearing a pale blue-green dress and turquoise necklace. She carried a small wooden box, which she opened to reveal four vials of clear liquid. Queen Latuh took one of the vials, pulled out the cork, and handed it to Mac.

"Drink," she commanded.

Mac hesitated.

"It will cure you of your ailments," said the queen.

Tipping back the vial, Mac drank it all, wincing at the bitter taste. Then he handed it back and bowed his head in thanks. "You have my gratitude," he said. "I appreciate—"

"I don't want your gratitude," Queen Latuh interrupted.

She grinned, but there was something off in that beautiful smile. Something cold, calculating—something evil.

"Now you will rest," she said. "Once you get your strength back, we will discuss the future."

CHAPTER 20

The bones of a horse lay across the road. There were human skeletons too. Wild beasts had gotten to most of them, scattering limbs and dragging them off to their lairs. Among the remains, Nick noticed weapons: machetes, knives, a pitchfork. That told him this graveyard was old, perhaps dating all the way back to just after the bombs, when villagers and city dwellers used whatever they had to stay alive.

The convoy of trucks drove slowly through the remains of a city laid low by fires long ago. Nick looked out from the back of the pickup truck at the charred structures. Another day had passed on the road, and they were stopping for the night.

Near the border of the old town was a single surviving structure that Nick recognized as one of the old big-box stores he had seen in books. Places where people came to buy things in bulk. There were even gas pumps.

El Pulpo directed the trucks into a parking lot overgrown with weeds. The rusted-out hulls of vehicles sat where they were left centuries ago. A chain-link fence still bounded much of the parking lot. It was mostly open out here—hard for anyone to sneak up on the area.

The captain barked orders as soon as the convoy parked. Cazadores hopped out of the vehicles, spreading out to set up a perimeter. Machine guns were heaved up and mounted to turrets, and sentries ran to find sniper positions.

Nick walked past the truck with the prisoner, who was no longer sitting up. Looking through the bars, he found the man curled up in a fetal position, his head a mess of bloody, suppurating wounds.

Hammerhead reached inside and nudged the man, but he didn't respond. Reaching down, he put a finger to his neck, then cursed.

The prisoner was dead.

Nick tried to stifle his emotions, but he felt for the man, who had suffered greatly. Still, there was nothing to be done now. El Pulpo came over, took a quick look, then turned to Nick.

"You like him so much, then you dispose of his corpse, Small Dog," he said. "Take him far enough that his stink won't attract predators."

Nick sighed and went to the truck. He climbed up into the bed, waving away the flies that buzzed over the body.

Whale met him at the back and reached up to help.

"I got him," Nick said.

"No, I help," Whale replied. Fuego pulled on his flamethrower pack, and Zorro loaded an assault rifle to head out on patrol duty. They escorted Nick and Whale out to the edge of the parking lot, where a hill sloped down to an old drainage ditch. A road lay just beyond that, and then the jungle canopy, stretching to the horizon under swollen skies.

"I say we dump this fool right down there," Whale said.

Nick shook his head. He didn't want to anger el Pulpo again. "I'll drag him myself."

"No." Whale pounded his chest, grunted, and lifted the body

back up. They heaved it down into the drainage ditch, then up the other side to the road. Fuego and Zorro followed them, watching for hostiles in the dense foliage as they were stopped by a wall of dirt, rocks, and debris that blocked the street.

Nick struggled as they made their way out onto the rocky terrain separating the road from trees. He spotted a recess in the loose dirt that looked like as good a place as any to dump the corpse.

Whale swung the body for momentum and gave a three count. On three, they both let go, launching the body into the dirt grave.

I'm sorry, Nick thought.

He looked down at the corpse buzzing with insects. Whale just rubbed his gloves together and walked away.

Suddenly, Nick felt the sensation of being watched. He scanned the jungle and reached over his back to draw his cutlass. Weapon in hand, he quietly retreated back to Whale, who had unslung his assault rifle.

"*¿Qué pasó?*" he asked.

"*No sé,*" Nick said, shrugging.

He backed away, searching for red eyes or the Horse Lords' helmets. Fuego and Zorro waited for them on the other side of the road, and together they fell back to the hill overlooking the drainage ditch.

When Nick returned, el Pulpo had already broken out a jug of the bootleg tequila back at the camp. He raised his helmet and took a gulp. Then he handed it off to Hammerhead, who chugged enough to make most men vomit.

The captain took the jug back, then climbed up on the hood of a truck. He yelled in Spanish, "Small Dog, stay out and patrol with the rest of your little friends."

Whale kicked a chunk of dirt, and Fuego cursed, but Zorro

simply turned with his rifle and started patrolling. They stayed on the road, walking back and forth for the next hour while el Pulpo and his Barracudas cooked dinner and drank.

They had positioned the trucks in a defensive circle. Nick counted ten more Cazadores standing guard and a sniper on the partially collapsed roof of the adjacent building.

The night wore on, and Nick fought the fatigue. He hadn't eaten all day or drank any water since he handed his bottle to the now-dead prisoner. But he was also out of water thanks to that—a worthless decision since the guy hadn't lived much longer anyway.

He walked over to Zorro and asked if he could spare a sip.

"*No hay problema, Perrito,*" he replied.

Zorro pulled the bottle from his outer vest as Nick tilted his helmet up. Just then Nick saw movement in the glow of the storms. A shadowed figure mounted the barrier of earth and broken asphalt ahead.

"What the…" he started to say.

A flash of lightning captured the silhouette of a centaur—half man, half horse—watching them from the pile of debris. Nick flipped his helmet back down over his head, and Zorro turned—right into two arrows that zipped out of the jungle.

"No," Nick gasped.

Zorro staggered back to Nick, who reached out and caught him as he fell. A gunshot cracked, and gore plastered Nick's visor. He fell under the weight of his friend.

"Ambush!" Nick shouted. He pushed against Zorro, moving him enough to see Fuego unleash a wave of fire at the mound of rubble in the road. The flames revealed the figure in detail. This was no centaur. It was a man, mounted on a horse that shrieked in pain from the liquid fire.

Nick squirmed out from under Zorro. Pushing the body up, he saw blood trickling from a bullet hole in his helmet. Shaking away the shock, Nick picked up the dropped assault rifle and scrambled over to the side of the road, keeping low. Snorting and whinnying echoed up out of the drainage ditch.

He raised the rifle at riders charging down the dry waterway. Ten of them, maybe more. Several loosed arrows from their bows, forcing Nick to the dirt. He watched as most of the group loped up the hill toward the camp. Cazadores rushed for cover from flaming arrows that flew through the air, falling right over the trucks where el Pulpo and his comrades had been eating and drinking. Screams of pain rang out.

Gunfire cracked, and muzzle flashes came from across the parking lot, where another dozen cavalry charged three patrolling guards. Using spears, the horseman skewered two of the Cazadores. The third managed to use a flamethrower, dousing a horse and screaming rider in fire.

El Pulpo flung his spear, knocking a rider out of his saddle. Another Horse Lord barreled toward him, leaning down for the saber stroke. El Pulpo ducked the blade, grabbed the man, and yanked him from the saddle to the ground. In the same fluid motion, el Pulpo's axe swung down and split both head and helmet.

A flaming arrow hit el Pulpo in the upper chest. He snapped it off and then hurled his axe at a charging horse, the blade cutting through a foreleg above the knee. The horse crashed to the ground, pinning its rider.

"*Perrito!*" Whale shouted.

Only seconds had passed, but it felt much longer as Nick raced back to the debris barrier with Zorro's assault rifle. The first horse was on the ground, burning along with the screaming rider pinned beneath it. But two more Horse Lords had ridden their beasts from the drainage ditch up onto the road. Fuego had been hit by something and lay injured on the ground. Whale tried to pull him over to the ditch, away from a Horse Lord about to hurl a spear.

Nick fired a burst. One of the rounds hit the warrior in the chest, knocking him backward, the spear falling from his grip. As the horse bolted, the man leaned in the saddle, then toppled all the way out, but his left boot caught in the stirrup. The horse stampeded past Nick, dragging the dying man away.

He shouldered his rifle at the second Horse Lord, but this man managed to throw his spear before Nick could fire a shot. The blade hit his shoulder plate, spinning him and knocking the assault rifle out of his hands. The rider kicked his horse in the flank, launching it forward while he drew his saber.

On the ground, Nick searched for his rifle, but the spear that had nearly killed him was closer. He scooped it up and rose to his feet. Screaming at the top of his lungs, he ran at the charging horse. Moments from being trampled, he darted to the side and thrust the point under the rider's helmet. The spearhead sliced open his neck, releasing a spray of arterial blood.

The horse kept going, but the rider fell off onto the road with an audible thud. Panting, Nick drew his sword and went over to the writhing soldier. He kicked the helmet off and looked down at a youthful face staring up with terror in his eyes. He had both hands clamped around his neck in a vain attempt to stanch the spurting blood.

Nick thought himself a bit young for war, but this was a mere boy.

"Prince Rin!" someone shouted.

Nick turned to see a third Horse Lord emerge at the top of the ditch with a rifle aimed at him. A massive armored figure slammed into the shooter, knocking him to the ground. It was Whale, and he began bashing the man's helmeted head into the concrete.

Meanwhile, the prince tried to speak, blood gushing around his fingers.

Nick looked down ruefully.

"I'm sorry," he said.

Rin's eyes widened, and blood bubbled from his mouth as he tried to say his final words. Nick thrust his cutlass down, into his heart.

The rumble of a motorcycle carried from the camp across the ditch. Nick ran over to the hill, making sure no Horse Lords were using it as a flanking path. Whale had just finished bashing the last warrior's head into pulp, and Fuego was burning down the jungle with his flamethrower.

Nick took a fleeting moment to watch the scene back at the camp. A Cazador on a dirt bike burst out from the four parked trucks, which were now trapped between circling horses. Two horsemen pursued, firing pistols at the rider on the bike.

Muzzle flashes came from inside the fort of vehicles, but it looked as though most of the Cazadores there had been injured by arrows. Flaming bolts stuck out of the trucks and burned on dead warriors.

Suddenly, a Cazador warrior leaped to the back of a truck and grabbed the mounted machine gun. He turned it on the horsemen pursuing the dirt bike, firing a burst that cut down one of the horses and took out the other rider.

Arrows flew at the Cazador on the machine gun. Some of them caromed off as he swiveled it around to fire on the circling horsemen, but several pierced the armor on his back and one arm. It was Forge, screaming not in pain but with a bloodcurdling war cry.

A large explosion went off between the trucks, sending up a fireball that tossed Cazadores back like rag dolls. Screams rang out from within the caravan that was meant to shield them but had trapped them all. The Horse Lords had the trucks completely surrounded.

Burning Cazadores tried to escape, only to be picked off. One of them scrambled over a truck hood, his body consumed in flames. He made it a few steps before he dropped to the ground, six arrows sticking out of his armor.

"We have to help," Nick said. He started down the hill when Whale grabbed him and pushed him to the ground. Then he pointed out the Horse Lords advancing on foot in the drainage ditch. Some were already charging up the hill toward the camp. One of them looked in their direction.

Fuego whistled, then waved from the edge of the jungle with his sword. He dropped his flamethrower pack off into the mud as Nick and Whale hurried over. All three of them looked back to Zorro, who lay in the road, a pool of blood around his helmet.

Nick knew there was nothing to be done for him now, and so did Whale and Fuego. They fled into the dark jungle, hoping to survive and fight another day.

The screams and gunshots faded behind them as they ran. Even Whale kept up the fast pace, using his sword to hack through anything in their way.

An hour later, they finally stopped at a clearing in the dense canopy. There, they beheld a stone pyramid that towered above the jungle. This was a massive, ancient structure that looked older than anything Nick had seen in the wastes.

A twig snapped behind him, and he whirled to find a slender figure holding a sword.

Nick had his own cutlass half drawn when he saw the Cazador armor covered in mud. The warrior lowered his weapon, then motioned for Nick to come over.

As he approached, he saw that this was no man—it was

Wendig. And for the first time, he was glad to see her. Whale and Fuego also turned.

"How'd you find us?" Fuego asked.

She looked down at the mud, and Nick gazed at his tracks.

"If I can find you, so can they," she replied. "We have to go to the swamps."

Nick remembered seeing them. When no one came up with a better idea, the three followed her a quarter mile back to the edge of a large reeded expanse of stagnant water.

"You want to go *that* way?" Fuego asked.

She nodded. "Crocodiles, or arrows and spears. Dealer's choice."

Nick nodded, but Whale hesitated. He looked back to Fuego, who also seemed undecided.

"We hide in the swamps until the Horse Lords are gone," Wendig said. "Then we come out and kill them all."

*   *   *   *   *

"Wake up," said a female voice.

Mac opened his eyes. He lay in a bed inside a stone room. His eyes found a beautiful woman standing at the foot of his bed.

"Whoa," he said.

At first he thought he was dreaming, but then he saw that beautiful face he had seen outside the pyramid. He remembered: This was Queen Latuh of the Horse Lords, wearing a black dress that emphasized the curves and cleavage of her shapely body.

She moved closer, the light from flickering candles capturing her beauty—dark brown eyes and perfect thick brows.

She gave a dazzling smile of straight, white teeth. "How do you feel?" she asked.

"I feel good."

Mac thought back to the medicine she had given him. It appeared that the time for talking about the future was upon him.

He sat up in the bed, shirtless but wearing pants. He felt something heavy sticking on his back. As he twisted to look, she drew a knife from her belt.

Mac froze.

She chuckled. "If I wanted to kill you, I would have done so the moment we met," she said. "Now, turn. I will remove the last sucker."

She brought the blade to whatever was stuck on his back. After a short prick of pain, he felt pressure release, then heard a pop.

The queen held a glistening black leach that squirmed in her grip. Walking over to the table, she dropped the writhing creature into a jar.

"You had an infection in your back," she explained. "This magnificent creature helped draw it out."

Mac thought back to the wound he sustained on the warship—the same wound that Elena had treated. Like this queen, the nurse had been beautiful, kind, and competent.

So what the hell had Elena meant about these people being worse than the Cazadores?

"Come with me," the queen said.

He swung his legs off the bed, the sheet falling away. She took a quick glance at his muscular form, her eyes tracing him up and down. Then she tossed him a white tunic.

"Get dressed," she said. "We'll get you some food and water shortly."

Mac threw on the tunic, expecting his back to hurt. But aside from a little soreness, his upper body felt great. His legs, on the other hand, felt weak, as if he had been lying in that bed for quite a while. At this point, he had no idea how much time had passed since he was captured, but judging by his recovery, it was a few days at least.

He walked to the door and opened it to find two guards in polished leather armor waiting with the queen. The tails from their helmets hung like capes over their backs as they escorted Mac into a hallway.

Queen Latuh walked by his side. He wanted to ask her if there was news about Prince Rin and his horsemen, but he decided to remain silent. The guards led them to a wide passage with light streaming in from open doorways on both sides.

Mac looked inside chambers thrumming with activity. Inside large stone chambers, overhead lights shone down on troughs of growing plants. People wearing masks and goggles tended to crops of beans, corn, spinach, and tomatoes.

"These grand rooms were once used to store gold, jewels, and diamonds," Latuh said. "Now they store real treasure: our food."

Mac thought of Lord Portatormentas, who was weighed down by the gold he wore and the food he ate. The fat bastard was the embodiment of greed. He ate enough to feed a large family.

The queen stopped as an elderly male worker carried a basket out into the hallway. She held up a hand, and the man stopped and bowed. Taking the basket, she offered it to Mac.

Mac looked at the fresh tomatoes inside.

"Go ahead," said Latuh.

Mac pulled out a ripe tomato and took a bite. The sweet, tangy juice ran down his throat. Another worker brought over a jug of water.

A few minutes later, Mac had eaten two tomatoes and drank half the water.

"Thank you," he said.

Both workers bowed and backed away.

The queen and Mac passed more of the chambers brimming with crops. They had an entire farm down here—not just plants but livestock too. Chickens, hogs, cows. The animal sounds echoed into the passage, and the pungent scent of manure drifted out of open doors. Blue light flashed across those rooms, which Mac assumed had skylights to the surface.

In another section of the pyramid, giant water tanks were installed in the vaulted chambers. An engineer with a tool belt tended to a giant boiler with pipes extending in all directions.

They came to a gate blocking off the next passage. Through the metal bars, Mac could see only more stairs leading down into the structure. One of the guards unlocked the gate as Queen Latuh took a torch off the wall and lit it.

"Follow me, Mac," she said.

Holding the burning torch down, they started down the stairwell. The flickering glow fell on paintings. But these weren't old like the pyramid itself. These were newer, depicting a man on a horse in a field of crops, looking out at a distant mushroom cloud and fireball.

"Mateo," she said. "The first Horse Lord and my great-great-great-great-grandfather."

She lowered the torch to the next image, showing Mateo riding away on the horse, smoke choking the sky over a village where a woman held two small children.

The torchlight swept over another scene—Mateo again, putting on a cowboy hat in front of the woman and the two kids. Behind him were two mounted riders holding shotguns.

A few steps farther down, they came to a painting of the three men riding toward a group of filthy people with blades in their hands, who were scowling and snarling like wild animals. They looked like unarmored Cazadores.

"We have faced many threats over the years," said the queen.

She kept walking down the stairs, her torch revealing scenes of warfare. The horsemen transformed from a small group to a large cavalry led by Mateo, now bearded and scarred. In the next painting, he traded his cowboy hat for one of the metal helmets that the Horse Lords still wore today.

In the final scene, the man led a company of warriors on horses, guiding their families and livestock toward a temple—this temple.

"This structure became our salvation after many years of fighting," Queen Latuh said. "We have lived here for over two hundred and thirty years. These walls have protected us from many enemies, and they will protect us from the Cazadores."

She kept on to the bottom of the stairs, which opened to yet another chamber. A stone altar and a semicircle of stone benches were the only furnishings in the sprawling, echoey space. The guards went inside first, holding out their torches and lighting wall sconces that captured more of the ancient frescoes. They were faded, but the symbolism of animals and people remained poignant.

The light fell over maps strung up on the wall. Most of them seemed to depict surrounding countries. Mac stepped up, examining the red markings on cities.

"Our former enemies," said the queen.

She waved her torch in front of the maps, showing the red dots that marked the battles.

"But I didn't bring you here to show you who we have conquered," she said. "I brought you here for *you* to show *me* who I will conquer next."

She handed the torch to Mac.

"Show me where the Metal Islands are," she said coldly.

He took the torch while looking into her brown eyes.

Of course, he thought to himself. In his gut, he had known she wanted this from him.

"These Cazadores destroyed your home, killed your people, enslaved you, forced you to fight," she said.

Mac nodded. He felt the deep-seated rage in his belly for what they had done to everyone he cared about and to him. The queen seemed to sense that rage.

"Then show me their home," she said. "Guide me to these metal rigs, and I will destroy them and take what they took from you."

He looked at the maps and found one of the Caribbean Sea, then Puerto Rico and the Virgin Islands, which lay close to where the Metal Islands were hidden. He wasn't sure where, exactly, just the general area. But with ships, it would take them mere months to find the sunshine.

"You can join me," said the queen.

He looked at her and saw that sly, beautiful grin return.

"Together we can kill every last one of them," she said. "We can erase their kind from this planet, cleansing it of evil."

"Every last one?"

"You do not save a diseased crop by leaving any in the ground. You burn it all, then replant with fresh stock."

Mac stared at her. She meant children.

"Don't give me that look," she said. "You leave any kids alive, and they will hunt you many years later."

He again considered what Elena had said about doing worse to him than the Cazadores.

And not just me. She would kill everyone, including every woman and child.

Footsteps from behind drew his gaze back to the doorway they had entered. A guard rushed up, panting.

"The horsemen have returned with dire news, my queen," he said.

She hurried out of the chamber. One guard stayed with Mac,

escorting him back up the stairs. From there, he was taken to a new passage. As he came topside, he was greeted by ten mounted soldiers in the rain. Behind them, a growing group of Horse Lords on foot surrounded wounded men, most of them half naked and covered in tattoos.

Hundreds of people issued from tunnels into the pouring rain. Youth, elderly, men, women. Farmers, engineers, cooks. Everyone gathered to watch their enemies marched before them by the proud Horse Lords.

Mac pulled back into the shadows when he saw the shaved head of el Pulpo, snarling with his jagged teeth as he was pulled by a rope around his neck, tied to the saddle of a horse. Blood dripped from wounds on his shoulder, arms, and belly as he trotted forward, trying to keep pace. Hammerhead and six more Cazadores stumbled along in chains.

El Pulpo pulled on the rope, only to have the rider on the horse give it a kick, pulling him to the mud. He pushed up from the muck, howling like a wild beast. Three Horse Lords closed in, kicking and hitting him.

Queen Latuh ran over with her guards to one of the warriors who had just returned. He dismounted from his horse.

"Where is my son?" she asked.

The Horse Lord went down on one knee, then looked up. "He was gravely wounded, Your Majesty," he said remorsefully. "I'm sorry, but he succumbed to his injuries."

Mac expected her to howl like el Pulpo, but she simply stared, perhaps in shock.

The rest of the prisoners were escorted toward aboveground animal pens. Inside were hogs, but these weren't like the hogs Mac had seen below the surface. These creatures snuffled with hunger. Two of the wounded Cazadores were stripped naked.

Then they were strung up by their hands on a pulley system that hoisted them above the pens.

Queen Latuh made her way over to el Pulpo, looming over him as he lay pinned in the mud. She put a boot down on his neck, pressing hard enough that his eyes bulged.

Raising her hands to the heavens, she let loose a shriek far louder than the one el Pulpo had made. Her enraged voice echoed off the stone walls that had protected her ancestors for centuries.

Mac was starting to understand how they had survived out here, and he had a feeling el Pulpo was about to find out what Elena had meant about their brutality.

CHAPTER 21

Wendig swam to the other side of the swamp and waved from the bank.

Nick had to admit—her bravery out there was impressive. She had some balls to back up her need to prove herself, that was for sure.

Now it was his turn. Spear up and ready, he waded out. As the water rose to his thighs, a faint ripple rolled toward him. Whale yanked him back as the jaws of a crocodile exploded from the murky water, snapping where Nick had stood a second earlier.

Fuego thrust his spear at the beast, and it flopped back into the swamp with a splash and was gone. Nick retreated a few steps into a shallow cave at the edge of the marsh. Two tall, spindly trees rose above it, drooping red branches over the water. Whale pushed one aside and looked out at the water, waiting for the croc to resurface. In the residual glow of lightning, Nick spotted the fifteen-foot-long beast cruising across the swamp to the bank where Wendig had climbed out. An elongated snout poked out in search of easy prey, but she was already gone.

"Guess she's on her own," Fuego said in Spanish. "You lucked out."

Heart still pounding from the close call, Nick nodded. He huddled with the other two men as the monster waddled up the muddy shore.

"I'm so hungry I could eat that," Whale said.

"You can have my share too," Fuego replied.

They had only the rations they were carrying during the ambush. Nick could deal with thirst and hunger—he was more worried about getting eaten. And the croc wasn't the only predator out there. He had seen a snake as thick as one of those trees growing above the shallow cave. The jaguars, too, were on the prowl, their roars floating out from the depths of the jungle.

The plan was to hunker down and wait for reinforcements, but Nick wasn't sure they would ever come. Lord Portatormentas was probably sitting on the *Golden Sentinel,* ripping through a roasted chicken with passion fruit.

Nick thought of Zorro, who had fallen in the ambush and died in his arms. Of all the Cazadores, Zorro had treated Nick the best. Respected him, defended him, and made him feel like one of their own. It was the closest Nick had come to making a friend among these people.

And with Mac more than likely dead, he felt that lonely dread creep back into his mind. Despair set in as he waited for Wendig to return.

An hour passed. Then two. Nick remained alert the entire time, watching the jungle around them for hostiles.

At the start of the third hour, a distant human scream silenced the chirp and drone of the insects. He turned to look at Fuego and Whale, sitting inside the small hollow in the rocky bank. They got up and joined Nick again at the edge of the cave, a few feet back from the water.

The anguished call was likely a captured Cazador, being tortured at the temple of the Horse Lords, deep in the jungle. The scream rose in a ghastly crescendo that sounded like someone being burned alive.

"Is that Wendig?" Fuego asked in Spanish.

"She was stupid for going out there," Whale said.

"Who you calling stupid?"

Nick looked up at a muddy figure standing above them, holding an assault rifle in each hand. Wendig dropped down in front of the cave, covered in mud. She laid the weapons down, then peeled off her backpack. Whale picked it up and started rummaging inside for food.

Wiping muck off her armor, Wendig heaved a long breath. "I saw the prisoners," she said.

"How many?" Nick asked.

"Five."

"Did you see Mac?"

"I didn't get a good look, only at Hammerhead, but some of them are still alive. Not for long though. That scream you heard was one of them being executed. We have to do something—fast."

"You want to sneak in there and free them?" Whale asked.

"Better than sitting here and waiting to turn into crocodile shit."

"I get Hammerhead is your kin, but we're vastly outnumbered," Fuego said.

"Fine," Wendig replied. "Sit on your ass, then. I'll go alone."

She reached down for one of the assault rifles she had brought back.

"No, wait," Nick said. "I'll go. Show me where they are, and maybe we can come up with a plan to free them."

"At least one of you isn't a coward. I'm just surprised it's Small Dog."

"Want to say that again?" Whale said, rising to his feet and towering over Wendig.

She stood, too, staring into his eyes a foot above her.

"This is insanity," Fuego said. "We're outnumbered a hundred to one, and you want to fight *each other*?"

"No, I want to fight the enemy," Wendig said. "We are Cazadores. Did you forget what that means?"

Wendig ejected the magazine, checked the cartridges, and palmed it back into the weapon. "We're hunters, so let's do some hunting," she said.

Nick grabbed the other rifle and nodded.

Whale groaned. "At least give me a minute to eat." He lifted his helmet and took a bite of jerky from the bag Wendig had found. She walked down to the edge of the swamp while the three men passed around the rations.

Nick took a bite and washed it down with some water. Already feeling better, he joined Wendig. They surveyed the murky water, but Nick saw no sign of the croc.

Whale grabbed his spear, grumbling.

"We need to stay together," Nick said.

Nods all around.

All four warriors waded cautiously into the water, leaving their sanctuary. Spears up, Whale took point and Fuego went to rear guard.

Nick felt his boots sinking into the muck as he struggled to move. Scanning the swamp in all directions, he spotted movement on the bank a hundred yards to the right.

Sure enough, a croc slipped into the water.

Whale heaved forward, up to the bank. He slipped and flopped on the ground, as if one of his namesake creatures had beached itself. Nick tried not to laugh, but then he, too, slipped and fell. He got his feet under him, then turned to help Wendig. She hesitated before taking his hand.

Fuego was still in the water as the croc closed the distance. If he slipped in, there would be no saving him.

The crocodile was only fifteen feet away when Nick helped Fuego up onto solid ground. He scrambled up to safety as the crock watched. It went under when the four Cazadores climbed up a hill, into the trees.

Wendig waved them into the jungle. They stalked through, avoiding the barbed bushes and another mound of fire ants. Seeing the insects made Nick think of Zorro again, but he pushed the thought of his friend away. No use dwelling on the dead right now.

Ahead, Wendig raised a fist, halting in front of a towering tree. She looked up, then nodded at Nick. He went over and checked the massive tree. Its many sturdy limbs looked as if they could support the weight of their armor. Most of them, anyway.

Nick grabbed a branch and pulled himself up, with Wendig following. They climbed up thirty feet while the other two Cazadores held security below. A fierce wind howled across the jungle canopy, and Nick wrapped his arms around the tree, hugging it until the wind died down.

Near the top branches, he was greeted with a sprawling view of the jungle and some sort of ancient stone temple rising out of the clearing maybe a thousand feet away. This magnificent building was different from Old World structures he had seen before. It appeared to be truly ancient.

Wendig handed him binos for a better view. He zoomed in on a wall built of rubble, including vehicles, rocks, metal sheets, and tires. The twenty-foot-high barrier surrounded the entire area. Torches burned over it, illuminating guards along the parapets.

Outside the wall, box-shaped wooden structures had been built up in the trees. Checking one, he saw a guard inside. There were at least ten of these watchtowers, all but invisible in the jungle outside the fortress perimeter.

Nick moved the binos back to the walls surrounding the temple. Surrounding the pyramid were twenty, perhaps even thirty, structures—metal shacks, pole barns, and tall, cylindrical silos.

He identified multiple tunnels in the side of the temple. Judging by the number of people coming and going, there must be tunnels leading underground—perhaps where they lived. An entire culture had developed out here in the middle of nowhere, with the ancient building as the hub of their civilization.

Wendig pointed to a large recessed area that reminded Nick of the Sky Arena. Through the binos, he saw that this pit wasn't for fighting; it was a corral full of horses—fifty or more of them.

Finally, he located the Cazador survivors of the ambush. There were only five left, all of them wearing just their hazard suits. He zoomed in with the binos, but Mac wasn't among them. He did identify Forge, Hammerhead, and el Pulpo, who, judging by his bandages, had been given medical attention. That was a surprise.

But not everyone had been so lucky.

Two Cazadores hung from ropes over a hog pen, the creatures chewing on their dangling bare feet. Both corpses had great gashes and were missing parts—whether from torture or the battle, Nick couldn't be sure.

He searched the bloody faces for Mac.

Wendig pointed higher up the pyramid, to the very top ledge.

Nick dialed in on a sixth Cazador prisoner, who lay curled up on his side. A sudden wind nearly knocked Nick out of the tree before he could get a good look. He grabbed another branch and held on until the gust died.

Shouting drifted from the top of the temple. Nick looked back up to the ledge, where the prisoner was now on his knees, head lowered. Behind him were two people in black and gold clothing with feathers on the shoulders, arms, and legs. Some sort of priests or magi.

Two Horse Lords pushed a cart laden with three barrels.

"Guerrero!" someone shouted.

In answer, a giant warrior emerged. The man wore only tattered shorts, sandals, and a bandanna holding back his shoulder-length hair. He had an unusually large head that vaguely reminded Nick of a horse, especially with his long mane. His thick muscles flexed as he lifted one of the barrels off the cart with ease.

A loud humming of many voices began across a stone terrace where several hundred people stood gathered in front of the temple. Two men with torches set fire to stacks of wood inside a pair of giant stone bowls. Flames leaped up, illuminating the colorful clothing of the crowd. All ages were present, from children to doddering oldsters.

They watched the prisoner, who was about to be sacrificed, just like the two dead Cazadores hanging from ropes in the hog pen.

Nick heard shouting in Spanish that he understood to mean, *I'll never tell you! None of us will!*

He looked up at the prisoner at the top ledge, struggling in the grip of the guards. One of the Horse Lords smacked him with the hilt of a sword, knocking him to the side. Leaning down, the soldier pried open the Cazador's mouth. A second Horse Lord forced a tube into his mouth. That tube was hooked up to a barrel that the giant, Guerrero, held against his chest.

His massive arms raised the barrel above his head, dumping thick fluid over the Cazador. After drenching him, the mammoth Horse Lord lowered the barrel to the stone ledge, leaving a trail of black as he moved back.

A woman emerged, wearing an elegant black dress and crown. She raised her arms outward, like an eagle taking flight. The feathered priests handed her two lit torches.

"No, no!" the Cazador pleaded as he spat and hacked on the ground.

"The enemy has come for oil!" she shouted. "So we shall give it to them!"

She lowered the torches, igniting the dark trail. The fire traveled quickly toward the prisoner. His body erupted in flames as he tried to clamber away on all fours. Engulfed, he twirled and flailed, then ran blind right off the ledge. He fell a third of the way down before bouncing off a step and tumbling all the way to the bottom, where he lay still and eventually burned out.

Angry screams came from the cage holding the surviving Cazadores. El Pulpo and Hammerhead stood, pounding the bars and shouting profanities.

They would be next on the sacrificial pyre if Nick and his squad didn't find a way to save them soon. He climbed back down with Wendig to Fuego and Whale, and they explained what they had witnessed.

"We have to free them," she said.

"What do you propose?" Fuego asked.

Nick thought back to what he had seen. But it was the image of the horses that stuck with him. An idea formed in his mind.

"Have either of you ridden a horse before?" he asked.

Whale didn't seem to understand his Spanish.

"A what?"

"A horse—*caballo*," Nick said.

"You serious?" Fuego asked.

Wendig laughed. "I'm not sure there's a horse out there that could support Whale. He would need a rhinoceros."

Nick understood then, and they were right. With his armor on, Whale had to weigh 350 pounds or more.

"I will provide a distraction," Whale said.

"We'll need a really big one," Nick replied.

"I have an idea," Fuego said. "You said there are oil barrels?"

"Yeah."

"Then maybe I can make a big boom."

Nick nodded. "Okay, Wendig, as soon as those crowds move, we take down the guards on the wall, then head to the corrals to let the horses out," he said. "We'll bring whatever weapons to the prisoners while Whale and Fuego create the distraction."

Wendig punched him on the shoulder plate. "I'm starting to like you, Small Dog."

"It's mutual." He went back to the tree. "I'll signal when the crowds are gone."

He climbed back up with the binos, perching on the same branch. More women and children were emerging from tunnels underground, flooding out to stand in front of the pyramid steps.

Behind them, three mounted horsemen trotted forward. A fourth horse followed, its saddle empty. A rope from the pommel pulled a wooden sleigh with a body on it facing the sky.

The crowd went down on their knees, bowing and chanting, "Praise Prince Rin."

Nick froze at the realization: It was the youngster he had killed on the road. The woman in the dress stepped up to look down on what must be her dead son. Standing by her side was a new figure, flanked by two Horse Lords. Their torches illuminated a face that Nick thought he would never see again.

"Mac," he whispered.

*　　*　　*　　*　　*

"Soon your people will all burn for what they did to my son," Queen Latuh said. "But first one of them will tell me the location of the Metal Islands."

Mac looked down at the dead Cazador prisoners.

Now he understood what Elena had meant.

The Horse Lords, under their queen, were more brutal than he realized. From torturing two of the other prisoners and feeding their flesh to starving pigs to burning the other Cazador alive after choking him with oil. And that was just the beginning.

"They won't talk," Mac said. "No matter how hard you try to get them to."

"No? Then I'll burn them all to provide beacons for the rest of the barbarians, leading them here, where I will flay them, burn them, cut out their hearts, until one of them speaks."

"Those aren't men down there," Mac said. "They're animals."

"But you aren't." Queen Latuh looked at him. "You are a logical, good man, no?"

"I won't guide you to kill women and children. That isn't logical. That is evil."

She laughed. "You just told me those aren't men, and you somehow think their women and children won't end up like them? You lived underground far too long not to understand how things work in the darkness."

Maybe that was true, but Mac would never ransom his life by watching children be slaughtered. No, he'd rather be burned alive.

Over five hundred people had gathered outside in the light

rain to watch the sacrifice. Now they watched their prince laid on the stone steps of their temple.

Dogs ran freely, barking and fighting over scraps of food. Even the animals had come out to see the commotion. The lowing of cattle and grunting of hogs came from the livestock pens nestled against the western walls of the city.

All illusions of joining this society were gone. These people were not much different from the Cazadores, who understood only the sword and flame.

Queen Latuh held her arms up again.

"Listen to me, brothers and sisters," she called down. "For today, the gods have blessed us with a gift I have prayed for since I was a young girl."

She raised her chin to the storm clouds.

"Our ancestors have lived in this darkness for over two centuries," she said. "Through strength, determination, and bravery, they survived here, within these walls. Under the leadership of my husband, King Alexi, we expanded, but threats beyond our borders kept us from exploring more of the shattered world. Now those threats have arrived here, to take what we have."

She motioned, and the two warriors behind Mac escorted him to the ledge of stone overlooking the terrace. Flanking him on both sides, the men made sure he wouldn't be able to touch their queen.

"This is one of the infidels from the wastes," she said. "But he is not like the others who have come to raid and pillage our sanctuary. No, while he may be evil, he is from a place where the darkness has been defeated—a place of light."

Gasps and voices resonated up from the terrace below.

Mac saw el Pulpo stare, the rage in his eyes now directed solely at him.

"Silence!" Queen Latuh called down.

The crowd fell still.

"Our Horse Lords have already slain and captured the first of their forces," she continued. "I have deployed another contingent of fifty to finish off the rest of them and seize their warship, which will lead us to their home."

She raised her arms again, and the people below did the same.

"From the darkness to the light, I will lead you to a new world!" yelled the queen. "We will cleanse the Metal Islands of the evil that dwells there, and then replant, growing a new and better life for our people."

Cheers and shouts echoed off the pyramid's stone walls.

"I will show these Cazadores what it is to be hunted, and then what it is to live in the darkness, to know what real evil is," she continued. "I will eradicate them from history—every last one of them! But first we will honor my son, Prince Rin, who gave his life fighting for his people."

She looked down, past the crowd, to the area where the Horse Lords had stopped their beasts. The three riders dismounted and walked back to their fallen prince.

Queen Latuh looked on, showing no emotion. The warriors brought her son to the bottom of the stairs leading up to the temple. His horse climbed up a ramp that appeared to have been built specifically for that purpose. The hooves clattered up to the ledge, where the body was laid down on a stack of wood.

Three priests in their feathery attire made their way down the stairs to the bottom, singing a hymn that the crowd quickly took up. The horse let out a neigh. Extending its neck, it nudged the dead prince.

Seeing the beast's affection for its master reminded Mac that Rin had seemed like a good person. Perhaps it was just part of being that age, as Nick had been. Mac thought of the young prisoner-turned-Cazador, hoping he was still out there somehow, still alive. But the odds weren't good.

The wastes were not kind to youth. Most never survived to see adulthood.

Queen Latuh reached out as a Horse Lord handed her a bow. She nocked an arrow and pulled it back as the warrior by her side lit the tip. Then she aimed it down at her son.

"I will avenge you," she said as she released the bowstring. The flaming arrow streaked into the pile of wood, igniting it.

Queen Latuh lowered the bow, watching for a moment before turning away.

"Bring the infidel," she said in a cold tone.

The gigantic warrior named Guerrero grabbed Mac and pushed him toward the stairwell leading back into the pyramid. Down they went, following the queen and two more Horse Lords to a chamber deep down. On the floor were scattered bones and corpses in varying states of decay. The stench of decomposing flesh was overpowering.

Several crates lay on the stone floor. They reminded Mac of the treasure boxes that Lord Portatormentas had brought on his journey. The queen unfastened the sides of the center box, opening it to reveal a half dozen large glass jars filled with live scorpions, a hairy black-and-red spider, and a black-and-red snake.

"You tell us where the Metal Islands are, or you will suffer far worse than the others," Latuh said. "And to prevent you from lying, you will remain here until the islands are found. If you give us the real location, I'll show you grace."

She faced Mac, leaning up to him, their lips just inches apart. He could smell a sweet scent of fruit on her breath.

"Grace and pleasure beyond your wildest dreams," she said. Raising a finger, she dragged the nail across his cheek, softly at first, but then digging in. He reared back from the gouge, which drew blood.

"Open it," she said.

Guerrero left Mac and went to the stone door. He put his shoulder against the side and pushed, his calves flexing as his sandals found purchase. Heaving like a draft animal, he slid the stone away.

Queen Latuh held a torch up to reveal a small chamber filled with glinting jewels and gold bars. Mac had never seen so much wealth in his life.

Pulling the torch away, Latuh walked over to the altar and selected the jar containing the spotted spider.

"A single bite from this beautiful creature will paralyze you, rendering you unable to move," she explained. "But you will still be able to feel pain. In fact, the bite will actually amplify the sensitivity throughout your body."

She set the jar down and opened another box. Inside were blades, syringes, hooks, and pliers—the tools of torture.

"Unlike your comrades, you can choose," she said, licking her lips. "Pleasure and great wealth, or…" Her gaze went to the altar laden with poisonous creatures and the instruments of torture.

Mac felt a cold chill as he realized he was about to experience hell. It was either that or let thousands of kids and women die, which he could not do.

Mac took a deep breath.

I fucking hate the wastes, he thought.

CHAPTER 22

Nick thought he heard screaming coming from somewhere inside the temple. It seemed a familiar scream.

Or maybe that was just his mind.

He remained on a branch high in the tree, drowsy after being up there for over two hours. El Pulpo, Hammerhead, and two more men remained in the cage, but Nick wasn't sure where Mac had been taken. The crowd was finally starting to move away from the stone terrace facing the temple now that the bonfire had burned out, leaving only charred metal armor and the ashes of the young prince Nick had killed.

He said a silent prayer for the lad, then put it out of his mind.

It was time to move. And fight.

Nick climbed carefully down to the ground, where he exchanged a nod with his comrades. The four Cazadores set off through the jungle toward the towering stone wall. Wendig wasted no time clambering up the side, using the stones as foot- and handholds. At the top, she drew a knife. Then she skirted silently around, landing behind the guard. She crept up and thrust her blade in his neck while pulling him over the parapet.

He crashed to the ground in front of Whale, his twisted body still jerking.

"That was beautiful," Whale said in Spanish. "I think I'm in love."

"Pretty sure she doesn't like men," Fuego said.

"I'm not a man; I'm a god."

Nick couldn't help but grin when Whale raised his arm, pretending to flex. The big Cazador then bent down and stripped a pistol and spare magazine from the holster on the twitching body. He handed them up to Nick, who had already scooped up the dropped crossbow.

"*Gracias*," Nick said. "Good luck."

"You too," Fuego said.

Nick climbed up the wall using the rope Wendig had sent down. At the top, he kept low and went over to where she lay on her belly.

Looking over the edge, Nick saw el Pulpo, Hammerhead, and the other two men, one of whom was Forge. The lieutenant lay still and appeared to be hanging on by a thread.

Wendig held up three fingers, then pointed to the guards watching over the pit that served as a horse corral. Keeping low, Nick followed her to a staircase. She gave the all clear, and they hurried down to the ground, bolting to the stone building. The first guard was on the other side. She sneaked up behind him and slit his throat, then pulled him behind the structure and finished him with two thrusts to the chest.

By the time Nick got over there, she had relieved the body of a pistol, two magazines, and a hatchet.

The next two guards were both at the edge of the corral, looking up at the stone temple and the prisoners, whom Nick could now see clearly. He and Wendig advanced side by side, both clutching knives.

The man Nick selected suddenly turned, and Nick hurried

his attack, leaping outward and jabbing his blade into the guard's visor. It broke through into the eye, but not deep enough to kill instantly.

The guard cried out in pain.

Nick landed on top of him, almost falling over the side and into the corral. He pushed up and tried to pry the blade out. That just made the guard scream louder. An arrow *thwacked* into his helmet, and Nick looked over to see Wendig standing over her kill, with a crossbow in hand.

He gave her a nod, then unslung his crossbow. He raised it at the temple, but the guards and priests up there had retreated from view.

Nick turned back to the wall they had climbed over. Whale and Fuego were in position. They both pointed behind Nick at the same moment that Wendig pulled him away. He saw the guard with a torch coming toward them, moving slowly—he must not have seen them yet.

Wendig ran to the other side of the pit, where a ramp down was gated off. Nick turned toward the temple with the salvaged weapons. He didn't see a staircase, but the stones themselves were almost like very big stairs. He climbed up, making his way toward the cage.

Halfway up, he heard a whinny and glanced over his shoulder to see a mounted warrior aiming a rifle directly at him.

A vibration shook the stone he stood on, and the warrior turned in the saddle as dozens of horses stampeded up the ramp. Wendig rode one of them, with only a leather thong around its neck.

The Horse Lord aimed his rifle at her, but Nick had already aimed his crossbow. He fired a bolt that hit the man in the side of the head, knocking him out of the saddle.

Gunshots came from the wall, where Whale had opened fire with an assault rifle.

Nick kept climbing the rope, slipping but then pulling himself up. He got to the cage with all the prisoners standing inside. Quickly, he hauled out his weapons and tossed them inside the cage. Wendig arrived a minute later and did the same.

Arrows streaked up, cracking against the stone blocks. Despite the threat, Nick drew his cutlass and raised it high. He brought it down, shattering one of the two locks.

A bolt hit him in the side, punching through the armor and penetrating his flesh in a hot-icy jolt. He raised the blade again, then swung at the other lock, breaking it off.

With a war cry, el Pulpo pushed the gate open. He grabbed the cutlass from Nick and leaped off the ledge, falling nearly ten feet to the bottom level. Then he jumped to the ground and snatched the mane of a loose horse.

Wendig shouted from horseback for Nick to flee, but he couldn't leave without Mac. His friend was somewhere inside the pyramid. He snapped off the arrow shaft sticking out of his armor, growling at the pain. Then he raised his pistol and started toward a door in the pyramid.

A priest stood there with a torch. Nick motioned for the man to get back, but instead he swung the burning torch. Nick shot him in the thigh. The priest howled in pain, dropping to the ground.

"Where's the other prisoner?" Nick shouted.

The priest glared up at the pistol barrel between his eyes.

"Unlike you, I will see the Lord when I die," the man said.

"You sure about that?" Nick asked.

The man stared back at him.

"I'll happily send you to your Maker. You have two seconds to decide. One…"

The priest raised a shaky finger. "Take this passage, then the stairs down two levels, then go through a gate. The prisoner is inside."

"Good choice."

Nick smacked the priest in the head with the pistol, knocking him unconscious. Wincing from the arrow wound, Nick got up and started into the temple with the torch. A warrior burst around the corner ten feet ahead. They both raised their weapons at the same time, but Nick got off two shots before the man could fire his rifle. He crumpled to the stone floor.

Stepping over the body, Nick turned the corner with the pistol. *Clear.* Then he picked up the fallen warrior's rifle and slung it on his back. Finally, he took the dead soldier's knife.

With the priest's torch in one hand and his pistol in the other, he headed toward the stairs. The din from the battle raging outside grew distant. He knew he had very little time. Maybe no time, but he couldn't leave without Mac.

Two levels down, Nick blasted the lock off the gate and swung it open, moving into a chamber with an altar.

"Mac," he said. "Mac, you in here?"

A muffled voice came from behind a stone door across the room. Nick rushed over to the door and planted the torch in a wall sconce. He set his rifle down and began the search for a knob or handle of any kind by running his hand along the wall. When he didn't feel anything, he wedged his knife into the gap and pried. His side burned and bled from the force.

Taking care not to break the knife in two, he guided the blade against the stone edge, and a gap began to form. It widened, and a hand emerged, helping from the other side. Nick put his boot against the wall and pulled, expanding the gap enough for Mac to slip through.

When he stepped out, Nick didn't quite believe it was him.

"Mac," he murmured.

"You got to be kidding me," Mac replied. "Nick, how the hell—watch out!"

Nick whirled as a guard burst into the room. He drew his pistol and fired a shot that missed. The next pull of the trigger clicked, the magazine empty. The guard rushed him with his sword, but Mac yanked Nick backward. He hit the wall, saw the torch, grabbed it, and tossed it at the guard.

Mac picked up a glass jar from the altar and plucked the lid off to toss a furry black spider at the Horse Lord. The man screamed, swatting at it as it landed on his helmet.

Nick used the moment's distraction to shove the knife through the man's neck. He collapsed, dropping the sword as his hands went vainly to his neck. After grabbing the sword, Mac led the way back to the exit. They raced up the stairs as sporadic gunfire echoed outside.

Nick took point, guiding them to the tunnel where he had knocked the priest out. The man was still there, curled up, unmoving. Nick limped forward, gripping the bloody knife.

Keeping to the shadows, both men peered out over the terrace, where dozens of horses ran loose over the stones. Nick scanned the distant walls for Fuego and Whale and saw Fuego helping a severely injured Forge up to the top.

"There," Nick said.

After Forge was up, el Pulpo went next, climbing the rope. Searchlight beams shot across the terrain, raking over the ground and walls as arrows flew from guard towers.

"Come on," Nick said.

Mac grabbed him, saying, "It's too far to the wall. We won't make it. We have to find—"

Voices echoed out of the passage behind them. Cornered now, they had no choice but to try to escape this way. Mac took point down the stairs to the ground level of the pyramid. He kept close to the base, moving in the opposite direction of the wall where the other Cazadores had escaped.

Distant gunshots cracked, and panicked voices called out. Thunder masked much of the noise, booming as if the very Horse Lords, or perhaps their gods, were bellowing in rage. Nick and Mac skirted around the edge of the pyramid, coming out near the aboveground livestock pens.

Shouting drew Nick to a commotion on the other side. He crouched with Mac as a Cazador in armor rode a horse in circles, surrounded by enemy spearmen on foot. The rider yelled in an arrogant tone that Nick recognized—it was Wendig.

A burst of automatic gunfire exploded from the temple above them. The bullets hit the ground in front of the horse, who rose up on its back feet, dumping her from the saddle. She crashed to the ground but was immediately on her feet, holding a knife.

"Down there!" someone shouted.

Lights hit Mac and Nick. In the bright glow, he saw a humanoid figure above them, but the arms were wrong, as if it had wings.

"Ah, shit," Mac said.

The lights centered on the queen, her dress whipping in the wind behind her as she stepped down the stone stairs. She shifted her submachine gun from Wendig to Mac and Nick.

"I need them alive!" Latuh screamed.

The forces moved in toward Wendig as she snarled and slashed out. One of the Horse Lords threw a lasso at her but missed.

Along the bottom of the pyramid, Nick and Mac came together, back-to-back, as four Horse Lords surrounded them.

"Don't let them take you," Mac said. "It's better to die fighting."

Heart pounding, Nick nodded.

The enemy soldiers strode forward, feinting with their spears, testing them. Mac slapped one of the blades away with his sword.

"That's him," shouted a Horse Lord above Nick and Mac on the pyramid. "The demon who killed Prince Rin."

Queen Latuh fired another burst into the air.

"Halt!" she shouted. Then she handed the weapon off to a guard beside her. Reaching to her belt, she pulled out a long, curved knife. She walked across the tier of stones, stopping just above Nick and Mac, glaring down at them.

"Take Mac," she commanded. "The other one is mine!"

The four Horse Lords simultaneously attacked Mac, knocking his sword away and slamming him to the ground, where they pinned him. The queen jumped down in front of Nick, slashing outward with her blade. He jumped back, but there wasn't much room to move—only a few feet to the temple wall.

She slashed at him again, her dress billowing up around her, and forced him back another step. Nick knew he only had one chance. As she drew back to strike again, he lunged with his knife, the tip cutting through the silver necklace around her neck. The black obsidian pendant fell away, but there wasn't a spray of her blood that followed. Only an icy jolt that ripped through Nick as she jabbed her own blade into his upper chest. She grabbed him by the shoulder and pulled him forward onto it. His gaze went down to the blade sticking in his flesh.

"This is just the beginning of your pain," she hissed.

✳   ✳   ✳   ✳   ✳

Mac shuddered at the screams that rose over the clash of thunder. He forced himself to remain quiet, knowing that any protest from him would only make it worse for the young man.

A violent storm had swept over the jungle, deluging the pyramid and its surroundings. Waterfalls cascaded down the stone stairs to where two horses stood with ropes tied to their saddles. The other end of each rope was attached to one of Nick's wrists or ankles. Wearing nothing but a loincloth, he lay stretched out in the mud.

Queen Latuh clearly had no interest trying to learn the location of the Metal Islands from Nick—only in avenging her son, whom Nick had apparently killed out in the wastes.

"Again!" Queen Latuh shouted from the top of the pyramid, her wet dress clinging to her. Two priests, also drenched, stood beside her.

Mac shivered from the cold in the same cage where the other Cazadores had been held captive. It was just him and the young woman, Wendig. She crouched in the corner, looking away from Nick as the horses drew the ropes taut.

They took another step, until every muscle and tendon in his body felt stretched to the limit.

Mac forced himself to watch. Part of it was awe—Nick had strength and spirit unlike anything Mac had ever seen. Making it this far wasn't merely amazing; it showed the grit and determination of that spirit. And Nick had risked his own freedom and life to come into the pyramid and try to save Mac.

Blood oozed from the bandages on his stomach and chest as his body came taut.

"Where's the rest of the army?" Mac whispered in Spanish.

"The Black Order is with Lord Portatormentas," Wendig replied. "Last I saw them, they were in the harbor on that golden ship."

Nick let out a terrible scream that made Mac clench his jaw. The scream lasted several agonizing seconds before the horses stepped back, dropping Nick into the mud. He rolled on his side, spitting out dirt and gazing up at Mac.

Their eyes connected, and Nick gave him a nod as if to say, *I'm okay.*

The young man had the mental strength and resolve to endure the pain, but his body would eventually succumb to the torture. Seeing no way to rescue him, Mac considered an alternative—find a way to end his suffering.

A horn blared from a guard tower flanking the main gates. They drew apart, letting in a horse and rider. The warrior dismounted at the bottom of the temple stairs. Taking off his helmet, he rushed up to the top, bowing before the queen and priests.

Mac couldn't hear the message, but whatever it was, it drew her gaze to the jungle. She turned to the giant warrior Guerrero. He made his way down the stairs to their cage. Using a key, he unlocked it, then stepped inside, looking from Mac to Wendig.

The big man strode forward as Wendig stood up in front of him, a good two feet shorter. He grabbed her by a fistful of hair and dragged her out. Kicking and swearing, she fought until he slapped her on the side of the head.

The door slammed in Mac's face, and he watched the giant take her down to the pens. She was strung up by a rope and dangled over the hogs, who looked hungry.

Wendig kicked up, holding her feet above their hungry mouths, but she wouldn't be able to hold on forever. Her screams were masked only by Nick's as he was stretched once again.

"Stop!" Mac shouted, unable to control himself another moment.

Guerrero pulled him from the cage next, marched him up the steps, and pushed him to his knees in front of Queen Latuh.

"Who is this man to you?" she asked.

Mac ignored her, keeping his gaze down and trying to silence the screams of both Nick and Wendig.

"You know him; he came for you," said the queen. "He risked his life for you. Is he your son? Wouldn't that be ironic!"

She used her knife to lift his chin.

"You can't save his life, but you can end his suffering." She licked her lower lip. "Tell me where the Metal Islands are, and I will give him a swift death. The girl too."

Mac forced his chin down against the knife, feeling the sharp blade cut into his flesh. The prick of pain made him pull up out of instinct. The queen withdrew, standing and shaking her head. Then she raised her hand.

"Again!" she shouted.

The screams that followed were the worst yet as the horses pulled, threatening to pop arms and legs from their sockets. Soon they would rip out altogether.

"You *will* tell me," said the queen.

Mac closed his eyes, recalling how Nick had come screaming into this world back at the bunker. He would be going out the same way.

Wendig let out a howl of her own, joining the chorus of pain.

For the next agonizing hour, Mac listened to their voices until Guerrero hauled him to his feet. The giant pushed him down by the back of his head, forcing him to look at both Nick and Wendig. She was still hanging, trying to keep her legs above the hungry jaws.

Over their sniveling noises came screams from Nick as he was dragged away by his strained limbs.

"Still not ready to talk?" asked the queen. "I guess we will move to stage two."

She nodded at Guerrero.

"Give the filthy abomination a bath," she ordered.

The warrior pushed Mac to the stone, then lumbered down the stairs to a fire pit beneath a massive iron cauldron of water hanging from metal beams. The guards dragged Nick there, dumping him at Guerrero's feet. He bent down to grab Nick, leaning right into a lazy, slow punch Nick threw up with his good arm. The behemoth didn't even flinch at the impact. He grabbed Nick in a bear hug and squeezed.

Nick headbutted the man in the nose. The crack echoed

across the grounds. Mac couldn't believe his eyes. Somehow Nick still had fight left in him, even after being stretched and beaten.

The giant lumbered over to the edge of the fire pit with Nick in his grip, then tossed him into the iron cauldron with a splash.

Queen Latuh held out her arm, and another Horse Lord handed her a bow. She put an arrow in, raising it and aiming at the wood under the bowl. Another soldier lit the arrow. She loosed it immediately, the bolt streaking right into the oil-soaked wood, which burst into a bright blaze.

"No," Mac whispered. He wasn't sure he could watch Nick be boiled alive.

"You don't have long," Queen Latuh said. "Tell me what I want, and I'll end his pain."

Nick thrashed in the cauldron with his stretched, injured arms. Even in the sheeting rain, it wouldn't be long before his skin peeled off like a boiled chicken.

Mac shook as the seconds ticked by with the impossible decision.

"You can end this," said the queen.

Lifting his bloody chin, Mac looked at her. No longer did he see the beauty of her features. He just saw the same evil he had seen in el Pulpo.

The stone suddenly trembled under his knees. Queen Latuh must have felt it, too, as she faced the dark wall of jungle.

Whatever Mac was feeling grew more powerful, like a small earth tremor. *The Horse Lords she deployed are returning,* he realized. The vibrations came from hundreds of hooves pounding the ground at a dead run. *That must have been what the scout told her,* Mac thought.

Cracking and crunching sounds came from the jungle.

Mac tilted his head at the odd racket.

Horses didn't destroy trees.

A horn blared in the distance, and Queen Latuh turned to her guards, who raised their bows with arrows nocked.

"Queen Latuh," Mac said, "you don't need to go to the Metal Islands, because the Metal Islands are coming for you."

CHAPTER 23

Nick flailed in the warming water. He let out a scratchy scream into the air. As if in answer, lightning forked out of the storm clouds. Rain poured down, keeping his face cool but doing nothing to fight the rising temperature of the water.

He turned, his injured shoulder touching the scorching metal rim.

"Ahhhh!" he groaned.

His battered, cut body was a world of pain. He closed his eyes, wanting it all to end. In his mind, he saw a single face—Sofia, telling him not to give up, to keep fighting.

And fight he did, trying to keep his head above water. But the water was quickly warming, and every part of him hurt.

A distant explosion roared through the night. But this wasn't thunder.

Shouting came from all directions, including the temple far above him. He glimpsed Mac on the ledge above, being yanked back by a Horse Lord.

Automatic gunfire chattered in the distance. Booms from bigger explosions shook the pot. Somewhere beyond the agony,

Nick managed to register the reality: Those noises meant the Horse Lords were under attack. Lord Portatormentas had sent the rest of their forces.

But for Nick, it would be too late.

He screamed again.

A voice answered him in Spanish.

"Hold on, Small Dog!"

Nick opened an eyelid to a dark blur surging toward the pot. The blur took on a humanoid shape, then became Whale. Fuego was right behind him, firing an assault rifle.

Whale slammed into the pot, knocking it on its side and dumping Nick in the mud.

Gunfire boomed above him, hurting his ears. He raised his head as hands grabbed his feet and dragged him away. Through blurred vision, he focused on the main gate, some five hundred feet to the east. A group of fifteen Horse Lords on foot were running in that direction. Flaming arrows arced away from guard towers along the wall facing the jungle. A brilliant burst erased the tower on the right side of the gate, the guard cartwheeling away.

Whale suddenly stopped dragging Nick. A grunt came from behind, then a cracking sound and a pained cry. Nick turned to see that Whale ran a Horse Lord through the chest with his sword. He pulled the blade out, and the man fell backward into the mud.

Nick tried to push up with his stronger arm but collapsed in agony.

Another blast rocked the wall to the east. The gate burst outward, sending metal and wood shrapnel flying through the air. Smoke curled out. A figure on a horse emerged where the gate had stood. Smoke swirled around the beast and the half-naked, bandaged man in the saddle.

"El Pulpo!" Nick cried.

The warrior raised an axe and let out a war cry as armored

Cazadores rushed through the destroyed gate, hurdling over the burning wood debris and following their captain. Burning arrows and gunfire flashed across the grounds from dozens of Horse Lords who had emerged from the underground tunnels. The few civilians caught out in the open scattered for cover.

"You okay, Small Dog?" said a voice in Spanish.

Nick turned to see Wendig limping over to him, using a spear shaft for a crutch. From what Nick could tell, there was no one else behind her. The entire terrace to the western wall was abandoned, giving them the perfect opportunity to escape with Whale and Fuego.

But Nick wasn't leaving without Mac. He glanced up the pyramid to see Mac on his knees on the highest platform, with Guerrero holding a sword to his neck. The queen was up there, too, firing down with her submachine gun, surrounded by a phalanx of Horse Lords.

The archers and snipers fired down from the pyramid, taking shots at the destroyed gate and beyond, where Cazadores were still coming from the jungle.

Horse Lords on foot used cover on the ground to slow the attackers' advance. El Pulpo, on horseback, charged toward a pair of warriors standing behind a stone slab. The horse leaped over it, and he hacked with two axes while the beast was airborne. It came down on the other side of their position as both Horse Lords crumpled with grisly head wounds. Dozens of Cazadores charged in a roaring wave of war cries, the ground rumbling under their feet.

"I have to help Mac," Nick said.

He knew that likely meant death, but he was prepared for that after getting this second chance. Holding the arrow wound in his side, he limped over to the stairs, but he wasn't alone. Wendig hurried after him while Fuego and Whale moved ahead. The squad crept up the back side of the pyramid while the Horse Lords were focused on the frontal attack by el Pulpo. Explosions burst across the walls, sending defenders flying like rag dolls.

Nick stopped when he heard loud crashing and smashing from the jungle in the respite between bursts. To the east, trees swayed from side to side, cracking as if some giant monster were rampaging through the jungle. A flash of light streaked out, smashing into the stone wall near the gate. Chunks of stone blew outward.

"What in the…" Nick started to say.

Another projectile fired from the jungle, punching through the wall and opening a massive doorway. Through the opening chugged an armored vehicle with a turret cannon.

A tank…

Stones bounced harmlessly off the vehicle's armored sides as it crashed through the wall.

Nick moved again for a better view. More Cazadores were leading the tank. But how had they gotten here so fast? El Pulpo couldn't have returned to the coast and brought them all this way in mere hours, unless…

They had been on the way all along.

Lord Portatormentas had used el Pulpo and the Cazador greenhorns as bait and then attacked at the perfect moment, while the queen and her people were grieving their dead prince and torturing captives to find the location of the Metal Islands.

The gun on the tank rotated right, toward the pyramid. Another boom echoed across the terrace. Then came the detonation, sending rock and pieces of Horse Lords flying through the air.

Behind the tank came more crazed Cazadores, screaming war cries.

The Horse Lords on the ground abandoned their posts,

fleeing back to their temple. The tank's gun turned on them, firing into a group of four and sending up a geyser of bloody dirt and armor.

Machine-gun fire cracked from all directions, cutting through the retreating Horse Lords. Tank shells burst, leaving bloody, smoking craters across the temple grounds. The tank motored through, bullets pinging harmlessly off the sides while its cannon wreaked wholesale havoc.

Nick kept going up the stairs, each step more agonizing than the last. His vision dimmed, but he pushed on. Wendig grabbed him as he wobbled. She helped him, moving side by side as the battle raged to the east.

At the top, Whale surprised Guerrero, grabbing him from behind and tossing him down the stairs, one of his arms snapping from the impact. He howled in agony before his voice was drowned out by the crack of Fuego's assault rifle, killing two of Queen Latuh's guards. She turned toward him with her submachine gun and pulled the trigger.

Nothing happened.

She tossed it away and pulled her knife.

The gunfire and explosions grew sporadic. Distant cries echoed up as Cazadores clashed with the last defenders. The battle, by the sound of it, was already over, and Queen Latuh seemed to know it.

Whale had Guerrero subdued, a foot on his neck below, ready to stomp his spine. But that was a last resort, Nick realized, for this man would be a valuable addition to their army if he made the decision to join them.

Queen Latuh walked over to Mac, her dress whipping in the wind.

"Deep down, I knew that evil would eventually take this place," she said. "I thought brutality might save us, but I was wrong."

She looked out over the terrace and her defeated people.

The tank stopped in front of the temple, the barrel raised up at the queen. A hatch on the turret popped open, and out came a warrior with a horned helmet.

El Pulpo's son.

"You want my treasure, and our flesh to feast on?" Latuh shouted down. "I'll kill us all before I allow that."

Thunder boomed above as she raised her hand. In it was an electronic remote control.

"One touch of this, and this entire pyramid and everything underneath it explodes."

As the thunder faded, Nick heard the clatter of hooves on paving stones. He noticed a shadowed beast loping up the ramp to the top of the pyramid behind them. In the saddle was el Pulpo, a grin on his bloody face. He whistled, and the queen spun about, brandishing the remote control. El Pulpo's axe met her halfway, and the remote fell to the stones, still clutched in her severed hand.

She howled in pain, retreating to the edge of the stone. Bending over, she gripped the gushing stump. El Pulpo rode over to her, then pulled on the reins, causing the horse to rear up. A hoof kicked her in the face, erasing her beautiful features and sending her over the edge to the level below.

El Pulpo dismounted with his axe. He hopped down to the platform where she lay crumpled, blood gushing from her missing wrist. Grunting, she tried to spit as he brought the axe down on her neck.

Two hacks later, he held the queen's head by the hair. He stood and raised it into the air, to the cheers of his Cazadores below. He then took the head over to Guerrero, holding it over the defeated giant.

El Pulpo said, "Mac *Suertudo*, tell him if he wants to keep that ugly head, then he will fight with us."

Mac relayed the words in English, and after a moment of consideration, Guerrero bowed in defeat, just as Mac and Nick had done three years ago at ITC Star Station.

"*Perrito*," el Pulpo said, gesturing to Nick.

Nick limped over to stand beside his own conqueror.

"If not for you risking your balls to save us, I would be pig shit," el Pulpo said. "Stand tall, Small Dog. You have earned a great reward. Whatever you want is now yours."

*   *   *   *   *

Two days after the defeat of the Horse Lords, el Pulpo and his son had led the convoy of the tank and three trucks back to the harbor to reunite with Lord Portatormentas and his forces. Nick rode in the back of a pickup truck with Wendig sleeping by his side. They were lucky to have survived their capture, but healing would take time—and not just for their physical injuries.

For Nick, it was the mental side of what he had witnessed on his first raid. He had lost pieces of himself out there, parts of his soul. And this was just the beginning. El Pulpo had singled him out on the stone temple, in front of the Cazador troops, making it clear that Nick was a warrior to be respected and honored. And that he could have a reward.

Nick could think of only one thing he wanted: to free Sofia.

That was the one thing that kept him from wallowing in guilt over all the people he had killed for the Cazadores under el Pulpo.

He could see the captain now, riding in the turret of the machine that had breached the walls of the Horse Lords for the first time in over two centuries. The tank rumbled in front of the convoy, pulling cages full of captive women and children. Some had escaped into the jungle during the attack, but Nick knew they would likely die out there without food, water, weapons, or protection from the radiation.

The survivors would face the same horrors he had encountered before he decided to fight for his own freedom and for Sofia.

He tried not to look at the faces of the captured people. In them, he saw her, Smitty, Ron, and himself.

The convoy emerged from the jungle, hitting the coastal city that bordered the outpost that had cost them so dearly. Before them stretched the endless dark expanse of sea. In the harbor, the *Golden Sentinel* sat at anchor. Boats were already motoring away from it to receive the slaves and plunder from the temple.

Nick nudged Wendig, stirring her awake. She blinked a few times, then followed his finger out to the *Golden Sentinel*.

"Didn't think we'd see that again," Wendig said in Spanish. She looked over and grinned, showing off a newly chipped front tooth. "You did good, Small Dog."

"You too, Chipper."

She cocked an eyebrow, then reached up and felt her tooth before breaking into a chuckle. "Good one, Small Dog. Maybe you do have a sense of humor."

Nick didn't feel like laughing, but he cracked a smile.

By the time the convoy drove through the gates of the outpost, two trucks and an armored personnel carrier were driving up to meet them inside. The tank rolled to a stop in front of a charred silo, nothing but the husk remaining.

El Pulpo jumped down from the tank to the dirt, holding a bag. Mac, Hammerhead, and three other surviving Barracudas moved up behind their captain to receive Lord Portatormentas. The hatch popped open, and Horn climbed up in the turret but said nothing.

Nick and Wendig went back to stand with Whale and Fuego and watch.

"Maybe he'll get to keep his head now," Whale said.

"Keep his head? El Pulpo will get a promotion for the gold he brought back," Fuego said.

Nick watched four soldiers unloading the captured treasure in wooden crates stowed in one of the truck beds. They lugged it over to the front of the tank, setting it down in the dirt where el Pulpo pointed. Behind them, sobbing rose from the cages where the slaves huddled together, terrified. Again Nick was transported back to his own experience of being captured. Now he was doing the same to others.

If he hadn't tried to rescue el Pulpo, maybe this would never have happened. Those people would still be free.

They attacked the Dragon *first*, he reminded himself.

His mind turned to Sofia, the person he cared about more than any other. Joining the Cazadores, rising through the ranks—all of it was in the effort to save her. He had to remember that, to keep himself focused through the horrors of the wastes. Maybe he had accomplished that. Maybe el Pulpo would grant her freedom for the sins Nick had committed out here.

The loud rumble of an armored personnel carrier snapped him from his thoughts. The brakes squeaked as the vehicle entered the outpost and came to a stop. Two pickup trucks pulled up and disgorged six Cazadores in black armor from the cabs. Twelve more climbed down from the beds in back.

A door on the APC opened, and Colonel Vargas jumped down. Colonel Santiago came next. They both stood and saluted as Lord Portatormentas grabbed a handhold and extricated his jiggling mass from the vehicle. Another six of his Praetorian guards got out of the back of the APC, along with Ernesto the scribe and the mage, carrying a golden box.

El Pulpo walked over, bowed, and pulled the head of Queen Latuh from the bag.

"The leader of the Horse Lords, Queen Latuh," el Pulpo said in Spanish. "A gift for you—one of many."

Lord Portatormentas took the head and handed it to the mage, who stuck it into the golden box. Raising a finger, the lord motioned for the scribe.

"Document my victory over this Queen…" Lord Portatormentas looked to el Pulpo.

"Latuh," he said.

"Queen Latuh."

Ernesto flipped a page up and began writing on his clipboard. He followed Lord Portatormentas as he surveyed the convoy, stopping to look at the slaves. "I thought there would be more," he said.

"They put up an honorable fight," el Pulpo said. "There are mostly just women and children left, but I did save a few of their men."

Portatormentas went over to examine them. He stood outside the bars, looking in, as if deciding which tasty morsel to eat first. There were twenty-one women and fifteen children, ranging from three months old to about ten years. The mother with the baby was surrounded by four other women who seemed to be protecting them.

The lord walked around those cages and stopped at the men. Four were Horse Lords who had surrendered during the battle, including the giant, Guerrero. They all agreed to join the ranks of the Cazadores.

The other five men might also be considered for the Cazadores, but they would likely be put to use here at the outpost, to keep it running. Or brought back to the Metal Islands for manual labor.

Lord Portatormentas went back to the women. He pulled off a glove and pointed a fat finger with a large gold ring at a young woman of perhaps nineteen or twenty years.

"Bring her to my quarters," he commanded in Spanish.

El Pulpo grunted something.

Colonel Vargas went over to the cage with two of his soldiers in their black armor. The women closed in around the girl, trying to hold on to her as the warriors pulled her out.

Nick thought of Sofia again, seeing her in this youthful woman.

Anger seethed in his belly. His fingers wrapped around the hilt of his cutlass as Lord Portatormentas moved away from the slaves, clearly unhappy.

He went to the chests in the dirt.

Then he turned to el Pulpo, waving him forward.

"Where's the rest of the treasure?"

"That's all of it," said el Pulpo.

Lord Portatormentas let out a deep, bellowing laugh that ended as fast as it started. The noise echoed away.

"Your bastard son took my tank without a scribe, and I'm to believe it was all documented?" He raised his golden rings and pointed at the convoy. "Search the vehicles—all of them."

The warriors of the Black Order spread out, surrounding the trucks.

Whale and Fuego backed up to Nick and Wendig, the tension palpable. Hammerhead, Mac, and the other Barracudas were also surrounded.

"You take this outpost, then lose it, then get captured by the enemy," said Lord Portatormentas. "Your son learns of this fate and decides to take the tank. I knew of this plan, and I let it happen. You know why?"

The king pulled off his helmet and went up to el Pulpo.

"Speak," he said.

"I do not claim to know your plans, my lord," answered el Pulpo.

"I used you like a minnow on a hook, to guide me to this

temple, with plans to come slay these Horse Lords with my own blade," he said. Reaching down, he drew the jewel-encrusted curved sword. "Tell me where the rest of the gold is, and I will take only your bastard's hand for his treachery."

Lord Portatormentas turned to wave his scribe over. In that moment, Nick noticed el Pulpo give a subtle nod in the direction of the tank. When the king turned back, el Pulpo grabbed him by both wrists, easily prying the sword from his grip. Then he thrust it right through the center of Portatormentas's chest.

It happened so fast; Nick had difficulty processing what he was seeing.

Portatormentas put a hand on el Pulpo's shoulder, trying to push him back. But el Pulpo heaved the blade up and twisted it.

The guards in black drew their swords, but before any of them could strike, an explosion boomed. The tank thumped back from the recoil of the shot. Then it jerked forward, nearly crushing two Black Order soldiers who were forced to dive out of the way. The turret rotated toward Colonels Vargas and Santiago. They both froze, along with the warriors who accompanied them.

El Pulpo lifted his helmet, staring with satisfaction at the moaning Lord Portatormentas, who had fallen to his knees.

"I've dreamed of this, you fat, greedy pig," he said in Spanish.

Portatormentas tried to speak, but el Pulpo twisted the blade again. His eyes widened in agony, and he gave a pained gasp.

In a slow pull, el Pulpo withdrew the curved blade. He stepped away from his former lord, now lying on the ground. He writhed in the dirt, blood pouring from the wound just above his heart.

El Pulpo gestured for the scribe. He took the piece of paper, ripping it from his clipboard and crumpling it up.

"Document this," he said in Spanish, crouching down.

"King Mayac, the Stormbringer, choked on a chicken wing. I tried to remove it from his chest but failed. However, because

I conquered the Horse Lords and took all the spoils that come with it, his final words were…"

El Pulpo leaned down, putting a hand up to his ear.

"What's that?" He grinned. "Oh, you declare me the new king for my amazing victories?"

El Pulpo rose up, his grin gone and his face a stony mask. He drew his axe from over his shoulder.

"Is there anyone here who wants to dispute what I just said?" he asked.

The Black Order all watched their lord let out a final sigh. He flailed one last time with a fat fist, then fell still.

Santiago muttered, "His time was over. A new reign has begun."

"Yes, the era of the Octopus Lord," Vargas said.

They both bowed down.

Hammerhead raised a spear into the air. "All hail the Octopus Lord," he shouted in Spanish.

El Pulpo pumped his axe in the air as they chanted his name.

With Portatormentas lying dead in the dirt, realization passed through Nick that Sofia would be free from the chains that had bound her to the king. She would still be a slave, but Nick would have a better chance at keeping her safe, and maybe even freeing her totally from the bondage to this barbaric empire.

"Small Dog!" shouted el Pulpo. He motioned for Nick.

Trying not to limp, Nick went over to the new king of the Cazadores.

"Tell the scribes to write that it was *el Perrito* who risked his neck to bring this victory," he said. "As soon as you recover from your injuries, you will join the Barracudas. We need men like Small Dog, with huge balls and brave hearts."

Yes, men like me, Nick thought. *Monsters.*

El Pulpo gestured for his son.

Horn climbed down from the tank and walked over.

"I hereby claim Outpost Iron Reef, to be overseen by my heir," he said. "Horn will defend this terrain and keep the oil flowing so I can embark on new raids, expanding our territory and building the empire that this pile of lard failed to do."

He spat on the corpse of the former king.

The Cazadores raised their swords into the air.

"All hail the Octopus Lord!"

Nick raised his fist in the air, joining the chant.

PART4:
THE OCTOPUS LORD

CHAPTER 24

A Klaxon sounded on the *Golden Sentinel,* marking the moment everyone on board had been waiting for. Nick was one of those anxious souls. He rushed up the ladder to the upper deck, hoping to see the Metal Islands. But all he saw was darkness.

Almost three months had passed since the fall of the Horse Lords. The Cazadores had spent much of that time helping Horn transform the Iron Reef outpost into a fortress that could be defended from enemies. But it was also retrofitted with technology from the Horse Lords' pyramid to be a sustainable base. They had set up a farm and water filtration system and put the slaves to work making sure it all functioned.

Nick spent much of that time recovering from his injuries, but in the final two weeks, he had deployed back into the jungles, all the way to the pyramid to see if any of the escaped Horse Lords had returned.

Standing on the deck of the warship, he thought back to his last view of the abandoned structure and the rubble skirting the ruined wall. All he had found out there with his squad were skeletal remains of the dead. What the jaguars didn't get, the insects finished off.

Still Nick held on to the hope that some of the innocent civilians who escaped would find a way to survive and make a new home for themselves somewhere in the jungle.

It had taken work and cost the Cazadores greatly, but in the end, this Iron Reef oil facility belonged to el Pulpo, the king.

He had further cemented his power by killing a lieutenant who was loyal to Portatormentas—not because the lieutenant threatened him directly but because he had tried to send a message back to the Metal Islands saying what really happened.

And now, after what felt like an eternity in the darkness, Nick was headed back to the sunshine on a warship packed full of gold and fresh slaves. Guerrero stood in the cage below, looking out over the ocean. The greatest warrior of the Horse Lords was now a prisoner, just as Nick and Mac had been.

In the distance, a glow emerged. This man was about to see the sun for the first time.

"There it is," said a voice.

Nick felt a hand on his shoulder as Mac stepped up.

As excited voices rose in anticipation, he leaned down to Nick.

"You would have made a hell of a Ranger," he said.

Nick wasn't sure what to say. He felt conflicted. Mac seemed to sense that.

"You're doing what it takes to survive," he said quietly. "Don't forget that. Maybe someday we will find peace and freedom, but we're it now. The last male survivors of our home."

His mind raced at the thought of their bunker as the sun lit up the horizon. It didn't seem all that long ago that he had seen it for the first time. Now it had been almost four years.

He thought of all they had lost since then: Silvio, Hyena, Ron,

Smitty, Glock. Their deaths came to Nick in detailed flashbacks, especially the two that came at his own hands.

But he would do it a hundred times over again if it meant saving Sofia. And now he might just have his chance. With Lord Portatormentas dead and Nick having saved el Pulpo's life, he hoped the new king would free her if Nick asked. He would continue to serve, to fight, if it meant she could have her chains removed.

She wouldn't have to grow up fearing the Cazadores. She could live among them in peace. Maybe someday Nick could even find peace with her, as Mac suggested.

Shouting came from the command center, drawing their gazes to the deck where Lord Portatormentas had sat on his throne, eating grapes and chicken. El Pulpo was there now, hands on the rail, looking out over the deck where he had new prisoners, new loot, and barrels of oil.

The new king of the Cazadores had a thirst for conquest and the resources to keep expanding his territory.

Nick stared at the man who had killed so many of his people—his friends.

Then he looked at the warriors who had become his new friends. Whale, Fuego, even Wendig. Over the past five months, Nick had trained with them, fought with them, bled with them, and mourned the loss of Zorro.

But deep down, Nick never let up hope—not just of freeing Sofia but of escaping all this horror. That dream seemed so far off, though, as he became more entrenched in the giant war machine. That dream needed to die. It seemed only one of them could be free.

Brilliant sunshine glinted off the deck, and Nick turned, shielding his eyes. As they adjusted after months in darkness, he made out the metal rigs rising out of the clear, blue water. The *Golden Sentinel* cruised toward the largest of them all.

The warship wasn't the only vessel en route to the tower. Nick went up to the rail and looked out at hundreds of boats—skiffs, fishing trawlers, ferries packed full of people. All were heading toward the marina at the base of the rig.

A whistle blew from the command center of the warship, and Colonel Vargas strode out, barking orders for everyone to prepare for docking and to disembark in *full* armor. The reason for this was simple.

They had the rotting corpse of Lord Portatormentas on board—a secret that el Pulpo had kept from getting back to the islands. When the slain king's supporters found out he was dead, murdered by el Pulpo, there could be trouble.

Nick returned to his bunk and put his suit on over new scars and new muscles. Even on the trip, he had gained more weight, feasting on the plentiful food they had taken from the Horse Lords. By the time he got back up to the deck, the warship had eased on final approach to the giant tower, but it wasn't stopping.

The ship cruised right up to one of the slips, slamming into a fishing boat with a crunch. Deckhands and fisherman ran down the pier to escape. Rope ladders were thrown off the bow of the *Golden Sentinel*. El Pulpo stood in front of one of those ladders, no longer bulwarked in his dented armor. He had swapped it for the golden armor of Portatormentas.

As his most loyal warriors surrounded him, the new king of the Metal Islands turned to them with his infamous axe. Dozens of men chanted the Spanish motto that Nick knew by heart.

"*¡Todos alaben al señor Pulpo!*"

They followed el Pulpo down the rope ladders to the pier. From there, the soldiers marched toward the tower, the rhythmic rap of their boots crisp and loud. All around them, civilians looked on, called here because they thought Lord Portatormentas had returned.

The guards at the hatches stepped back as el Pulpo approached with his men, letting them inside the structure without a word. Nick flooded in with them, climbing the internal stairwells to the top of the tower. From there, they passed the forest of blowing palm trees and the crops growing in the fertile soil.

Thousands of people had already arrived in the Sky Arena and were standing among the many rows of seats. And they weren't alone.

In the dirt and sand below stood a middle-aged lieutenant with slicked-back hair. Nick had seen him a few times and knew him as Lieutenant Casimiro, a respected warrior who had served for many years under Portatormentas. Behind Casimiro were thirty troopers armed with blades and guns.

Casimiro drew his sword as el Pulpo and his loyal soldiers marched out onto the sand of the arena. Nick swallowed as he stood there, near where he had stood as a slave not four years earlier. Not far from the spot where he had killed Smitty. And the place he had seen Sofia with the former king. He glanced up at the skybox, which was now empty.

But the rest of the arena was packed, with thousands of Cazadores filing into the stands.

Pulling his axe from over his shoulder, el Pulpo strode over.

"Lieutenant Casimiro," he said.

"Captain," Casimiro replied, eyeing his golden armor. "Where is Lord Portatormentas?"

El Pulpo raised his hand, and the group of Cazadores behind him parted. A metal box was brought out and dumped onto the sand. Using a boot, el Pulpo kicked the lid off, revealing the head of the former Golden General and lord of the islands.

Casimiro heaved a deep breath and looked past el Pulpo, to Colonel Vargas and Colonel Santiago.

"El Pulpo has claimed the crown," Vargas said in Spanish. "Step aside so we can officially coronate him."

The men around Casimiro shifted slightly at the news, their spears lowering and swords rising in a defensive position. The heavily armored group behind el Pulpo did the same. All across the arena, civilians gawked, speaking in excited whispers.

Nick watched as el Pulpo grinned and then spat in the dirt.

"There is no need for many to die today," Casimiro said. "Only one more need join Lord Portatormentas."

In a swift stroke, he slashed upward with his cutlass, nicking el Pulpo in the nostril and eyebrow before he could react.

El Pulpo grunted in pain and pressed his thumb against the wound.

The warriors all moved in as Casimiro lunged with his cutlass, striking el Pulpo's armor over his left ribs as he managed to side-step and deflect the thrust. He swung his axe with his other hand, forcing Casimiro back.

The leaner, faster man danced around el Pulpo, striking at him with his cutlass. Blood ran from the painful facial wounds, getting in his eyes and obstructing his view as he swung wildly to keep Casimiro at bay.

The crowd watched in silence, knowing better than to cheer until it was over.

El Pulpo backed away from the strikes, then stood his ground. As Casimiro brought his cutlass down, el Pulpo pulled his hand away from his nose and blocked the blow with the thickest part of his armguard. The blade hacked into the thick leather armor and stuck there. El Pulpo smashed Casimiro in the face with the haft of his axe, crushing his nose.

The lieutenant fell to the ground. El Pulpo tossed his axe

away and grabbed the smaller man by the neck. He heaved him up, holding him in the air. Blood trickled from el Pulpo's slit nose as he held the man higher. Dazed but conscious, Casimiro stared into his eyes until, with a quick snap, el Pulpo broke his neck.

The warriors behind Casimiro bowed instantly as el Pulpo snorted blood out of his nostrils and dropped the dead lieutenant on the sand of the Sky Arena.

"Lord Portatormentas grew weak and delusional!" he shouted in Spanish. "He lost his fighting spirit. His heart no longer beat for our people, but rather for his own lust after gold. So I removed his heart. His gold is now *your* gold."

The other boxes that his men had brought were put down on the bloodstained sand across the arena. Then they were propped open, revealing treasure from the Horse Lords, to the crowd's delighted surprise. Applause and cheers rang out from all directions, echoing louder than they had for any gladiator victory that Nick had ever seen.

Imulah strode up with prepared remarks on his clipboard as a medic handed a towel to el Pulpo. The scribe then took a mic and spoke about the fuel outpost and how the new king would use that fuel to reach farther into the darkness. To find new pockets of civilization and bring them into the Cazador empire.

"A new age is upon us," Imulah said. "An age of plenty."

But not of peace, Nick thought.

There would be more war.

El Pulpo raised the bloody rag up as his people chanted his name. He placed it back over his face as a crowd of women were brought out onto the field, along with servants who had belonged to Lord Portatormentas.

As they crossed over, el Pulpo walked over to his soldiers, stopping at Nick. But he was too busy staring at Sofia walking among these women.

"You helped make this day possible, *Perrito*," el Pulpo said. "Have you thought about your reward?"

Nick continued to stare at the woman, much to el Pulpo's amusement.

"Not them," he said with a grunt. "Those are mine now."

Nick's heart skipped. He looked to the king, who laughed, snorting blood out of his nose. He clamped the rag back over it and went to meet his new brides.

Suddenly, Nick saw himself back at the Horse Lords' temple, being stretched by four horses. He had gone through all that for nothing. Sofia wasn't going to be free.

What was Lord Portatormentas's was now el Pulpo's.

Nick forced himself to look at Sofia, who had seen him now. She stared back at him, and for the first time in their lives, he saw pure terror in her innocent eyes.

*   *   *   *   *

Almost five months after returning to the Metal Islands, Nick woke up to a conch being blown. The sun poked over the horizon, marking another day at the rigs. He stretched his muscular arms in the hammock on the upper deck of the *Golden Sentinel*, now dubbed the *Sentinel*. Every day started like this, with training before dawn.

And every day, he continued to grow stronger. He had made a full recovery from his wounds in Belize. Those wounds were now just part of the patchwork of scars covering his body.

Four and a half years after his capture from the bunker in Texas, he hardly recognized his own body. Not just the scars but the musculature. Weighing almost 240 pounds, he was more than twice his size when he first came here. He had tattoos now, too, on his back, arms, and thighs, each representing part of his travels. From the skull of a monster to the pair of crossed spears on his back.

But it wasn't just his body that had changed. His heart had changed too.

It beat for Sofia, and that had interfered with his ironclad mental effort to stay alive. Most days, all he could think about was her bondage to el Pulpo. The king had yet to take her as a wife, for she was still too young. Even the Cazadores had rules about that. But soon, Nick knew, he would want her for more than peeling his grapes and polishing his crown.

"¡Levántense!" Lieutenant Forge shouted to the few warriors still in their hammocks. The scarred lieutenant nodded at Nick. He was lucky to be alive after taking multiple arrows back in Belize. Since then, he had shown Nick respect, clearly grateful for what Nick had done to free them from that cage at the temple pyramid.

Nick nodded back.

The men went over to the rack of armor rigs. Five minutes later, Nick was suited up and jogging up and down the deck of the ship, already sweating, his mind still on Sofia. After a ten-mile run, they got out of their armor and jumped off the deck into the ocean to cool down. The cool plunge finally snapped him out of his dark thoughts. This was training he couldn't afford to lose focus on, with the threat of sharks and other creatures out in the water. With the protection of two skiffs following them, they swam in the sea for two miles.

From there, it was to the mess for chow.

Wendig took a seat in front of Nick, placing a bowl full of mush on the table. She shoveled a scoop into her mouth. Nick had hardly touched his own food—more of the meat from the eyeless beasts, which had helped him grow to proportions he never imagined. He knew he needed the protein today, but he had no appetite.

"What's wrong, Small Dog?" Wendig asked.

Nick took a bite, forcing it down while ignoring her.

Whale sat down, the bench groaning under his weight.

"You still feel bad about the Horse Lord prisoners?" Wendig asked.

Again Nick ignored her, knowing he couldn't share the real truth. If any of his squad found out about Sofia, it would put them at risk, too, likely pitting them against Nick.

"You can be honest." Wendig put her spoon down. "Your people were destroyed like the Horse Lords. I'd be pissed as all hell too. But you're one of us now, Small Dog."

"One of *us*," Whale said, pounding the table.

Fuego nodded.

"Okay, anyway," Wendig said. "I want a rematch today."

Nick glanced up from his food to see she was looking at him.

"Not scared, are you?" she asked.

"Of what?" he growled.

Wendig narrowed her brow, then scowled. "What's up your ass, Small Dog? Seriously."

"Something I ate," he lied. "Gonna go take a crap."

"Without finishing breakfast? Never seen that before."

Nick left the mess, changed, and then went to the top deck, squinting in the scorching glow of the sun. By midmorning, the temperature had already soared into the nineties. Fortunately for the trainees, Lieutenant Forge allowed them to practice without their suits.

Today Guerrero joined them on the deck, his broken arm healed but his wrists cuffed and held by a thick chain. Lieutenant Forge had tried to break him in a few times in training, but like a wild horse, Guerrero refused to submit even though he had bowed his head back at the temple in Belize. He didn't speak either. Nick wasn't sure whether he couldn't or just didn't want to.

Most of the Cazadores thought it was a mistake to keep him around—that it would be better just to eat him. It was a widely held belief among them that eating a valiant enemy after killing him would fill one with the strength of the deceased warrior.

Nick thought it was all bullshit. But there was no denying that eating the humanoid beasts had helped him and the other new boots bulk up.

For now, no one would be killing and eating Guerrero. El Pulpo wanted him alive for unknown reasons.

Nick studied Guerrero, who stood stoically, his pale flesh now red from the sun. His long, dark hair blew in the wind across his long-jawed face. He stared at Nick with a burning rage in his dark eyes. Perhaps the same rage Nick had felt for el Pulpo when he first arrived—the same rage he felt now but had learned to hide.

"All hail the Octopus Lord!" Lieutenant Forge shouted in Spanish.

Nick stiffened.

El Pulpo and his entourage made their way across from the port side, where a rope ladder hung over the side. Hammerhead, Mac, and a rising star named Warthog guarded the king of the Metal Islands. Imulah, the scribe el Pulpo seemed to favor, walked in stride with them.

He translated as the king spoke to the gathered troops.

"Lord Pulpo says the day is upon us to claim our next dominion," he said. "You will all be on this raid, which will take us to Los Angeles."

Nick had heard of the Old World city and remembered one of the disc stories that told of the once-popular megacity for the rich and the famous.

"King Pulpo will sail the *Sentinel* to the Panama Canal, where King Mayac deployed the *Anaconda* and *Sea Sprite* over ten years ago, both failing in their missions to reach the other side. But where they failed, we will be victorious."

El Pulpo gestured for Guerrero. The manacled slave lumbered over. Hammerhead drew a sword, gesturing with the blade.

Guerrero spat, earning himself a kick to one of his thick thighs from Hammerhead. The prisoner kicked back and then strode forward, halting when Hammerhead swung his cutlass to keep him back.

"*Bruto sucio,*" Hammerhead muttered.

It took three armored Barracudas, including Mac, to get the filthy Guerrero to hold still and face el Pulpo. The king laughed but became agitated when the man wouldn't bow his head.

"*El caballo sucio,*" el Pulpo said.

Imulah translated. "Our king says you will have a new name, the Dirty Horse, for you are no longer a lord of anything. However, if you follow orders, you can achieve great honor among the men and women standing here with you."

Imulah gestured to Nick, Mac, and another prisoner-turned-warrior.

"You can become like them," he said.

"Why don't we just lop off that big head?" Hammerhead asked in Spanish. "I'll do it in a single swing."

El Pulpo snorted, then spoke quickly, Imulah translating again for Guerrero. "Our king says the dirty horse has been where we are going, and we need him to lead us there."

Of course, Nick thought.

Imulah pulled a rolled-up document from his satchel.

"This map was discovered in a treasure vault at the Horse Lords' temple," Imulah said. "It marks a location of powerful Old World technology that the Horse Lords went in search of. Technology they believed could power their home and expand it."

Guerrero tried to pull free of the three Cazadores and lunge at el Pulpo, but the king was fast. He swung a fist, knuckles cracking against the long jaw and knocking him to the deck. Then el Pulpo commanded Hammerhead to bring them each a spear.

The soldier trotted over to the racks of wooden staves, but el Pulpo whistled, pointing to the *real* blades. Hammerhead hesitated, *"Pero…"*

"¡Ahorita!" el Pulpo shouted, spittle spraying from his mouth. He reached up, catching one and then the other of two spears that Hammerhead tossed to him.

The king's next order surprised even Guerrero when Hammerhead came over and unlocked his cuffs. He backed away, and el Pulpo stepped up with the two spears, asking Imulah how to say something in the foreign tongue.

The scribe answered.

"Okay, Dirty Horse," el Pulpo said in broken English. "Time to break you in."

He tossed the spear to the deck, just to the slave's right. The giant picked it up, gripping it in both hands. The Cazadores formed a tight circle around the two men.

El Pulpo took off his light armor, then his shirt. Scars crisscrossed his body, including the burn marks on his shoulders and neck, from the Iron Reef, where some of his back had melted off. A tattoo of an octopus covered most of his thick back.

"What happens if this guy wins?" Nick asked Mac.

"Good question, but I think it means the crown goes to the victor."

"Not to a slave," Imulah answered. "If Guerrero bests el Pulpo, he will win his freedom."

El Pulpo and Guerrero struck at the same time, their blades clanging together in a flurry of sparks. Guerrero pulled his shaft back, then thrust it forward, the spear slicing through the air with deadly precision. El Pulpo sidestepped with surprising agility, his spear darting forward in a series of quick jabs that forced his opponent back.

But Guerrero wasn't some novice, nor was he a wild brute. His own strikes were calculated and measured.

The dance of their blades became a blur of motion, clashing and then recoiling. The crack of wood on wood, and clang of metal on metal carried across the deck.

Guerrero drew first blood, his spear finding an opening and grazing el Pulpo's side. Blood streaked out. The onlookers roared, and Hammerhead stepped forward, but Lieutenant Forge held him back.

After spitting on the deck, el Pulpo narrowed his eyes as Guerrero swung outward with enough force that it would have taken off el Pulpo's head if he hadn't ducked.

With a fluid motion, he spun around, his spear sweeping low to hook Guerrero's ankle. The wooden shaft cracked against his heel, taking the big slave down. He fell to the deck with a thud. Before he could recover, el Pulpo jammed the butt of the spear into Guerrero's crotch. The big man groaned.

"Imulah," el Pulpo grunted.

The scribe scurried over, bowing as el Pulpo told him to translate.

"King Pulpo says if you refuse to submit, he will take a testicle." He looked at the king, who went on.

"He says if you refuse again, you will have nothing but that dainty little prick between your legs. Then he'll take that, too, and feed it to the rats."

Hammerhead started laughing, but el Pulpo glared him silent. The other Cazadores watched as the king turned to them.

"How do you get someone to fight who has lost everything he cares about?" he asked in Spanish.

No answer.

"Find something they *do* care about," el Pulpo said. "Something no man wants to live without."

Guerrero held up a hand and spoke for the first time as el Pulpo's axe hovered above the slave's groin. He quickly got the point.

In a raspy voice, he said, "Okay, okay, I will lead you there, octopus warrior."

"So he can speak," Nick whispered.

El Pulpo reached down, offering his hand.

Several beats seemed to pass before Guerrero took it. The king heaved him up to his feet. The surrounding warriors watched the two mortal enemies coming together, bonded by their duel.

With a nod, el Pulpo headed off to the command center. From there, he grabbed a rail and shouted down in Spanish, "Tonight you are free to leave the ship and head to the rigs to drink, fuck, or do whatever else you desire. For tomorrow, the *Sentinel* departs for Los Angeles."

Cheers rang out, but not from Nick. While the other warriors all celebrated and laughed about what they were going to do in their few hours of leave, he simply stared up at el Pulpo.

What Nick wanted was to see Sofia again, and that was less likely now than on the day he first saw the sun. The only way he was going to do that was by killing the octopus king.

CHAPTER 25

After a quick shower, Nick returned to the barracks to change into his civilian clothes. All he had were a pair of brown trousers, which hardly fit, and a torn green shirt—both hand-me-downs that Whale wore when he was probably ten years old. The waist of the pants fit Nick, but the cuffs came up to his knees.

As he buttoned them, laughter rang out.

"You look like Peter Pan on drugs," Wendig said in Spanish.

"Surprised you know who Peter Pan is," Nick said.

"I can read."

Nick thought to crack a joke about her reading level but let it go. He just wanted to get to the rigs, get some decent grub, and get some sleep.

An hour later, he was sitting with Wendig, Whale, and Fuego on a skiff heading to the two connected Cazador rigs. Whale planned to say goodbye to his mom, and the rest of them were heading to a place called "the pit."

"You're coming with us," Fuego said.

"I'll pass," Nick said.

"What? With those clothes?" Wendig laughed. "You can't

pass; you'll fit right in. Then we'll all head to the Sky Arena and give you a mic to take over as the jester!"

Nick sighed inwardly, realizing he would be joining his comrades for a short while at the pit.

As they got off the boat at the capitol rig, he pictured an underground fighting ring where Wendig might want to go a few rounds with him. It wasn't until they took a stairwell filled with a driving bass beat that he realized the pit was a bar.

A hard-looking man wearing a bandanna and an eye patch guarded the hatch. As soon as he saw the Cazador warriors, he got off his stool and opened it to another long stairwell. Wendig shouldered past the guy, then led the way into the bowels of the rig.

The thump of bass and raucous voices grew louder. Sconce torches flickered along the way, guiding them down to a landing overlooking a cylindrical chamber five stories deep. Four balconies wrapped around the exterior were already filled with people drinking from mugs. At the bottom, a dance floor was packed with bumping and grinding bodies of scantily dressed women and muscular men covered in tattoos.

Wendig stood at the rail beside Nick.

"*Bienvenido al cielo*," she said, elbowing him in the side.

To Nick, this place was light-years from heaven. But not for the Cazadores. An excited Whale lumbered past, moving quickly down the flights of stairs to the bottom, where the mandible of a whale served as a bar, with a few empty stools in front of it.

Like all places, this one looked to have a hierarchy. As soon as the civilians on the occupied stools saw the Cazadores approaching, they hopped up and scattered.

Nick went up with his comrades to the bar, resting his back against it and looking out over the dance floor. There were booths, too, packed full of mostly young people, but a few middle-aged or older. A hefty fifty-year-old Cazador man with thick black hair and gold chains draped over his hairy chest sat in one of them, surrounded by four women half his age. Two middle-aged men stood in front of the booth, armed with swords. But they didn't look like Cazadores, although they were just as rough. The main giveaway was their long hair, which was forbidden in the military.

"That's Martino," Wendig said in Spanish. "Owns most of the fishing fleet and a few pirate boats."

So those guards were pirates. Their eyes found Nick as he observed, and one of them sneered at him.

Wendig saw that. She slugged down a shot of liquor, then strode away, pushing her way through the dance floor.

"Shit. Trouble already," Whale said. He finished off his mug, slammed it down on the bar, and followed with Fuego. Nick took off after them. He noticed passageways on the margins of the pit, with shadows of the people inside dancing on the walls: a man behind a bent-over woman, a woman on top of a man. Their ecstatic moans were abruptly masked by loud shouting in Spanish.

"He isn't one of us!"

"He's a Barracuda," said a deep voice.

Hammerhead broke through the crowd that had parted behind them. Mac and Warthog were with him. They went up to the booth where the two pirates guarding Martino had their hands on their sword hilts.

Martino palmed the table, using it for support to push his husky body up so he was standing in front of them. "This is just a misunderstanding," he said. Then he looked at the pirate who had disrespected Nick.

The man nodded, then looked at Nick and said, "*Lo siento, Perrito.*"

Nick nodded back, then turned at the sound of heavy boots.

He froze at the sight of el Pulpo, surrounded by a group of women in white dresses. He saw Sofia, and his heart leaped.

Her eyes found Nick, then quickly flitted away.

All sense of time seemed to stop. Seeing her with the king sparked in him a rage that he had never felt before. It made him feel insane.

He forced his gaze away to the other women. The oldest of the group, Carmela Moreto, guided the dolled-up women to a horseshoe-shaped booth on a platform across the dance floor. Waiters were already putting jugs and plates of fruit and fish on the table.

"*Perrito!*" el Pulpo shouted. He came over and grabbed Nick hard by the back of the neck, then turned him toward the booth. Sofia sat wedged between two older women. Nick knew better than to look too long at her in front of her new owner.

Owner, he thought, the warm rage spreading through his chest like a wildfire.

He also knew not to turn down a drink from the king, who handed him a jug of the potent tequila. Nick tipped it to his lips and drank, feeling the burn of the liquid and the burn of Sofia's eyes on him.

"*Perrito, Perrito!*" el Pulpo chanted.

Hammerhead laughed and raised a fist into the air. Even that psychotic warrior had taken a liking to Nick after his bravery at the Horse Lords' temple. The fiery liquid burned down his throat, warming his empty gut.

He handed the jug back and avoided Sofia's gaze again.

Bowing, Nick stepped away from the crowded bench. "*Gracias.*"

El Pulpo showed off his sharpened teeth in a grin, then slid into the booth, putting his arms around the women, including Sofia.

"*Siéntate con nosotros,*" el Pulpo said, gesturing to Nick to have a seat.

A hand tugged on his arm, and Mac then stepped up, saying something in Spanish about how they had food ready and would join later. Nick simply stared, his heart beating so hard he couldn't speak. He wanted to kill el Pulpo—slit his throat and let him choke on his own blood.

El Pulpo quickly lost interest as he groped the woman on his right, a Cazador who didn't look much older than Sofia.

"Come on," Mac whispered to Nick.

He backed away, returning to the whale-jaw bar. Wendig, Fuego, and Whale were there, sharing a plate of fried bread and fish. Fuego tossed Nick a piece of the puffy bread, but he had lost his appetite again.

Whale handed him a mug, insisting he take it.

Nick took a slug, doing his best to avoid looking at Sofia across the room, sitting with the monster whose life Nick had saved. But the more he tried, the harder it was. He drank more, numbing his senses—and with them, his ability to reason.

After he finished the second mug, the liquor was having an effect. He felt a sudden flash of fear.

He had to get his mind right. He couldn't throw everything away and do something stupid now. If he was going to kill el Pulpo, he needed a plan.

Head spinning, Nick pushed back into the crowd that had retaken the dance floor. Sweaty bodies bumped against him as they danced to a hip-hop song in Spanish. He forced his way out and into a passage where signs pointed to the head. Inside, he found an empty stall and heaved into a toilet.

When he came out, a hand pulled him to the side, down to a dark corner. Sofia put her finger to his lips.

"I was wrong," she said. "I don't want you to forget about me, because I can never forget about you."

She pulled her hand away.

"I know you're leaving tomorrow," she said.

Standing on tiptoes, she pulled his neck down and kissed him on the lips.

"Come back to me," she said. "No matter what it takes to survive out there."

Then she was gone, melted back into the darkness.

Heart thumping harder than it ever had during battle, Nick stood there for a few moments. When he finally stepped out, another much larger figure cut him off in the corridor. Nick went for the knife on his belt. But then he saw the face of Mac. He didn't look happy.

"You fucking crazy?" he asked. "You're lucky I'm the only one who saw you. You can't trust any of them, Nick—not Whale, Wendig, or Fuego."

Mac poked him hard in the chest. "If anyone knows your heart beats for Sofia, el Pulpo will rip it from your chest and eat it raw."

*   *   *   *   *

El Pulpo entered the command center of the *Sentinel*, dressed in a velvet robe with gold trim—no doubt from the former king's wardrobe. Mac snapped to attention with the Barracudas, Colonel Vargas, and Captain Villanueva, all saluting their king.

It was early evening, but el Pulpo already reeked of ale and the perfume of his warrior wife Moreto, who had come along for the journey to Los Angeles. The scents followed the king as he made his way to the front of the oval table covered in plastic tubes that Imulah had brought from the archives.

Mac thought of the sailors who had stood around this very

table in times past. Men of war, at sea to protect their country and to strike enemies who dare threaten them. Conquerors, like el Pulpo.

"All hail the Octopus Lord," said Colonel Vargas.

The warriors all repeated it—everyone except the man to Mac's right. Mac turned his head just enough to see Nick glaring at the king, nose sightly crinkled in anger. Mac nudged him with his elbow.

Nick stiffened and relaxed his face, but Mac was starting to worry. Back when they departed the Metal Islands, he had thought the distance might help Nick put things into perspective. But if anything, it had only made things worse. Nick had withdrawn from his squad, and Mac often saw him staring at el Pulpo as he was now.

If the kid kept this up, he was going to get himself killed—not because of raiders or mutated beasts but because of a woman who now belonged to a different sort of monster. Mac had to persuade the kid to forget about her before he did something stupid.

But how?

Mac had experienced love before. He knew it could drive a man mad and make him do things. *Stupid* things. He had grown to care about Nick, as a brother or even a son, seeing him as one of the last connections to their old life—a life of peace between humans, for the most part.

Imulah shook a rolled-up map from one of the tubes and laid it across the table. Captain Villanueva picked up a tiny gold statue of a ship and placed it on their current location, just outside Limón Bay and the city of Colón. He used a finger to trace their route through Gatún and into the Panama Canal.

Reaching over to the little pile of tokens, he picked up a second warship.

"Eight years ago, the *Anaconda* was deployed with the *Sea Sprite* to pass through the Panama Canal and look for new territory on the other side," he explained in Spanish. "The *Sea Sprite* vanished, but a search party found the *Anaconda* at anchor in Limón Bay."

He placed the *Anaconda* ship token on the map.

"Captain Zaragoza was an experienced sailor, but something happened out there. When we found the ship, it was abandoned. Not a soul aboard."

El Pulpo grunted as he leaned over the table. "This ship will destroy whatever lurks out there, I assure you."

The words in Spanish sounded arrogant, but el Pulpo wasn't just a homicidal brute—he was a strategist, who backed his play with his axe.

He motioned for Imulah to spread out the next map, showing the Pacific Coast of Mexico, California, and finally their target, Los Angeles.

Guerrero was brought over to look. It only took el Pulpo touching his sword to inspire the slave to point out their destination: an air force base.

"Three black mounds conceal an underground tunnel that leads northeast," he said. "You will need excavating equipment that we lacked."

El Pulpo tilted his head slightly as Imulah relayed the info. "Ask him why they just gave up and went home after traveling so far," the king said.

Guerrero's eyes flitted away slightly before rising back up to meet his gaze.

"We lost four men in a cave-in and decided to return with better shoring someday." He looked at the king. "We never got the chance. Now you do."

El Pulpo held his gaze. "Maybe you're telling the truth, maybe not. But we have plenty of time for you to get your story straight." He motioned to the guards. "Put him in the cage on the deck."

As el Pulpo turned to leave, he ordered the captain to put the ship on high alert as they approached Limón Bay. Something told Mac the king wasn't going to be on the lookout for anything besides more debauchery.

The rest of the Barracudas had the same thing in mind when they got belowdecks. As the night wore on, a game of dice started up, and jugs of liquor cracked open. Nick camped out in a dark corner, lying on bags of rice with his face buried in a book, while the rest of the Cazadores gambled and drank. A few years ago, he might have been teased about his reading, maybe even beaten for it. But everyone down here respected him.

Some feared him.

Mac observed from across the space, hardly believing the transformation from the runt whom no one expected to survive long after birth, to grease monkey in the machine room of the bunker, to defender in the assault on the bunker, and all the hell that followed.

Nick hadn't just survived; he had thrived, until just recently. And through it all, he had remained a good-hearted, caring person. But Mac had seen some of that spark dim in the young man as anger ate at his insides.

He had to talk to the kid—bring him out of this funk before they reached Los Angeles. Deciding that now was as good a time as any, he went over to sit on the bunk next to Nick, but Wendig beat him to it.

"I want that rematch, Small Dog," she said.

Mac cleared his throat, but Wendig moved ahead of him with two wooden swords. She tossed Nick one, nearly knocking his book away. He placed the book down, careful not to bend the cover. Then he grabbed the practice weapon, stained by the blood of previous fighters.

Wendig taunted Nick with her wooden sword, giving Mac an opportunity to grab her wrist.

"*¡Qué diablos!*" she shouted.

The other Cazadores looked up from their dice game.

"You want to fight, take it topside," Mac commanded in Spanish, his voice rising with just the right note of annoyance. He needed to talk to Nick away from his squad.

Wendig glared at him, furious. It was no secret that she didn't care for outsiders like Mac, and she had only recently started to like Nick after they narrowly escaped death together in Belize.

Nick got up and went to the ladder. Mac tried to beat Wendig to it, hoping to catch Nick's ear for a minute, but she pushed ahead of him, muttering something about a dirty old man and not to look at her ass.

"You're not my type," Mac shot back. "I prefer women."

His plan to talk to Nick collapsed as Whale, Fuego, and most of the Barracudas followed them up to the stern with jars of liquor. Thunder boomed as they went topside. In the short time they had been belowdecks, a violent storm had descended.

Lightning slashed the sky in a brilliant jagged fork, illuminating a distant shore littered with rubble from Old World resorts. Ravaged high-rises and condos lined the shore like shattered sandcastles.

Wendig wasn't deterred by the weather.

"*Ahhhhrrrr!*" she shouted, lunging at Nick.

He parried the blow with an upward arc of the wooden blade. She threw a punch with her other hand, hitting Nick on the shoulder as he turned. The thump was loud, but he hardly reacted.

That seemed to enrage her even more.

Wendig came swinging wildly for his face. He stepped back, meeting each sword stroke with one of his own. The crack of wood on wood carried across the deck. The other fighters stopped their sparring to watch as Wendig screamed in her fury.

Nick waited for his opportunity, then seized it, striking her across the back with his sword and knocking her to the deck. He brought it down on her neck just as she thrust her own weapon up, the tip at his heart.

A draw.

He stepped back to let her get to her feet. Then she came at him again, snarling as Nick countered her blows, easily deflecting them. Shouting rose up around them, cheering for "Small Dog," and "Psycho Girl."

He knocked her down again, but this time she rolled away behind him. Slashing backward, he nearly hit her in the head, but she avoided the blow. Then she kicked his leg hard. And again Nick hardly flinched.

Wendig screamed, striking at his neck. He reached up and grabbed her wrist, applying leverage and tossing her to the deck. She hit the surface hard, yelping in pain.

Several of the half-drunken spectators laughed, including Hammerhead, who stumbled over, clad as usual in only a loincloth. He leaned down to Wendig, offering her a jug of the liquor.

Mac noticed it wasn't just the Cazadores watching. Guerrero, who was stuck inside the open cage, sat cross-legged and stoic. But when Mac looked, he saw that the prisoner was actually looking toward the bow, completely ignoring the violence going on in front of him.

Wendig pushed off the deck, looking at Nick as she took the jug. She slugged down a long drink, then dragged a wrist across her bloody lips.

Hammerhead took the jug back but held it instead of taking a swig. His crooked gaze went out to sea. Mac noticed the water glowing on the horizon, growing brighter by the second. The group of Cazadores all turned from Nick and Wendig as they continued thrusting and parrying.

The yellow glow, almost fluorescent, burned like an underwater flare.

Hammerhead took off, shouting, *"Monstruos brillantes del mar."*

Mac knew enough to understand that this wasn't a warship. This was something alive, a bright monster of the sea—possibly what had killed the crew of the *Anaconda*.

Whatever it was, this was the biggest living creature he had ever seen or even imagined. His hand went to his belt, but he realized he had left his cutlass below, not that it would be of much use against such a behemoth.

"What is that?" Nick asked. He had stopped his bout with Wendig to gape at the glowing leviathan that appeared to be on a collision course with the ship.

A Klaxon wailed, and the ship began to turn as Captain Villanueva shouted orders to his gun crews.

Several of the Cazadores had wandered over to the rail to gawk.

"Get out of the open, *idiotas*!" el Pulpo barked from the command center behind them. The king stood at the bow rail, entering commands into the golden cuff that Lord Portatormentas had used to control the four-barreled energy weapon on the bow of the ship.

Mac suddenly understood: El Pulpo was up there activating the device, manifesting a storm for cover so they could cross the bay without being attacked. And Mac had inadvertently put them all in harm's way by suggesting a fight on the top deck at the worst possible time—all for a chance to talk to Nick in private.

"Son of a bitch," Mac muttered.

The Barracudas raced back to the hatch they had entered, when a loud, low whistle resonated from the ocean—the call of the giant beast. A humped back of gray flesh mottled with orange patches broke the surface. The broad, flat head that looked almost square exploded above the water. Long, fleshy tubercles hung from the jaw of an impossibly huge mutant whale.

Thick, cable-like arms writhed up from the water, waving back and forth as it surged toward the ship. This wasn't just a whale; it looked like the product of some bizarre coupling with a giant squid. It was becoming clear now what had happened to the sailors on the warship *Anaconda*.

Turrets on the deck of the *Sentinel* rotated toward the monster as it charged the ship.

"*¡Abran fuego!*" el Pulpo shouted.

Three cannons fired, sending up huge geysers of water around the glowing shadow surging toward the port side of the ship. But the sea monster kept coming.

Mac could see now just how massive this thing was— almost half the size of the ship. The cannons fired again, and two .50-caliber machine-gun turrets blazed to life, firing tracer rounds into the big, blunt head with no apparent effect.

"Brace!" someone yelled in Spanish.

The leviathan slammed into the portside hull, jolting it so hard that Mac flew off his feet. All around him, Cazadores ran for cover, ducking the huge, flailing arms. The massive limbs rose high above the ship before slapping down against the deck. One of them snatched Wendig, yanking her away, as another wrapped around the cage holding Guerrero.

El Pulpo threw off his predecessor's velvet robe and jumped down from the bow rail. He hit the deck, gripping his axe. Sliding, he ran forward, troops flanking him with spears to keep the terrible, whipping arms back from their king. Hammerhead ran with them, tossing out spears.

Mac caught one, almost laughing at the thought of using a toothpick to fight off a bull.

A warrior darted out of a hatch, holding a chainsaw. He tried to duck under a swinging limb, but it grabbed him by the head, plucking him away. He dropped the chainsaw, and Mac scrambled over to pick it up. He turned to a screaming Wendig, wrapped in a snaking coil. She plunged her knife into the thick hide as it raised her into the air.

"*Perrito!*" she shouted.

The limb slammed her down on the deck, hard enough to knock her out. Nick ran over as the thick limb dragged Wendig's limp form across the deck. Mac dashed over to help, when el Pulpo shouted his name.

"*¡Mac Suertudo!*" He pointed at the cage, where another limb had wrapped around the bars protecting Guerrero. The bars started to bend inward.

Mac knew that if they gave, it would crush their one guide for Los Angeles. He changed course with the chainsaw. Pulling on the cord, he tried to fire it up, but the damn thing coughed and died.

Guerrero, on his knees, reached through the bars, but he didn't scream for help even as the bars bowed in.

Mac pulled on the cord again, and again the motor failed to fire.

"Come on, you dumb pile of shit!" he shouted.

Another hard pull with the choke set, and the spark finally caught. Revving the saw, he angled it downward, the chain sizzling. The teeth cut through flesh, spraying him with purple fluid.

The limb seemed to react by squeezing harder, crushing the bars. Blinking, Mac bore down, and the arm finally retracted, half severed. It slapped Mac away, knocking him onto his back. His head bounced off the deck.

Suddenly, a blast of white light lanced downward from the

four-barreled device, firing the energy, or whatever it was, into the water. An enraged whistle answered, followed by a loud crunching noise. Fleeing Cazadores screamed as the limbs began to retract back into the water. Hands scooped Mac up under his armpits. He looked up at Nick.

"You okay?" Nick asked.

"Yeah." Mac followed Nick to Wendig, who stirred on the deck. They helped her up and over to the bow of the ship. They were cruising out of Limón Bay now, almost to Gatún. El Pulpo stood at the bow, naked except for a loincloth and his golden wrist cuff. He had fought off the beast using the weather-modification technology, but at a dire cost. All four barrels were twisted and mangled by the leviathan limbs. Mac watched the glow of the enraged beast dimming on the horizon. It was injured but alive, and someday, when they returned, they would likely have to face it again—and without the technology that had just saved them.

First, though, they had to survive Los Angeles.

CHAPTER 26

At midnight, Nick went to the top deck of the command center on the *Sentinel* for a view of the horizon. Lightning flashed through the bulging storm clouds, creating a brilliant blue glow. Waves rose around the massive warship, splashing up over the bow and across the deck. The storms seemed to worsen as they neared their destination: Los Angeles.

They were close, just hours from having eyes on the former megacity. Now on day twenty-two of the journey, Nick was anxious to arrive despite the unknowns out there. He wasn't the only one. The crew and the warriors had grown tired of the long voyage. Fights had broken out among the Cazadores—some brawls over things like rations, others over nothing but a wrong look. Everyone was ready to get off the ship, even if it meant fighting monsters.

Nick thought of Sofia's words: *Come back to me, no matter what it takes to survive out there.*

He would, even if it meant using his fingernails to claw his way back there.

A Klaxon blared, interrupting his thoughts. Hatches swung open across the ship as the entire army of a hundred hunters disembarked. There were also a hundred sailors and support technicians on the ship with them, plus their guide, the former Horse Lord Guerrero. The prisoner had been given a hazard suit and helmet, but he stood unarmed among the other ninety men and ten women, who were divided into squads. Nick joined the Barracudas, along with his comrades Whale, Fuego, and Wendig. As the youngest members, they stood at the back of the group.

The warship pushed through turbulent seas toward Marina del Rey. Ten skiffs hanging in their davits shifted in the howling wind.

But the Barracudas weren't taking those. They followed el Pulpo over to the tank that his son had used back in Belize to destroy the Horse Lords. He climbed onto the turret and looked out over the city. The armored weapon sat on the top deck's elevator, alongside four dirt bikes and two trucks.

Lightning flashed, illuminating the skeletal remains of tall buildings. El Pulpo raised an arm and pointed.

Relays clicked and motors hummed as cannons and machine guns, freshly primed and loaded, were trained on the remains of the mysterious Old World city.

Nick wondered what was out there in the darkness. The only one who knew what awaited them was Guerrero, and so far, all he had said was something about a tunnel cave-in that forced his people to abandon their search.

That was difficult for Nick to believe. The man was hiding something.

But el Pulpo seemed intent on plowing ahead. He signaled, and the elevator started down to the lower level, where a landing craft waited that would take the convoy ashore. The warriors would be the first to land, clearing the way before the other squads were sent in.

Nick got in behind the prow, finding a spot between Mac and Wendig. The landing craft slid into the water with a splash that showered everyone aboard and motored away from the massive warship *Sentinel*.

"Eyes peeled at all times," Mac said. "I got a bad feeling about this place, just based on the storms alone."

A loud, grinding jolt cut him off.

"What'd we hit?" Nick asked.

Mac shook his head, but el Pulpo just grinned and shook his axe at the sky.

"*¡Prepárense para la cacería!*" he roared.

The hunters raised their weapons and chanted, "All hail the Octopus Lord!"

Lightning cracked, capturing the king's golden armor, straddling the tank's cannon like a child on a hobbyhorse. The front ramp of the craft lowered into the water.

The convoy's engines started, and the tank led the way down the ramp and into the shallow water. All twenty Barracudas charged out, four of them riding the dirt bikes. They scrambled up the beach to scout the route. On the shore, el Pulpo whistled down to Hammerhead, who brought Guerrero over to the tank. Next, the king ordered Mac and Nick to bring over the shackles hanging on the side of the tank.

Hammerhead didn't give Guerrerro a chance to run. He aimed an assault rifle at his head as Nick and Mac brought over the restraints. Five minutes later, they had the former Horse Lord chained to the front of the tank.

Glancing at his HUD, Nick checked the radiation. The reading was so high that he had to check again.

"Holy hell," Nick whispered.

El Pulpo raised his axe again, undeterred.

And the hunt began.

The vehicles rumbled up the ancient roadway, passing a graveyard of shattered boat hulls. Nick remained on foot, scanning northeast. Mutant palm trees grew out of the poisoned dirt. Red vines and barbed bushes had taken root in a few locations, too, but not like in Houston or Belize.

Very little life had adapted here, and not much of the city proper had survived. Most of the buildings had been leveled, leaving only foundations and rubble. That made an easy line of sight east to the airport. The runways were easily recognizable from the scattered wings and hulls of ancient aircraft.

A system of ancient highway interchanges spread out to the east. Some still stood, arching into the sky in long sections. Others had long since crumbled to the ground. El Pulpo surveyed the route, then pointed down a highway that cut through the remains of the airport.

The convoy advanced down the road framed by mountains of rubble, rolling over rocks, debris, and bones. Grinding the remains of people caught here when the bombs dropped.

Terminals, concourses, and row after row of maintenance warehouses stretched out in a pattern of charred rubble ahead. The flight control tower had toppled onto the roadway, partially blocking it. The top of the structure lay on its side in the dirt. The whine of an engine bounced around the rubble piles as one of the scouts returned. He raced over to the tank, skidded the dirt bike to a stop, and gave the all clear.

The tank rolled onward, passing the last of the airport and heading east toward the air base. Unlike the airfield they had just left, there wasn't much of anything out here besides rolling black mounds.

El Pulpo sat in the turret as the tank pushed on. A few minutes later, he raised a hand, halting the convoy. A hundred yards east, Nick saw another mound. This was different, forming a C shape. A half-buried road snaked up to it. Nick looked through binos to see tracks from one of the dirt bikes.

This was it—their target. Beneath those enclosed structures was a tunnel, or tunnels, that would lead them to this technology that Queen Latuh had sought for herself.

The tank's cannon rotated toward the mound. Twisted radio towers protruded at odd angles from the wreckage. At the top, several satellite dishes lay scattered in the dirt.

The low rumble of the convoy's idling engines resonated off the rubble piles, threatening to give away their position to whatever was out there.

For several minutes, they sat there, awaiting the scout's return.

El Pulpo flashed hand signals, sending out a patrol that included Nick. He moved away from the truck with his assault rifle. Using the infrared spotting scope, he searched for heat signatures as he walked to the road. Whale, Fuego, and Mac accompanied him, along with Hammerhead and Wendig. They fanned out as they entered the central open area within the C-shaped mound.

Hammerhead pointed left, at two giant doors that sealed off the tunnel they wanted. Nick checked his scope again, this time picking up a heat signature. He zoomed in on a dirt bike lying in front of a smaller, human-size access door. The bike was off, but the engine was still warm to the touch.

Shouldering their weapons, the Barracudas double-timed over to Nick. When they were ten feet away, he slowed and moved his finger to the trigger guard. Footprints led up to the door, which stood ajar. The scout had gone inside.

Nick decided not to call out, instead sneaking up as quietly as possible. Fuego took up position just right of the door. He gave Nick a nod, and Nick shouldered the door open. He moved into a dark chamber.

What he saw through the night-vision goggles made him freeze.

Looming in front of him was an airship, propped up on massive landing pads inside a concrete hangar. He gazed fifty feet up at the bulbous bow with its protruding cockpit.

"My God," Nick whispered. He had seen one of these before, when the Cazadores first came to Houston. They had shot that vessel down, killing the humans inside, and salvaged the parts and supplies. But this ship looked different from the one he had seen blown apart above the radioactive dirt of his former home.

For one, it was shorter and sleeker, with machine-gun turrets fore and aft. This was a flying warship.

Fuego gave a long whistle. "*Caballo del cielo*," he said.

Nick stared in awe at what his friend had called a "sky horse." Was this the technology the Horse Lords had come to steal? It certainly didn't match the stories about tunnels and a cave-in.

Wendig clicked her tongue—something she did when she was excited.

"El Pulpo is going to love this," Mac said.

"Whoa," Whale grunted. He lowered the Minigun as Hammerhead walked in front of them to study the strange sky horse.

Nick also moved closer, looking at the scout's footprints, which led to a ramp into the ship. The tracks ended abruptly a few feet from the bottom of the ramp.

He bent down and tried to look up into the ship but saw only a darkened bay.

Hammerhead gave him a nod to advance.

Switching the light on his rifle to guide him, Nick walked quietly up the ramp. At the top, his beam shot into a storage bay packed with steel crates, each about eight feet tall and three feet wide and deep.

He counted a dozen of them, six of which had been opened and were now empty. He started down a row, shining his light through a gap, to an offline computer terminal across the room.

Mac followed him inside, then Hammerhead. They crossed through the maze of crates to the terminal. Nick tapped the screen several times, but it remained offline. The power was off, the ship dead.

Rifle up, Mac started through the hatch, which opened to a mezzanine over an engine room. The steel footbridge, protected by a railing, spanned over electric propulsion units, turbines, generators, and power converters twenty feet below. Nick recognized a lot of the equipment from his time working in the machine shop. It was all covered in dust and cobwebs. This told him the ship hadn't moved for a very long time.

Maybe it couldn't move at all.

Something wet hit Nick's helmet. He reached up and pulled away a chunk of something slimy. Looking up, he noticed a blob of flesh and bits of metal, like some sort of alien nest, attached to the overhead.

"What the…" Nick took a step forward, straining to see.

Protruding from that blob were a boot and a hand. And in the center…

"No," Nick gasped.

A human face with one destroyed eye and one bulging eye looked down at him. Nick watched in horror as that eye blinked, and the swollen lips mumbled, asking for help.

The unholy amalgam of burned flesh and mangled armor was the scout.

Up ahead, Mac turned. "What?" he asked.

An orange glow flickered to life from an open hatch at the opposite end of the mezzanine. A red flash streaked out at Mac. He dropped his weapon to the metal platform with a loud clatter.

But the gun looked wrong. Somehow his hand was still holding it.

In that moment, all sense of time seemed to slow for Nick.

Mac raised the stump where his arm had been blown off. The end simmered, smoke curling away from the burned flesh. He staggered forward and collapsed in front of Nick.

"Ambush!" Nick shouted.

Still not seeing the shooter, he grabbed Mac and dragged him across the mezzanine and into the cargo bay. Hammerhead helped pull him in. As Nick started to shut the hatch behind them, he caught a glimpse of a shadowed figure, partly illuminated by orange light, lumbering across the mezzanine in light armor. He slammed the hatch shut and flipped the locking mechanism, then backed away to help Hammerhead carry Mac back to the ramp. They practically slid down to the concrete floor, where Wendig, Fuego, Whale, and three more Cazadores had gathered with their weapons aimed at the ship.

"¡Regresen!" Nick shouted. "Back!"

Confused chatter arose as they heard banging inside the vessel. Then came a crash—the hatch? But how could someone break it down that fast?

More questions entered Nick's mind as he tried to unsee the scout plastered to the overhead.

He brought his rifle up as he retreated. Heavy footsteps clomped toward him.

Faint orange light spilled down the ramp. Nick trained his weapon on the hatchway.

A ball suddenly rolled down, emitting a bright flash that blinded him. He squinted at the blurred shape of a metal figure striding down the ramp.

Three flashes of red burst away from some sort of barreled weapon.

Nick crouched down, blinking to regain his vision. He saw at least one Cazador in a heap on the ground.

Screams broke out around him. He swung his rifle at the

enemy stomping down the ramp with metal feet, metal legs, metal torso. The neck connected to a helmet that Nick recognized—the armet of a Horse Lord, with the tail draping over the back.

The realization hit him. This was an ambush. Some of the Horse Lords had never left this place.

Nick fired a burst at that helmet, knocking it off. But where there should be human eyes, there was only a flashing orange visor attached to the metal skull.

He blinked again, wondering if what he saw was real.

Nick aimed his rifle at a robotic face similar to one he remembered in a disc story he had watched back in the bunker. He fired another burst into the head, one of the bullets cracking the visor as it raised the energy weapon it had used to blow Mac's arm off.

Fuego lumbered forward, launching a stripe of fire that enveloped the machine. It clanked forward, the entire exoskeleton a torch. The flames appeared to disorient the robot, and it fired wildly, missing.

"*¡Corre!*" Nick shouted. "Run!"

He grabbed Mac under his arm and dragged him away. But that wasn't going to work. So Nick squatted down and heaved him over one shoulder. Wild bolts from the burning android flashed by as he carried Mac toward the door they had entered through. They passed the remains of a soldier Nick no longer recognized, his helmet a simmering mess.

The exit was only a few feet away now. He kept going, not risking a glance over his shoulder. Whale started through but got stuck in the small aperture.

"*¡Rápido!*" Nick shouted.

With a mighty push, Whale popped through. Nick went next, turning sideways, but one of Mac's legs hung them up. Wendig was right behind them and reoriented him so he could get through. She fired a burst from her rifle, then followed.

"*¡Agáchate!*" Whale shouted up ahead.

They ducked as his Minigun whined and then roared to life.

The squad backed away, heading back toward the convoy. Nick saw the tank ahead, el Pulpo in the open turret as it rotated in their direction.

Nick hunkered down, then dropped Mac to the ground as the tank rolled ahead. Turning his head, he saw the burning robot emerge in the open hatchway. The tank's cannon fired, scoring a direct hit that sent the machine flying backward.

A dozen Cazadores moved out, weapons shouldered.

Nick looked down into the small crater just in front of the hangar door. The machine lay still, twisted and smoldering.

As Nick stood, the machine moved too—an arm at first. Then a leg.

The robot slowly rose, laser rifle gone, the arm that held it now mangled. The head hung to the side, crooked but apparently still operational.

A loud grinding sound drew the Cazadores' gun muzzles to the two main hangar doors. They parted. In the darkness of the gap, an orange glow of a visor appeared. Then a second—two more of the machines.

They moved out, raising their energy weapons. Then the doors parted all the way, revealing the airship and the ramp. A bulky robot the size of a rhinoceros clambered down the ramp. Armored plates covered its back like the shell of a beetle. Attached to its head were twin weapon barrels that reminded Nick of mandibles. They glowed an angry red as the robot moved forward on long, thick legs.

Uncharacteristically, el Pulpo hesitated for a moment, which passed. "*¡Abran fuego!*" he shouted. "Open fire!"

The tank fired in front of the open hangar doors, sending dirt and debris exploding outward. Machine-gun fire clattered from all directions as Nick got back down. Through the smoke, he saw two of the orange visors from the machines moving. They returned fire with energy rifles that cut through the bulky Cazador armor like arrows through fat. Two men near the tank went down.

Nick grabbed Mac and pulled him away, keeping low. Behind them, the huge beetle-like robot turned toward Whale, who was too busy firing his Minigun to notice. Releasing Mac, Nick raised his assault rifle, firing a burst into the dirt next to the big quadruped droid just to get it to move. The enemy laser slammed into the ground with an impact that launched Whale backward.

The robot's twin barrels turned toward a truck, firing into the front as the driver tried to back up. The explosion left the cab a smoking wreck.

Laughter came from the tank, where Guerrero remained chained down. His laugh grew louder—the laugh of a man who had tricked them all and was getting his revenge.

The tank fired again at another machine—a direct hit. Limbs and part of the torso flew in different directions. This time, the machine stayed down, destroyed.

The two remaining bipedal androids and the beetle robot halted abruptly, perhaps communicating over an encrypted network. Bullets pinged against their armor as they plotted their next move.

In that stolen moment, el Pulpo brought his axe down on Guerrero's head, silencing his maniacal laughter. But in that fleeting moment, he failed to see the machines raising all their weapons at the tank. They had made their decision.

They fired at the same time, bolts spraying the armor in a brilliant barrage of light. A concentrated blast slammed the turret as el Pulpo ducked behind it. The muscular giant that was Guerrero vanished in a pulpy spray.

For several seconds, the lasers pounded the front of the tank and the turret that the king tried to hide behind for cover. It all finally gave, armored plates bursting outward and the turret exploding upward and cartwheeling away.

Nick didn't see el Pulpo, but he saw his axe, which had landed in the dirt not far from Nick. The smoking laser rifle wasn't far either. He scrambled forward and grabbed it as he heard a Spanish word he understood but had never heard the Cazadores use.

"*¡Retírense!*" Hammerhead shouted.

Cazadores fled the battle, running in all directions. Gripping the enemy rifle, Nick scrambled over to Mac, who lay curled up in the dirt. He bent down and tried to pick him up, but Mac pushed him back.

"Leave me, Nick," he groaned.

"No chance, amigo."

CHAPTER 27

Smoke billowed up on the western horizon, where the machines had decimated the convoy hours earlier. In the chaos, Nick had escaped with five Cazadores and headed several miles north, into the city. They had been on the run for hours now, trying to put distance between themselves and the air force base where the machines had ambushed them. Nick was so focused on trying to survive he had little time to reflect on el Pulpo's death—and the fact Nick hadn't been the one to kill him.

But at least he was finally gone, and his reign of terror would end. Sofia would never have to be subjected to his disgusting hands again.

Nick turned to find the group dragging worse and worse. Everyone was exhausted and dealing with injuries from the battle. Whale lumbered along, carrying Mac over his shoulder. Fuego, Wendig, and Hammerhead staggered along with their useless weapons.

Nick kept rear guard with the one useful weapon they had: a laser rifle. He kept the heavy weapon up, watching for the orange glow of the machines behind them. But it wasn't just the demons on the ground he feared—that airship was just as scary.

So far, it hadn't taken off from the hangar.

Maybe it couldn't fly at all. Maybe the Horse Lords had taken the fuel cells, leaving it idle and trapping the machines here. That would make sense based on what he had seen. The terminal that didn't turn on, the engine room covered in dust and cobwebs. Now that Guerrero was dead, they would never know.

Nick scanned the skyline. Rain drove at an angle, sluicing down his visor. He wiped it away and kept going. The heavy rainfall turned the ground to muck, making it impossible not to leave tracks. He headed to a copse of mutant trees for cover, keeping well away from the thorned limbs. Through the thick vegetation, he could see rows of overgrown parking lots that bounded a group of collapsed buildings. Heading that way seemed a bad idea, and though Nick wasn't in charge, Hammerhead could hardly speak, let alone give orders. The normally hardened Cazador lieutenant had fallen into a daze since the attack that killed el Pulpo. All Nick could do was continue to offer advice on which way to escape, and hope Hammerhead would snap out of his shock.

He spotted an old drainage pipe jutting from a hill on the western edge of the parking lots. At the top of that hill was a roadway littered with burned-out vehicles. It was a good place for an ambush, but he didn't see the orange glow of the machines' visors. Nor did he hear the clank and clatter of their steel bodies. If the beetle machine was coming, he would hear it.

"Should we go that way?" Nick asked Hammerhead.

The man simply nodded.

Rising, Nick took point. As he approached the pipe, he got a view of the other side. It stopped him midstride. It was the same view that had stopped him back in Houston: the crater from the bomb that destroyed the city.

Nick gazed out over the earthen bowl during a flash of

lightning. He looked for a way forward, but there was only more radiation that way.

Death ahead, death behind.

Their only chance was to head west to the ocean, then work their way to the *Sentinel* before it left them here—and before Mac died. Even with his arm cauterized, the wound was exposed to toxins and radiation.

Nick returned to Hammerhead and explained his idea to make it back to the ship. But Hammerhead didn't reply.

"Lieutenant, we have to get back to the ship," Nick explained in Spanish. "We stay out here, and the radiation will kill us. We must take our chances with the machines. I'll even head out to scout us a path. You can stay here."

"Like hell," Wendig said.

"Yeah, no way," Fuego said. "We all go."

Nick considered looking at their map, but there was nothing recognizable out there to identify where they were. He must rely on his compass. He went over and checked Mac, lying on the ground.

"Hang on, okay? We're going to get you out of this hell," Nick said.

Mac mumbled something indistinct.

"Okay," Nick said with a nod to Whale.

The big Cazador heaved Mac up over his shoulder.

Nick retreated out of the tunnel the way they had come. Laser rifle up, he led the group up the hill to the road above. Their boots made some noise, but the wind masked it. Still, they were easy targets.

The likelihood of getting back to the Metal Islands and to Sofia was getting slimmer by the minute. To do so, Nick needed to become something greater—to transcend to another level, pushing emotion aside. Thoughts of Sofia or Mac couldn't break his focus.

His eyes swept their surroundings, searching for threats, moving constantly as he led the group through the blasted terrain. They walked through a mile of city blocks reduced to their foundations, then through an area where mounds of rubble were all that remained of once-grand structures.

Finally, Nick saw a landmark he recognized: a highway marked by a rusted sign with a faded shield that read INTERSTATE 10. He knew it was dangerous to take it, but it would lead them straight to the ocean. Then they could head south, back to the *Sentinel*.

Nick climbed up on a concrete wall bordering the eastern edge of the highway to look around. There were plenty of scattered vehicles—good cover. The entire road had been one huge traffic jam when the bombs fell, trapping people in their cars.

Hammerhead stepped up by his side and gave a subtle nod to advance.

It was good to have him functional again.

They set off, up the on-ramp to the road. Another hour passed as they weaved through the maze of wrecked automobiles. Ahead of them, a plane had crashed long ago, taking out an overpass. A mutant tree grew from the wreckage, and red vines twisted out of broken windows in the tail section.

As Nick approached the eerie sight, a voice stopped him.

"Help me!" someone yelled in English.

Nick hurried for cover, puzzled by the youthful sound. He crouched behind an upside-down car, wondering if his mind was playing tricks on him.

Was he hallucinating?

Turning, he saw that his comrades heard it too. Wendig crouched beside him. For several minutes, they listened to the whistling of the wind. Nick prepared to move again, right when that same voice came again.

"Is anyone out there?"

The voice was female and young, reminding him of Sofia.

It seemed to come from the other side of the plane.

Nick popped up for a look, but Wendig pulled him back down. Then she pointed to a hill beside the road. He nodded. They took off for a better look from the crest overlooking the highway. Shuffling toward the plane wreckage was a girl dressed in a hazard suit.

When Nick saw her, he knew this was no trick.

As she approached the wreckage, Nick caught a momentary flash of orange coming from a structure on the neighboring hill. He grabbed Wendig's arm and motioned for her binoculars.

Nick brought them up to his visor and zoomed in on a machine perched behind the foundation of a house, watching the highway. It was using the girl as bait.

He flattened his body on the ground and told Wendig what he had seen. She sneaked a look, then nodded. "Okay, we sneak up on it together. I'll flank and try to grab its weapon."

It was a risky plan, especially since the machines had human prisoners, which meant there were likely *more* machines.

He crouch-walked back down to the others and relayed the plan. Then he set off with Wendig around the hill, searching for the best way to flank the machine.

"Anyone, *pleeease*," the girl cried.

Nick cut through a traffic pileup that happened over two centuries ago. Keeping low, he circled back and up the hill to a block of dilapidated houses overlooking the highway. He scanned the street and other structures, knowing there could be another machine out here.

Using the destroyed houses as cover, he made his way with Wendig up to the foundation where he had seen the enemy. He shouldered his rifle, hidden behind a chimney and partially attached wall. Wendig moved into position on the other side.

The machine had set the trap, unaware that it was trapping itself.

This time, the Cazadores were the hunters.

Nick crept along the foundation as he went in for a shot. The faint voice of the girl carried up from the highway, and Nick used it to mask his approach. Coming around the side of the house, he popped up, finger on the trigger guard.

A steel-and-titanium fist punched Nick in the center of his chest. The impact threw him back against the chimney, and he slid to the ground.

Wendig darted around the side, firing her assault rifle into the robot's head. The bullets knocked it back, but the robot still managed to fire a burst from its laser rifle. She dove over a broken wall, the bolts pounding the concrete.

Nick tried to get up as the machine strode forward. It reached down with skeletal fingers to pick him up by the helmet. He scrabbled for the dropped laser rifle, but the machine had him.

Grabbing him by the throat, the nearly seven-foot-tall metal behemoth lifted him in the air. A blur moved in his peripheral vision. Another large bipedal figure in metal—a second machine!

Nick knew it was over for him then, but he squirmed and kicked as tiny dots swarmed his field of vision. The second machine fired a laser bolt into the arm gripping Nick. The metal cracked at the wrist, but the fingers still tightened around his neck.

In the next second, the new machine swung a bladed object down on the arm, severing it. Nick fell back with the mechanical hand still wrapped around his neck. He landed in the dirt and looked up to see not a second machine but a Cazador in soot-covered armor, firing a laser rifle into the chest of the robot. It went down on its back, reaching up with its remaining hand.

The warrior stepped over it, aimed down with the laser rifle, and flashed a molten tunnel through the skull.

The orange visor blinked off.

Gasping for air, Nick sat up as the Cazador who had saved him turned in his direction, and he caught the glint of gold beneath the soot.

"El Pulpo," he gasped.

"Paying you back, Small Dog," he said in Spanish, reaching down. Wendig joined them, carrying the laser rifle the machine had fired at her.

Footfalls came from behind them.

Warthog jogged over, along with two more Cazadores who had survived the initial ambush. A few minutes later, Fuego, Hammerhead, and Whale arrived with Mac.

"Three down, one left," el Pulpo said.

"The beetle," Nick said.

The armored behemoth would be the hardest to destroy. But maybe they could get back to the ship without engaging it. He looked back down over the highway, searching for the girl.

"What about the kid?" he asked.

"Not real," Fuego said. "Some sort of hologram."

Nick stared down, glad, in a way, that the child wasn't real.

"*Vámonos*," el Pulpo said, waving his axe.

The ocean wasn't far now, Nick realized as he spotted a damaged carousel that he remembered from pictures. That had to be the Santa Monica Pier.

Fanning out in combat intervals, the Cazadores charged toward it. From there, it was only a short trek down the beach to the warship. Nick hung back from point this time, letting el Pulpo lead the way. He still couldn't believe the king had survived, nor could he deny that he was actually happy to see the crazed barbarian.

The sound of waves crashing on the beach filled Nick with hope that they might actually make it out of here. When he saw the silhouette of the *Sentinel* on the horizon, that hope grew. They were almost back, almost out of this radioactive hell world.

"Just a little longer, Mac," Nick said.

Mac hardly responded as Whale lugged him across the beach parking lot. As the Cazadores hit the sand, Nick turned to check their six. As far as he could see, nothing moved out there.

The crashing waves made an almost soothing white noise on the trek back down the shore. As they drew closer, el Pulpo radioed Captain Villanueva.

Static crackled back, but no answer.

He tried again.

Nick halted when he heard a whirring. The rest of the ragtag group heard it, too, and began to turn in different directions. The noise grew louder, somewhere east of them. It seemed to be coming from the sky.

El Pulpo gestured wildly for everyone to take cover, but on a beach, there was nowhere to go. Nick dropped to the sand, aiming his rifle at the clouds. A glint of metal reflected in a flash of lightning.

His heart sank. The airship!

It was barreling right toward them. He used the infrared spotting scope to capture the smooth craft. But this wasn't the airship after all. It was far smaller, with legs folded up against an armored carapace. Two gun barrels tilted off the bow.

The beetle could fly.

Nick aimed but held his fire, waiting for the right moment. The thing zoomed closer, almost on top of them. Then, as he was about to squeeze the trigger of the laser rifle, it blasted away, arcing over the ocean.

It swooped down over the *Sentinel*. Lasers flashed down across the hull. On the beach, the Cazadores hugged the sand, watching in horror. But el Pulpo stood, walking out toward the water, axe in hand.

The *Sentinel*'s cannons remained idle, the turrets abandoned. He heard no shouts or screams. Unable to do anything, the Cazadores could only watch as the flying machine ravaged the warship, lasers cutting through the hull in vital areas as if it knew right where to strike. The hull was breached in multiple places, with flames gouting up through the jagged rents.

Not a minute into the attack, a massive explosion burst through the aft section. Subsequent blasts ripped across the bow in a chain event that obliterated the entire vessel.

El Pulpo fell to his knees, his axe dropping to the sand, as the warship began to sink.

Home just got a lot farther away.

*   *   *   *   *

Mac was going to die. Nick had accepted that. With the destruction of the *Sentinel* by the machines, there was nothing he could do for the man now. But Nick wasn't ready to give up. There had to be a way to get out of this accursed city.

He perched on a shelf of concrete, watching the sinking ship. Smoke billowed from the mangled hull across the stern, which was still above water. The lasers had cut through the hull like a fillet knife through a mackerel.

What remained of the Barracudas had taken shelter in an oceanfront building. Fuego and Whale tended to Mac, doing their best to make him comfortable. There were four more Cazadores, including Warthog, who had multiple shrapnel wounds and a bad burn to his leg.

Nick had come outside to search the pier with Wendig for a way out of this awful place. She was across the harbor, searching for something to sail back to the Metal Islands. But even if they found a suitable vessel, they had eleven mouths to feed, the injured to care for, and limited water.

Making it back home seemed impossible now.

Nick wanted to fire his rifle into the sky and draw the mechanical beetle back to them so he could at least die fighting. It beat starving or wasting away from radiation poisoning.

No, Nick wasn't going out like that.

He looked back toward the city. The rain had stopped, but the relentless electrical storm raged on, the clouds thick and black enough to hide an airship.

A thought occurred to Nick: What if they could get the airship up and running?

It was a long shot, but it just might be their *only* shot. Although it likely meant they must face the beetle machine.

Nick worked his way back to Wendig, who was shaking her head at the broken vessels in the water. She shook her head again when he explained the idea.

"What makes you think you can get it running?" she asked.

"It's worth a try, no? I don't see a single vessel that is seaworthy here."

She looked out over the water, then nodded. They returned to the building where el Pulpo was taking an inventory of their weapons and supplies.

"Crazy, Small Dog," el Pulpo said in Spanish after Nick explained his idea again. "I like it. We die fighting, on our feet, like men."

"And women," Wendig said.

El Pulpo laughed. "Yes, yes. We die like Cazadores."

Warthog sat up where he rested on the floor next to Mac.

"*Lucharé*," he said. He would fight.

Nick went to check on Mac as everyone assessed their weapons and equipment, laying out what they had left. There wasn't much: five assault rifles with twenty magazines, three laser rifles, five grenades, and five cutlasses, one with a broken end. Tech-wise, they were down to their individual battery packs plus four fresh packs. Nick planned on using one to access the terminals on the airship—to see if it could even fly.

It was a plan. They had hope.

Crouching, he nudged Mac, who laid on his back.

"Hey," Mac whispered.

"I'm going to get you out of here," Nick said.

Mac grimaced but managed a smile. "My time's over, Baker. I had a good run."

He coughed, then grabbed Nick by the wrist.

"If you do make it back, remember what I told you," he whispered. "Let her go."

He tightened his grip on Nick for a moment, then released him.

"*¡Vámonos!*" said el Pulpo.

It was time to move out. Nick patted Mac on his shoulder armor, then stood and unslung his laser rifle. Fuego, Whale, Hammerhead, Warthog, el Pulpo, and Wendig walked out of the shelter, into the darkness.

They trekked west down the shore, toward the airport. El Pulpo led the way across a runway. The warriors fanned out as they crossed toward the air force base. Nick alternated his gaze between ground and sky, scanning for the deadly flying machine. By the time they got within view of the hangars, sweat dripped down his forehead. El Pulpo crouched behind a concrete slab, waving Nick and Hammerhead up.

They each took a grenade, which they would use to disable the beetle if they encountered it. Then all three of them would blast it with the laser rifles.

With a nod, the king gave the order to advance, once again leading his troops into battle. They took the same road they had used with the convoy, and soon came upon the remains of the trucks, bikes, and tank. Mangled piles of metal lay scattered among charred pieces of armor. A few of the Cazadores had been blown apart.

Lightning forked behind the C-shaped mounds, striking the rubble with a sharp crack. It felt like a warning to stay back.

But Nick pushed on, scanning the ground for tracks and listening for the click of metallic joints and wings. Nick kept between el Pulpo and Hammerhead as they moved quietly toward the hangar. The door still hung open, the ship right where they had seen it last. Sprawled in the dirt was the first machine they had destroyed. Nick checked it and saw that it wasn't getting back up. Whatever battery or computer it had looked completely destroyed.

El Pulpo stared up the ramp, with Hammerhead behind him. Nick followed, stopping to look over his shoulder. Everyone moved up to the wreckage, weapons ready.

Wendig raised a hand, and Nick nodded back. He walked up the ramp into the cargo hold, past the metal crates. He took the railed footbridge over the engine room to the hatch where the first machine had emerged. From there, the corridor led to a few closed hatches and a ladder up. El Pulpo went first, then Nick. At the top, Nick saw the command center, looking perfectly preserved. It was as if the ship were about to take its maiden voyage.

Except that it wasn't going anywhere. Nick plugged his battery pack into the terminal to see there was no power anywhere. Completely dead. With the battery pack, he activated one of the screens. He pulled up a log, which looked like flight data—starting 270 years ago. He scrolled through it. The ship had been to several countries and had arrived in Los Angeles over twelve years ago. Then they had experienced some sort of engine failure.

Hostile threat present. Fuel cells extracted.

Critical systems going offline. Power failure imminent.
DEF-Nine units deployed to find additional resources.

His theory that the Horse Lords had come here and taken a fuel cell was all but proven now. They had somehow escaped with the fuel cell, trapping the ship and the machines here until the Cazadores came back and poked the hornet's nest. It was all one big trap, a final trick from Guerrero to avenge his people and kill el Pulpo.

Nick recalled his maniacal laughter right before he died.

He looked up from the monitor and explained to el Pulpo what he believed now to have been an ambush all along. The king stared for a long moment, then cursed and kicked a bulkhead. As he kicked it again, gunfire cracked outside the airship, drawing them both up to the viewports.

Outside, streaks of red light came from the sky, slamming into the already-destroyed tank. The explosion sent two Cazadores flying in different directions. Lowering with its thrusters over the destruction was the beetle-like killer machine, blasting away with its energy weapons at fleeing Cazadores. The thrusters burned blue as it extended all four legs to land. The twin barrels rotated, searching for targets.

El Pulpo and Hammerhead bolted outside from the vessel, but Nick had a better idea. He used the battery pack in his suit, giving the dashboard enough juice to activate. Then he scanned the screen, looking for something to make a distraction, and finally saw the control for the lights. He tapped the button, and weak beams shot out from the bow.

Sure enough, the robot oriented itself toward the ship. Nick pulled the grenade off his vest. Outside the hangar, the eyeless machine seemed to stare at him, processing in milliseconds this new threat—not to itself but to the ship. Nick held up the grenade, taunting the enemy.

It bounded forward, kicking up dust with its padded feet. Bullets pinged against its armor as it left the surviving Cazadores. The four-legged droid clambered into the hangar, ignoring el Pulpo and Hammerhead, who fired their laser rifles as Nick looked down from the cockpit. His heart thudded. He had its attention now.

After hooking the grenade back onto his vest, Nick grabbed his laser rifle and bolted to the bridge over the dusty equipment below. He halted at the sound of clanking metal in the cargo hold ahead.

The machine was inside the ship.

It slammed into the steel crates, knocking them aside. Nick aimed his rifle as it bounded toward the open hatch. In that frozen moment of time, Nick felt pure, raw fear—not from man or beast but from machine.

"*¡Dispara!*" el Pulpo shouted from the other end of the cargo bay.

Nick pulled the trigger, firing at the robot as it raised one of its twin barrels at him. He dove away from the return bolts flashing across the room as Hammerhead and el Pulpo flanked the machine from behind. Using its thrusters, it blasted crates like so many toy blocks while firing in all directions. Something hit Nick before he could get up, launching him back to the bridge over the engine compartment, losing him his weapon in the process. He heard it clatter through the railing and hit something below.

He pushed himself up onto his forearms and looked down into the cargo bay, where the machine was back on the deck, firing at the golden-armored shape of el Pulpo, who dashed about like a madman between crates while firing his laser rifle.

The enemy return fire was almost continuous, and at least two bolts hit el Pulpo's heavy armor. Nick was amazed that the king could still be moving at all, but the armored suit was far more powerful than normal Cazador armor. Still, it wouldn't hold forever, and Nick had to help.

He got up and looked over the railing on the bridge to see that his rifle had landed on a generator below. Nick turned at the sound of heavy footfalls drawing closer. And he realized that the firing from el Pulpo had stopped.

The beetle machine clambered toward him, having neutralized the other threats. The square plates were speckled with red, glowing holes like stings from mutant bees. Nick pulled out the grenade again. If he was finished, he was taking this infernal machine with him.

Nick took a step back, enticing the beast across the bridge. It aimed its lasers at him but didn't fire.

"That's right," Nick murmured. "Just a few more steps."

The machine charged, slashing out with a bladed foreleg that could cut him in half. He leaped backward, hitting the low railing of the bridge and toppling over the side. Somehow he managed to grab a rail support and dangled there, twenty feet above the airship's engines.

The robot leaned its big, square head down, examining Nick as if *he* were the insect. He held up the grenade, ready to hit the button, when a big Cazador came through the open hatch with a chain.

"Whale!" Nick shouted.

The massive Cazador tossed the thick chain around the metal neck, then jumped onto the back. The machine bucked and pitched like a wild bull. Two more Cazadores dashed inside, blasting the metallic hide with assault rifles. A third used a spear to try to lever the thing off the bridge.

Whale rode it right into the railing above Nick, then over the side. He slid off onto the bridge as the beetle bot crashed into the engine compartment below. Still clinging to the walkway of the bridge, Nick let go with one hand long enough to drop the grenade after arming it. Then he swung a heel up onto the bridge and manteled himself over. He scrambled over on his knees to Whale.

El Pulpo emerged behind them, smoldering from spots on his arm, side, and lower leg where the lasers had hit the dense golden armor.

The king pulled the pin of another grenade and dropped it onto the wreckage of the mechanized beetle. The warrior with the spear leaned down and grabbed Nick, and he saw then it was Wendig. Fuego and Whale rushed off the bridge with them as the grenades detonated behind them. More explosions followed, the blasts growing louder and louder.

By the time they got into the cargo hold, the entire ship trembled from a massive explosion. The group rushed down the ramp, then out of the hangar. A final blast tore through the airship, sending out a shock wave that knocked them all off their feet.

Nick hit the dirt hard headfirst, and it hurt. But pain was good. For one thing, it meant he hadn't broken his neck. He looked up at approaching figures.

Either he was seeing double, or more people had arrived.

He heard a quiet, measured voice that he recognized as Imulah's. Then a furious female voice—Moreto, yelling at her husband.

Nick twisted around to see a second group of Cazadores, in black armor—Colonels Vargas and Santiago and ten more warriors. Dazed, Nick found himself jouncing along on a stretcher, being carried back to the ocean, where a large landing craft from the *Sentinel* waited in the water.

He was going home to the Metal Islands after all.

PART 5:
THE RHINO

CHAPTER 28

An alien light pierced the darkness of Limón Bay like a burning Cazador spear. The beam flashed from the cylindrical tower of a lighthouse on the western shoreline. The steel structure was once used to warn ships during storms. Now the Cazadores had rigged it to lure their prey.

Of the original two hundred souls who had set off for Los Angeles from the Metal Islands over six months ago, only thirty-two remained. And they were starving. The rations they had managed to save from the *Sentinel* were almost exhausted, and water was in short supply. Medical supplies had run out completely on the return voyage, resulting in the deaths of five more Cazadores from radiation poisoning. The way Nick had felt, he expected to be next. It got so bad during the journey that he had even *welcomed* the idea of dying.

And yet, once again, he had pulled through after losing ten pounds to malnutrition and illness. He was still recovering, but he was strong, still very much in his prime.

Four months had passed since they fought the metal demons in the former City of Angels. The journey home was taking almost twice the time as the trip out, due to the assault craft breaking down repeatedly, forcing them to scavenge parts from places along the way, as they were now.

During those scavenging missions, Nick had seen more strange apocalyptic terrain teeming with exotic mutant plants and monsters. He recalled the man-size turtle-shelled crab beasts skittering across the banks of rubble along the Panama Canal, and some glowing orange abominations that appeared out of nowhere, like apparitions in the darkness.

Then there were the horrifying whale-squid creatures that had attacked the *Sentinel*. Nick stood in the observation gallery at the top of the lighthouse, watching one of them now. The behemoth had emerged a few minutes ago in the open sea before making its way into Limón Bay to hunt. If the Cazadores could ever get their landing craft back up and running, they would still have to get past that beast. For now, the vessel was docked in the marina, undergoing repairs. This was the third time since leaving Los Angeles that they had been forced to stop, this time to replace the alternator and a blown belt.

The Metal Islands were only twelve hundred miles away, but it didn't really matter when the giant monsters in their path could swallow the landing craft in one enormous bite. They no longer had the firepower of the warship *Sentinel* to keep them safe.

Nick studied the monstrous sea creature as it surfaced in the distance, blowing out a cloud of breath before vanishing back into the depths. An oscillating tone resonated on the wind, pulling his attention from the north to the southeast. He rushed around to the other side of the lighthouse.

It was midnight, and he was exhausted—not to mention hungry—but he couldn't let his guard down. There were other threats out there too. Eyeless creatures hunting in the darkness, prowling closer, unaware that they were being lured into a trap.

Raising his bolt-action sniper rifle, he used the mounted infrared scope. Heat signatures flickered across the optics, but the beasts moved too fast to track them. He lowered the weapon and glanced down at the waterfront area, where they darted and disappeared. The long-limbed creatures hunted over the rubble of an old industrial area where ships had off-loaded their cargo. Hundreds of rusted containers lay scattered, along with the twisted cranes that once pulled them off the ships. The Cazadores' boat was hidden away near the wreckage of a container ship.

Even from this high vantage point, Nick could barely see it.

Hearing a noise from the ladder behind him, he turned to see el Pulpo climbing up. The grizzled king gave him a nod. Below, Cazadores lay in wait to trap the beasts.

"*La carne vuelve al plato,*" said the king.

Meat would indeed be back on the menu, but it was going to take some effort—and some risk.

One of the creatures below took to the sky, flapping upward on tattered wings. Nick raised his scoped rifle, but el Pulpo waved him back. He pulled out his spear and stepped outside.

The creature let out an ethereal screech as it sailed under the low clouds to investigate the strange light from the tower. According to the Cazadores, the energy drew them out like moths to a flame.

El Pulpo cocked his arm back as the creature homed in on the tower and then on him. It flapped downward, angling into a dive. Nick resisted the urge to open fire—he knew better than to take the king's kill.

As the creature speared downward, el Pulpo hurled his spear. It hit the abomination in the shoulder, knocking it from its dive into a tailspin that slammed it into the side of the tower with a loud thud.

Nick looked over the railing to watch the limp body bounce off the lighthouse and crash to the ground with an audible crack.

El Pulpo laughed. "*Hora de cenar, amigo*," he said. "Time to eat."

He started down the ladder to the ground while Nick stayed at his sentry post, hoping the king would send a steak up for him.

Nick checked on the other creatures that had clambered over the rubble. They retreated in the distance, ducking into holes or vanishing into tunnels. Those creatures had evaded the trap, but for the winged beast, it was too late. As the Cazadores carved off strips and prepared to cook them, the lighthouse flashed again, sending another beam out to sea.

Moving back to the other side of the tower, Nick watched for the glowing leviathan. It had surfaced in the bay, no doubt curious about this strange light.

He watched the oceanic monster long enough to see that it wasn't heading in their direction after all. The glowing monstrosity bore to the south of the bay, which lay covered in a low curtain of fog. He lost sight of it but stayed there watching.

Just as he was about to turn away, he spotted movement deeper in the fog. A ship—not large, maybe sixty meters in length, with a beam of ten meters. The vessel was moving at a good clip, throwing up a large wake. But the glowing beast was catching up to it.

"*¡Contacto entrante!*" Nick yelled.

He looked down at el Pulpo, who was just a few rungs off the ground. The king changed directions, climbing back up in his golden armor. Nick raised his scope at the ship, trying to make out any markings that might tell him if this was a Cazador ship. Whatever it was, it had to have seen their light.

He searched the deck for sailors but saw no one. Whoever was on board had brains enough to stay inside. He zoomed in between the radar dishes of the command center, marked with a white trident. If his eyes weren't playing tricks on him, one of those dishes was rotating.

A low-pitched noise like a moan resonated out of the bay. To Nick, it sounded almost like music—a rhythm following a complex pattern that repeated several times.

The glow of the leviathan monster seemed to dim with the noise, slipping back down into the depths. Nick stared in awe as the ship turned right toward the lighthouse.

It was clear now this wasn't a Cazador vessel. El Pulpo shouted orders down to his troops on the ground, before returning to the ladder.

"Stay here," he commanded.

Nick gripped his rifle, looking out over the water at this mysterious boat. What had been a hunt for mutant meat had turned into an opportunity to attract something far more valuable: a ship to get them out of this hellhole.

It wasn't the first time the Cazadores had used a lighthouse to draw out survivors. But this time, their forces were weak, hungry, and few in number—not in their usual fighting form. But el Pulpo appeared to have a plan.

Nick noticed Cazadores running down the pier, moving into position. The troops on the ground for the monster trap were already dug in and ready.

The ship cruised in closer, and Nick hunkered down to stay out of view. His heart pounded from the implications. Ambushing beasts was one thing, but people? Again confliction tore at what was left of his heart. He had no idea who these sailors were, or where they came from, but he did know that el Pulpo wasn't just going to make them surrender. No, the king and his forces were starving, and they would much prefer eating men over monsters. It was another Cazador tradition to feed on the flesh of one's enemy, believing it would transfer strength to the warrior. To Nick, it was as stupid as it was barbaric.

He looked down at el Pulpo, resisting the urge to gun the man down right here. All it would take was a single bullet into that demented brain.

Outboard engines snapped him back from his fantasy.

Nick shouldered his rifle and trained it on the mysterious ship displaying a trident symbol. A rubber Zodiac craft was being lowered into the water by three men wearing metallic armor. He zoomed in on one of their armets. It reminded him of medieval knights he had learned about in school.

These men were indeed warriors, carrying rifles. They climbed down a ladder into the Zodiac when it hit the water. Its two engines growled as it motored away from the ship, toward the marina.

On the docks, Nick saw Cazadores shedding their armor. Hammerhead guided a group of four troopers who had stripped down to their hazard suits. They jumped into the bay, going under and swimming out toward the main ship to board it. They closed in as the rubber craft landed on the shore. All three men jumped out, rifles in hand.

Nick aimed down at these odd knights trekking up the shore. A bright glow flashed inside the tower. It took him a beat to understand that it was the lighthouse beam firing out to sea, but by then it was too late. All three of the foreign soldiers looked right up at him.

"Sniper!" one yelled in strangely accented English.

Gunfire cracked out from multiple locations below, and a muzzle flashed on the ship. But this gun was much bigger—a rocket launcher firing a missile right at the lighthouse. Nick had only a second to move. He dove to the deck as the projectile hit the side of the steel structure below the observation gallery. The boom drowned out the crack of gunfire below.

Ears ringing, he got up and tried to shake off the shock. He found his rifle a few feet away and scrambled over broken glass and debris to the exit. As he stumbled out onto the platform, he looked down, taking in the scene rapidly.

Two of the knights were down. A third man was on his knees, arms up, as Cazadores closed in around them.

On the ship, Hammerhead led the charge across the deck, slaying the two knights operating the rocket launcher. A sailor opened a hatch, right into Hammerhead's spear. Two Cazadores stormed past him, skewering more of the enemy.

One of the downed men on the ground below the tower suddenly got back up, raising a pistol at el Pulpo. Lining up the sights on the enemy armet, Nick pulled the trigger.

The rifle cracked, and he lowered it to see the man hit the ground. The knight kneeling with his arms in the air looked up at Nick, who had just gunned down his comrade.

Nick moved the scope to el Pulpo. This was his chance to end the man who had caused so much terror.

Moving his finger to the trigger, he gritted his teeth.

Do it! Kill the evil bastard!

He put pressure on the trigger, then eased off as el Pulpo turned to see who had saved him. Nick lowered the rifle and nodded down.

If Nick was going to kill him, he would do it with a blade. And he would make him suffer.

As he pulled the rifle away, Nick noticed movement to the east. He swiftly aimed the weapon at the rubble, expecting to see one of the blind, hairless monsters sneaking in to scavenge flesh.

A target emerged in the scope. Not a beast but a single knight, watching the massacre with binoculars. Nick checked for others but saw no one except this single warrior. He lined up the helmet and again moved his finger to the trigger.

And again, he hesitated as he considered who this man might be.

Did he have kids? A wife? Loving parents? All people who would hurt terribly if Nick pulled the trigger.

With a sigh, he pulled the weapon away. There had been enough killing on this journey.

*　　*　　*　　*　　*

Darkness gave way to light and the applause of the starving, sick, exhausted Cazador survivors from the mission to Los Angeles. Six months had passed since they last saw the sun. But they had indeed made it back to the Metal Islands on the Trident vessel they seized back in the Bay of Limón, Panama.

El Pulpo strode out onto the deck with the other Cazador survivors.

Only thirty-one of the original two hundred Cazadores who had set off on the *Sentinel* were returning. Another had died after leaving Panama. Every warrior standing before their king had new scars and fresh fuel for nightmares to come. Inside, Nick felt as though more pieces of his soul had flaked away as recompense for lives he had taken for el Pulpo.

But on the outside, he had grown ever stronger, building muscle and honing his fighting skills. Despite all odds, Nick Baker had clawed his way back here, defeating beasts, foreign soldiers, and killer machines. He had upheld his promise to Sofia.

"Remember what I told you," Mac said quietly. He leaned closer, his prosthetic arm scraping against Nick as he whispered, "Forget about her."

Nick gazed down at his friend and mentor, a man Nick had looked up to as a beacon of morality and strength. But the

Cazadores had broken him, and raiding had shattered his body, leaving him with an injured back and only one arm.

"Please," Mac said. "You have to forget about her."

There was fear and pain in his voice, further eroding the pedestal that Nick had put this man on for so long. Nick didn't want to be a source of more pain, so he gave Mac a nod. It was a lie, of course, but it wasn't the first thing Nick had kept from him. His eye caught the faded trident symbol on the side of the vessel that they had tried to scrub off on the way back to the Metal Islands.

He had no idea who these people were, only that it was another group of survivors the Cazadores had slaughtered.

All but one of them.

Nick held a secret that he would take to his grave about the knight he had spotted scouting them out after they seized the ship. Standing on the lighthouse with his sniper rifle, Nick could have killed him, but he had held his fire, just as he had held his fire instead of killing el Pulpo.

Not even Mac knew about that man, or that Nick had let him get away after that initial ambush. He was probably drawn to the screams of the knight el Pulpo had captured, interrogated, and then eaten.

Before that prisoner died under torture, he had given up information about his civilization. A place called the Coral Castle, hidden somewhere near Australia. Thousands of miles away. El Pulpo hadn't spoken much about it during the return journey to the Metal Islands, but Nick had no doubt the king would some-day deploy a raiding party to that place, to destroy yet another pocket of civilization.

The first glimpse of home appeared in the distance. Nick gazed out at the rigs, wondering where Sofia was now. He had thought of nothing else on the way home, racking his brain for ways that he could save her—from asking el Pulpo to free her, to lopping off the king's head and freeing her himself.

The thoughts consumed him.

And now that they had arrived, he had to make a decision. Freeing her might get him killed, but doing nothing would just kill him more slowly from the inside.

On the horizon, he spotted the capitol tower, the largest of the rigs, glinting in the sun. A giant warship had already pulled away from it and was turning in their direction. Three speedboats raced out toward their stolen vessel but then halted, still too far away for Nick to make out who was piloting them.

The warship, which Nick could now see was the *Elysium*, kept coming.

El Pulpo stood at the bow of the small research ship, smiling as he raised a proud hand. But this was not the welcome they had all expected.

A warning shot fired over their bow, forcing el Pulpo to duck down. The shell hit the ocean behind them, sending up a geyser of water.

The king shot back to his feet, screaming, *"¡No disparen, cabrones!"*

Both Nick and Mac retreated from the railing as machine-gun turrets and cannons rotated toward them from the *Elysium*.

"What in blazes is going on?" Mac whispered. "Don't they see us?"

Nick nodded. It wasn't a matter of not knowing who they were, he realized. Something had changed in the six months since they left.

Maybe one of the colonels had mounted a coup and had given orders to kill el Pulpo if he returned. Or maybe it was someone else. Either way, Nick prepared to fight. He unslung his rifle and pulled back the charging handle.

El Pulpo screamed orders, raising his axe and pointing. Something about sending another radio message. But Nick had a feeling that wasn't going to do any good.

The warship began to slow as it closed in, now only about a thousand meters away. On the deck far above, a group of fifty warriors emerged with rifles, which they aimed down. Far too many to fight with el Pulpo's small and starving force.

El Pulpo grew more furious by the second, shouting up, spittle flying from his mouth.

Barracudas closed in around him, forming a phalanx of metal and flesh around their king.

The warriors clustered above parted suddenly, and a muscular warrior looked down. But this wasn't one of the colonels; it was el Pulpo's son, Horn.

El Pulpo went quiet for a single moment, staring up in disbelief. Horn backed away, much to the ire of his father, who resumed screaming.

Using an extendable ramp, Horn descended with a dozen of his warriors. Those on the deck above remained, lowering their rifles slightly as el Pulpo screamed up at them. He swept his axe over them, screaming in Spanish, "I'll have all your heads!"

Then he stepped up to his son, who was wearing el Pulpo's crown. Nick followed most of the conversation in Spanish as he stood anxiously with the other fatigued and famine-ridden survivors of the failed expedition to Los Angeles.

"You better have a good explanation for this, boy," el Pulpo said.

"You were gone for so long; we thought you were dead," replied Horn.

"As you can see, I'm very much alive."

Horn looked behind his father, at the surviving Barracudas.

"Where are the rest of your men, and the *Sentinel*?" he asked.

"We're all that's left. We faced many threats, but we prevailed, and we have discovered something worthy of our sacrifices to the Octopus Lords."

Horn made another visual sweep of the deck, including Nick, who half expected him to laugh at their sickly, famished remaining forces. It was clear that el Pulpo had overextended himself in Los Angeles, wasting resources and many lives.

"You left me at a fuel outpost," Horn said. "What good is fuel if the ships we need it for are destroyed? And if the men who fight for it are killed?"

Nick couldn't deny it—the bastard had a point.

"There will always be more ships, and there will always be more slaves," el Pulpo said. "What is in short supply is bravery and honor. I refuse to sit back like that fat fuck of a Golden General."

El Pulpo snarled inches from his son's face. "I will return to the wastes and find more ships and more slaves," said the king. "I will extend *my* empire, with, or without you."

Horn glared up at his father.

"Now, you can hand over my crown, or I can take it, making you a head shorter in the process," said el Pulpo. He raised his axe in his right hand.

The men on the top of the ship aimed their rifles, and Nick and el Pulpo's Cazadores did the same, everyone picking out a target. He felt the tension ready to explode.

"Stop this nonsense, both of you!" came a female voice in Spanish.

Moreto walked out of the hatch and down to them.

"We have lost much, that is true, but we are still blood," she said. "So start acting like it, for the sake of the Octopus Lords."

Horn looked at her, then stared at his father. Finally, he reached up and took off the crown. El Pulpo snatched it in hands trembling with anger.

"It's time to return to our throne and celebrate the future," Moreto said. "For we have a world to conquer."

She gestured, and Imulah walked up to document the exchange.

The shivering rage seemed to subside in el Pulpo when Moreto put her hand up on his thick neck. Nick squinted into the sunlight and saw the rifles come down, both above and below him. He did the same, though he had a feeling this wasn't over.

CHAPTER 29

The Sky Arena buzzed with excitement. Thousands of excited citizens from the rigs had gathered to celebrate the homecoming of el Pulpo and his Barracuda warriors. The king had kicked off two weeks of festivities, including gladiator matches between men and beasts.

El Pulpo, with his freshly shorn head and polished chest rig, stepped out onto the sand. Behind him, twenty-five Barracuda soldiers followed, dressed in brown leather vests, their ceremonial light armor. Holding spears and with cutlasses sheathed on their belts, the Cazadores marched out with their leader, chanting, "*¡Todos alaben a los señores Pulpo!*"

Nick muttered the line, unable to muster any vigor to his voice.

The king raised his muscular arms, roaring like a lion. The crowd roared right back. They worshipped him, believing him a demigod, capable of anything. Stories of the Horse Lords, infernal machines, and Trident ship had spread like a fire across the Metal Islands, resulting in epic, highly exaggerated tales about his victories out in the wastes.

El Pulpo had gone from a crazed lieutenant raider of the Barracudas to the most popular and powerful king in the history of the Metal Islands. Partly, Nick thought, because he was one of them—a warrior who had scratched his way to the top. He wasn't born into the position; he had fought sharpened tooth and nail for his victories.

But to Nick, what had happened out there were hardly victories. They were all lucky to have come back alive. El Pulpo had lost the warships *Dragon* and *Sentinel,* along with two hundred warriors and crew, between Belize and Los Angeles.

It was no secret how many souls had been lost. For each warrior killed in the field left behind loved ones. But the widows and orphans also understood what it meant to be a Cazador— with duty came sacrifice.

He looked from the sands of the Sky Arena up into the seats, squinting in the glow of the bright sun, searching for the one person he truly cared about. But he didn't see Sofia in the stands, and he dare not break formation to look for her.

The troopers marched across the arena with el Pulpo still pumping his axe, hyping up the audience. He stopped in the center of the sand, where the jester pranced over with a microphone, bowing slightly before handing it off.

El Pulpo brought it up to his mouth and said in Spanish, "I stand before you today, brothers and sisters of the Metal Islands, to celebrate great victories and announce a new future. But first we remember those we have lost in these conquests."

The crowd went silent, bowing their heads. Nick thought not just of the Cazadores like Zorro, who had been his friend, but of all his own people from the bunker: Chubs, Ron, Gus. The irony wasn't lost on him as he stood in the sand not far from where he had split the head of Smitty almost five years ago.

Had it really been that long? It had been even longer since he arrived here at the islands, when he was just a thin, frightened kid. Now, of the men and boys from the bunker who had come here, it was just Nick and Mac. Nick lifted his gaze to the former Ranger-turned-Cazador, who now had a prosthetic arm. He stood in the front row of Barracudas, between Fuego and Whale.

El Pulpo raised his head and began to call out names: Hammerhead, Warthog, Fuego, Wendig, Mac, Whale, and then *el Perrito*.

Nick stepped up with the other warriors. They stood proudly in front of the king, who paced. Nick scanned the crowd again for Sofia, wondering what she would think of him now. He squinted in the sunlight at the sky booth, and the women standing inside it, looking down at el Pulpo and his Barracudas.

"My victory would not be possible without these brave bastards," el Pulpo said while holding up his mic. "But there is one standing among us who has surprised even me."

He turned to Nick just as Nick spotted Sofia in the booth. She looked older, her blond hair in a braid that hung over her breast. The happy-go-lucky girl he knew had transformed into a strong young woman.

"For his bravery and actions under fire, I hereby promote Small Dog to lieutenant," el Pulpo said. "And I dub him with a new name to reflect his thick hide and relentless charge into every battle, no matter the risk to his own life."

El Pulpo grinned and shouted, "Lieutenant Rhino!"

He slapped Nick on the back hard enough that it would have knocked him to the ground five years ago. But today he didn't even move. Standing six feet tall with his boots on and weighing 260 pounds, almost all of it muscle, he was indeed a rhino.

The runt born in the bunker was dead. Nick Baker had transformed, too, and, without noticing, earned what he always wanted: respect. He was a warrior, a lieutenant of the greatest fighting force left in the known world.

And it made him feel sick to his stomach.

Was this what he wanted?

He looked up to Sofia, trying to gauge her reaction, but the sun dazzled his eyes.

"Today we begin a new era of the Cazador, focusing on North America," el Pulpo announced in Spanish. "The warriors standing in front of you will lead missions to find new communities, restoring our resources. And back home, we will train a new generation of soldiers, creating a powerful army to extend our empire."

He looked up at the crowd with his maniacal gaze. They cheered him on, roaring louder than before. And el Pulpo did not disappoint them.

Reaching to a chain around his neck, he pulled out the bone whistle he had used to summon the octopus on the way to Belize. The noise it made when he blew it today was different, evoking a different response—a real roar.

The Barracudas shifted their gaze to the grate now rising from the tunnel that Nick had emerged from for his first fight. Chains clattered over the ground as a furry orange animal with extended claws burst out, the chains yanking it back as it growled. The noise echoed through the arena, silencing the crowd.

El Pulpo smiled from ear to ear as he went over, holding up a hand to the monstrous spotted cheetah. This was no mutant behemoth from the wastes, but a majestic animal straight out of the pages of the book Nick remembered.

With his whistle, the king tamed the creature. It submitted as he approached, going down on its haunches.

"*¡Un regalo para mi nueva esposa!*" el Pulpo called out.

A small procession of people walked out onto the sand, with them a short woman whose face was covered with a veil. A braid hung forward over her shoulder. And Nick knew there were freckled features underneath that shroud. This was Sofia. A servant held up the end of the flowing white dress.

In the past, his heart might have leaped seeing her, but today it broke at the sight of her walking across the sand. She lifted the veil when she got to el Pulpo, and looked at his hideous, scarred face.

The urge to draw his cutlass and hack the king down burned through Nick like fire from Fuego's flamethrower. Every muscle tensed in the body that Nick still hardly recognized as his own.

He tried to force his eyes away, but he couldn't.

The rage consumed Nick as he watched el Pulpo lean down to Sofia. She looked away but allowed his disgusting cannibal lips to touch her own.

Nick growled under his breath like the chained cheetah.

The king gestured for the cheetah, who popped up and trotted over. Unafraid, Sofia reached out and stroked the rich orange-and-black fur. Then her eyes found Nick, and he saw the defeat there, all sense of strength gone.

She had accepted her fate.

But Nick would not. He would free her, whatever it took.

* * * * *

While el Pulpo sealed his marriage to Sofia in a lavish ceremony at the islands, Nick was back at sea on yet another raiding mission. But this time, he hadn't said goodbye to Sofia, and this time, he wasn't going to kill monsters. He was returning to Texas, not far from his former home at ITC Star Station. He wasn't sure why—only that the orders had come from el Pulpo himself.

What he did know was that he wasn't returning to his home-land as Nick Baker, or Small Dog. He was *Lieutenant Rhino*.

Almost four years after he met Fuego, Whale, and Wendig, they all stood around a table in the cabin of the midsize patrol boat taken from the knights in Panama. The trident logo had been scrubbed off the hull and replaced with a barracuda.

The image evoked a range of emotions as he thought of everything that had happened over that time, and how he was returning to where it all started. Soon he would see the land where he was born, captured, and conscripted into this life—a life he had thrived in, like the mutant flora growing in the wastes that killed Luigi, the young Ranger.

As the ship closed in on the coastline, Rhino went back to studying the maps. They were headed to a city on the coast called Galveston, where they would establish a forward operating base at a lighthouse and then begin to search for survivors. Mac was there to help lead them, but with a prosthetic in place of his missing wing, he had been pulled from the front lines of combat.

Rhino was in charge now.

Inside the cabin were new members of the Barracudas, as well as some potential candidates along for the ride. Ten warriors stood around the table, including a bull of a man with an unusually large head, named Jorge Mata and known to all as Gran Jefe. They had trouble finding a helmet that would fit his dome.

He was about as young as Rhino had been when he joined as *el Perrito*. But unlike Rhino's younger self, Gran Jefe had a mouth on him. He loved to talk smack, loved to pick fights, loved to argue. Today he was not happy about his assignment to guard the lighthouse.

"Let me come with you," Gran Jefe said in Spanish. "I'll prove I'm a boss."

Rhino raised a brow. That reminded him of his own words when he was younger. Mac smirked at what probably sounded familiar to him as well.

"You'll do what Lieutenant Rhino says," Wendig snapped in Spanish.

Gran Jefe shot her a glare, and she walked over. "Got something to say?" she asked.

"No, he was just shutting his mouth," Rhino said.

He looked back down at the maps, and a theory about their mission began seeding in his mind.

"Dismissed," he said.

Everyone started out of the cabin.

"Mac, you stay."

Mac turned and walked over to the table. After the hatch closed, Rhino said, "What did you tell el Pulpo about this place?"

Mac let out a sigh. "I'm sorry."

"For what?"

"I told him about this place to *save* you, Nick."

"Save me from what?"

Mac smirked again. "From doing something stupid at the royal wedding."

Now Rhino was the one to sigh.

"You and I both know you wouldn't have just stood by and watched," Mac whispered. He looked over his shoulder to make sure no one could eavesdrop.

So far, the secret about Rhino and his love for Sofia had stayed between the two of them. Otherwise, Rhino wouldn't be breathing.

"What did you tell el Pulpo?" Rhino asked again.

"I told him about a place I heard of on the comms at ITC Star Station, between the time the airship crashed and the Cazadores returned. Survivors living in Galveston. Minister Silvio was going to head there with the new Rangers."

Rhino snorted, angry at not learning this earlier. His freshly pierced nostril burned as he drew in a deep breath.

"If we go there, those people will end up like us," he said.

"Not if we don't find anyone," Mac said with a shrug. "That's up to you, Lieutenant."

He walked over and put a hand on Rhino's shoulder.

"El Pulpo wanted you at that ceremony. I had to come up with a reason to send you out here, and this being our former stomping grounds, figured it would be a nice vacation."

"Vacation." Rhino snorted again. "Thanks for that."

"*De nada, amigo.*"

They returned to the lower deck, where the troops were placing bets on a fistfight between Wendig and Gran Jefe. The agile woman danced around the big lug, throwing punches into his face, neck, and ribs. He reached out to grab her, but she had learned things fighting Rhino. He watched with his arms folded over his chest.

The fight ended when Wendig's luck ran out, and she danced right into a reverse punch that knocked her out. Whale carried her away to a table where Fuego and three other Cazadores were filing their teeth down.

An hour later, shouts came from above, drawing them back up to the top deck. Rhino looked west, where the thin line of shore emerged on the horizon. He asked to borrow a sailor's binoculars.

Rhino raised them to his helmet to study the coastline. It didn't take long to see the lighthouse. They had arrived.

After a few scans, he gave the order to ready the skiffs. The all-terrain truck with a mounted .50-caliber machine gun would stay aboard the ship. Everything out of sight for now.

Rhino finished his gear check, then climbed aboard the skiff with Wendig, Fuego, Whale, and Mac. Unable to row with just one arm, he had to content himself with critiquing the others. The banter helped Rhino keep his mind off Sofia.

Their skiff pulled into a marina, entering a thin layer of fog that made it difficult to see as they navigated past the shattered hulls of mired ships and boats. They curved around a pier and got their first view of the muddy shoreline.

Whale gave the boat a good heave, pushing them up onto solid ground. Rhino hopped out with the others, and they carried the craft up past the high-tide mark, again with the benefit of Mac's critique.

The team fanned out, rifles up, toward the lighthouse. This structure had taken punishment over the years—stripped of all paint, and with the exterior ripped open in multiple locations. Normally, they would climb up and rig a light, drawing out any survivors or at least the eyeless beasts. But not today.

Rhino had other plans. He didn't want to find anyone here. The killing and crushing of the Horse Lords had left him broken inside. If he could avoid more bloodshed, perhaps he could get a piece of himself back—a piece that Sofia might recognize if he ever saw her again.

He halted abruptly to stare at a track in the ground. A boot print. Glancing over his shoulder, he checked to see if anyone else had noticed it. But the other hunters had spread out without pausing.

Rhino looked ahead. The footprints hadn't continued over the concrete shelf surrounding the lighthouse. He discreetly dragged his boot over the track in the dirt, then pushed on.

Senses on high alert, he scanned the terrain beyond the structure—mostly just mussel-encrusted boulders and the hulls of boats washed up over the years. There were buildings farther inland—two-story dwellings on concrete legs built to withstand hurricanes long before the bombs. Rhino focused on each of the four structures in turn, scanning for anything moving, any sign of life. Smoke from a fire, or discarded trash, or clothes hung out to dry. Going by the radiation readings, it was unlikely anyone could survive up here. But he had been surprised before by life in places where it shouldn't exist, including the jungles of Belize.

He searched, but there was only the single track. Maybe it was old, although he knew that was unlikely.

After securing the lighthouse, he gave the order to bring the greenhorns up. Gran Jefe was first to arrive, excited like a little kid on his first fishing trip.

Mac joined Rhino as the soldiers set up the FOB, pitching secure tents and bringing up the truck with the .50-caliber machine gun.

"Doesn't look like anyone's here," Rhino said.

"Yeah, seems that way," Mac said.

"I'll take the truck inland, scout it out."

Mac nodded. "I'll drive."

"No, you stay."

"Come on, I'm not *completely* useless."

Rhino thought on it, then nodded.

Whale took shotgun as Mac got behind the wheel. Fuego and Wendig climbed up into the bed of the truck with Rhino. He took the handles of the .50-caliber and gave the roof a tap. The engine growled, and the tires jolted over rough terrain until they found the road leading away from the lighthouse.

Rhino looked over his shoulder at the Barracudas and greenhorns setting up what he planned on being a temporary base. The sooner they got out of here, the better.

The truck hobbled over the broken road, but Mac was an expert driver. He navigated the terrain just as he used to in the Stryker, not far from this very location. Rhino swept the machine gun in a long arc, scanning the wastes for signs of life.

Patches of mutant vines twisted out of the ground as they drove through thickets of red bushes bristling with barbs. They passed a few trees with dangling purple branches.

Wendig stepped up with infrared binoculars, scanning the area for life. "*Nada*," she reported.

Rhino trained the glasses on another cluster of buildings amid the destruction. They seemed to emit a faint glow, but it didn't look like the red hue he was used to seeing from the flora. Fuego saw it, too, and pointed.

Whatever it was, Rhino couldn't hide it from the others now. They had to check it out. He patted the top of the truck, and Mac eased to a stop.

Wendig took over on the .50-caliber, and Rhino took her binos before jumping out of the truck. He went to the driver's side and opened the door. "Back up; stay out of sight. I'm going to check out the structure with the yellow glow."

Mac looked out the window at it and nodded.

"Fuego," Rhino called.

The man jumped down with his flamethrower, and together they started off. They crossed an open field of foundations from a block of houses that had fallen apart over the years. Half-buried vehicles protruded from the toxic dirt. A wooden boat lay on its side, rotted down to the struts. Rhino used one to climb up for a view of the structure ahead. They were close, only about a hundred yards away now. He put the binos on a two-story domed building he hadn't seen earlier. The yellow glow bled through small holes in its dome. At first it looked like an optical illusion, but then he realized this dome was covered by a tarp, with holes letting out the glow from inside the building.

His heart skipped. There were survivors here.

He scanned the outside of the wide building. No vehicles or people within view. But that meant nothing, as he well knew.

Rhino stalled. He had a difficult and painful decision to make after discovering survivors. Something he hadn't wanted to do. Now that he had, he couldn't just continue on his way. It was like poking a hornets' nest—most of the time, they would swarm out. Question was, how many wastelanders were there, and how hard would they fight?

He hoped the answer was not many and not very hard.

If Rhino could let them escape, he would, just as he had with the knight back in Panama.

Climbing back down, he gave Fuego the nod to advance. They started out across the field separating them from the dome. Halfway across, a distant gunshot rang out. Rhino halted, turned, and dropped to the ground as gunfire exploded from the domed structure behind them.

So much for these people not fighting hard.

Rounds ripped into the dirt around him as he scrambled for cover behind a foundation to his right. Fuego plopped down right beside him.

The enemy gunfire stopped, but more distant cracks came from the lighthouse. Rhino poked his head up over the concrete, only to be forced down by a burst of bullets.

But these weren't coming from behind—they were coming from in front of them!

Rhino hugged the dirt next to Fuego, well under the lethal spray. The growl of an engine in low gear filled the brief respite. Both men looked up to see their truck, with Mac behind the wheel. He drove like a madman, careening around wreckage while Wendig unleashed hell with the machine gun mounted in the bed.

The truck screeched to a stop. "Go, go, go!" Mac shouted out the window.

Wendig laid down covering fire, and Rhino and Fuego jumped and vaulted into the back.

The truck fishtailed on its dual tires, trying to find purchase. Then Mac straightened its course and pushed the pedal down, kicking up a plume of dust. Over it, Rhino could see the strangely glowing dome, and plants growing under hanging grow lights. Outside, a single body lay crumpled over a concrete barrier pocked with bullet impacts.

Rhino lost sight of the building as Mac sped off toward the lighthouse. It soon came into view. The shooting was over there, too, from the sounds of it.

By the time Rhino caught his breath, he could see the FOB. A group of Cazadores had surrounded several bodies in tattered clothing and wearing breathing masks. Mac braked, and Rhino jumped out of the truck. At least ten bodies lay scattered around the lighthouse, riddled with bullet holes or skewered by spears. Some of the fighters gripped archaic weapons: pitchforks, a machete, a grain flail.

The circle of Cazadores parted, letting Rhino through, where he found a young boy of perhaps nine years clutching the limp body of a man. Rhino felt anger rising in his chest as he approached the child, who snarled at him like a feral animal. The anger grew, not at the boy or the people who had died defending their home but at himself for letting it happen.

He crouched down in front of the snarling child, thinking of himself back when el Pulpo had arrived with the other demons clad in metal and leather.

Now Rhino was one of them. But unlike the cannibalistic barbarian king, Rhino reached out. "I'm not going to hurt you," he said. "I'm sorry about your father."

He took off his helmet.

"My name's Nick. What's your name?"

The kid growled.

"I heard them call him 'Zuni,'" someone said.

The boy looked over, seeming to recognize the name.

"Come with me, Zuni," Rhino said, extending a hand. "Let's get you something to eat."

CHAPTER 30

Another six months had crawled by out in the wastes, away from the Metal Islands. Mac spent those months on scouting missions along the Gulf Coast of the former United States. Now their warship was anchored outside New Orleans.

The city, like every city he had seen, was shrouded in constant, oppressive darkness pierced only by the occasional flicker of lightning from the turbulent, ash-filled clouds above.

Three months ago, Rhino had split off with a squad of Barracudas when two fresh Cazador ships had arrived in Galveston. He stayed in Texas on a mission to find sky horses that the youngster Zuni had spoken of after they captured him in Galveston. The kid had been sent back to the islands, along with the large cache of food discovered in the domed farm his people had established. The crop wouldn't help the Metal Islands much, but el Pulpo would be pleased with the salvaged technology, which included grow lights and a watering system.

But it wasn't food or tech that the king was after in New Orleans. Mac, Hammerhead, Warthog, and the other Cazadores had deployed here to hunt a monster. At least, that's what Mac assumed the giant cage on the deck of the ship was for.

As Hammerhead finished unloading the cables they would use to capture this beast, Mac considered heading down and asking him about it, but he decided not to stir the pot. There was no way he would be heading out there anyway with his severed arm.

Four troopers moved in around the cage, using a cable hoist system to get it loaded onto the back of a truck moored to the ship's deck. Another group of warriors loaded a single skiff on the port side with spears, a flamethrower, and electric cattle prods.

"Mac."

He turned to the open hatch across the room, where the company scribe, Ernesto, now stood. "Hammerhead said suit up. You leave in an hour."

Ah, fuck me, Mac thought. "Uh, did he say what I'm doing?"

The scribe handed him a piece of paper with nine numbers. "This is an access code to a terminal that Hammerhead and Warthog will escort you to. We need someone with computer knowledge—which you have, no?"

"Yeah, yeah, I'll take care of it."

Mac snatched the paper and folded it up. Then he went to change into his hazard suit and armor. An hour later, he met Hammerhead and Warthog at the skiff. Both of them grunted, complaining about how long they had been waiting.

"*Lo siento, amigos*," Mac said.

He climbed into the skiff, taking a seat and pulling out his submachine gun. The weapon was small enough that he could operate it with the prosthetic arm that he had retrofitted with a weapon mount. He checked the magazine and chambered a round.

Hammerhead and Warthog climbed inside the skiff. It splashed into the water, and they motored away from the warship. A dense white layer of fog blocked their view of the city now.

Minutes later, the fog broke, and they could see the shore and the ruins beyond. Hammerhead piloted them toward the mouth of the Mississippi River, once the city's lifeline back in its heyday. Now the dark, murky waters meandered through a desolate wasteland of cattails and lily pads.

Mac kept away from the side of the boat, knowing that monsters likely dwelled in the waterway. He kept his submachine gun out, ready to blast whatever burst up from the depths. Mutant plants grew in clusters out of the poisoned ground along the river, pulsating with an eerie red light that he knew well.

Not long into their journey, Hammerhead piloted them toward a concrete pier. He cut in, angling the boat up along the side, shut the engine off, and hopped out.

Warthog tied the boat up, then threw a tarp over it while Hammerhead scanned the area with binos. Then he waved them on toward a fenced-off facility with a crooked sign that read zoo.

The structures that once housed a diverse array of wildlife were now ruins overtaken by wild, mutant vegetation. Vines and moss clung aggressively to crumbling walls. A large, twisted tree had broken through the cracking concrete, toppling the very enclosures that once defined the boundaries between the wild and the civilized.

Nothing living remained inside the fenced-off areas and cages that once held exotic animals where tourists and locals came to gawk with their children. Today it appeared that Mac and the Cazadores would be the tourists exploring this Old World attraction.

Hammerhead led the way through a broken gate, his rifle cradled across his armor. He didn't seem nervous, and he appeared to know where he was headed. They passed a water feature where penguins or otters once likely swam. What had once been a clear, sparkling pond was now a stagnant, murky pool reflecting the distorted silhouettes of broken bird statues.

In some areas, phosphorescent algae lent an unnatural reddish hue to the water.

They continued through the facility to an underground section that once housed large snakes in glassed-off enclosures. Shards of windows lay on the floor. Hammerhead climbed into one of the displays and went to a wall covered in faux vegetation.

"Where the hell are you going?" Mac asked.

The answer came when the Cazador pulled back one of the webs to reveal a hidden door. He opened it and shined a light down into a stairwell. They took it down three floors, deep into the ground. At the bottom landing, a steel door was marked with a pane that had hardly faded over the years.

"ITC Zoological Research Station. Authorized Personnel Only," Mac read.

Warthog grunted, waving him forward into a chamber full of computer equipment. Beyond were intact glass walls revealing laboratories. A corridor passed between them, leading to another thick door. To his surprise, the area beyond had electric power.

"How the hell did you find this place?" Mac asked in Spanish.

Hammerhead responded with a simple word: "*Rata.*" Spanish for "rat." The Cazadores often used the term to describe survivors. Mac figured that was how they had come to learn of this hidden location, from some people they had captured in the past. He looked at the computer equipment, but Hammerhead motioned him to a door at the end of the corridor ahead. When he got there, he asked for the access code.

Mac pulled out the paper and tapped the numbers into a touch screen. The doors hissed, letting out a blast of cold air. Through the cloud, Mac made out a massive honeycombed chamber containing glass enclosures of various sizes. Through the frosted glass, he could make out the shapes of creatures. He stepped into the room cautiously, wondering if these were some sort of monsters. But as the frost cloud dissipated around them, he saw hundreds of pods holding different species of animals.

Hammerhead strode over to a section of wall, pointing up at a pod containing what they had come here for—a cryogenically preserved cheetah. Mac had no doubt that the empty enclosure beside it had housed the cheetah they took years ago, when el Pulpo first came here.

"You got to be kidding me," Mac muttered.

They had seriously wasted fuel and endangered lives coming here so the king could have a second pet?

As Mac looked around, he saw empty enclosures across the space. He went over to a shattered section of the wall that once contained pigs, chickens, cows, and goats. Exploring further, he saw that most of the exotic creatures, like pythons and lizards, were left untouched. Obviously not a good food source for the Cazadores, who had come here before to take livestock for their farms back at the Metal Islands.

Mac left the room as the two Cazadores climbed up a row of pods to reach the cheetah. Hammerhead pulled out a knife and wedged it behind the pod to pry open the glass lid.

"Better be careful," Mac said.

He went back to the computers and was happy to find them functional. Sitting at a terminal, he tapped in the access code.

"Welcome to Industrial Technology Corporation," said a cordial but firm female voice. "My name is Leah. How may I assist you today?"

She reminded Mac of the AI from back at ITC Star Station. But that AI would never answer questions about anything other than their own facility, no matter what the prompt.

"What is this place, Leah?" Mac asked.

"This is Industrial Tech Corporation Zoological Research

Station Z-One," she replied. "Established in the year two thousand fifty-four."

"What was the purpose of this facility?"

"That information is classified."

Of course it is.

"Please insert your credentials in order to retrieve classified information," Leah said.

Mac gave the access code.

"Denied," she replied.

Cursing echoed down the corridor and into the computer lab. Hammerhead and Warthog were working to retrieve the sleeping cheetah. That gave him an idea.

"Leah, my name is Mac. I am a former resident of ITC Star Station," he said in a voice that he thought sounded nervous. "That facility was destroyed by hostiles that now threaten this very lab. I need access to protect it, to save the specimens."

There was a pause. "ITC Star Station does not show any IDs for Mac."

Damn, she's good.

"Furthermore, the specimens here have already been compromised," Leah continued. "The classified hard drives remain in their solid state and will be protected at all costs at this facility and the sister facility at ITC Communal Nine."

"Where is ITC Communal Nine?"

"That is—"

"Classified," he interrupted.

"Correct."

"Okay, if it is, then I'll just have to hack into the hard drives and get it—"

He was interrupted by a loud thud. Mac stood and looked down the corridor at the chamber, but this noise hadn't come from the two Cazador brutes.

Mac turned as a door began to open in the wall across the room. Cool air hissed out.

"Leah," he said calmly. "What's behind that door?"

"Security."

A massive humanoid foot stepped through the door. Strangely, it seemed to be made of *bone*. Mac stared, trying to make sense of what he was seeing, as the second foot appeared. It articulated with a leg, also impossibly big, also of bone.

Mac brought up the submachine gun, aiming as a gigantic skinless beast sniffed through slots in its bony face and opened a jaw set with sharp yellow teeth. Rippling red muscles stretched and flexed behind the bony armor as it rose to its full height of almost seven feet.

Staring mute, Mac stepped away from the desk, tripping on the chair and falling on his backside. The creature turned glowing red eyes in his direction. He raised his weapon as it lumbered forward with a heavy huff that sounded like a snorting grizzly bear. And it had to be every bit as big as one of those Old World carnivores.

Mac fired a burst and then scrambled across the floor as it came at him.

"Help!" he shouted.

Warthog dashed down the corridor, firing his assault rifle. Three quick bursts slammed into the bony, spiked back. The nightmarish creature whirled toward him, raising both hands over its head.

With a quarter twist, Mac locked the gun onto his prosthesis. As he lined up the sights on the red flesh beneath the bones, the beast hunched over. So he held off lest a stray shot hit one of the Cazadores now retreating down the narrow corridor between the labs. Warthog, for his part, didn't seem all that worried about hitting Mac as he fired away at the monster.

Diving for cover, Mac heard bullets whizz overhead. He cursed, watching the beast run right into the hailstorm of lead. Another furious howl echoed through the facility as the thing crashed through a wall. Reaching over its shoulders, it plucked out a long, sharp lance of bone and hurled it like a spear at Warthog, who fired at the same moment. Hammerhead screamed something indistinct.

On the ground, Mac aimed his submachine gun at the fleshy part between the titan's skull and spine. Holding in a breath, he waited, waited… then pulled the trigger.

Bullets bounced off the bony plates, but one punched through into flesh, and blood spattered out. The creature staggered, reached over its shoulder and pawed at the wound, then collapsed to the ground.

Hammerhead approached the downed monster cautiously and fired his rifle into one eye, then the other.

Mac let out a sigh of relief. Then he saw the cheetah cub lying in a puddle of blood. An arrow of bone from the monster had pierced the sleeping creature.

He went back to the computers. "Well, looks like your security guard failed," Mac said. "How about you tell me where ITC Communal Nine is now, Leah, or we're going to turn this place into a smoking crater, including you and the hard drives."

There was a slight pause again, probably as the AI ran a cost-benefit analysis. Another second elapsed before she replied, "Miami, Florida, at the following coordinates."

Mac looked at the screen, then leaned down to examine a marked map of the city in Florida. The facility was huge, far bigger than this little place, which told Mac there were many more frozen animals there.

Hammerhead returned, huffing and cursing.

"El Pulpo is going to be pissed," he said in Spanish. He lifted the dead cheetah cub by the scruff of its neck, then dropped it.

"Good thing you brought me," Mac replied with a grin. "I know where we can find another one of those—and a whole lot more."

*　　*　　*　　*　　*

Rhino sat on a lower deck of the warship with his comrades, listening to Gran Jefe whine and groan while getting his new tattoo from Wendig.

"Hold still, anvil head," she said in Spanish.

It was hard not to laugh at their banter, but Rhino was exhausted after spending months in Texas. The darkness, bleak terrain, death, and radiation had sent ripples through his normally ironclad mental state. He just had to hold on a bit longer. They were almost back to the Metal Islands. Almost back to the sunshine—a good thing, for their food supplies had dwindled. He sat around a table with Whale and Fuego, eating some of the last rations they had salvaged from the domed farm back in Galveston.

As he scooped up a bite of roasted potato, he thought of the people they had killed there. The boy Zuni's father, who had fought back just as Rhino had when the Cazadores showed up in Houston. He raised the hunk of lightly salted potato to his mouth, then put it down.

He wasn't hungry.

Fuego and Whale both looked up but knew better than to say anything when Rhino got up and left the table. They had known him long enough to know he was in a mood.

Wendig, on the other hand, called out, "LT, don't you want to see me screw this tat up on Jorge?"

Gran Jefe turned his massive head on the bench where he lay. "What the fuck, *puta*?" he grumbled.

Wendig smacked him on the ear. "Who you callin' *puta, puto*?"

For a moment, Rhino lingered, wondering if he was going to

have to break up a fight. Gran Jefe was a loose cannon, and danger-ous. On their last raid, Rhino had tested the man by letting him take point when they were looking for a mining facility. The kid had almost gotten eaten by some mutant manatees. But he had also proved himself by sneaking into the facility, where he found a nest of sick feral humans and what they guarded—sky horses.

Rhino had decided to pull out, returning to the Metal Islands to deliver the location of those aircraft to el Pulpo, who would likely want to return in force to cleanse the facility of the mutant freaks. Then he would seize the helicopters.

"Don't worry. I won't mess you up too bad, Jorge," Wendig said after the second of tension passed. She flashed a gap-toothed grin. "Now, turn around."

Rhino left the communal area and returned to his quarters to rest his troubled mind. It wasn't just the bloodshed from the raid in Galveston, or even all the bloodshed over the past five years as a Cazador. His thoughts remained on what he had lost—his home, his family and friends, and now Sofia.

He picked up the weights on the deck and began doing curls. A cracked mirror hung from the bulkhead, showing him a reflec-tion that he hardly recognized. Not just the burly muscles and bulging veins on his 270 pound frame but the many scars and tattoos marking his body like a canvas. Each mark told a story of his journey from ITC Star Station and back.

A knock came on the hatch, and Fuego stepped in with unsur-prising news.

"Gran Jefe is fighting Wendig," he said in Spanish. "She fucked up his tattoo—drew a penis instead of his sword."

Rhino groaned and followed his big friend out to the upper deck. And there, he paused. The first rays of sunshine were peek-ing through.

The wall of darkness faded away, and Rhino beheld the

homeland of the Cazador empire for the first time in over a year. He could already tell that things had changed significantly.

In the distance, half a hundred boats of various sizes had surrounded the capitol tower.

Rhino barked orders for the two biggest pains in his ass to get themselves cleaned up.

Gran Jefe slammed Wendig in the shoulder as he walked past. She punched him in the face and kicked him in the shin. Rhino pushed her away and caught the fist that Gran Jefe launched at her head. Gripping it, he pushed down until Gran Jefe was on his knees, wincing in pain.

"*Lo siento, teniente,*" he said.

Rhino released him and looked out at the horizon, hearing the rumble of motors. A war boat sporting twin vertical exhaust pipes sped out to the Barracudas' midsize ship. Standing in the cockpit were two faces he hadn't seen since they parted ways back in Galveston: Warthog and Hammerhead. They motored up alongside as if confirming that it was Rhino and nodded to him.

Hammerhead waved for them to follow, then turned the boat back toward the capitol tower.

Whale and Fuego moved next to Rhino, remaining by his side as their ship cruised toward the fleet. Rhino counted three new warships. On the decks, he noticed many figures, some of them sparring with weapons. There were hundreds of them.

New warriors, just as he had once been.

As they got closer, he could tell these weren't just Cazador youths. Some were prisoners from raids, and like Rhino, they would never speak of their homes, for to do so was forbidden. Their histories would be erased, just like the Horse Lords' history. These people were Cazadores now, after surviving the monsters at the Quill and earning a spot in el Pulpo's war machine just as Rhino had done.

As he boarded a skiff to the marina, he noticed the king standing on a balcony near the top of the capitol tower, watching over his growing dominions. Even from a distance, Rhino could see the jagged grin on his face.

Hammerhead waited on the pier with Warthog, nodding again to Rhino. After tying up the skiff, he walked with Wendig, Fuego, and Whale into the tower, where they took the long stairwell up to the hall of kings. As they strode along the polished tile corridor, the sculpted likenesses of great Cazador warriors greeted them. And hanging on the wall were two fresh portraits of the royal family: el Pulpo, his son Horn, and his eldest wife, Moreto.

Seeing them, Rhino couldn't help thinking of the king's other wives and the children they would bear him. The thought had crossed his mind countless times over the past year, ever since he saw Sofia, wearing a white dress at the Sky Arena.

Hammerhead waved ahead. "*Ven.*"

Rhino followed, tensing as if he were preparing for battle. Two Praetorian guards waited at the double doors to the chamber where the king gave audiences. He had only heard of this place and had never been inside.

The great wooden doors creaked open to a chamber filled with pews, all facing an ornate dais with steps of carved palm logs and topped by the throne. Behind the throne, windows were open to a balcony where el Pulpo stood gripping the railing, his robe blowing about him in the breeze. He turned away and staggered, nearly knocking over a table with a bowl of fresh fruit and two jugs of tequila. One fell to the floor, empty.

The king lurched away from the railing.

"*Perrito*—Rhino!" he called out. "You return!"

He raised his arms, and the robe fell away, showing off his chest covered with scars, tattoos, and lipstick impressions.

Rhino shuddered at the thought of them being from Sofia.

He put that thought away as the warriors gathered in front of the table.

"Eat, drink," he said, picking up a jug. "You must be hungry and thirsty after your long journey."

Whale required no further coaxing and snatched a mango out of the bowl, while Rhino refrained.

"Thank you, but I would like to show you what we found on our journey," Rhino replied. "Sky horses."

He reached into his vest and pulled out a map, which he spread out on the table as el Pulpo raised a curious brow.

"The aircraft are located here, protected by feral humans—maybe a hundred of them," Rhino explained. "With your forces, you can crush them and take those machines."

El Pulpo looked at the map for a moment, then shrugged.

"Perhaps, but what good are sky horses when we have no pilots to fly them?"

"I'm sure we can learn how to operate—"

"No." El Pulpo belched the word. It reeked of liquor. "I've already planned a new raid. Thanks to Mac, who found something better—a facility that can support my growing army. In a few months, we're taking the fleet to Florida."

He went back to the railing and looked down at the sundeck below, grinning and waving playfully. Rhino could see them on the deck below—women in bathing suits sitting around a pool surrounded by a beautiful manicured garden. One of them looked up.

"She loves the water," el Pulpo said.

When Rhino saw that he was talking about Sofia, he stepped back from the railing, out of view. Then he bowed and retreated.

"I will start my preparations," he said.

El Pulpo snorted. "You need to relax, Rhino," he said. "Enjoy the sunshine for a while."

He turned back to the railing, waving again like a stupid little boy.

Rhino resisted the urge to kill the man, as he had so many times. In the king's current drunken state, it would take but a shove to send him plunging to his death.

Soon, he thought. Soon the world would be rid of this tyrant.

CHAPTER 31

As the landing craft pitched and wallowed in turbulent seas, Rhino thought of Sofia sitting on that sundeck, dressed to titillate her new husband and master. That was two months ago. Since then, Rhino had been back at the Metal Islands preparing for this raid to Miami. He had spent the ocean journey to the city either training or trying to come up with a plan to rescue Sofia.

But did she even want him to save her? Or had she surrendered to el Pulpo in exchange for a life of comfort and wealth?

Rhino shook away the thought. He couldn't bring himself to believe it. Like him, she was acting, biding her time until she could escape the clutches of the barbarian king.

"Prepare to beach!" Mac shouted.

Shifting to a gridded viewport, Rhino looked out at the fast-approaching shoreline of what was once Biscayne Bay. The landing craft thumped into the surf, catching the inbound wave. He was with twelve Cazador warriors, the best of the best—the Barracudas. Hammerhead, Warthog, Whale, Fuego, and Wendig were aboard, with Mac in the pilot's seat of the assault craft. Chained to a lift in the cargo bay was a rusted two-cab pickup truck with all-terrain tires, and a plow blade in front. A secure tarp covered the mounted .50-caliber machine gun in the bed.

They had some fresh faces with them today, including that cocky Jorge Mata, or Gran Jefe. Despite his flaws, he had the makings of a great warrior and had already proved himself on several campaigns in Texas over the past two years. He was brave, strong, skilled, and a colossal prick.

The warriors checked their weapons and hazard suits one final time as surf sprayed back on them. The landing gate began cranking down toward the sand.

Rhino waded out first. Before him lay an apocalyptic cityscape far vaster than any he had seen outside Houston. Lightning cleaved the skyline over flooded streets that once bustled with locals and tourists from around the world. Now those playgrounds were completely submerged after tsunamis ate miles of shoreline.

Beyond the water, the few remaining structures were covered in thick moss and creeping vines, creating an eerie red contrast with the eternal black clouds churning overhead.

For a fleeting moment, Rhino thought he saw the outline of an airship up there. He thought of the one that el Pulpo had shot down over Texas all those years ago. It had always occurred to Rhino that maybe there were more airships out there.

His next step put him on dry sand, and he led the Barracudas up onto the beach. The pickup truck rolled down the ramp, Mac behind the wheel. The plow blade splashed into the waist-deep water and over dark heaps of seaweed. He drove them up to the beach, where the rear all-terrain tires began to spin in the gritty sand. Rhino could tell from the sound that it was going to get stuck. He grabbed one of the cables attached to the front bumper and began to pull. Gran Jefe grabbed the other without being told. With some help from Whale, they pulled until the tires found purchase and the rig thumped up to solid ground.

"You getting soft, Rhino?" Gran Jefe asked in Spanish. "I feel like I did that all by myself."

"Dream on! It was all me!" Whale proclaimed.

Rhino snorted. "Both of you, shut your clam holes. We have work to do."

Laughter came from the truck ahead, where Mac had rolled down the window.

"Glad I lost my arm back in LA," he said. "I'm getting too old for that shit. But you, Rhino—you were born for it."

Rhino thought about it. This was what he had always thought he wanted. And now all he could think about when he wasn't trying to survive was how to escape the war machine with Sofia.

If she even wants to be saved…

With a grunt, Rhino raised his hand and gave the signal to advance. They began the trek overland to the adjacent road. Rubble from fallen high-rises littered the shore, though some of the structures farther inland had survived, somehow. Shards of Old World towers formed a skyline as jagged as a Cazador's teeth.

Rhino pulled his telescoping spear from over his shoulder, shaking it out to its full length as he scanned the destruction all around them. A faded sign hung from a rusted pole. He read it out loud: "Welcome to Beautiful Miami!"

He had seen this place in a disc story he watched in the bunker as a kid. Little did he know back then that he would one day come here in search of another ITC bunker.

Rhino pulled out the map marking the coordinates Mac had located back in New Orleans. But there was little point in trying to guide them there based on line of sight. They must try to locate actual roads in this chaos of ruination, and even that looked nearly impossible.

But that was what the scouts were for—a man named Feather and another called Camarón, who had to be one of the smallest men in the army. Not unusual, considering scouts were often chosen for their ability to get in and out of places, like he had once been in the machine shop.

The two scouts walked over, awaiting orders to search for a way forward through a city vastly altered by the bombs and tsunamis. What the inferno didn't destroy, Mother Nature had reclaimed by swallowing it into the ground or covering it with mutant plants.

Finding the bunker wouldn't be easy, and it came with serious risk. Everything out there would try to kill the Barracudas—the terrain, the monsters, anyone who might be hiding among the ruins, and the weather.

Rhino checked the rads on his gauge—even higher than he had expected. Miami was bright red—hit directly by one of the bombs, just like Houston.

The squad wended their way around pits and rubble piles to the road and remounted the .50-caliber machine gun in the bed of the pickup truck. Wendig hopped up, grabbed the handles, and pointed the weapon into the darkness.

"Move out and clear the area!" Rhino commanded in Spanish. "Camarón, Feather, go see if you can find the bunker."

The two men ran ahead, into the wastes.

Fuego led the way with his flamethrower, marching ahead of the truck. As they advanced, the ruined pavement all but disappeared, shrinking to a narrow causeway through swamps that had once been residential neighborhoods. Structures poked from the murky water, some with signs for once-bustling bars and nightclubs.

But the Old World city wasn't completely abandoned. Long, scaly shapes cruised through the water. Modern-day *dinosaurs*, Rhino thought, *otherwise known as crocodiles*. He looked at Gran Jefe, who jogged ahead eagerly near the edge of the road. Fortunately, the greenhorn had learned his lesson from their last raid in Texas, when he almost lost his legs to a mutant manatee.

Gran Jefe stepped back from the edge and turned to Wendig, pointing.

"*Lo puedo ver, tonto,*" she said.

Rhino grinned at the sarcastic comment that meant "I can see it, dumbass."

The narrow roadway widened as they reached terra firma and the first city blocks of dry ground. Debris lines showed where the area had flooded over the years. They were lucky it was dry, for there were plenty of sinkholes and caverns for crocs and other predators to lurk.

It took a while, but Rhino finally identified the road they needed to take, thanks to Feather's scouting. Only problem was the rubble and wrecked vehicles covering it. The path forward required them to make some noise.

Rhino gave Mac the go-ahead to use the blade on the truck. Mac lowered it, then pushed down on the gas, slamming into a rusted-out automobile with a loud, grinding crunch.

They spent the next hour punching a doorway through the rubble. As they worked, Feather returned again, panting.

"We found it," he said in Spanish. "But Camarón fell into a pit."

Rhino signaled to advance, and they pushed on. The pit wasn't far, but an electronic wail made him pause. A similar call came in answer, confirming that it wasn't just a pit. The small Cazador scout had fallen into a nest.

Standing near the edge, Rhino looked down at a single helmet on the rocky ground below. Thin, muscular bodies darted by in the shadows. Crunching bones and tearing flesh told him it was already too late for Camarón.

"Fuego."

It was all he needed to say. The warrior stepped up and flicked on the pilot light to his flamethrower.

Rhino watched the jet of flame roar into the darkness. Fire chased away the shadows, some of them igniting as Fuego raked the barrel back and forth.

Rhino motioned for the squad to continue to where Feather had found the bunker. It took another half hour to get there. Somewhere deep under a demolished high-rise was ITC Communal Nine, along with whatever it was that el Pulpo had come looking for inside.

The scout took Rhino to a half-collapsed ramp heading underground. Examining the roadway, he noticed tracks all over the grit-covered path.

He bent down to examine them.

Clawed feet, human sized. Definitely the eyeless creatures. But not just a few. This seemed to be a massive grouping of them—a nest of immense proportions.

Standing, he looked back to his platoon, then signaled for Fuego. The warrior lumbered over. His pilot light would be the candle to guide them.

The squad set off, with Fuego on point, the little blaze at the nozzle of his flamethrower guiding them through the darkness. Humanoid skeletons lay scattered across the ground, their bones chiseled and chewed many years ago. Not all the remains were ancient though. Fuego lowered his flame toward a man wearing something like a space suit with a helmet.

Mac stopped beside Fuego.

"Ever seen anything like that before?" Rhino asked.

"Once," Mac said. "The day we saw the sky people."

Rhino thought back to that day so long ago when he had sneaked outside the bunker. He remembered the strangely dressed people from the sky who had come to save them all, only to be murdered by the very brutes he now fought for.

Fuego pulled his burning wand away and moved ahead.

They were now about five stories beneath the surface, in a section of the passageway that had suffered some cracking and erosion over the years. Fuego moved his pilot light back and forth to make sure it was safe, and they found what looked like a barricade ahead.

What appeared to be bullet impacts scarred the concrete walls, and rubble littered the ground. More corpses lay ahead, some holding mangled weapons.

A battle had been fought here many years ago.

Passing through the carnage, Rhino realized the guns were pointing not outward to keep some attacker at bay, but inward. It didn't take long to figure out that these were some of the former occupants of the bunker.

But why had they turned on each other?

Or maybe they hadn't. Maybe something had somehow gotten inside.

"Come on already," Gran Jefe said in Spanish.

Rhino grunted. "Still eager to die?"

"Eager to kill."

"Go first, then," Fuego said.

Rhino shook his head. As much as he wanted to put Gran Jefe in his place, he didn't want a needless death on his hands. The past few years had cost them dearly, with too many Cazador deaths and too little to show for them.

Fuego walked on, guiding the Barracudas to a blast door that was cracked ajar. They moved through, Fuego's "candle" creating a small pool of light in the stygian blackness that surrounded them. They paused at a large chamber filled with rows of toppled shelves and crates. But it was the sight of bones that made him freeze. Skeletal remains lay scattered randomly in some places; in others, they were stacked in neat mounds.

Even the impetuous Gran Jefe stopped in his tracks.

"Holy shit," Mac said. "What happened here?"

A dripping sound caught Rhino's ear.

Everyone went still at the distant sound.

Rhino gave hand signals, and the squad spread out across the ransacked storage chamber. They came to broken-down barricades at a pair of doors. One was broken open, and a trail of bones led them into a passage that in turn led to another open door.

Another vast chamber greeted him, this space filled with towering pillars that comprised stacks of human-size pods made of some transparent material. He and Fuego walked over to the nearest pillar, and Fuego raised the burning nozzle to the pods, capturing their broken surfaces.

The glass was broken outward.

Across the room, Gran Jefe yelped. Stumbling backward, he fell on his backside. Small, shadowy humanoid silhouettes scampered forward, shrieking unintelligible sounds.

Fuego walked over, squirting a jet of flame that chased away the little screaming things. The fire lit up sticky bulblike structures stuck to the walls.

Rhino held up a fist as the troopers spread out.

An electronic wail echoed, rapidly answered by another that came from overhead. He looked up at another silhouette, this one far larger than the others.

Raising his spear, he saw not just one but dozens of winged abominations hanging from the ceiling like roosting bats. Their lean, muscular bodies shivered as they awoke from their slumber. It was obvious what had happened to the people here all those years ago.

Rhino lowered his spear and gave the retreat order.

They were going to need more warriors to explore this place.

"Mac, send a message back to the Metal Islands," Rhino said.

"Tell them we located the ITC facility, but there's a swarm inside. I'm establishing a base to await reinforcements so we can cleanse it of these demons."

*   *   *   *   *

The crackle of a radio distracted Rhino from the map spread across his desk.

He got up from his chair. He now weighed 275 pounds without his armor and stood just over six feet tall in boots. Nick was dead now, that part of him shed away like the skin of a snake that had outgrown it. He went by only one name now: Lieutenant Rhino.

But as strong as he had become physically and mentally, the sound of the radio alarmed him. He still couldn't say for sure that it was real. The thing hadn't buzzed in fourteen months.

Fourteen months of living in the darkness, of hunting monsters and waiting for el Pulpo and his new army and fleet to arrive at Miami. There was no denying it—his mind had begun to weaken over the long stay in the wastelands. It was starting to play tricks on him. He was hearing whispers from his past, the voices of the dead. Seeing them, too, sometimes.

All these brutal days in the wastes had given Rhino time to reflect on the dead. And the living. This campaign had taught him more about himself than he ever knew. When he wasn't on missions exploring the city, he spent his time eating, lifting weights, and practicing with his double-bladed spear for one thing: to slay el Pulpo and free Sofia.

His gaze went to the map marking places the Barracudas had already raided while awaiting reinforcements. And places that Rhino had searched on his own and that would play into his plan to take out el Pulpo and put an end to his reign when he finally arrived here.

The radio crackled again, and it was real, no question. Rhino picked up the handset off the docking station and went over to the office window in what had been a military outpost during the war.

He pressed the talk button. "Does anyone copy?"

Static hissed back.

He gazed out through the thick, reinforced glass. Before the war, the view would have been blocked by art deco high-rises. The bombs had given him an ocean view.

Mounds of rubble surrounded the station, like islands in the sea. The two-story concrete building had been a police station made of concrete and brick before the military took it over. Some of their notes remained, and Rhino had spent many nights reading over the horror those men experienced in their final days here.

Twenty-foot-high walls surrounded the building, which went three floors belowground, with a secure garage now housing two Cazador trucks. Rhino had spent the first few weeks adding razor-wire fences, motion detectors, and mines buried in the poisoned dirt outside.

The radio buzzed again. This time a voice said, "Barracudas…"

Rhino felt himself grin. An odd sensation, considering he hadn't in as long as he could remember. He rushed out of his office, down to the communal area, where the thirty Cazadores of the platoon loitered. They slouched on chairs or lay on their bunks, looking bored or depressed.

They all got to their feet as he walked out among them. Mac threw up a salute with his left arm. He had dark hollows under his eyes, and his skin was as pale as one of the eyeless beasts that prowled outside the fortress.

The wastelands eventually broke the hardest Cazadores. Even the garrulous, energetic Wendig had begun to withdraw, and

Gran Jefe's constant joking around gave way to frequent angry outbursts.

Today all that would change.

As soon as everyone had gathered, Rhino said, "Armor up. Reinforcements are coming."

Cheers and shouting broke out. Fists were bumped and backs slapped, and a few of the warriors even embraced in celebration. Mac walked over to Rhino as the troopers gathered their gear and headed to the underground parking garage.

"El Pulpo?" Mac asked.

"We shall soon see," Rhino said.

They got into their armor in half the usual time. Rhino took shotgun in the lead truck, with Mac behind the wheel.

The two armored pickup trucks headed up the ramp to a gate that a sentry cranked open manually. Two of the guards would stay behind while the Barracudas went out to wait for the fleet. Mac drove out into the street, bulldozed over a year ago to open a route to the marina. Headlights illuminated the blasted landscape that Rhino knew as well as the scars and tattoos on his flesh.

He looked out at the ocean, his heart beating with anticipation. As they drove out onto a pier, a light blinked on the horizon.

El Pulpo had indeed arrived, and he wasn't being discreet. His ship, the *Octopus*, was lit up like a damn torch, riding at anchor in Biscayne Bay with four other warships and an oil tanker. They were equipped for a lengthy campaign.

Mac turned off the truck, and the Barracudas all piled out. Rhino walked out onto the concrete pier, where he wrapped the head of a spear in a grain sack he had soaked in gear oil. Fuego touched it with his flamethrower pilot light, and Rhino waved the flaming torch to signal the fleet.

They watched as a skiff pushed away from the *Octopus* and came to shore, drawn to his beacon. The two Cazadores aboard stood and saluted Rhino. He got aboard the skiff, and it motored back out to the fleet.

An hour later, Rhino was walking through the dimly lit corridors of the flagship, on his way to meet with the Black Order. El Pulpo met him in the war room, along with Colonels Vargas and Santiago. Moreto was standing there as well, and she did not look happy, perhaps because el Pulpo was clearly intoxicated.

"Rhino," he slurred, waving him over to the table.

Rhino took a few steps, then froze when he saw a young woman near a viewport across the room, standing in the shadows. Her blond hair fell in a thick braid over her shoulder.

Sofia.

He felt a sinking in his belly.

Had el Pulpo found out about them? Was he about to kill them both? He resisted the urge to reach for the telescoping spear on his back, eyes darting about the room, looking for assassins.

But he didn't see any unexplained personnel. Just two Praetorian sentries, a pair of naval officers—one of them the captain of the ship—and Imulah the scribe.

If this were an ambush, el Pulpo would have far more men to subdue Rhino.

No. He would want to kill me with his own axe.

The king strode over, reeling slightly.

"You know *mi novia*," el Pulpo said.

Rhino couldn't resist looking over at the king, who rarely spoke any English. He glared at Rhino and then motioned to Sofia.

"Mi wife," he said. "*Tú* know her, *¿sí?*"

Rhino knew better than to lie.

"She is from your bunker," said Imulah.

"Yes," Rhino admitted. "I know Sofia."

She nodded too.

"She a child when I... *¿cómo se dice 'liberar,' Imulah?*" el Pulpo said.

"Liberate," Sofia responded. "Although I don't see it that way."

El Pulpo grunted. "You little girl when I rescue you from that dark box, no?"

She was hardly a little girl now. She had blossomed into a beautiful young woman of eighteen years. Rhino caught Moreto glaring at her, and then he understood her sour mood.

"I give you good life, no?" el Pulpo said. "I learn *tu* native tongue. This what love is."

Sofia glanced at the deck.

El Pulpo frowned at his ungrateful bride and reached out for her chin. Rhino tensed, resisting the urge to pull his spear and lop off the offending hand.

"Sofia has expressed her gratitude many times, Your Majesty," Imulah cut in. "She is proud of your achievements and has requested to come along on this raid to see you in action and cheer for your success."

Still holding Sofia by her chin, el Pulpo turned to the scribe.

Rhino stared ahead, trying to understand what was happening and, at the same time, not give his heart away. To his eye, Sofia appeared to despise el Pulpo, but Imulah's words said otherwise.

The king pulled Sofia's face toward his lips, kissing her cheek.

"Have you found it?" he asked, turning to Rhino. "The ITC bunker?"

Rhino nodded.

"*¡Excelente!*" El Pulpo strode over, clapping him on the shoulder before moving on to Colonel Vargas. He gave orders in Spanish.

"Prepare the war party," he said. "Tomorrow morning, we raid."

Rhino tried to look away from Sofia as he was dismissed, but he couldn't stop himself. Their eyes connected, and he saw the defiance. The strength.

She hadn't come here to cheer for el Pulpo.

She had come here to escape him.

As Rhino left the war room, he realized Sofia had been acting the entire time. By coming here, she had done what Rhino had failed to help her do—escaped the Metal Islands.

This was his chance—the best opportunity he would ever have to free her.

Now it was his turn. He would kill el Pulpo and take her away from this place. The wheels were in motion. He just needed some luck for his plan to work.

CHAPTER 32

Rhino stood on the tenth floor of a high-rise with a view of the shore.

White light bloomed around the forward operating base that el Pulpo had already set up—the first artificial illumination in the darkness in over two hundred years.

Bulldozers rumbled and growled as Cazador workers and engineers dug in for what could be an extended campaign in Miami. Half the five hundred troops were already on the beach. More boats arrived each hour, shuttling new soldiers from the fleet. Not so long ago, Rhino had been one of them, heading out to Belize on his first raid.

He zoomed his binos in on the *Octopus*. The flagship was heavily guarded by el Pulpo's men. Rhino had just learned that the king had grown paranoid over the past year, after the divide between his son Horn and him had deepened. Rhino still didn't know exactly what had happened, only that the prince had fled the Metal Islands with his warriors, vowing to come back and take the crown. This was why it had taken the king so long to get to Miami with his fleet.

Rhino kept his binoculars on the *Octopus*, watching movement on the deck as the king and his forces prepared to kick off the raid.

It was time.

He turned to look out over the city where he had spent the past fourteen months. Over that time, he had discovered several places that might serve as temporary safe houses—an old metro station and a handful of old military posts that had been established after the first bombs fell. But he had decided on this building as the most suitable to hide Sofia once he freed her from the *Octopus*.

Rhino went down the stairs to a blast door at the very bottom level of the building. Not even his own squad knew about this place. It was hidden and safe, but he knew the only true way to be safe out there was to slay el Pulpo. When that opportunity came, he would seize it. But as much as he wanted to take the man down with a blade, he had come up with another way.

By Cazador tradition, killing the king would make Rhino the new king of the islands. He would inherit everything that was el Pulpo's. Technically. But it wouldn't be that easy. El Pulpo was far more powerful and more popular than King Mayac had been. And there was his wife, Moreto, and his son Horn, who would return for the crown.

No, Rhino didn't want it—or the fights that would follow.

He just wanted Sofia, even if it meant living out here. So he had come up with a plan to have someone else kill el Pulpo—or, rather, *something*.

Rhino opened the door to a former data center. He went to the rows of black racks that had once been processing units for AI. They had several of these racks in ITC Star Station. Beyond the equipment were shelves of miscellaneous electronic devices and parts. He scavenged through them, finding a box of transmitters.

When he had turned one on, he discovered that when activated, the devices emitted a frequency that attracted the eyeless demons from the ruined city. The electronic-sounding calls had answered immediately, then closed in on him. He had only barely escaped.

Reaching into the box, he grabbed four of the four-inch-long tube-shaped transmitters and slipped them into his tactical vest pouches.

After erasing his tracks from the data center, Rhino hurried to the mound of rubble marking the facility known as ITC Communal Nine, just two miles away. He placed the transmitters in a variety of places, making sure they were hidden from view.

The plan was simple. Once his Barracudas were safely on their way back to the fleet, Rhino would activate the transmitters to draw the beasts to the facility while el Pulpo and his forces were inside. If all went to plan, the king would never see the sun again. He would live his final moments in terror as the beasts fed on his flesh.

Rhino gave his work a final scan, then headed back to the police station. The guards on duty nodded to him. They were used to him slipping out whenever he wanted, and he had made a point to tell them as he left that he was heading out to recon the facility for the raid that was scheduled first thing in the morning—which wasn't a lie.

There was no point trying to sleep. Instead, Rhino spent the time meditating, thinking of his past and then his future. By the time the sun rose over the storm clouds, he was dressed, armored, and ready for the biggest challenge of his life.

In the underground garage, his comrades waited. Whale, Fuego, and Wendig stood at the head of the platoon that had served Rhino over the past fourteen months. But one person was missing from the helmet count. Where was Mac?

"*¿Dónde está…?*" Rhino started to say.

Footsteps came from behind him, at the top of the ramp

leading outside the garage. Mac walked down holding his subma-chine gun.

"The king is on his way," he reported.

Rhino turned back to his hunters and gave the nod. They had waited a long time for reinforcements. Now they could finally go home. Excited for the first time in months, the haggard warriors followed him out into the street. He watched them in the intermit-tent flashes of lightning. Part of him would miss these comrades. But he would not miss the fighting or the death.

The thunder faded, and there was only the growling of engines coming from the shore. A convoy of ten trucks and two jeeps chugged down the cleared road with a hundred fresh troops marching behind them. That was good. It meant fewer warriors Rhino would have to deal with back at the warship *Octopus*.

An armored jeep broke away from the middle of the convoy and pulled to the front. A man stood in the back, gripping the iron roll bars.

The driver skidded to a stop, and the warrior jumped down. It took Rhino a moment to see that it was el Pulpo. His golden armor had been painted black, and skulls of the eyeless beasts had been added as a sort of epaulet or shoulder pad.

Hammerhead, Warthog, and four other Barracudas-turned-Praetorian guards joined el Pulpo on the road.

"You have spent many months in the darkness waiting for me to arrive, and for that I thank you," the king said in Spanish. "Drink. Eat. Sleep. You will be on the next ship home to see your families."

The king pulled the axe from over his back and strode over.

"You stay, Rhino," he said with a grunt.

Rhino felt the stab of fear. Was the king toying with him? Did he know about him and Sofia after all?

El Pulpo raised the axe, and Rhino took a step back.

El Pulpo's deformed face crinkled in mirth. "What? You think

I try to kill you?" He closed the distance between them again. "Why would I do such a thing to my best *perro*?"

"I do not think that, Sire. What orders may I execute for you?" Rhino bowed slightly.

"You will lead me to this swarm that your warriors could not cleanse."

Rhino tensed as he slowly looked up. This wasn't part of his plan, but he could still make it work. It just meant activating the transmitters while he was inside the facility and not on his way to the shore.

You can do this, he thought. But fear and doubt plagued his mind.

El Pulpo faced his army, pumping his axe at the sky.

"*¡Para los señores Pulpo!*" he shouted.

Mac stepped up as the rest of the Barracudas carried their bags to a truck at the end of the convoy.

"Permission to come along?" he said to Rhino.

Rhino began to shake his head, but el Pulpo waved him forward, saying, "*Bien, Mac Suertudo.*" He added something about how the one-armed former Ranger was his good-luck charm.

Mac climbed up onto the back of the jeep with el Pulpo. Rhino took over for the driver, sliding in behind the wheel. The short drive would give him time to consider what he was going to do, knowing that it could put Mac in harm's way. But when he saw the rubble over the ITC facility where he hid the transmitters, his decision was ironclad, and so was his heart.

No more waiting. Today el Pulpo would die, and Sofia would be free.

Rhino parked at the top of the underground road. Leaving the engine running, he got out and went to look at the claw prints of the eyeless monsters that he had found when he first arrived.

There was also a new type of track, and not from a beast.

He examined what looked like a motorcycle track. That wasn't here when he came earlier this morning. Someone had beaten them here. It had to be a Cazador.

"Did you send a scout, Your Majesty?" he called out to the jeep.

El Pulpo came over and crouched down to study the track. Then he stood up, shaking his head.

"*Hay ratas*," he growled. Removing his helmet, he sniffed the air with his mutilated nose. "I smell them!"

"I found no evidence of other humans during our campaign," Rhino replied as he looked around them for contacts. That wasn't a lie. He had never seen anything to indicate that people had managed to live in this radioactive hellhole.

El Pulpo growled low, like an animal about to attack. Rhino felt a flash of anxiety that somehow he was being played. That he had been followed and that someone had watched him plant the transmitters.

"I will find the rats," Rhino said confidently. "I will slay them with my spear and bring you their heads."

El Pulpo turned from the rubble and looked at Rhino for what felt like a full minute before slipping his helmet back over his face.

"*¡Tráeme las ratas!*" the king roared.

Rhino guided the troops into the dusty tunnel. Mac walked up beside him along the ramp down into the garage. Over the years and decades, dirt and grit had covered the concrete in a thick carpet that allowed them to follow the tracks. They ended inside the underground facility, but there was no sign of the bike.

The door leading inside the building had been pushed open. Lowering his spear, Rhino saw boot prints, but only one set. This seemed to be a single person.

Rhino saw this as another good sign. It gave him another distraction, and a chance to slip away to hunt with Mac. He pushed the door wide and shined a light into a passage littered with trash and debris.

El Pulpo kept close behind, flanked by Warthog and Hammer-head. The four Praetorian guards and twenty more troops followed. They were packing a lot of firepower, but in here, the monsters had the advantage.

Rhino guided the Cazadores past the desiccated remains of the facility's former occupants. He didn't stop until he got to the chamber of columns bearing shattered pods, where the lair of the monsters was located.

El Pulpo stepped through the open door for a look. Then he motioned for two warriors with flamethrowers. A shriek echoed out of the room as heavy footfalls pounded the concrete floor.

"Go, find the *ratas*," el Pulpo said to Rhino. "We will burn these *demonios*."

Rhino nodded and stepped back. His plan was coming together almost too perfectly now.

"Hope you know what you're doing," Mac whispered. "I've done all I can to save you from a horrible death."

The realization hit Rhino. Those tracks weren't left by a rat. It was Mac. He had followed Rhino here in the early-morning hours.

He turned to his friend and mentor.

"They will feed you *both* to the Octopus Lords," Mac said. "But first he will torture you both in ways you can't imagine."

Rhino reached into his vest.

"Go and try to free her from that ship and see how far you get," Mac said. "You might kill ten guards. Maybe twenty. Hell, maybe you kill them all. But el Pulpo will send his entire *army* after you, and when he finds you, it won't be pretty. Remember the honey bath he gave that Horse Lord back in Belize?"

"I remember, but he can't do anything if he's dead." Rhino held up the transmitter. "Get ready to run when I tell you."

"Run?" Mac stepped forward. "Just wait—"

"I'm done waiting."

"What crazy shit do you have planned?"

"A grisly end to the octopus king."

"I like the sound of that. Count me in, then."

Rhino looked at his friend, aware of the sacrifice he was offering to make.

"Someone of our people has to survive, to carry on their story," Rhino said.

"That's why I must help you if you're intent on this insane plan. Because I'm not carrying on shit. The future of our people belongs to you and Sofia."

Rhino reached out to Mac, putting a hand on his shoulder.

"Thank you," he said.

Mac shrugged. "So what's that thing do? Make a big boom? Bring this place down?"

"Something like that. Just remember to run, old man."

Mac chuckled. "All right, then. Get on with it."

Rhino pushed the button, activating a signal from all the transmitters. Almost instantly, the electronic wails of the creatures answered from within the facility walls. Distant shouts came, then the crack of gunshots.

"Follow me," Rhino said. He pointed his spear down the passage that went east. They passed a group of living quarters from the former residents. Inside were shredded mattresses, ragged clothing, and discarded belongings. Rhino took a stairwell that he remembered from his solo visits here and went up two floors, above the surface. As he opened the door at the landing, a message from Warthog hissed in his helmet.

"*Veo la rata en el subnivel B, médico.*"

Rhino paused as his mind sorted the message about a rat on sublevel B, medical. A second message followed about a team of Cazadores pursuing the hostile.

So maybe there *was* a rat.

Rhino turned to Mac and said, "I thought you made those tracks."

Mac laughed. "What? I thought it was you."

They stared at each other, then looked back into the hall the way they had come. Someone was out there, all right—a survivor from Miami. But that didn't matter now.

"Come on," Rhino said.

He pushed open the door and hurried down the passage, seeing the first sign of the outside—a pulsating blue light peeking in at them through the collapsed wall. Concrete and struts had collapsed ahead, blocking the way.

Rhino cursed. He had taken the wrong passage. As he turned around, another transmission broke in his helmet. He missed some of it due to the crack of gunfire and shrieks of the monsters back where el Pulpo was engaging the nest. But the transmission came again.

"*El convoy está siendo atacado por múltiples hostiles en el exterior.*"

The beasts were attacking the convoy outside.

Rhino felt his heart skip at a third message—something about the queen. Some of it was jumbled, but he picked up an important part: "*Joven reina.*"

Young queen.

Sofia.

She had arrived in a vehicle at the convoy that was now being attacked by monsters that Rhino had summoned to kill el Pulpo.

His plan to save Sofia may have doomed her.

Rhino steeled himself for a bloody, brutal fight with the beasts.

*   *   *   *   *

Rhino heaved a hundred-pound piece of concrete debris outside. Gunshots and screams echoed through the building behind him, mixing with similar noises from the road below. Shrieking abominations of nature put up a din that made Rhino shudder. It also inspired him to work harder.

Lifting beams and heaving them aside, he fought his way through the blocked passageway to get down to the road. After several minutes of grueling work, he lifted away the last major piece. His shudder transformed to a chill up his spine when he saw the battle raging at the convoy, not two hundred feet away. Dozens of giant beasts closed in on the trucks, using claws and teeth to tear apart sentries and drag them into the darkness.

Only about fifteen Cazadores were still fighting. The rest had come inside to help el Pulpo, leaving the trucks mostly unguarded. The truck carrying Sofia had pulled right up to the front and was bottlenecked in now. A beast crouched on the hood, pounding at the windshield. The driver tried to reverse, but the tires spun in the mud, stuck. He opened the door, raised a pistol, and shot the monster through the skull.

Another darted from the left, snatching him by the arm before he could react. It ripped his arm from the socket, then slashed his neck open. Two more creatures bounded up, grabbing the fallen Cazador and dragging him away. Sofia pulled the front door shut.

Rhino climbed over the last pile of rubble with his assault rifle dangling over his chest. The sling caught on a piece of metal, holding him up for a moment and perhaps saving his life.

A winged creature flapped overhead down the passage, swooping down on a mounted gunner in a truck. The gunner turned the barrel at the last second, but the creature plucked him away, carrying him off into the sky.

Rhino looked up to make sure the sky was clear. A dozen winged beasts circled above before dropping like meteors into the gunfire.

Tracer rounds rose from two mounted machine guns in the trucks. One of the gunners held steady, blasting away even as the predator swooped down into the rounds. It jerked from multiple bullets but held steady. Spearing downward, it slammed into him with enough force to knock him out of the turret. Those tattered wings wrapped around him, and talons plucked his body from the truck.

"Holy fucking shit," Mac said. He put a hand on Rhino, but not to hold him back. "I'll cover you. Go," he said.

Rhino climbed out onto the rubble slope rising three stories over the road below. At least fifty of the pale, long-limbed beasts scrambled from beneath foundations, culverts, and collapsed buildings in all directions, answering the call of the transmitters Rhino had buried. Their high-pitched wails reminded him of the Cazadores' Klaxons and the emergency sirens from his original bunker.

Mac fired a covering burst, giving Rhino time to climb down the mound. Chunks of concrete broke loose on his descent, tumbling away with the loose scree. He slipped and slid down to the final stretch, right above the road. Five Cazadores lay bleeding out on the ground, spread along the road where they had been crushed and torn apart. A winged creature plucked a man with broken legs from the ground as he was firing a pistol. With a claw, it snapped his head to the side, breaking his neck as it flapped away.

Rhino jumped to the ground, running toward the convoy. Gunfire cracked at the end of the line of vehicles. Muzzle flashes captured the armored shapes of four Cazadores still in the fight. Another had climbed into a machine-gun turret in a desperate bid to keep back the tide of beasts swarming up out of their lairs.

Moving fast, Rhino raised his rifle at the spiked back of a beast that had jumped onto the hood of Sofia's truck. It pounded on the shattered window and began prying away shards of glass. Rhino could hear her screams, but he held his fire, afraid of hitting her.

Instead, he ran over, using his rifle butt to smack the beast in its spiky spinal column. Then he yanked it to the ground, where he stomped its head with his boot, shattering teeth. He placed the rifle barrel where the eyes should be and pulled the trigger.

Blood spattered his armor. He ran over to the driver's-side door and yanked it open. Sofia was in the back seat, screaming and kicking at him as he leaned in, dripping gore on the seats. To her, he probably looked like one of the beasts.

"It's me," he said. "Nick."

Sofia froze, staring at him through the visor in her helmet. Then she climbed into the front seat and hugged him around his neck.

"I'm getting you out of here," he said. "I know a place we can hide. It's all planned, but we have to hurry."

She pulled back, looking at him again, and for a moment he feared he had misjudged, that she didn't want to leave with him. But then she reached up to the collar around her neck.

"It's got a tracking device in it," she said. "If I go anywhere, they will find me."

Rhino bent down to look for a way to remove it as a scream rang out behind him. He whirled with his rifle and fired at a creature bounding toward them, blasting it in the chest.

In what seemed like slow motion, he took in the scene. A dying Cazador lay on the street, howling for help as four beasts ripped at his armor. Everyone else was dead, or gone to the front of the convoy. Here in the middle, he saw only a single muzzle flash. He heard a few random gunshots and shouting at the tail end of the trucks. Glancing up at the mound of rubble he had descended, he searched for Mac, but he was nowhere in sight.

Rhino felt something fall from his eye, not realizing it was a tear until it blurred his vision. This was his fault. He had doomed his best friend *and* Sofia.

But he would not let her die.

The claws of a creature slashed at his back, and he turned and kicked it away. Then he raised his assault rifle and gave it a burst in the chest. In the glow of lightning came the snarling faces of four more demons, prowling in the darkness, waiting to strike.

Knowing he had only a few rounds left, he handed the rifle to Sofia.

"Use this if I can't stop them," he said.

"Nick, no!" Sofia screamed.

"I love you, Sofia. I always have and always will."

"I love you too, Nick. Don't—"

He shut the door as she pounded against the other side. Standing in front of it, he drew his double-bladed spear and shook it out to its full length. An extended lightning strike allowed him to take an inventory of the attacking creatures. They were everywhere, shrieking and dashing over the rubble, feeding on corpses on the road, jumping onto trucks.

The first ones came in a pack of three, two leaping in the air while the other bounded forward on all fours. Rhino slashed outward with his spear, nearly severing the heads of both jumpers. They crashed to the ground at his sides as he swept the other end of the spear up into the jaw of the monster charging on the ground. Prying it free, he kicked the creature away, then ducked and thrust the blade up at a winged beast swooping down at him. He skewered it through the heart, pulling the spear free as the giant creature planted headfirst in the roadway. At the sound of claws on metal, he slashed backward, taking the arm off a creature that had scrabbled up onto the truck behind him.

Beast after beast charged, lunging at Rhino. He cut them all down, slinging blood everywhere. A ring of bodies formed around him as he fought.

The strange oscillating calls closed in as more of the monsters answered his transmitters.

He knew he couldn't kill them all.

After hacking down a slavering beast, he worked his way to the back of the truck, cutting off the head of a monster that jumped in front of him. Thrusting his spear into the ground, he leaned down and grabbed the bumper of the vehicle to try to free the vehicle from the mud.

Squatting, Rhino gave a mighty heave and managed to lift it a few inches before he heard snarling from the side of the road. He dropped the truck and swung his spear, disemboweling a creature that lunged too close. As its viscera dumped onto the road, he fell to his back. Reaching down to his vest, he unholstered his pistol and fired at two more creatures coming from the rear of the convoy.

In the distance, he spotted headlights. Reinforcements.

He grabbed his spear, then went back to the door to protect Sofia. Voices and gunfire also came from the front of the convoy now, in the direction of the garage. His heart skipped again when he realized that the racket was from Cazadores who had gone inside the facility.

Had el Pulpo survived?

An enraged shriek snapped him back to the road, where a tall, lanky beast charged his position, along with four of its smaller but quite lethal brethren. Rhino fired his pistol, squeezing off .45-caliber rounds into their leader as it kept coming. At ten feet, he fired again, and the trigger clicked, the magazine empty.

Rhino holstered the handgun and charged with his spear, thrusting it into the monster's shoulder and pushing it back. He swung it with all his might, knocking the two beasts behind it to the ground. He yanked the spear free and went to work slashing and stabbing the other creatures. Their claws slashed back, at least one getting under his leg armor. Bleeding from his calf, he stumbled back to the truck, where he heard Sofia shouting louder.

"Get down!" she yelled.

Rhino moved to the side when he saw her raise the assault rifle. She held the stock against her shoulder and fired a burst. A roar of pain behind him startled him, and he turned to see the giant beast he thought he had killed, down for good this time.

It slumped over, part of its skull gone from her blast.

Two trucks squealed to a stop at the end of the convoy, unloading troops. On the back of one was Wendig, firing the .50-caliber into the sky. Fuego unleashed a wave of fire, and Whale's Minigun whined, blasting the monsters with a hundred rounds per second.

They sidled their way toward Rhino as he staggered back to the truck. Sofia remained in the open door with her rifle, looking up at him. He stood tall, the spear still in his hand. He was injured but alive.

And so was Sofia.

"Nick!" shouted a voice. He turned to Mac, who limped forward, gripping his chest. Blood leaked down his armor, but he was alive.

"Watch out!" Mac shouted. He raised a pistol at the sky.

A shriek from above answered, so close it sounded right overhead. Sofia lifted her rifle to fire at the creature, but the weapon didn't fire, the magazine empty.

Rhino knew then that he had let his guard down.

Powerful limbs ripped his massive frame off the ground, lifting him into the sky. He looked down at Sofia, who reached up, screaming, "NICK!"

He pulled the knife from his belt and thrust it into the

creature's ropy muscles over and over. It pulled him higher, flapping and shrieking. The claws tightened their grip, but he kept stabbing, plunging the blade deeper. Finally, when the convoy looked like toy cars below him, the powerful wings ceased their rhythmic beating, and then he was falling with the monster, for what seemed long seconds. Too long. He knew this wasn't survivable. All he could do was try to reposition his body over the beast and pad his fall.

The monster was beneath him when they hit a mutant tree, breaking a limb that then impaled the flying beast. The talons lost their grip on Rhino, and he blasted through many thin branches. They slapped against him and flipped him about and broke, dropping him through more branches that did the same. Then he hit something immovable—a steeply sloping pile of scree and rubble. Sliding and tumbling, at last he reached the bottom and could fall no more.

He stared up at the towering black tree he had fallen through. His body felt numb.

Numb was bad.

In the past, pain meant he was alive and could fight, that he could come back from whatever injury he had suffered. But he couldn't feel anything or even move. His fingers wouldn't respond. Or his toes. Only his eyes.

He used them to watch his Barracudas closing in on the road, pushing back the monsters with bullet, blade, and flame. Seeing them filled him with pride, and also relief that Sofia would be safe...

The thought faded when he saw a phalanx of troops flooding out of the garage tunnel. Four of the warriors carried someone in black armor with skulls on the shoulder plates.

The king still breathed.

Sofia was not safe.

"No," Rhino grunted in a whisper.

He tried to move again, but nothing would respond, and there was no pain. His warrior body was broken, his legs shattered. Frustrated tears blurred his eyes as they found Sofia, who was trying to push past Mac. She almost succeeded, but he grabbed her, and forced her back to safety.

On the ground, he saw Wendig running up toward the declivity in the rubble where his broken body lay. He looked back to the king, who screamed and fought free of the men holding him to look at someone else being pulled from ITC Communal Nine.

A man in a hazard suit, wearing plates of armor and a helmet that reminded Rhino of the helmet on the corpse he had seen when they first arrived at the facility. Some sort of soldier or skydiver—the rat.

EPILOGUE

Lightning cleaved the invisible wall that bordered the Metal Islands. This place was truly a miracle, a sanctuary in a cold, dark world of death and despair. But it had also required violence and fear by those in charge to protect it from factions within, and envious survivors dwelling in the darkness.

Mac stood in a lookout at the top of the rig with his binoculars, watching for enemies. Clouds scudded across the blue sky like foam blowing on the ocean. Curtains of rain fell on the most distant rigs of the Metal Islands and on the fleet of Cazador warships being readied for the next raiding campaign.

With el Pulpo as king, the bloodshed would never end. And the cannibalistic barbarian of the sea and wastelands had no intention of stopping. He was ramping up his campaigns, preparing to annex new territory.

Banners displaying the names of the raiding squads whipped in the wind on the ships. Mac zoomed in on the most famous of them all: the Barracudas.

Six months after returning home, he would soon be heading back into the wastes with the team. They had a new mission now:

Find the sky people who the man in Miami had told the king about while a prisoner of the Cazadores. A man named Xavier Rodriguez, a Hell Diver who had dwelled in the sky for most of his life. Xavier had done what Mac and every other survivor kidnapped from the wastes had failed to do. He had escaped the clutches of el Pulpo.

Since then, the king had become obsessed with finding the "rat" and his people, fearing they would be looking for the Metal Islands or somehow had followed them back here.

Mac was more worried about el Pulpo Jr. The bastard son, Horn, had taken off into the darkness with a small army of a hundred loyal, bloodthirsty warriors. They would be back someday, and they would come for the crown in what would be a bloody civil war.

El Pulpo wasn't stupid. He had planned for that. Half the fleet would remain here guarding the rigs, as they had when he traveled to Miami to raid ITC Communal Nine. He rotated the binos to the ship currently sailing away from the marina below, packed full of Cazador scouts. They were embarking on a hunt to find Horn and bring him back, dead or alive.

Mac left the lookout and headed toward the sound of shouting. Today was the send-off for the fleet, which meant bloody celebrations at the Sky Arena. But right now it was reserved for training. The clatter of wooden weapons rose from the sand.

Another Cazador relieved Mac, and he walked over to the railing around the upper levels of the Sky Arena's seating. Below, a single man wearing nothing but tattered shorts fought four greenhorn Cazadores with a wooden spear shaft.

From Nick Baker to Small Dog to the great Rhino.

Two of the new trainees lunged at him wielding wooden swords. Rhino dropped one of them with the sweep of a muscular leg, then caught the other trainee across the diaphragm with his staff, knocking the wind out of him. The next two charged, swinging their swords, which Rhino deflected almost nonchalantly with a flick of his shaft. He hit one of the youngsters across the shoulder, knocking him to the sand, then thrust the pole out toward the face of the other kid, who froze, staring at the end of the shaft, an inch from his forehead.

Rhino pulled it back, twirled it, and fell into a ready stance as the four greenhorns recovered.

Mac couldn't help but smile.

Screaming, the four youthful warriors charged together, and again Rhino knocked them all down on the sand. This time, only one of them got back up. Spitting blood, the ambitious little bastard charged. Rhino swept the kid's legs with his pole, then held the end to his throat, forcing him to submit.

Victorious, Rhino tapped the shaft on the sand, summoning the next batch of kids who wanted to test themselves. He looked over his shoulder, clearly sensing he was being watched. Their eyes connected, and they exchanged a friendly nod. The two warriors were the last men from their bunker now, having survived the unthinkable when el Pulpo showed up at their former home.

Rhino was lucky the king had never taken his head back in Miami. Mac had been in the medical ward on the *Octopus*, in the bed next to Rhino's, when el Pulpo visited him three days after the battle. He figured the king was there to kill both Rhino and him. Instead, he had thanked them both for saving Sofia, gave them each a medal, and granted him whatever he desired. But the one thing Rhino wanted, Mac knew, was Sofia. If the king ever did find out about their love, he would make them both suffer.

Even more miraculous than surviving his injuries, Rhino was almost fully healed. Mac knew he shouldn't have doubted him. The doctors had looked at his broken back and shattered legs and said he would never walk again. Three and a half months after that, Rhino had taken his first steps.

Four months later, he had started walking.

Five months later, he was doing a light workout.

Six months, and he was fighting again.

Even from the top level of the arena, Mac could see the scars on his torso as he took on the next pack of four greenhorns. His legs were covered in long, vertical scars where the doctor had set his broken bones. His back, shoulders, neck, and arms had slashes, burns, and raised flesh. Every inch of his muscular frame told a story.

As the rain clouds passed by, Mac stood watching the gifted young warrior train. Each stroke and movement of his choreographed strategy was pure art. His victories had lifted him to the top ranks of el Pulpo's barbaric army.

As the first patrons began to gather for the evening's gladiator fights, Mac took the stairs down into the arena. He gathered with the other Barracudas already standing in the sand. Fuego, Whale, and Wendig watched Rhino beat the cockiness out of the last three Cazadores hoping to prove they had what it took to stand against him. He had bested thirteen of the trainees, giving them all some nice welts and a good story to tell.

An hour later, the stadium was packed with people. Over two thousand spectators gazing down at the ranks of Cazador warriors standing stiff in a ceremonial parade rest. El Pulpo arrived with his wives, including his favorite, Sofia. They stood side by side in the sky booth, where a four-foot-square platform with handrails had been added. El Pulpo walked out, wearing his modified armor with the monster-skull shoulder pads. His pet cheetah followed him on a chain to the end of the walkway, where it sat on its haunches to look out at the crowd.

The jester, perky and hollering, the bells on his shoes jingling, pranced across the field.

"Gooooooood evening, ladies and gentlemen!" he shouted in Spanish. "Are you ready to witness some of the most ferocious fights in the history of the Metal Islands?"

The crowd whistled and roared through sharpened teeth, prompting a roar from the cheetah. El Pulpo used a remote connected to the electrical collar to subdue the beast. It growled but went down, resting its massive head on its front paws.

Across the arena, the gates to the dungeons squealed open, disgorging the gladiators who would fight tonight. Many of the men were slaves taken from other communities, like Mac and Rhino, and given their chance to join the Cazador war machine.

Some of them sobbed, stared at the ground, or pissed down their leg. Others prayed quietly, and a few steeled themselves to fight just as Rhino had fought on this very ground.

"Tonight el Pulpo has a special treasure for you all!" the jester shouted. "The champion of the wastes, the legendary Barracuda, our very own Rhino!"

The champion bowed to el Pulpo, then raised his fist into the air.

Mac again remembered the day Nick had come screaming into this world, and the skinny little boy who had grown up dreaming of becoming a warrior. He had transcended to something far beyond being a warrior, becoming almost a demigod among the Cazadores. Sofia looked down at him for a single moment that Mac noticed, and in that fleeting second, he saw the love in her gaze. Mac realized then that their love couldn't be extinguished by sword or flames. Rhino and Sofia would never give up in their quest to be together. And if anyone could end the reign of el Pulpo, it was likely Rhino.

Until then, Mac knew that Rhino would see Sofia in the

shadows and would fulfill his promise to her, doing whatever it took to survive in the hellish wastelands until the day they were free from el Pulpo.

*　　*　　*　　*　　*

And thus, Rhino continued leading the Barracudas into the darkness, discovering more pockets of survivors while searching for the sky people. For the better part of a decade, with his spear and sword, he slew any foe that threatened their empire, helping el Pulpo fulfill his promise to expand territories. But it was one single man they had found in Miami who would threaten that empire and the king himself.

But that is another story.

Start *Hell Divers* to dive into the main storyline, in which you will be introduced to the legendary Xavier Rodriguez, the Hell Diver from Miami. Follow his adventure as his people battle for survival in the sky and search for a place they can call home.

ABOUT THE AUTHOR

Nicholas Sansbury Smith is the *New York Times* and *USA Today* bestselling author of more than forty novels with two million copies sold. Before his writing career, he served at Iowa Homeland Security and Emergency Management, a background that inspired many of his story concepts. A two-time Ironman triathlete, he enjoys running, biking, and hiking. Nicholas also loves traveling, especially to his cabin in Northern Minnesota where he weaves his tales. He lives in Iowa with his wonderful wife and their son and daughter.

Join Nicholas on social media:
Facebook: Nicholas Sansbury Smith
Twitter: @GreatWaveInk
Website: www.NicholasSansburySmith.com